ONE

THE HOCKEY GOAL TAUNTS GIL, sun shining on the red pipes, white netting bright in the morning light.

He wipes blond hair off his forehead, adjusts his shirt stuck to his back, and grips his hockey stick.

Carefully, he pulls the puck back, sets it on the heel of the blade, squinting through the heat and the sting of salt in his eyes to focus on the top corner of the net. Shifts his weight, moves the puck forward, back, and then shoots with a quick snap of his hands, the push-pull of his arms, the sweet sail of the puck toward—

"Shit," he says.

"Can't hit the side of the barn there, can you, Gil?"

Gil has better aim throwing his stick like a javelin at his youngest brother. Joey sidesteps it, laughing, and the stick clatters to the driveway.

"Remember how good you used to be at scoring? Maybe you can ask the other team to make the net bigger when you're on the ice," Joey says.

"I can score. I'm just lulling you into a false sense of security for when I play you this fall." Gil grabs the puck where it sits against the garage door, the paint scuffed from years of shots and bank passes. "If you make the roster, that is. I hear your team has a seat with your name on it to watch the game from the press box with the rest of the scratched players."

Joey grabs Gil's stick and holds it just out of reach. "Front row seat to watch you hit the end boards over and over and over again instead of the net, Gilbert."

Joey's tall, but Gil's always been taller, and he yanks the stick back. "Don't call me that."

"I'll stop if you can beat me. Target shooting, best of ten. Tommy, you get to play winner."

Tommy doesn't even bother to look up from where he's lounging on the grass, scrolling through his phone. "No."

Joey kicks a stray puck at him. "You're no fun."

"Shut it, Joey. I gotta practice." Gil lines up another shot.

"Clearly."

Gil ignores him, eyes on the net, feeling the weight of the puck as he stick-handles, moving it gently front to back on the blade of his stick. Easy, familiar, just as he's done since he was old enough to stand up, Dad bending over him and guiding his hands, drawing the puck back, shifting his weight, sending the puck toward the net.

And off the post.

The metal rings and the glint of the sun hurts his eyes.

"Nice," Joey says.

"Leave him alone," Tommy says. "We're having a pleasant morning together."

No, Tommy's having a pleasant morning, lazing in Baltimore's September sun with a cup of coffee. Gil's working and absolutely sucking at it, fewer pucks finding the back of the net than the scarred garage door beyond it. Embarrassing for an NHL center heading into his tenth professional season. Even more so when Joey grabs Gil's

LIGHT UP THE LAMP

KIT OLIVER

For my hockey team
Please never read this

Light Up the Lamp:
To score a goal in hockey, and thereby set off the goal lamp
behind the net

LIGHT UP THE LAMP

stick and pots a goal right away, spinning in a circle as he cheers for himself.

Gil taught him how to shoot like that, back when they'd been kids and the only way to tell them apart was their staggered heights. Gil used to line Joey and Tommy up, lecture them on how to stand, how to move their hands, how to flex the stick to store up power and release the puck with a snap, flinging it past the goalie before he could react.

Though Tommy had eventually signed up for choir, the middle school play, and trumpet lessons, Mom driving him while Dad took Gil and Joey to the rink. And then Joey had taken a puck off the nose, Tommy had needed glasses, and so they no longer looked identical. Now they've scattered: long-legged, broad-shouldered, and blond still, but off on their own lives, back together for just this week.

Tommy rolls onto his stomach, ignoring it when Joey whacks his ass with Gil's stick, prodding him to move.

"C'mon," Joey says.

"I can't. I'm allergic to hockey. And I have to practice my speech," Tommy says.

Gil glances over him, the same slim, long frame as Joey and Gil, but none of the bulk from life as a professional athlete. *You should work out more*, Gil had told him when he'd arrived the other day and Tommy had tucked his finger into his mouth and aimed it for Gil's ear, as if they weren't all in their late twenties but in middle school all over again.

"Nobody cares about your speech," Joey says, "and it's family game time. You and Gil against me. I can take on my two big bros."

"Give me my stick back," Gil says.

"Give Gil his stick back," Tommy says, grabbing it from Joey and trying to wrestle it away. "He'll break out into hives if he goes too long without obsessing over his shot.

And please, everyone cares. How often do I get any recognition compared to my famous brothers?"

"I have work to get done." Gil plucks his stick back. His training binder laid out on the edge of the driveway lists all his off-season workouts: morning cardio and mobility exercises and a series of skill work, strength training tomorrow, and a set of conditioning drills before his flight takes off back to San Diego. He's got only days until training camp starts and with it preseason, and then the eighty-two games waiting for him between October and April. Maybe when he was Joey's age, four years younger, he could get away with shirking his workouts, but at twenty-nine, he feels it when he doesn't get his stretches done.

And he can quite clearly tell when he doesn't work enough on his shooting.

Whatever. He can score. Joey's being an ass. Gil's just a bit off today, feeling the oddness of being back here at Dad's house, in this old neighborhood with too many memories.

Gil stares at the net, visualizing the puck flying from his stick and hitting the top corner with such force the net rocks back, unmoored from the pavement. Eighty-two games and then as deep into the playoffs as the San Diego Mountain Lions can manage. Farther than last year, hopefully, if he can do enough to help the team forward from the first round to the second, and from there to the conference final.

It's possible. Their general manager is making the right trades, the new rookies on the team are filling spots in the lineup that were weak last year, and more than for any of the last nine seasons Gil has played on the team, this is the one where there's a real chance at winning the cup.

He lets that excitement spread through him, energy pumping in his arms, his hands, as he moves the puck back and forth, setting up his shot and letting it fly.

Straight past the side of the garage and over the lawn in an arc that clears the back fence.

Gil throws his stick onto the grass. "What the hell is wrong with this thing?"

"Hey, remember," Tommy says as he climbs to his feet. "We're having a nice morning gearing up for tonight when you two clap politely as I, and I alone, get recognized at our old high school for my accomplishments. I'll go get your stupid puck. Try counting to ten, Gil, deep breaths."

"Don't," Gil says.

"Don't get your puck?" Tommy laughs. "Don't tell me that missing the net, of all things, is what'll make you finally take a break. Can we do literally anything other than hockey? Please, pretty please?"

"I have another puck," Gil says. An entire bucket of them.

But Tommy's walking backward toward the back gate, hands clutched over his chest, eyes comically wide. "If I return the wayward puck maybe we could talk about something not related to hockey. The weather? Dad's awful attempts at cooking? Gil's chronic singledom?"

"Don't bug the neighbors," Gil says. "And I'm not chronically single."

"Try a little move called dating, not just hooking up with a revolving cast of characters. And it's not 'the neighbors,' it's the Martins. Not that you'd remember, avoiding them for years."

"I haven't been avoiding—Tommy, no."

"Tommy, yes." Tommy grabs the top of the fence to peer over it.

"You're going to break it." The wood of the fence is old and worn with winters and summer sun. Once too tall for any of them to see over it, now Tommy's barely up on his toes as he waves.

"Mrs. Martin," Tommy calls over the fence. "Hi, good morning, can we get our puck back? I take full blame for it nearly sailing into your pool. You know neither my adorable younger brother or my perfect older brother would in any way possibly be responsible for any hockey paraphernalia ending up in your yard."

The Martins' pool. Gil grabs his stick, picking at the tape on the blade. Had he forgotten that? The diving board, the ladder that always pinched his fingers, the pool vacuum he'd once been terrified of and then had later laughed at as Joey madly splashed away from the same harmless thing.

No, he remembers. The shining, clear water, the yard, the back porch, all on the other side of the tall, weathered fence, behind the gate that's been latched closed for so long.

It swings open on hinges that squeak, Julie Martin already smiling as she steps through.

"Tommy, look at you. And it's Julie, please, you're all grown up." She reaches up to hug Tommy, her brown hair pulled back, streaked with gray that never used to be there. "How are you? Oh, all of you are here? Joey, Gil, look at you three, it's been so long."

Gil digs the toe of his stick into the grass, poking at a dandelion that's managed to work its way up next to the driveway, a lone weed in Dad's neat lawn. "Hey," he says softly.

"Gil's fault this ended up in your yard," Joey says, taking the puck when Julie hands it to him.

"I think I've heard that one before," she says. "I didn't know you three were visiting. Joey, how's Texas?"

"Hot," Joey says. "But it's good, the team's alright."

Walk over there, Gil tells himself. *Be polite, say hello, and apologize for bothering her.*

He manages a quick, small wave as he eyes the yard behind her, the edge of the trampoline, the patio with its grill, the old elm tree with the tire swing hanging from a branch, the rope frayed and faded.

"Joey, I'll play. First to ten goals, let's do it." Gil gestures for Joey to toss him the puck, trying to talk loudly enough that he doesn't have to listen to Tommy and Julie—*Mrs. Martin* still sounds more natural—catch up. *Close the gate*, he wants to call to Tommy. Latch it, lock it, the Martins on their side of the fence and the Roussins over here.

"Phone call." Joey scoops his phone out of his pocket. "I'll be right back."

Gil stays rooted in the driveway. He can see the gate, still hear them chatting. He needs to focus. He has his training plan he has to finish. His lunch to eat, plain chicken breast and spinach and brown rice and a protein shake, the right mix of fuel to recover from his workout this morning and prepare him for tomorrow. Then, reviewing plays the assistant coach just emailed to the team, working through drills ahead of the first day of training camp—and hammering shots into the net until he's so well practiced it's impossible to miss.

Which he should be. Ten years of professional hockey and here he is, sending the puck wide of the damn net. *How good he used to be at scoring*, he hears Joey say and frowns.

So no, he's not going over there to catch up with the neighbors. The Martins. *Focus*, he tells himself. Stick in his hands, puck on the blade, pulling it backward, forward, shifting his weight—

"Holy shit!" Tommy yells, loud enough Gil looks up.

His chest goes cold, and then hot.

Sebastian.

Sebastian with a beard and short hair.

He—*oh*. He grew up. His hair combed over, the sides clipped, and his body filled out, a dark blue T-shirt clinging to his chest, jeans hugging his thighs.

Grinning too, hugging Tommy, muscled arms around Tommy's back, a smile dimpling Sebastian's cheek, shining in his brown eyes.

The smile fades when he sees Gil.

Gil ducks his head. The puck, his stick, his hands—it feels like there's thick mud he has to drag against as he moves the puck back and forth.

He's working. He's practicing, he's not—

"Gil, look who it is!" Tommy shouts. "Get the hell over here! Sebastian fucking Martin, it's been so long, I missed you, man!"

"Tommy, I didn't know you were in town," Sebastian says and his *voice*.

That hasn't changed, the deep rumble it had settled into after the awkward change of adolescence, or how his mouth moves over the words, the shape of his lips as he—

Yeah, he's still hot. Still really, nearly unbelievably attractive, distracting in how he stands, long legs and the frame of his torso, how he moves, just the way he talks.

No. Focus. Gil stares down at the puck, moving it faster, back and forth and back again. He's worked hard to get Sebastian out of his head, and right now, the beginning of the season waiting for him, isn't the time to let the past creep back in.

"Just till tomorrow," Tommy says. "Two of us have training camp, and I have the good sense to go back to my job that doesn't involve getting crushed by oversized men while vulcanized rubber is flying around, trying to hit me in the face." He laughs and smacks Sebastian's arm. "Look at you, how are you? It's been ages."

"I'm good," Sebastian says and Gil moves his hands even quicker like he can drown out that voice with the *tap tap tap* of the puck against his blade. *One, two three*, he counts. *One two three, one two three.* "Heading out later today, or I'd love to catch up."

"Aw, too bad, we're off to the high school tonight. They're doing a whole start-of-the-school-year arts thing and I got invited to talk about the music program. Can you imagine that? A Roussin up there, not talking about hockey, but instead my own glorious career in teaching kindergarteners how to play piano?"

"Not hockey?" Sebastian asks and Gil doesn't look, he can't look, he won't look, but he can hear the ghost of a smile in Sebastian's voice. "No way."

"Way," Tommy says. "Come over for a couple minutes at least, 'cause you'll never guess what we're doing. Playing hockey, what a surprise, right? Rescue me, please."

Gil pulls the puck to his backhand, twisting to handle it smoothly, the muscles in his arms burning with the effort. *It's good practice*, he tells himself, to be off balance like this. It takes more of his attention to keep a steady rhythm, to move the puck as naturally as on his forehand.

"I would, but I've got to get packed up. Hey, good to see you though," Sebastian says. "If you're ever in town, give me a shout."

Yeah, because Sebastian can't pick up the fucking phone himself.

Gil aims for the net, hands slippery on the stick as he shoots.

He hits that top corner. *One*, he thinks. Four more in a row and he'll be satisfied.

Tommy probably will call Seb, knowing him. Good luck getting Sebastian to answer, though. Plenty changes over the ten years since they last talked, but that? Gil drops another puck onto the pavement. No, it's Sebastian and some things always stay the same.

TWO

In the kitchen, Gil fills a glass with water and drinks it straight down. When he fills it again, he presses the glass to his forehead, letting the chill soothe the burn of his face.

Seeing Sebastian again. Seeing him here, in their little neighborhood outside Baltimore, suburbia stretching around them with cul-de-sacs, cookie-cutter houses, trees all the same height and shape.

It was a stroke of good fortune that of the maze of streets they'd moved to when Dad had bought the place, their house shared a fence with the Martins' backyard. *A boy your age, maybe you'll make friends*, Mom had said, smoothing his hair back from his face, bouncing Joey on her hip when she'd dropped them off here, Tommy wailing in his car seat.

Friends.

Yeah, they'd certainly become friends. And then some.

He chews a piece of ice so hard his teeth hurt.

Enough. The season's starting; he can't be just standing around playing memories over in his mind. Dad's home, tucked upstairs in his office as he gets ready to coach his team's training camp, going over the drills he plans to run, putting together the lines he'll use for preseason games. Gil should go up there, while he's got Dad face to face, ask if he can interrupt him with a question or two, rather than the distance between them all season so that Dad has to message him after games with pointers.

Don't make that pass, Gil finds on his phone most mornings after a game, the text coming through late in the night after Dad's watched his and Joey's shifts and made notes for them. *Shoot that yourself. You're not out there to let someone else play the hero.*

At least Dad bothers to text. Gil casts a look at the window over the sink and its view of the backyard, the Martins' roof beyond it.

Yeah, he'll go upstairs, sit with Dad, and get back to stick-handling and shooting tonight, when it's cooler out, when he doesn't have to deal with the glare of the sun making aiming harder than it has to be. For now, he can enjoy the peace and quiet of being back here in this kitchen he grew up in, the living room with its huge couch, Dad's office with the walls covered in framed jerseys and team photos. His old bedroom too, decorated the same ever since Mom took him to get a bedspread more suited for a teenager than a kid and then bundled him inside with it when Dad was out. He still loves that deep green she'd picked out for him, no matter how small that twin bed feels now.

Joey crashes down the stairs, swinging around the bottom of the banister and jumping onto Gil hard enough he rocks back a step. "Guess what?" he shouts into Gil's ear.

"What?" Gil flails for the counter to hold onto, trying to make sense of Joey's words. "You got what?"

"Traded," Joey yells again. "Gil! San Diego! We're going to play together!"

"Wait, what?"

"That was my agent on the phone. The trade just went

through. I'm not going back to Houston, I'm playing with you!"

Gil lifts him off the ground in a hug. "You're coming to San Diego? To the Mountain Lions? With me?"

"With you, you fucker! I'm calling your equipment manager right now. I want the locker next to you, I'm gonna tie your skates together before every practice."

"Rookies in the back," Gil says. "Nice try, you little shit. You get a seat next to the bathroom, gotta work your way up if you want to sit with us big kids."

"Party in the hot tub at your place. Dibs on your spare bedroom, 'cause I'm bringing—"

"No, no cats, you're not bringing that mangy—"

"Mr. Stanley and I are moving in," Joey crows.

"Get your own damn place."

"No fucking way, your pool has a waterfall in it."

"Who'd they move to free up roster space for you? Or did you go for draft picks only? Poor thing, that's just embarrassing. What're you worth, a fourth-rounder?"

"I got drafted higher than you."

Gil messes up Joey's hair. "You got drafted in a year when the picks could barely roster an intramural team at any decent division one school."

"All I hear when you say that is drafted first round, baby."

Gil fishes an ice cube out of his glass and drops it down Joey's shirt. Drafted first round, but didn't get an entry-level contract until after college, he could remind Joey, though it always just devolves from there, one-upping each other with points per season, who's gotten more ice time, how much deeper the Mountain Lions have gotten in playoffs than Houston ever has.

Gil takes a picture of Joey trying to shake the ice cube out of his shirt and texts it to Mom, the photo flying through satellites to Annapolis with his message *My newest teammate.*

The stairs creak beneath Dad's steps, his hand on the banister appearing first, then the rest of him, slowly, stately almost in contrast to Joey pulling a face and dumping the ice cube back into the sink.

"Gil," Dad says. "Did you hear?"

"Not sure how I couldn't have," Gil says. "Tommy heard outside, and Mrs. Martin and—" *Sebastian.* "Yeah, I heard, we all heard."

"You mean that horrible shrieking noise?" Tommy pushes into the house. "Joey, what happened? Did you see a bug?"

"I got traded." Joey tosses his arm over Gil's shoulders. "San Diego Mountain Lions, a second Roussin coming their way."

"Two for the price of one 'cause your agent sucks," Gil says, digging a finger into Joey's ribs. Joey, living with him in San Diego, filling up the corners of his house, someone to ride to the rink with, chat with on the way home from games. He can't stop smiling even as he jabs Joey's side again. "I'm charging rent for that mop of fur you call a pet."

"Mr. Stanley is gonna rule the house," Joey says. "Houston, you were great, but we are out!"

"Gil," Dad says again, his quiet voice cutting beneath Joey's noise.

"Yeah?" Gil turns at a soft jingle, the click of nails on the wood floor. "Is that—Buddy?"

Joey claps his hands, barging past Gil and kneeling to fuss over the dog. "You here 'cause you heard my big news? Are you, big boy? Look at you, you got old, Buddy! Or is it Mr. Martin now? What'd you do, slip through the gate?"

Buddy is older, gray around his brown muzzle, stiffness to his joints as he wiggles, putting his head down to get his

13

ears scratched. And no, Mr. Martin was Sebastian's dad, pushing them on the swing, tossing them around in the pool, throwing a football with them, until the day he just wasn't there anymore, gone in a flash of ambulance lights and then silence as it fled to the hospital.

"He's here to help us all celebrate," Joey says. "Aren't you? Yeah, you are, what a good boy."

But Buddy pushes past him, tottering toward Gil, nosing into his hand, tail whacking against his knees.

"Hey big guy," Gil says.

"Buddy!" comes a shout from outside.

Gil freezes. That voice he's tried so hard to forget lodges in his chest, a dull ache of a bruise he's ignored for so long, pretending it's healed.

Quickly, he turns Buddy toward the door. "Go on, go home, that's a good boy."

But Buddy backs up into Gil's legs, tongue lolling from the side of his mouth, head tipped up into Gil's hands in a demand to be petted.

"Bud!" Sebastian calls from the driveway. "C'mon, I got a treat for you."

"Hear that?" Gil tries to push the dog toward the door again. "You get a treat, go on now."

"The treat of the day is getting onto a team that has seen the playoffs in the last decade," Joey says. "Houston, you ain't the worst in the league, but damn have I been ready to leave."

"Dad, aren't you just so terribly proud of them, playing together? And of me too, standing in a high school auditorium tonight, of course," Tommy laughs. "Sebastian! Buddy's in here, and if he wasn't going deaf from old age before, he is now that he's gotten so close to Joey."

"Go," Gil pleads. "Buddy, go on."

But Buddy only spins in place, smiling his doggy smile

up at Gil, shaky on stiff legs. Sebastian peers in the door, a leash clutched in his hand.

Tommy waves him inside. "Seb, Joey got traded. He's really shy about it, so I figured I'd tell you."

"Mountain Lions!" Joey shouts, hands pumping in the air. "Me and Gil on the same team, can you believe it?"

"Buddy, c'mere" Sebastian calls, patting his thigh. "I'm so sorry, he just darted over here when he saw the gate was open. Come, Bud, let's go."

Gil pulls back from the dog, shoving his hands in his shorts pockets, hoping that without petting Buddy, he'll turn and shuffle away again.

Buddy licks Gil's knee, his tail wagging harder.

Hey, he should at least say to Sebastian. *What's up, how you been?* Something easy and casual, and make it utterly clear how little he cares that they happen to be bumping into each other again.

Though Sebastian could say hi, too. Bother to look at him, not keep his eyes on Buddy, and acknowledge that Gil's in the room at all.

"Gil," Dad says. "I need you for a minute. Come upstairs."

"Of course," Gil says quickly, and when Buddy still won't move, Gil steps over him. In his pocket, his phone rings. *Melissa*, the screen reads. He shows it to Dad as he crosses the kitchen. "My agent's calling."

"You need to answer that," Dad says. "And then we need to talk."

"And Buddy needs to romp around the house again." Tommy ushers the dog deeper into the kitchen.

Gil frowns, stepping into the living room as he answers his phone. "Tommy, c'mon, no. Hey, Melissa."

"Gil," she says, and he pictures her at her desk in New York, glass windows overlooking the city, a stack of old pucks on her desk she's collected over the decades. *She's good*, Dad had said when Gil had run the idea of hiring her past him. "Glad I got hold of you. You doing alright?"

"Yeah, I'm doing great. Did you hear? Joey just got traded. He'll be in San Diego with me." Gil turns his back to the door, trying to ignore the click of Buddy's nails just outside in the hallway and Tommy's voice cooing over him.

"I did hear." She must be in her office because there's no sound of an airport around her, the hum of a car as she drives to a meeting, or flies to visit a client. *Lunch*, she'd suggested last time she'd been in San Diego, and he'd found her already at the restaurant, her gray bob easily identifiable at the table, her phone in her hand until she'd spotted him too and slipped it into her purse.

"I'm so excited. He's totally a missing piece for our offense," Gil says. "What a great move for the GM to snag him. I didn't see it coming."

"I can't say I saw it coming either," Melissa says. "Gil, his trade came out of left field, and I'd say that it was behind my back, but I don't think the GM knew he'd make the move until it was done."

Go away, Gil mouths at Tommy, who only grins at him, encouraging Buddy through the living room door toward Gil. Buddy spots him and wags his tail so hard his entire body wobbles.

Gil turns away from them. "The trade for Joey? Whichever way it happened, it feels right, don't you think?"

"For you," she says. "Gil, it was a three-way trade. Joey to San Diego, and in exchange a draft pick and a prospect from Sacramento to Houston."

"Sacramento?" Gil asks. Buddy totters into the living room in a jingle of dog tags, his breath huffing in excitement. He shuffles over, his gait an unsteady sway where it was once a bounding leap across this same room, landing on the couch where Gil and Sebastian sprawled, legs tangled, shoulders pressed against each other, the dog wiggling in until there was room for him too. "Isn't that the minor league team for San Francisco?"

"It is," Melissa says. "And San Diego's sending you up there."

"Me?"

"Gil," Melissa says gently.

He laughs. "No way."

"There was an opportunity and your GM in San Diego took it. You're off the team, Gil, and you'll be hearing from the folks in San Francisco any minute now."

"San Francisco?" Gil laughs again. "C'mon."

"I'm not sure who'll be calling you. They just hired that new coach and I think they've had a lot of front-office turnover too over the summer."

"They have a new coach because that team is an absolute shitshow." Gil steps back from Buddy trying to nose at his legs, hoping for a head scratch.

"Buddy!" Sebastian calls.

"In there," Tommy says from the doorway, pointing toward Gil.

"No," Gil says, turning away from their voices. "I'm not going. I'm playing in San Diego with Joey."

"There's a flight leaving Baltimore for San Francisco this afternoon, and I've got you booked on it."

"This can't be right."

"For what it's worth, I'm sorry."

"San Francisco?" Gil asks again. "The Sea Lions?"

It's the wrong city. The wrong team. The wrong damn animal, because Gil can't trade the Mountain Lions for a goofy-ass seal. His head swims and Buddy leans against his knees, staring up at him with soft brown eyes.

"Buddy," Sebastian says again, his footsteps behind Gil.

"Please," Gil says. "No."

"The Sea Lions practice this afternoon. Their training camp started early this year," Melissa says. "Given the time change, the flight I have you on will get you to the rink in time."

"They're the worst team in the league," he says.

"Sorry," Sebastian says and oh, he's right behind Gil, reaching for Buddy's collar.

Gil jumps a step back from him. Ten years Sebastian's avoided Gil and he's here right fucking now?

"I can't go to San Francisco," Gil says, and Sebastian finally bothers to look at him, a quick glance up so Gil's pinned by both Buddy's adoring gaze and the sharp flick of Sebastian's eyes. Gil steps back again, but the couch is there and he's hemmed in, stuck between the dog and the furniture, his hand gripping his phone too tight. "I can't play there. Tell me there's a chance I can get out of this."

"I know it's not where you want to be," Melissa says. "But it's my job to point this out, so I'll go ahead and say it. This could be an opportunity for you to play on the first line, to be a real leader in the locker room. You could be the big name on the team, work with the new GM as he builds up the roster. They have a brand-new coaching staff and—"

"No."

A pause, and then he can hear Melissa's quiet exhale.

"Buddy," Sebastian says softly. "Come with me, please."

"I can see what I can do about getting you traded again," Melissa says. "Their GM is new to the NHL, so there might be some strings I can pull there. You have a preference for where you want to go?"

I want to play in San Diego, Gil nearly says. He lives there. His house is there. His buddies on the team, Giffy and Little and Hux, they're all flying in tomorrow. The guy he's been sleeping with, Dave, he's there, and oh yeah, Gil will have to figure that out if Joey's staying at his place, either put up with his teasing when Dave comes and goes or drive to Dave's place—

No.

He won't. Because Gil will be in...

Fuck.

"No, I don't care," he says dully. "Anywhere but San Francisco."

"I'll see what I can do, but in the meantime, just think about it, okay? The Sea Lions could be a really interesting spot for you."

"Get me off that roster."

"Okay, if that's what you want, then I'm on it," Melissa says.

"Thanks." Gil hangs up.

"Buddy," Sebastian says. "Buddy, come on, let's go, okay?"

Gil closes his eyes. *Buddy, get out of here*, Sebastian used to say, laughing, pushing at the dog, wrestling him and grinning.

Gil draws in a deep breath and bends down, pushing gently at the dog. "Go," he mumbles, coaxing him toward Sebastian.

He needs to sit down. Pace. Go outside and hurl pucks into the net until the burn of his muscles incinerates that phone call.

"Sorry," Sebastian says. "He's just, yeah, sorry."

Buddy's doing what he always did, him and Sebastian as familiar with this room as Gil and his brothers are, the huge TV, the gray couch, the framed pictures of Dad playing, the colors faded, the image grainy. Another of the day Dad's jersey got raised to the rafters, Joey with a missing tooth, Tommy with his hair barely tamed, and Gil on the verge of adolescence, acne covering his chin. More, of Gil playing as a tiny kid, Gil playing in high school, Gil on his college team, lined up with all those guys—

Sebastian was one of them. Gil frowns and turns away from the picture.

Sebastian without a beard, his hair a messy brown mop, not cut so stylishly.

Gil pushes Buddy toward him, a hand on his rump, and Sebastian snags him by the collar. He clicks the leash on and they both step back, Gil too quickly, catching his ankle on the foot of the couch. "Shit."

"You okay?" Sebastian asks.

"Yeah, just stings." Gil shakes his foot out.

"San Francisco?" Sebastian asks. "The, uh, the Sea Lions?"

Now you'll bother to talk to me? Gil wants to ask. *What happened to all those times I called you?*

He tests his weight on his ankle. Yeah, he's fine, not getting out of this trade with another ankle injury, this one delightfully timely. "Seems like," he says.

Sebastian licks his lips. "Gil..."

Gil looks away. A decade ago this fall, Gil had gotten called up to the NHL, a flurry of excitement and nerves and delight at his dreams finally coming true, and in that same moment Sebastian had started closing the door on him. Them. Everything they'd been and everything they were going to grow to be, gone in a dwindling number of texts, calls Sebastian took a long time returning, voice-mails Gil left and never heard back about, all of it so strange, so abnormal for Sebastian that Gil still feels like he's floundering, a missed step in a familiar staircase, the jolt of such a sudden change sweeping through him yet again.

You had ten years, Gil wants to snap at him. And right fucking now is not the best time.

No, Gil can't handle this. The Sea Lions, Sebastian—Gil pushes past him. "Dad?"

"Gil," Dad says softly as Gil walks into the kitchen. "We'll fix this."

"You know already?" Gil asks.

"Fix what?" Tommy asks. "Are we screaming again? Or is that just Joey in the other room, calling absolutely everyone he knows?"

"Gil just got traded," Dad says, his voice quiet. "But no son of mine is playing for that joke of a team. Gil, this'll be alright."

"Okay," Gil says, because if Dad says that, then it will be.

"Traded where?" Tommy asks.

"San Francisco," Dad says.

"No way," Tommy says. "Sebastian, isn't that where you're living these days?"

Slowly, Gil looks up. Sebastian? Living in San Francisco?

Oh.

Oh *no*.

Sebastian's cheeks flush red as he pulls Buddy along through the kitchen, toward the door. "Yeah, I'm out there."

"That's so great, you two can hang out," Tommy says.

"I'm not playing there." Gil's mouth feels numb, his lips, his throat, his whole body. He's not playing there and he's certainly not living there.

"Not for long," Dad says. "I'm calling Melissa back right now, and then I'm getting on the phone with San Diego's GM and giving him a piece of my mind."

"Gil and Sebastian together again, just like old times," Tommy says, ignoring Dad like he always does. "You two gonna hang out? Finally, right? How long has it been?"

Gil nearly laughs. He can picture it now, standing in

some bland hotel room in San Francisco, phone pressed to his ear, listening to it ring until Sebastian's voicemail picks up. Typing out a text that never gets a response, leaving a message that Sebastian doesn't bother to return. *Missed call*, Sebastian's phone must have read for all the times Gil called him, text after text Gil sent, Sebastian's reply a handful of words only, until no replies had come at all.

No, Gil's not doing that again. He's not playing in San Francisco and he's certainly not chasing after Sebastian again.

And besides, the real old times between them? Those was here in this house, on that couch, upstairs in Gil's twin bed with its green comforter, laughing, lips chapped, hands searching. *Best friends*, he'd thought, until that had unspooled and everything fun and perfect and amazing about Sebastian was replaced with a growing wave of silence.

"Sebastian? Buddy?" Julie Martin calls from outside.

"Coming, Mom!" Sebastian shouts back to his mom. "I gotta—um—"

"Bye," Gil says.

"See you soon," Tommy corrects, but Sebastian's backing away, tugging Buddy with him.

No, Gil won't. Sebastian made that clear enough once and a lot can change in ten years, but not that.

Gil can't look. Doesn't look as Sebastian walks away. Just presses his fingers to the bridge of his nose, waiting until he hears the click of Buddy's nails on the floor, footsteps trailing off, until he can focus his thoughts, a clear, smooth sheet of ice in his mind and he tries to hold onto that image for as long as he can.

THREE

In the kitchen, Dad paces, his phone pressed to his ear.

Tommy spreads mustard over a slice of bread and arranges pieces of ham just so. "Gil, you hungry?"

Gil sits with his elbows on the kitchen counter, fingers clutching his hair as he slumps forward.

San Francisco.

The Sea Lions, embarrassment of the league.

A new expansion team, only a few years old, and floundering since they began. The most impact they've made since their first puck drop is memes of a walrus unable to hold a hockey stick in its flippers, and even better, the team protesting it's not even the right animal, which just made everyone laugh that much harder.

Tommy takes a bite of his sandwich. "Well, the good news is that wasn't awkward at all between you and Sebastian."

"I can't go there," Gil says, pressing his face into his hands. To move from San Diego, contenders for the Western Conference, to San Francisco? No. It's impossible. It's not happening. He's going to jerk awake any moment, his heart pounding, sheets sweaty and tangled around his legs. Laugh about this and go for a long run until his head is clear again.

Today won't have happened. No call from Melissa, no Buddy charging into the house, no gate opening in a fence that's kept the Roussins and Martins politely separated for years, and no puck sailing into their yard, because Gil potted that shot he took, never missed the damn net in the first place.

"Normally when I haven't seen a bestie in ages, I jump on them," Tommy says. "Now, you walking Greek statue over here, I get the restraint. You might have straight-up crushed him, but Sebastian's tough, he could probably take it."

"Can we not?" Gil asks.

"I can't believe he was visiting his mom this whole time. What a little shit to not come over. You and Joey make enough noise he couldn't have not known."

"Tommy, please."

"I knew you and Seb, whatever, let things cool off, but have you not kept in touch at all?"

Gil sits up. "He's the one who didn't keep in touch, not me. Shut up, would you? I want to hear what Dad's saying."

"I think it's cool you'll both be out in San Francisco. Good time to catch up, no? I haven't seen him since high school, I don't think, but I figured you two at least still chatted now and then."

"I'm not going to San Francisco," Gil says. "I'm—"

"Gil." Dad jabs at his phone to hang it up. "Call for you."

Sure enough, Gil's phone rings, a 415 area code staring up at him. Gingerly, he answers it. "Hello?"

"Gil? Gil Roussin? Frank Weinhaus here, GM of the Sea Lions."

"Oh. Hi."

"Just spoke with your dad," Frank says. "Real treat."

That's sarcasm, Gil is sure. And this is not the way to start off a relationship with the general manager of a new team.

"Thanks for calling," Gil says. *I'm real excited to be joining you*, he coaches himself, but he can't get the words out.

"Our training camp just started," Frank says. "And we've got our first preseason game coming up soon, so I've got you on a flight that'll get you to practice later today."

"Right," Gil says. *Great*, he needs to add. *I'll be there, I'm ready to work hard, can't wait to play for you.* "Yeah, my agent said."

"We're looking forward to having you here," Frank says. "Big season ahead of us. We've got a new head coach, and we're working to get our assistant coaches in place as well."

Gil squeezes his eyes shut. They have a new head coach because the last one left, fleeing the team to take an assistant job in Florida, anything to get out from under the slump that is the Sea Lions. Some issue with payroll had been the rumor Gil had heard, checks not being cut because the front office was in such disarray, and the owners didn't give a single crap. Entirely fitting for a team that plays in a rink that's falling apart, and that hasn't scraped itself off the bottom of the standings since the whistle blew to start their first game.

"Listen, we're excited about adding you to the roster. I think we can really make something of this team and you're a key part of that."

Embarrassment crawls through Gil's chest at the sincerity in Frank's voice. "Great," he gets out.

"So we'll see you this afternoon. I'll have a car at the airport for you. Be ready to jump on the ice."

"Course," Gil says, but that's not enthusiasm in his

voice, he knows, as he hangs up. The edge of nausea, maybe. Absolute, unfettered dread.

Outside the window, the sun glints on his training binder, the green and yellow of San Diego's team colors on the heading of each page.

Slowly, he walks outside. Picks up the binder, flips it shut, the mountain lion logo snarling up at him.

"We'll get this sorted out," Dad says from the front steps.

Gil turns, the binder clutched to his stomach. "When?"

"Maybe even before the regular season starts," Dad says. "You talked to your agent?"

"She said she'd try to get something done."

"I'll make some calls too. Now c'mon, I'll take you to the airport."

No, Gil wants to say. No, because he's not going.

Dully, he picks up his stick. His equipment bag is down in the basement and he'll have to pack his gear into it. Gather his clothes from his old bedroom, plastered with posters of hockey stars he'd idolized as a kid, doing pushups until his arms ached, picturing one of them passing him the cup to hoist over his head as the crowd cheered.

He'd only packed enough clothes for the short trip out here, a duffle he'd thrown in the overhead bin on the plane, his hockey bag checked with his sticks. It feels too empty now as he slowly fills it, most of his clothes the green fabric and yellow print of San Diego. Does he even have anything clean to wear on the plane? No, so he sorts through Tommy's clothes in the room down the hall with the bunkbeds he and Joey had fought over until Tommy started spending more nights than not at Mom's and her then-girlfriend's apartment.

The shirt he finds is too small and the fabric chafes at him as he sets his bag in the back of Dad's car, the cuffs snug against his biceps. Of course it doesn't fit him. Tommy goes running a few times a week, at most. Gil should have taken one of Joey's.

Should have left his own green and yellow shirts for Joey in return. *Roussin*, all of Gil's Mountain Lions shirts read. Joey could just slip into them and the team will barely know the difference. Take his number sixteen on the roster too, and it might as well be Gil there.

He rubs at his eyes as Dad starts the car.

"Um, bye," Tommy shouts through the window, tapping on the glass with one finger.

"Bye," Gil mutters as he rolls it down. "I took your shirt. See you in—" *November*, he nearly says, but no, that's when Joey will see him because that's when San Diego plays in Baltimore.

"Yeah, you did steal my shirt," Tommy says. "And hey, asshole, apologize to me, would you?"

"I can send it back to you," Gil says.

"Tonight," Tommy says, enunciating the word. "Sorry, Tommy, for missing your big night."

"I—what?"

"Oh, Gil." Tommy reaches into the car to poke his forehead. "You absolute fucker. Have a safe flight, okay?"

"Sorry," Gil says, a beat too late. "Um, have fun?"

"Um, okay, I will. Joey! Gil's leaving!"

"Thanks for this!" Joey shouts across the driveway, Gil's training binder in his hands. "Hey! Your keys!"

"Yeah," Gil mumbles and works his house and car key off his keyring, handing them to Tommy as Dad backs out of the driveway.

Get the mail, Gil should call back to Joey. Don't eat all his food, don't go through his things, don't mess up anything, he'll be back, he'll be—

27

Somewhere. He rubs at his face. Some other city. Not San Diego, not home.

Not San Francisco, either. Not if there's any chance in hell he can get out of there.

"The league's a chess game of moving players around," Dad says. "You know this. You got lucky sitting in one spot so long, so you just have to deal with this now."

"Yeah, I know."

Friends traded in the middle of the night, players pulled off planes and sent to a different city than the team was flying to. Heading out on a road trip only to not go home again, but landing in a new locker room, a new team, new teammates while food spoiled in the refrigerator at an apartment that would stay empty.

"This could be the start of dominos falling that'll send you somewhere great. Boston, can you picture that? Because you never know where you'll end up."

"Didn't think San Francisco would be a stop along the way."

"And it's time you move up the roster and get off the third line anyway," Dad says. "It's really been too long."

"I would have been this year," Gil says. "I'd have been playing center for the second line. And gotten to play with Joey, too."

"He'd have lit a fire under you, that's for sure," Dad says. "The two of you, fighting to outdo each other in points? That would've been something to see, keep you from slumping into a scoring rut."

Gil frowns. "I'm not in a rut."

"Nothing like someone nipping at your heels to get you going. But you'll stand out in San Francisco. They can barely field a team, so this isn't the end of the road. You gotta believe that."

"Think I'll manage a trade?"

"You go there, tear up the ice, and show scouts and other teams what you're made of? You'll have GMs ringing Melissa's phone off the hook," Dad says. "That's what Joey's done in Houston, and it certainly worked to get him out of there."

"I've been working so hard already."

"And what do we say to that?"

"Always room to work harder," Gil murmurs.

Dad glances at him. "What was that?"

There's a reason Dad's won Coach of the Year three times over. Why his players glow when they speak about him, and wear their Baltimore jerseys so proudly. Why he doesn't have to raise his voice on the bench. It's in that look on his face, the one directed at refs when they miss a call, at his players when they mishandle a puck, at his assistants when they miscalculate a play. Confident, stern, and sober all at once.

"I can always work harder," Gil says, louder.

"You got it, kid," Dad says. "We'll get you out of there."

So simple, the way Dad says it, and so matter of fact. If Dad thinks Gil will get traded, then it's true, as easy as that. So if Dad says Gil's not staying in San Francisco, then he isn't. Okay. He can...yeah, this is not ideal, not at all, but it's okay. It'll be okay.

And he can work harder. He can always work harder. Dad's right, and Gil lets that thought warm his chest, the same quiet, confident guidance Dad's always given him.

Because he can't play for the Sea Lions and he really, really can't live in the same city as Sebastian.

It's huge, he tells himself over the knot in his throat. They won't see each other, have awkward run-ins, spot the other on the street.

But it'd be better if Gil were gone. If he could breathe knowing Sebastian might not be around the next corner, if they could go back to the silence that Sebastian started and Gil had eventually found some peace in. Joey and Tommy had stopped asking about Seb, and even Mom had stopped talking with Julie Martin as much, so the constant chatter and reminder about the Martins had faded with the years into a distance that had felt so safe until today.

Gil closes his eyes and leans his head against the window. He'll have that again. The sharp cleave of his life from Sebastian's, an emptiness that they each stay on their own side of, an unspoken agreement that whatever they had together, it's gone now and there's nothing of it left to linger over.

And he'll get out of San Francisco too. Whatever it takes. Absolutely anything.

FOUR

AT THE AIRPORT, Gil shoulders his duffle as Dad drops his hockey bag on the curb.

The green and yellow mountain lion stares up at Gil from the bag, caught mid-growl, teeth bared.

He'll be issued a new bag in San Francisco's red and gold. And this one from San Diego... he can keep it, if he wants to. Memorabilia, like Dad's old equipment in neat boxes in the basement. Or he can sell it to fans like some guys do, or auction it off for charity. Sign it, leave his autograph on it just there, near the zipper, and some kid somewhere will get it as a present, stuffing their own gear into it with the delight Gil felt under those posters in his bedroom, close enough to the glory of professional hockey to nearly touch it.

"Roussin? Bert Roussin, I can't believe it—huge fan." A man bustles forward, rolling a suitcase behind him, his hand stuck out toward Dad. "I was there the night you scored your double hat trick. I can't believe you're here! What luck, it's so nice to meet you."

"What a great memory," Dad says in his soft voice. He smiles, shaking the man's hand and gripping it in both of his like he always does, that specific handshake he reserves for fans, as if his usual sincerity doubles around them. "So glad you could share it with me."

The man is nearly breathless. "Could I get a picture?"

"Of course you can, I'd be delighted. Gil?"

"Yeah." Gil takes the man's phone as he sidles up to Dad, grinning ear to ear.

"On three," Gil says by rote. Once, this was fun, pulling the camera away from Tommy and Joey because Gil was the tallest, the oldest, the most responsible, so he got the privilege of being the photographer of fans and their famous dad.

He has to step over his bags to frame the image on the screen: Dad smiling politely, the man with his grin splitting his face, a car behind them that Gil pauses to let move so it's not just a picture of the two of them with bumper stickers plastering a hatchback.

It pulls away and a man's standing there, a messenger bag across his navy blue T-shirt, jeans slung low on his hips, dark brown hair and a beard.

"Sorry," Gil says, his finger slipping and pressing the shutter too quickly. "Okay, ready? Three, two, one, got it. Looks great."

Always do it right, Dad used to tell him as Gil clutched the fan's camera in his hands, tongue between his teeth as he concentrated. *This is every day for us, but this is one day out of their lives for them.*

Yes, the picture is fine, it's good. And the guy he'd glimpsed, Sebastian's same build, his height, that beard, is gone, not in the background of the photo and not on the curb anymore.

Gil hitches his duffle bag higher on his shoulder. That wasn't Sebastian. He's just jumpy today.

It could have been, though.

No. He adjusts his bag again. He's got to get his head on straight. The start of the season isn't the time for distractions, especially when he's pushing for a trade. He needs to bring his best game to San Francisco, make sure his play doesn't suffer for the circus of the team around him. *Stand out and get seen*, he'd told himself over and over again those last years of high school as he counted down the days to the draft. Make sure it's his name on the top of scouts' lists, that GMs bring up in their meetings, that coaches dream of adding to their rosters. He might not be able to control whether the GM trades him, but he can play well enough that he's worth something, and that starts today when he hits the ice.

Sea Lions practice, he thinks and his stomach churns.

"You go on, now," Dad says. "Let me chat with this gentleman, give him some of my time."

"Yeah, of course." Gil gathers up his sticks and hockey bag. *Let me get you a luggage cart*, Mom would say if she were here, but Gil doesn't need one, not with a summer of building muscle, his life of professional sports.

"Bye, kid," Dad says. "Remember, San Francisco is only a bump in the road. Do the work and we'll get you out of there."

"Bye," Gil says, stutter-stepping in hesitation as a car passes too close before he heads across the lanes of traffic. Yeah, a bump in the road. Temporary. Impermanent. A funny, mildly embarrassing story to tell in the long arc of his career, derailed for a moment before he finds himself back on track.

At the gate, he sprawls in a hard plastic chair, legs kicked out in front of him as he stares at his phone. *Don't worry, I'll take care of your pool waterfall*, Joey's texted.

Call me if you want to talk, sweetie, Mom messaged just after.

He rubs at his eyes. He'd seen her and Lex, her wife, a few days ago, when he'd landed here in Maryland for this trip. They'd had dinner together and shared a walk near the City Dock in Annapolis, but then he'd headed to the rink and to Dad's house so he could keep up his training.

Tommy must have told her about the trade. Probably called her right away as Dad drove Gil out of the driveway. With one more day in his schedule, Gil could have seen her again, let Mom hug him, given himself a moment to pretend hockey is far away, distant—

No. He flicks away from his texts to check his email and frowns at the *Welcome to the San Francisco Sea Lions!* message someone in the team's front office has already emailed him. *Practice Details,* a message from Frank is titled, though when Gil opens it, it's just an address for the rink and their ice time.

He sighs, shifting in his seat.

"You mind?" a guy next to him asks.

"Sorry," Gil mutters, pulling his feet back under him.

"No, your seat," the guy says. "So I can sit with my girlfriend."

"Yeah, course." Gil slips sideways into the seat next to him, freeing up the chair the guy was eyeing.

Gonna miss you, Rooster, a text appears on his screen. Hux, his buddy down in San Diego, his left wing.

Previous left wing. Joey's now, maybe, depending on how the roster shakes out without Gil there.

He flicks to Instagram to clear the text off his screen. *Welcome Gilbert Roussin,* a red and gold image reads, his face staring up at him, superimposed over San Francisco's logo of a sea lion. *We're flipping happy to have you,* the caption says.

Gil locks his phone and shoves it into his pocket, hard enough his elbow pokes the guy on his other side. Not the one who already made him move, at least. Still, Gil mumbles, "Sorry," with a quick, apologetic glance.

He freezes. Worn jeans, a blue T-shirt with *Rideau University, Minnesota* stamped across the chest in white, and an old-fashioned watch that was once—

"It's fine." Sebastian shifts in his seat so he's as far from Gil as he can get.

Mr. Martin's. That's his old watch on Sebastian's wrist, the one he used to take off before playing with them in the pool, wrestling with them in the backyard, tossing the football to them.

"I didn't, um..." Realize. Know. Mean to find himself nearly pressed against Sebastian's arm, given how crowded these seats are. Gil moves too, putting a few inches between them. "You also on this flight?"

"Yep." Sebastian doesn't look up from his phone, his thumb scrolling across the screen.

"Oh." Gil nods. To himself, apparently, because Sebastian still isn't looking at him. "Yeah, me too."

He just said that. Repeated himself, so it's real damn clear he's very much getting on this plane.

Without turning his head, he casts a look at Sebastian, whose lips are pursed as he reads his phone.

He looks the same, just older than the version carved in Gil's mind. None of the coltish youth of college on his frame, the last lingering softness of adolescence on his cheeks, covered now with his neatly trimmed beard, but it's still Sebastian. A couple inches shorter than him if they stood back to back like they used to, jockeying for height like they had any control over the ongoing competition. Narrower shoulders than Gil's, which meant an extra bit of power Gil could put into his slapshot that Sebastian could never quite match. Same size shoes, like always, Sebastian wearing scuffed sneakers next to Gil's leather boots.

When he looks up again, Sebastian's watching him.

Gil's face heats.

"You're playing for the Sea Lions," Sebastian says.

Hi, Gil wants to blurt. *How are you, how've you been, what happened, where did you go?*

"Yeah," he gets out. *Bye*, he maybe means instead of an entreaty of conversation, *leave me alone again, you did it so well for so long*. "I was in San Diego. Got traded."

"You're flying out quickly."

"I've got practice this afternoon."

"Missing Tommy's thing tonight?"

"Yeah, I gotta."

"Right."

It hurts his ass to sit like this, shoved to one side in the seat. Gil shifts gingerly, as if it's too dangerous to let his leg inch toward Sebastian's.

Once, he would have. Laid his hand right there on Sebastian's thigh, tipped his head close and whispered something filthy about the mile-high club, his plan for the plane bathroom, how to slip out from under the eyes of their college coaches.

That feels so much longer ago than the ten years it's been, an entire different life from the flurry of his career in the NHL.

Or shorter, maybe, which makes sense in its own way too, being here with Sebastian once again, time stretching like an elastic band, contracting back on itself.

But what the hell had even happened across those years? Going from best friends, teammates, sharing the same clothes, the same dorm room, the same twin bed, to—what? A slow fade into nothing?

Tommy was right. Old teammates Gil has run into, long-ago friends—he's greeted them with hugs, back slaps, the loud, laughing reminiscing of practices and games they'd shared. They'd be causing a ruckus in the terminal, earning glares from travelers. And if he'd known Sebastian was also in Baltimore this past week, they'd have been up late each night, talking, laughing, touching—

No. No, they wouldn't.

Gil hunches forward, grabbing for his phone again. His shirt's too tight and he picks at the cuff around his bicep.

Sebastian glances at his arm and then crosses his feet so his entire body slants away from Gil's.

Fine. Gil would rather stare at the damn graphic of himself photoshopped into a Sea Lions jersey than try to make conversation. Text Joey and tell him to make sure to check that the freezer is actually closed, not hanging open an inch like it tends to do. Even call Mom and let her fuss over him, now that Dad's not around to quietly frown, just a dip of the corner of his mouth, an unsaid remark about Mom's "coddling" loud enough.

"Now boarding first class," an announcement blares.

Sebastian clears his throat. "Gil—"

"That's me," Gil says, already on his feet.

"Wait," Sebastian says, standing too. "I have to tell you."

I'm sorry, I should have never stopped talking to you. Gil sucks in a breath, hope shoving through the hurt in his chest. *I missed you so much, I want to hang out, grab dinner, share a cab from the airport and catch up.* "Yeah?" he asks softly.

"I'm coaching the Sea Lions."

"I—what?"

"So I'll see you there, at the rink."

"The Sea Lions?" Gil repeats. Sebastian? Coaching? Coaching...*him?* "What the hell?"

"I'm one of the new assistant coaches. The only one for now, actually. They gave me an extra day to sort a few things out back at Mom's, but I'm heading there for practice same as you."

"You're coaching San Francisco?" *Me*, he means. *Coaching me?*

"I wanted to let you know. And—" Sebastian's eyes dart away. "Well, being new to the team, I'd appreciate you not saying anything about, you know, our past."

Gil feels his mouth gape. Sebastian, coaching him. Coaching the Sea Lions, and Gil playing for him. And, what, keeping his mouth shut? Keeping quiet about...

Our past what? Gil wants to prompt. Twist the knife digging into his gut, make Sebastian say it. Sebastian who will be on the ice, who's on this plane, who's flying to the same city. What past doesn't he want Gil bringing up? Past teams they played on together? The childhood they'd shared? Their friendship? Roommates in college?

Past relationship, Gil thinks. *Boyfriend*, he'd introduced Seb as at parties in college, his hand tucked in the back pocket of Sebastian's jeans.

Gil's mouth opens, but all he gets out is a soft puff of air.

"I've got to get to know everyone on the team, and I'd like a chance to get started in the position on the right foot. So if we could keep it professional, I'd appreciate it."

A laugh claws up Gil's throat. "Professional."

"And at least not volunteer any information if we're not asked."

"Right," Gil says. He steps backward. Boarding, the flight is boarding. "No problem. We're good."

"Gil—"

"Professional, I got it." Gil turns away. "Sounds great."

Ten years Sebastian's kept him at a distance. This is just more of the same, round two of Sebastian drawing a sharp, clear line between them of what he'll give and what Gil gets.

Which is nothing, same as it has been.

Gil's numb as he makes his way onto the plane, sinking into the aisle seat he's assigned.

Sebastian's going to be coaching him. Stepping onto the ice with a whistle around his neck, sending him through drills, and what, giving him pointers? Tips and advice Gil doesn't already know?

He wants to laugh. To bury his face in his palms until all of this goes away.

But no, Sebastian will walk by any moment now. Gil stares at the tiny TV in front of him, scrolling through it for the latest sports highlights as his head swims.

And Sebastian does appear, his thumb through the strap of his messenger bag where it crosses his chest, his other hand in his pocket, eyes focused down the aisle, straight past Gil.

Gil grabs his headphones, flicks through his phone for the type of music he reserves for before a game, the jarring, fast tempo, the deep bass that thrums through him, muffling the flight attendant chatting about the bad weather they'll be flying through and a rocky landing in San Francisco.

Still, he can hear through the clatter of drums, the electric hum of the guitar, or maybe the way Sebastian's lips form words is just so familiar, mouthing at each other across the locker room during practice, inside jokes traded back and forth like the passes they sent each other on the ice.

"Let me help," Sebastian says to a woman struggling with her bag, taking it from her and lifting it overhead to set in the bin. The motion raises his T-shirt, the hem inching above his belt, the top of his pants, a band of skin exposed, the trickle of hair that leads downward, the jut of his hipbones.

Sebastian's stomach is less defined than when he was playing hockey. Gil clenches his jaw, staring at his phone, willing the difference to matter to him, to dip into the hot slick of resentment in his gut at Sebastian so close to him, and to stem the innate, automatic attraction that flushes through his body.

I'm over him, Gil tells himself. Of course he is. It's been ten years.

But his anger is a slippery, squirming thing and his grip on it skids, making him want to turn and catch a glimpse of Sebastian's back as he walks to the back of the plane.

No.

Gil's been here before. Longing after Sebastian, the yearning a hollow pit in his stomach, clutching his phone and willing it to light up with a text, searching the crowd when he played in Minnesota, craning for a glimpse of brown hair, bright eyes, that smile.

He tips his head back, staring blankly, music he doesn't listen to churning in his ears as he waits for the plane to take off and head toward the wrong city in California.

FIVE

A GIANT SEA lion waves to Gil at the bottom of the escalator and beside it, a woman stands with a camera, filming him before Gil can even smile.

My new best friend! reads the sign the sea lion holds up.

When it hugs Gil, it's like being smothered in a musty-smelling stuffed animal, one that grips him too tight, dancing around and pounding him on the back.

But maybe this is better than what he'd expected, given what he knows of the team: a car that doesn't show up on time so he has to catch a cab, the team not ready for him, the practice time incorrect, the address he was sent bringing him to a wrong arena.

Being greeted by actual staff is a step above what he was braced for. Quite a few steps, actually.

"Got it," the woman with the camera says, and only then does the thing step back from him.

"Mikey," the guy in the suit says, waving a flipper at Gil. "Good flight?"

"Hey," Gil says, waving back and then shaking the woman's hand. "Thanks for meeting me."

"Gil, hi, I'm Emery Millbury, social media manager,

website admin, brand expert, all of it, one-woman show around here. Really nice to meet you. We just have a few minutes before we're ready to get going, then we'll get you straight to practice."

"Great," Gil says. It's flattering that they came to see him as soon as he landed. They're planning to put this up as his big welcome to the team, splash it over all their socials and on the team's website.

Awkward, also, if he can manage to get off the team as soon as he'd like to. But kind of nice.

And what had Melissa said? He'd be the big name on this team. And big names are always more likely to get traded when they want to be.

He puts on a smile. "Whatever you need."

"Give him a high five, Gil," Emery says from behind her camera and yeah, he can do this, smile and slap the flipper Mikey holds up. "And the beach ball, just right here, yep, and if you toss it to him, it's magnetic to his nose. It's really a seal thing, but engagement is great on these GIFs. Three, two, one, toss it."

People are watching and Gil's cheeks warm, but he picks up the ball she nudges toward him and tosses it. Mikey ducks to catch it, acting like he's balancing it on his nose as the magnet connects.

"Can I get in the car now?" Mikey asks, giant stuffed head still tipped upward. With him standing like that, Gil can see his face behind a gray mesh panel in the mascot suit's neck. He waves his flipper at a little girl walking past. "I'm not paid enough for this. This thing is hot as shit."

"Soon." Emery glances at the escalator Gil came down. They must be waiting for someone else. For—

Sebastian.

Of course they are.

Professional, Gil thinks, but it's like he can't get purchase on the word, the idea of it too smooth to grasp.

He pivots to the baggage carousel, already turning with bags marked *Priority* and there, green fabric and yellow straps, the handle worn from so many trips.

He'll get a new bag this season, a replacement, since this one is showing its age.

No, he would have. Joey will. *Roussin* stamped on it. Maybe Gil's old number, too, a bright *16* on each end of the bag.

Joey, he thinks. In his green and yellow uniform. Swimming in Gil's pool, lounging on the couch he'd just bought, that cat of his sauntering through the house Gil loves so much.

"Grab his equipment for him, Mikey. Make it funny." Emery swings her camera around. "Do something to the Mountain Lions logo, okay?"

Mikey skips a step backward, acting like he's terrified of the illustration, the mouth open, fangs white, eye narrowed as it growls.

"Something else," Emery says. "C'mon, that just makes us look scared."

"I'm a fucking dude in a gross costume, not an actor. What do you want from me?"

Gil takes a breath. They sent the mascot and the social media manager. *A positive*, he tries to cling to. "I got it," he says, and hauls the bag and his bundle of taped-together sticks from the conveyer belt.

"Sea Lions?" Sebastian asks, suddenly behind Gil, and oh, his *voice*.

Answer, Gil used to think as his phone rang, Sebastian's voicemail message the only sound of him speaking Gil had to cling to. *Hey, must have missed you earlier*, Gil had left, unsure why it was taking Sebastian so long to call him back each time. *I'm sorry if I did something, I don't know what it was, can you call me, can you please just call me?* he'd pleaded later until the day he had finally stopped leaving a recording, still calling just to listen to Sebastian telling him to leave a message, until he'd managed to quit doing that, too.

"Coach Martin, right?" Emery asks.

"Sebastian," he says, and he does the same quick half step forward to shake her hand he's always done, something sincere and earnest about it that used to make Gil smile. "Hi."

It still threatens to make him smile.

Hockey. He has practice. And when he's angling to get traded is not the time to be distracted.

"Real excited to hit the ice," Gil says.

"Great, we can head out," Emery says. "If you have everything, Sebastian?"

"I do," he says. "Didn't check a bag."

"And I can take this off?" Mikey raises his flippers to grasp the head of his costume.

"No. This way, gentlemen," Emery says and leads them to a black SUV idling at the curb. "Mikey, get in the back."

"I don't fit," Mikey says, but he squirms into the third row of seats, leaving the two bucket seats in the middle for Gil and Sebastian.

Like old times, Gil could say, tumbling into Dad's car on the way to the rink. Back then, it was Joey shoved in back and Tommy riding up front with Dad because Gil wanted to sit with Sebastian.

He yanks on his seatbelt, refusing to look over. Couldn't answer the phone, and now here Sebastian is, waltzing back into Gil's life where they can both be so delightfully *professional*.

Gil must have grandly pissed off the universe to manage

all of this. *Sorry*, he thinks like he can make up for it, blink and everything will disappear.

But no stroke of luck waits for him, ready to sweep all of this away. Just hard work and his will to grind until he gets the results he wants. He finds his smile again as Emery settles next to the driver, twisting toward them with her camera. "Can't wait to get on the ice," he says and when Sebastian glances at him, he ignores it.

"The team's thrilled you're here too," Emery says. "Both of you, really. What a coincidence, right? You know each other?"

Anything for a trade, he'd promised himself. *Journalists and social media managers can make or break your career*, Dad always warned. Gil sits up straight. Smiles. "Yeah, we played together in college."

"And—" Emery glances down at her phone, scrolling through what looks to be a list of notes. "High school?"

Oh, she did her homework.

Okay, no problem. He can be absolutely, utterly professional. "We grew up near each other, got to know each other pretty well," Gil says as easily as he knows how.

"I was looking up some old articles about Rideau from your playing days, Gil. You two were best friends?"

He keeps his smile plastered on. "That was a while ago."

"So back together again." Emery's eyes are trained on her camera's screen. "How does that feel?"

Sebastian's leg jiggles.

Stop, Gil wants to say. Lean over and press his hand to Sebastian's knee to still it.

Or maybe snap at him, *I'm not going to fucking say anything*, the hurt of the past years boiling up in an anger that wars with the sympathy in his chest at how terrified Sebastian seems.

Enough. He's annoyed for noticing Sebastian's nerves and even more so for caring. Sebastian clearly wants this job to work out. And he needs Gil to not mess it up for him. *I didn't turn into an asshole in the last ten years, that was you who's the jerk*, Gil could say to him, but he just smiles for the camera again.

"Really great," he says. "What a huge surprise for both of us."

"Can we have some get-to-know-you facts about each other?" Emery asks. "I'd normally do this individually, but how fun that you two are already friends."

No, Gil nearly blurts. *Friends*, he thinks and wants to cringe. "Absolutely," he says.

The engine hums as the car accelerates onto the highway, and the driver flicks the wipers on against the patter of rain. Behind him, Mikey sneezes.

"Any time," Emery says.

"Yeah, no, just thinking. Sebastian—sorry, Coach Martin, I mean. What an adjustment, right?" Gil tries to laugh. "Um, some interesting things about him, let's see…"

Eats cereal straight from the box by the handful. Can't get a basketball through a hoop for the life of him. Snores when he's really tired.

Unless all of that has changed. Maybe he eats his breakfast out of delightfully matching bowls these days, plays basketball in his free time, and finally learned to lay on his damn side so he doesn't disturb the sleep of—

Who? Gil wonders.

"Gil?" Emery asks.

"Oh, yeah, um, well, his dad was a hell of a football player."

Sebastian turns toward him, looking across the back seat.

"Quarterback for his college," Gil says. "Taught me how to throw a perfect spiral."

Over and over again in the Martins' backyard, cheering at every wobbly ball he and Sebastian hurled at each other, until Gil's dad showed up at the back fence, beckoning Gil back to the driveway for stick-handling practice.

"Speak up," Emery says.

"Sorry?"

"A bit louder and try to remember to smile, both of you."

Gil straightens in his seat. He's not actually used to doing this. It was other players the Mountain Lions' social media team chased after for content. He was mostly left alone, all the better to get focused on his game. *Dog and pony show*, Dad calls all the videos for social media. Necessary, but an embarrassing business of hockey when they could be focused on playing.

"He played catch with us," Gil says louder, through his smile. "All the time. It was great."

"And Sebastian?" Emery prompts.

"Yeah," Sebastian says and then just sits there, silent.

He looks miserable. He always did, ducking away from any videos filmed of their college team.

So he's not just terrified that Gil will start in on their so unprofessional past. He's also still shy, all these years later, quiet around groups of people, faced with a new player in the locker room, a bus full of guys he didn't know, hesitant over what to say, following in Gil's wake as Gil made friends for both of them.

How is he going to survive the scrutiny of being an NHL coach, cameras trained on him on the bench every game, chased down for quotes and statements on his work and the team's play?

Badly, Gil imagines. No wonder he's so nervous Gil might throw him under the bus.

A small, hard shard of the resentment in Gil's chest splinters free.

No.

I'm so fucking pissed you wouldn't pick up the phone, he thinks, trying to grab onto the old, familiar burn of anger. *Stay away from him*, Gil had finally convinced himself. Away from their chain of text messages Gil had read and reread, from the clothes they had shared that had ended up in Gil's bag when he'd packed so quickly to leave for the NHL, from the side of the bed that for too long he thought of as Sebastian's, and from the damn backyard at his dad's house with its fence and its gate, like he could ease it open and step back into the life they'd shared, be the Gil of Gil and Sebastian, instead of this awful new version who lived on his own, surrounded by his new team but alone each and every day.

That painful, harsh separation between them had worked for so long. Memories barricaded away of how he never once looked Sebastian up online, didn't let himself ask after him when Gil ran into hockey-world guys who knew them both, never bringing him up to their old coach to learn what Sebastian was up to.

He needs to keep himself safe that same way now, focused on hockey and only hockey for as long as it takes to get traded. *Only a couple days*, he tries to imagine, fortune working for him for once, Melissa calling him with the news she's found him a spot on another team, and quickly too. Weeks at the most, because he'll work hard enough on the ice to make that happen, to catch the eye of some scout or some GM who can't possibly pass him over.

So don't, he tells himself now. Leave Sebastian to his own devices like he left Gil by himself, faced with a new career, a new city, a new team, and none of the support of their friendship. Let him drift out in the cold like Gil had, lonely and lost and so confused the bewilderment had nearly eclipsed the hurt.

But it's Sebastian and he looks miserable and so Gil prompts him, "That first hockey practice."

"What about it?" Emery asks.

C'mon, Gil thinks at Sebastian, as if that old simpatico between them can restart like an unused engine, the battery sparking to life and the gears creaking as they turn over.

"The—oh. Yeah," Sebastian says, his voice soft. "Gil got me into hockey."

"What?" Emery asks. "Can you say that again?"

"I started playing hockey because of Gil," Sebastian says, louder. "I don't—is that a fact about me or him?"

"I dragged Sebastian with me to practice one day." The memory trembles in Gil's chest, that autumn afternoon he'd convinced Sebastian to get in the car. "He was wearing all my old pads. He had no idea how to skate. Fell and bruised his butt and said he wasn't ever coming back."

"Meant it too," Sebastian says quietly.

Is that a hint of a smile on his mouth?

No, Gil doesn't care. Can't care. It's one thing to extend the tiniest bit of help, another to tumble back into Sebastian entirely. "He caught on," Gil says brusquely. "Eventually. My Dad helped."

"Helped," Sebastian says just as softly as before. "Yeah."

"Dad got him up to speed, because Seb didn't start skating until, what were we, eight?"

"Nine," Sebastian says.

Yeah, nine, that's right, because that was the year—

Gil glances at Sebastian's wrist, at the watch he's wearing that had been his dad's. "I think I was already on the junior high team," Gil says quickly. *The bad year,* Sebastian had called it once, his arm thrown over his face as they lay in his bed, as if any of the ones that had followed had been much easier at all. "But Seb caught up, went from clutching the boards to making varsity in high school same time I did."

Sebastian lets out a soft laugh. "I think you made them take me."

"I probably would've if they hadn't." Because at that point, how could he play without Sebastian? He needed him, getting dressed next to him in the locker room, sitting together on the bus rides, side by side on the bench. The laughing, fist bumps, wrestling that soothed nerves in Gil's stomach before puck drop. Pounding each other on the back after a win and then after a loss, *You're okay*, Sebastian would murmur to him as Gil sat slumped, replaying the goal he had missed, the puck turnover he had caused. *It was one mistake. You're allowed one mistake.*

No, there was no Gil without Sebastian by the time they reached high school, and there hadn't been for some time.

"Best memories playing together?" Emery asks.

Gil lets himself smile. "Winning states our senior year."

"Sebastian?"

"I was—yeah, winning states."

"What were you going to say?"

"No, just the—we went to a water park as a team once, it was really fun, it—but, no, states. That was huge. Gil got us the overtime goal."

"That was an amazing game." Gil gives himself permission to dart a quick glance at Sebastian. "Remember, Seb, the boards? At that rink? When you went to jump over them and—"

"Gil, that was you."

"Me?" *Hi*, Gil wants to whisper. *Is it really you? Sebast-*

ian, are you here, are you back? "It was not, you caught your leg on the edge of them and nearly wiped out."

"No, that was totally you. You were so excited to get on the ice and then you stepped on a puck and—"

"I did not! You're thinking of college."

"Oh," Sebastian says and his *smile*, it fills his face, dances up to his eyes. "Yeah, that first game at Rideau when you were getting on the ice and—"

"No, don't, Seb—"

"The seniors put clear tape on your skate blades? To take you down a notch?"

"C'mon, man."

"And you went and tried to skate anyway, 'cause Gil Roussin wasn't going to—"

"This did not happen," Gil tries to tell Emery.

"It absolutely happened. He fell and couldn't get up and you were completely determined to just go ahead anyway, so you—"

"Seb!"

"He had to crawl back toward the bench," Sebastian says. "And then of course you got a hat trick that game to make up for it, because you're you, Gil."

Gil squeezes his eyes shut, laughing. "Shut up."

"Two of the guys dressed up like him for Halloween that year, falling all over themselves."

"Don't remind me, please."

"The single time in Gil's life he couldn't skate."

"Any other good college stories?" Emery prompts. "Because that was the last time you two played together, right? At Rideau before you got called up to the NHL?"

"Yeah, that was our freshman year and then the fall before our sophomore season I got my entry-level contract," Gil says. "But we had a great time while I was there. We played on the same line, both loved Coach

Thompson and the team, it was—that was a great year. Amazing, honestly."

"Sebastian?" Emery asks.

But Sebastian's looking out the window, watching rain streak the glass and the foggy, rain-smeared skyline of the city as the car zips down the highway.

"Seb," Gil prompts.

"Oh, of course, no, college was great."

"Got other memories to share?" Emery asks.

But Sebastian just says, "Yeah," and turns back to the window.

Don't go, Gil wants to say. Sebastian was nearly right here, the old Sebastian, the real Sebastian, not this quiet, grown man.

But Emery tells Gil to smile as Mikey leans forward, a flipper hugging him from behind as she clicks a photo. She bends over her phone, posting it, he's sure, as Sebastian stares at the highway and beyond the rush of cars, the skyline of the city rises toward them.

Gil's used to arriving at San Diego's rink through acres of parking lots, banners hanging from the streetlights on the drive up to it, and the front of the building plastered in huge graphics of their goalie, the captain, and as of last season, one of Hux that they'd all given him hell about, threatening to climb up there and draw on an awful twirly mustache.

Gil's used to San Diego's cheerful sunny days too, not the dreary drizzle the car rolls through, turning off a steep hill to take them down an alley, trash bags lined up on one side of it, an old crumbling brick wall with a steel door they stop in front of.

Emery gives a soft laugh at the look that must be on Gil's face. "It's got charm. It'll grow on you."

"Is this the practice rink?" Gil asks, hesitating as he gets down from the car, an oily puddle beneath him. Gingerly, he steps over it.

"Practice rink, game rink, neighborhood rink, we've got it all," Emery says.

"You're joking."

"Welcome," Emery says. "Mikey, watch that puddle. We don't have a second sea lion suit."

"Shame if it got ruined," Mikey says as he works his bulk out of the car.

"Sebastian, the coaches' office is upstairs. Frank wants to see you before you get on the ice."

"Thanks," Sebastian says, shutting the car door.

"Hey," Gil calls out, jogging a step after Sebastian.

But he's walking too quickly, already halfway to the battered metal door of the rink.

A bubble of hope pops in Gil's chest, a lightness born on the drive, the memory of what it had been like to send quips back and forth with Sebastian, the rhythm they had that was so natural to fall into.

When Gil turns, Emery is watching him, though at least her camera is off, no red light staring at him as she records.

"We just, ah, fell out of touch," Gil says.

"Seems like it."

"Been a while. But it's no problem, it's fine."

So fine. Utterly and completely fine. All of this, the shitty alleyway, the crumbling building, this team he's found himself on.

But not for long, not if he has anything to do about his situation here and getting a trade. He shoulders his bag and walks inside the rink.

SIX

THE RINK IS DIM. *Just a loading dock*, Gil tells himself, the familiar concrete floor and metal struts of all rinks' player entrances.

But there's another puddle dripping onto the floor just there, the edge rimmed with a stain of rust, and a crack in the wall that's been patched over only for the patch to crack too.

Above him, the fluorescent lights hum and one flickers off and on and then off again.

He hasn't ever played here. He missed the road game last year due to an ankle injury, and the year before they'd hosted San Francisco at home, an absolute rout of a game. *Lucky you didn't have to go*, Hux had said, pulling a face when he'd tried to describe the rink. How had he put it? Way worse in person than on TV, like the most run-down of the places any of them had played as a kid, but with the embarrassment of housing a professional team.

No, it's more like a joke, now that Gil sees it. This rink can't possibly be real. Another car will pick him up, this'll be a prank the team's playing on the new guy, and he'll show up to an arena more befitting the NHL.

A lone banner hangs, *San Francisco Sea Lions* written across it, a water stain on the corner.

Mikey chucks the sea lion head onto a folding table and shimmies out of the suit, tossing it after the head so it nearly slides onto the floor, close enough to the puddle he should probably care. He walks past it, ignoring Emery when she calls to him to put it back on.

"Um," Gil says.

Emery shrugs. "Super old, historic building. Some sort of warehouse. What better spot to tie together the city's history with its first professional hockey team, right?"

Right, Gil should say but he can't get the word out.

"Yeah, we know. The owners were supposed to fix this place up before the team ever started playing, but that's what happens when it's a bunch of tech guys thinking they can own a sports team. Bet wrong on their crypto, a few key stocks tanked, and we were at the top of the list of what they couldn't care less about."

"They can't just sell the team to someone else?"

"It's not worth anything. The old GM and front office drove the place into the ground, and pretty much everyone who worked here walked out. And I don't blame them. I use the term 'GM' loosely, because he was just one of the owners' buddies they hired. He didn't know shit about the game. All the value's gone from the franchise but the owners don't want to lose on the sale." Emery gestures to the gloomy, leaking building around them. "So this is what it is. Charming, isn't it?"

She laughs when he just opens his mouth, unable to find any words.

"Yeah, well, look, it was either keep the team here or play in a college arena. Which is worse, really?" Emery points down the hall. "Locker room's to the left, players' lounge and coaches' offices are upstairs, ice is to the right. Sounds like they're already out there."

"Thanks," Gil gets out.

That means he should hurry. Slowly, he heads in the direction she pointed and carefully doesn't look at the ice. There won't be championship banners hung above it, he knows, and he won't get the thrill of the sheet of ice under the shine of arena lights he always does in any arena, a hitch of wonder in his chest at the sight.

No, there's none of that here. None of that splendor as he sidesteps another puddle, just the astringent smell of industrial cleaner that can't quite mask the musty age of the building, the awkward retrofit of an ice arena into a space where it doesn't belong.

He wants to go home, to San Diego's brightly lit halls, the pictures of players before him on the walls and the hope his own will hang there someday.

He bites his lip hard enough to hurt and pushes inside the Sea Lion locker room.

"Fuck," he whispers at the sight.

There should be a dressing room for them to change from their suits or street clothes into workout shorts and shirts. A trainers' room connected by an open door, clean and tidy and full of staff. Racks of extra sticks, tape, skate blades, an equipment room full to bursting and still somehow perfectly organized, and someone in there waiting for Gil to check over his skates, sharpen them to his preferences, get his sticks laid out and have his stall ready for him, his jersey hung up and waiting.

The room has low ceilings and the aged yellow lights do little to brighten the corners, just shine on the scuffed mats on the floor. The lockers stuffed into the space are too small for professional athletes, cramped even before Gil has hung his gear in the only empty one.

No nameplate greets him above the stall, the little brass holder screwed into the wood sitting empty. *Douglas Mitchell, #32* reads the next one over. *Ondrej Blomkvist, #4* the one on the left says, but it's a bit crooked, like the laminated strip of red and gold paper has been shoved in there and nobody bothered to straighten it.

Slowly, he sits on the bench in his stall.

It's fine. He's not staying here. This is an embarrassing moment in the greater story of his career. What had Dad said? Boston, maybe, waiting for him on the other side of this mess?

Focus. Work hard and the rest will come. He can't make Frank trade him, but he can play well enough that a team will make an offer Frank can't refuse.

Gil yanks his shirt over his head, tossing it into the back of his stall, trying to ignore the thoughts rising through him, borne on the misery of how today is panning out. He has worked hard. And this is what came. A dingy, awful locker room, not even a pair of hockey socks laid out for him, so he pulls his old green and yellow ones on over his shin guards, and his green pants from San Diego too. He pauses when he stands on his skates, wearing his chest protector and elbow pads, staring around like a jersey will materialize out of the damp corners of the room.

"Hey," he calls, sticking his head in the hallway.

A light flickers. Somewhere, something drips, a rhythmic, slow plop of water.

He closes his eyes. *Dad,* he thinks. *Fucking save me.*

"You good?" someone calls to him. Mikey, the guy in the costume, now in shorts and a sweatshirt.

Gil frowns. That's a baseball team on the sweatshirt. They don't even have team clothing for this guy? *Sea Lions* splashed across the chest, the proud red and gold of the team for him to wear so he matches every other employee and staff member?

Which...Gil hasn't seen. Not anyone other than Mikey heading toward him.

"Is there a jersey for me?" Gil asks.

"Oh, I gotcha." Mikey pulls open a door in the hallway. The equipment room, Gil hopes, but it's just a closet stuffed full with cardboard boxes, piled haphazardly so they nearly fall when Mikey starts digging through them.

"You work for the equipment manager?" Gil asks.

"That guy? He quit before last season ended. Got out before the rest of the staff and honestly, good for him. Here, one red, one white, if you need a different size good luck, I guess, 'cause I think that's all we have. Someone was supposed to order more, but guess what?"

Gil doesn't want to know. "Thanks," he says and steps back toward the locker room.

"They quit too," Mikey says helpfully.

Gil holds up the shirts. "Which color am I supposed to wear for practice today?"

"Dunno," Mikey says.

"Is there a list?"

"Maybe?" Mikey shrugs and he's gone again, wandering off down the hall as Gil stares after him.

There should be a list on the whiteboard at the front of the room. A practice plan on it. A schedule for the day.

There's a board, at least. Poorly erased, streaked with old writing, the stain of someone using the wrong type of markers.

Slowly, Gil pulls on the white jersey. Gathers his helmet, Mountain Lion stickers on it, the green he'd been so proud to wear. His gloves with their yellow stripes, and a stick. He stands there for a long moment and just breathes.

No, it's fine. It's hockey. The sport's the same everywhere. He's played around the world and here is no different, not in the heart and bones of the game, the feel of the ice beneath his skates, the tap of the puck on his stick blade, the cool air against his cheeks.

Go, he snaps at himself but it still takes another beat to move, out the door to the empty hallway, to where the lights flicker and the rink waits.

Seats arc up in a bowl around the ice, forming the dark edges of the arena. It doesn't seem like there are enough of them, not the arching tower of row after row that rings most professional rinks. It might be bigger than a college arena, but it's achingly far from the soaring space where San Diego plays, nearly too big when he stepped into it as a player for the first time, staring around.

Nobody skates over to welcome him. No team captain comes toward him, hand held out for a firm shake, a slap on Gil's shoulder, ready to introduce him to the guys. No taps from the sticks of the players gathered against the far boards as they notice him. No team of coaches there to make sure he gets a warm-up in and can fill him in on the plan for practice.

None of that. Just two dozen guys standing against the boards, and a single coach in front of them. *Taking a break*, Gil wants to hope, but the team isn't by the bench and its rows of water bottles. They're in line for a drill, idly chatting, one standing to the side bouncing a puck on his stick in the air. As Gil watches, the guy nearly misses his turn to go through the cones, so he fumbles the pass when it comes, the puck too far in front of him, and he doesn't bother to stretch to grab it, listlessly circling back to the end of the line instead of barreling forward.

The puck continues on its way past the gathered players, none of whom reach for it, and it slides to a stop at the far blue line, sitting there alone on the ice.

Gil skates to it, pulling it in with the toe of his stick and neatly tucking it back into the pile of pucks at the front of the line of players.

"Stephanie Morris," the coach says. She's dressed in coach's warm-ups, not the full equipment of the players, her long brown hair tied up and a whistle dangling around her neck. "You must be Gil. So glad you're here."

Thank you, he'd spluttered at his first professional practice when the coach had glided up to him, nearly tripping over his skates in his excitement until a vet had smacked his stick against Gil's shins and told him to calm the hell down before he embarrassed himself.

Gil's jersey itches where it brushes his wrist as he shakes her hand. "Hi, Coach Morris," he gets out.

"Just Steph is fine. Thanks for jumping straight into things. Gentlemen, Gil Roussin, here from San Diego. Gil, these are the guys. Bloomer and Mitcher right here in front. That's Pezer and Lomsy back there and—seriously, Millsy, we're working here."

Millsy just keeps bouncing the puck on his stick. "Ah, a member of the hallowed Roussin family. What a delight."

Sprints, the coach of any other team would snap at a player goofing around with a puck instead of paying attention. *Or get the hell off the ice.* Remind him that if he doesn't want to be here, there's a list of guys waiting to take his roster spot, call-ups from the farm team in the minors, or college players, or the leagues in Europe and Canada—a professional salary, a spot in the league, so many players who would jump at the chance to be here.

Or, well.

Maybe not *here*.

Gil digs his skate into a chip in the ice. The edges of the furrow are smooth enough that it means it's been here too long, the Zamboni tracking over the gouge time and time again but nobody bothering to properly fix it.

In one smooth motion, Steph snags a puck, draws it back, and shoots it, arcing it up in the air to neatly hit the puck Millsy's bouncing, sending them both tumbling to the ice.

"Damn," Millsy says. "Nice, Coach."

Steph continues like she never even moved. "Gil, like I was saying, that's Pezer and Lomsy back there and that's Hal down in net."

Gil turns. The goalie has his helmet off, his back to the team, *Halbe* written across his shoulders above his number *1*.

"Do it again, Coach," Millsy says, snagging another puck. "I wanna see you do that twice."

She's going to raise her voice. Get in his face, even if she's a head shorter. Or turn icily silent, so cool to him it'll take him weeks to crawl back into her favor.

But she just pulls a puck in and then shoots it, hitting the blade of his stick with enough force to knock it out of his hands. She grabs it before he can and tucks it under her arm, circling away when he reaches for it. "Nope, it's mine now. You can get it back when it's your turn to go through the drill."

Gil looks between them, Millsy who's laughing with the rest of the team and Steph who seems unfazed, pointing him toward the back of the line.

The hell?

This is not how you coach a professional team. Teasing a player, getting a laugh from the crowd. Sure, she can lean into that somewhere down the line once the season's underway, but this is the first week of practices and she's a new face here. She needs to be sure the team respects her, not whatever the hell this is, acting like they're all pals.

Gil's face heats for her, glad at least the rink is empty, no reporters here and certainly no fans taking the time to watch their practice, the only person on the other side of the boards...

Oh.

Gil grips his stick tighter. He's not ready. Won't ever be, he's sure, for the sight of Sebastian with his skates on, wearing his gloves, his stick in his hands as he steps onto the ice.

Steph waves him over. "Gentlemen, you'll also remember we're welcoming our new assistant coach today too."

Sebastian tapes his stick the same way he always did, not bothering to wind strips around the toe. *It wears down your blade*, Gil always told him, trying to tug it away from Sebastian to do it right.

He skates like he always did, too. A graceful, long stride as he glides over, the same movement of his body that Gil knew so well.

Gil didn't bring a water bottle out here. And there probably isn't one for him, no equipment manager to make sure he's got one bottle with water and another with an electrolyte mix.

"Great to have you," Steph says, shaking Sebastian's hand. "This is Coach Martin, everyone. Maybe we can show him how nicely you all can do this drill?"

Millsy puts his hand up as if asking a question. "Hey, new Coach, can I get my stick back yet?"

Sebastian glances at him, then at the extra stick Steph's holding. His mouth opens like he's about to answer.

Oh, this team eats coaches alive. Gil can already tell. The guys are milling around, chatting among each other, those two, Pezer and Lomsy, already laughing at the confusion on Sebastian's face, Millsy with a huge grin, knowing full well he's poking fun at the new guy.

Sebastian's not good with a crowd, not before he knows them. Too quiet, too soft-spoken, and too dependent on making individual friendships rather than capturing the approval of the group at large.

Professional, Sebastian had asked for.

Best friends, always, he'd promised Gil once.

So don't bother now, Gil tells himself. Don't take care of Sebastian when he couldn't bother being there for Gil when his entire life changed, upended in a phone call that drew him up to the NHL and into a different life entirely, terrified at what waited for him. And today too, rushing away from Gil the moment he'd gotten out of the car. It's clear what Sebastian wants from him and it's a big, aching *nothing*.

But Gil can't not care. Not when it's Sebastian.

And hasn't that always been his problem when it comes to Seb? Ten years and Gil's still hurt, dozens of breakups over the years fading so fully he can barely remember some of the guys, when Sebastian has always lodged like a bruise right in Gil's chest, dogging him across the decade.

A trade, he reminds himself. Professional. Here to do a job and only a job, and yes, that's why he glides forward, not to draw the attention off Sebastian and onto himself, but to start standing out among this group.

Not that it's hard to do, him and him alone looking at the cones, ready to get to work. "What's the drill? I'd love to give it a try."

Steph grins. "I knew we'd like having you here. Through the cones, get the pass—Martin, you can do the passing—and then Gil, take the shot." Steph taps his shin with her stick. "Go on, Gil. Welcome to the team."

Sebastian, he thinks as he starts skating. Passing to him. Ten years later.

It's nearly too much, rounding the cone and looking up to see the familiar way Sebastian stands with his stick on the ice, how his arms move when he sends it toward Gil, the shift of his weight, all entirely the same.

Gil's caught looking, drinking it in, and he almost misses the pass, so when he takes the shot his balance is off, the puck sailing wide of the net, hitting the boards with a loud clap that rings too loud in his head.

SEVEN

"So," Mitcher says from the stall next to Gil's in the locker room. "You're the lucky guy who got dropped in this hellhole. What did you do to your old GM to win a trade here of all places?"

"Is there a laundry bin?" Gil looks around the room, but there's no bin pushed into the middle of it for them to chuck their shirts and socks into.

No spread of sports drinks on a table, either. Protein powders, fruit, nutrition bars, none of it.

No, it's not the GM in San Diego who did this to him. This must be some crueler joke of fate.

Sebastian, *here*. Coaching. Talking with Bloomer after he went through a drill, pointing with his stick to the blue line and then the face-off circle as Bloomer nodded. Standing with Steph against the boards as they watched the team skate. Working with Hal between drills, Seb's shot still fluid and graceful.

Glancing at Gil when they'd practiced face-offs, Gil dropping his shoulder and yanking back on his stick to pull the puck between his own legs and behind him. *Perfect*, he knew, so at least there wasn't a reason for Sebastian to talk to him, try to give him a pointer or tweak his technique.

"No laundry bin. Just chuck it." Mitcher dumps his own jersey in the center of the floor.

But it's not an equipment staff—there are no equipment staff Gil has seen—who gathers up the jersey. Instead, it's a player who moves forward to grab the jerseys and socks, a young kid whose name Gil hasn't caught.

"Wait," Gil starts. "That's not—"

"The rookies got it," Mitcher says. "You're new here, but don't worry, we're nice to vets."

That's not right, Gil was going to say. That's not how things work, to have guys on the roster dealing with the team's laundry, but the kid walks over to him, still wearing half his equipment, a hand held out for Gil's jersey.

"I can—"

Mitcher grabs it from Gil and tosses it to the kid. "No worries. They like doing it."

"...take it myself," Gil finishes, sitting down slowly. By rote, he peels the tape off his socks, right leg and then left, unwinding it from around his calf where it held his shin guards in place. There should be a trash can next to the laundry bin that's not there. Gil tucks the tape onto the bench beside him, rather than flinging it into the room and making someone scramble after it.

"You'll figure out this clown show soon enough. I did, when I got stuck here at the eleventh hour of the trade deadline last season," Mitcher says. "And I thought the old coaches we had were shit. Didn't know this year would be even more fun. Steph's weird as hell, taking Millsy's stick."

Gil worries at the knot on his skate. "Can't say I've seen that tactic before either."

"I'm just hoping for some luck getting the hell out of

here now that Frank got hired, because rumor has it he's looking to move a player or two."

Gil looks up. "He is?"

"That's what I've been hearing."

"Your agent's been talking to him?"

"My agent, my mom, my next-door neighbor, my mailman." Mitcher grins, shimmying out of his pants and shin guards, and then his compression shorts beneath them. "You too, huh? Let me tell you, get off this team while you can, 'cause this place chews up good players and turns them into Bloomer over there."

Gil looks to his other side where Bloomer's sitting quietly, taking off one elbow pad and then the next, hanging them up behind himself. Silent, too, which is odd in a room filled with chatter, like everyone knows better than to try to engage him in post-practice banter, the idle chitchat of a bunch of guys who spend most of their days together.

Yeah, Bloomer looks done. With today, with this practice, and most certainly with the boisterous locker room, Pezer and Lomsy throwing a ball of tape back and forth over Millsy, who jumps to try to grab it.

Mitcher walks through their game as he heads to the showers. He's good-looking. A nice tight ass that flexes as he walks, broad shoulders, narrow waist. A gorgeous, fluid skater too, with a hell of a set of hands on him as he handled the puck, dumping shot after shot into the net.

That, or Mitcher's skill at scoring is a testament to the goalie not giving a shit. Across the room, Hal drops his leg pads in a pile on the floor, leaves his skates and pants on top of them, and stands naked, a hand on his hip as he scrolls through his phone, his mind already clearly far from practice.

It's not hard to take the temperature of a new locker room, to see how everyone fits into it, and for Gil to find his spot. Mitcher is as familiar as the rest of them, the type of player like Hux down in San Diego who Gil's always made an easy friendship with, a guy to hang out with in the locker room and on plane rides, surface level and easy buddies, tied together through a familiar will to compete that they recognize in each other.

The rest of these guys, though...quickly, Gil shucks off the rest of his equipment and his compression shirt and shorts so he can hurry after Mitcher.

"You hear those trade rumors from your agent? Or Frank himself? Or someone else?" Gil asks, stepping under the spray of the shower next to Mitcher.

A buddy here, that's exactly what Gil needs, both of them united in the goal of getting the hell off this damn team.

Competing for it too, probably, but what had Dad said? Nothing wrong with some rivalry to light a fire. It'll only do him good.

"A little birdie on the wind told me Frank's looking to adjust the roster before the season starts," Mitcher says. "He's new here, so he wants to make his mark by cashing in on some trades."

"So like one player, or more than that, and is he looking at forwards, or D, or—"

"Move."

Gil jumps, twisting to look behind him.

"Move," Hal says, slower this time, like Gil didn't hear.

"What?"

"That's my shower."

"That is his shower," Mitcher says.

The showerhead is identical to the rest, the tile cracked and stained, the nozzle sending water at odd angles from the mineral deposits lining each hole. The only difference is that it's at the end of the row, against the corner of the wall, and has the sole curtain in the room, mildew growing on the bottom and rusty water stains streaking its length.

"Sorry." Gil shifts to the shower on the other side of Mitch, but Hal ignores him, his head under the spray, water already dripping from his long hair and the unkempt stubble on his face as he yanks the curtain closed.

Right. Okay. Goalies are always a bit weird. Trust Hal to care that he's got the one private shower in the row of open stalls, cordoning himself off as the rest of the team files in to clean up.

By the time Gil gets his gear sorted out in the unfamiliar locker and a fresh set of clothes from his duffle, even the rookies are done showering, the last of them gathering up the final pieces of laundry on their way out.

He needs to hurry, then, if he's not going to miss a team meeting about tomorrow's game, but upstairs, the players' lounge is nearly empty, the huge TV turned off, none of the guys on the couches or sitting at the tables, just Steph with a laptop open.

"This is the post-practice meal?" Gil asks of the tray of sandwiches. *And is this really the lounge?* he wants to ask too. The couches are worn, like they were already used when they were brought in here, the windows that overlook the ice are streaked, and more than one of the table's chairs is mismatched, as if they've been dragged in from some other room.

"Sure is. Knock yourself out," she says, eyes on her computer.

San Diego has a team chef. A brightly lit kitchen, a full spread of whole wheat pasta, sweet potatoes, fish, chicken, salads with kale and cabbage, bowls of quinoa, brown rice, and then a stack of containers for any food he wanted to take home with him.

Slowly, he picks up a sandwich marked *Tuna*. "Isn't there a meeting?"

"No meeting." Steph finally looks up, waving at someone past Gil in the doorway. "Hey, there you are. Gil, this is Frank, our GM."

"Frank Weinhaus." He's a head shorter than Gil, perfectly bald, and has glasses perched on his nose.

Gil moves toward him, hand held out, and puts a smile on his face. This is the man who will trade him away from here, if Gil can make himself worth enough to another team. "So great to meet you," Gil says, shaking his hand.

Frank laughs, a deep, clear sound, and claps him on the shoulder. "Oh, you're a good sport, at least. That much about you is true."

"What else did you hear?" Gil asks. "I guess you know my dad, right?"

"Can't say I do, not personally, at least. I just know of you through the typical rumor mill. Great to have you here, Gil."

"Where'd you play?" Gil asks slowly. Where indeed, if Frank doesn't know his dad, the Bert Roussin around whom the hockey world orbits.

But it's the Sea Lions. *Did you play?* is maybe what he should ask.

"Steph and I came up through college together," Frank says. "Dabbled at the national level too."

Steph laughs. "Dabbled, yeah. Frank won gold on the US Olympic Team."

"You did?" Gil asks. Frank isn't old enough to be on the most recent US team that won gold in the Olympics, back when Dad was playing for the national team.

"I warmed the bench, more like," Frank says. "Steph did all the work."

"Oh," Gil says as he puts it together. No, the men's

national team hasn't won. The women, though, they've been something else these last few Olympic Games. "I watched that game. It was a good one. You won in a shoot-out, right?"

"Potted us our gold." Steph smacks Frank's arm.

Frank laughs. "And got benched through the second period for giving up a shitty play, but what're you going to do, right? A win over Canada is a win over Canada so we'll take it, won't we?"

Gil makes himself nod. Frank definitely doesn't know his dad from the world of men's hockey, not if he transitioned after making it to the Olympics with the women. Gil's stomach drops. That's one avenue of favors gone. All the harder to get out of here, if Dad doesn't hold sway over this GM, of all of them in the league.

"All the way from the Olympic podium to here in San Francisco with the Sea Lions, who could have predicted that," Frank says. "Though I'm sure it's a surprise to you too, Gil."

"I—I'm happy to be playing, it's great to be here, I—"

"So polite, I love it. Listen, Gil, we're not under any illusions, alright? The owners left us a steaming pile of shit shaped like a hockey team and the entirety of the help the league has extended is refusing to let the franchise fold. This isn't where you wanted to end up. I know that."

"It's alright." Gil casts about for something to compliment. "I mean, it's—"

"It is what it is," Frank says. "For now. Steph and I, we're here to change that."

"Great," Gil says. It sounds weak.

"I've been taking calls from your agent," Frank continues. "She's laying on the pressure to get you traded. But you ought to at least give us a chance, let us change your mind. And yeah, yeah, I know, it's a player's worst nightmare to get traded here. But we're changing things up. Steph and her coaching style is the first piece of that, but there's more coming."

What coaching style? Gil could ask. Being buddies with the players? Holding onto Millsy's stick for most of practice, joking around with Pezer and Lomsy? That's not a coaching style. That's barely even showing up to do her work.

Frank really believes it, though. Gil can hear it in his words, see it on his and Steph's face. They think they can change this team, shift the culture, rise through the league rankings and make something of the Sea Lions.

How absolutely mortifying.

"I did ask my agent to work on a trade," Gil says. "And yes, I'd like to ask the same of you."

Frank spreads his hands. "I'll do what's best for the team. If you can bring me more in a deal than what I can get out of you on the ice, I'm happy to let you walk, but a lot of that's up to you and what scouts and other GMs see in you."

"I'll put in the work."

"Well good, because we've got our first preseason game against Vancouver in a couple days and right now I have a single assistant coach to help Steph corral you lot. You know him, right? This Martin guy?"

Gil nearly takes a step backward. "I do."

"He was coaching college hockey here in the Bay Area for years. We're pulling him in since I don't know if you've noticed, but we're a little light on employees. He's at least one friendly face for you here, right?"

"Absolutely," Gil gets out. "I'm—it's been a wild day, actually, and I'm pretty beat." No, that's not right, he shouldn't be admitting he's tired, not to management and coaches, not ever. He clears his throat and tries again. "I want to be rested for tomorrow, is what I mean. Really looking forward to playing well. Who's the best person to ask about my hotel?" *If you got me a hotel*, he could add. If the team can come through on that, at the very least.

"You mean our fully staffed logistics department?" Frank laughs. "Look, we're hiring as quickly as we can. For now, we've got an intern and they got you a room until you can find a place to live. Let me get you the hotel address."

Gil won't be looking for a place to live, because he's not staying here long enough to bother. No, he's holing up in his hotel room and calling his agent all damn night if he has to, determined to get moved as absolutely soon as he can. Whatever it takes. He'll get a goal, get a truckload of them, step onto the ice like he's got afterburners on his skates and play so well that offer after offer will come in, so many that Frank will have his pick of where to send Gil.

Outside, the weather's cleared, and he stands on the sidewalk in the alley as he checks his phone, though Melissa hasn't gotten back to him. It means she's working, which is good news. Great news. Ideal, really, and maybe he'll be off to the airport sooner than he even hoped, ready to settle in a new city, a better one.

A car rolls up, gleaming red, the engine a low purr, too shiny and clean for this back alley, the trash bags, the crumbled bricks and potholed pavement.

Mitcher leans out the driver's window. "Want a ride? You're at that same hotel the team always uses, I'm guessing?"

"Please," Gil says. Yes, the familiar blandness of a hotel room after the hell of today. He can get some rest and get ready for practice tomorrow. Melissa will call by then. And Dad's working on a trade too, and if Dad said he's not staying, then Gil's not staying. "I appreciate it," Gil says.

"To be fair, I'm already going there." Mitcher hooks his thumb toward the passenger seat.

Gil can't see until he bends down, the car too low, the alley too dim.

Oh for fuck's sake.

Sebastian. His messenger bag on his lap as he sits in the passenger seat, his eyes on Gil before they flick away.

"Gotta be nice to the folks who make the lines," Mitcher stage-whispers.

"I can just walk," Gil says quickly, but Mitcher pops the trunk, leaving Gil the choice to go over and close it, or toss his bag into it and get in the car.

His knees nearly press to his chest with how far back Mitcher has his seat.

He could slide over. Sit behind Sebastian.

He stays, working his seatbelt across his chest just in time for Mitcher to floor it.

"So good practice, huh?" Mitcher asks, weaving around a truck stopped to make a left turn. "Nice that you can actually move a puck, Gil, what a change from the rest of the guys. Bloomer isn't bad, but you'd take him in a race, no problem. You're fast."

Yeah, because Coach Thompson at Rideau used to hammer on the sprinting drills. Edge work to start practice, long, boring exercises to lengthen their stride, and then relay races over and over until they were panting, sticks braced on their knees, sweat dripping onto the ice where it steamed.

He and Sebastian used to win those races. High-five at the end, red-faced and gasping.

Gil stares out the window at the city rushing past them. Coach Thompson, who had gone to the draft with Gil and his dad. Who'd hugged him tight the day Gil had left for the NHL, who'd flown out to be at Gil's first professional game, decked head to toe in green and yellow. Gil had gotten him a jersey that first year he'd been on the Mountain Lions, *Thompson* on the back with Coach's old number 17 on it. It had cost Gil a pricey bottle of whiskey for the equipment staff to custom make it and Coach still wears it every time Gil plays in Minnesota, getting seats against the glass and waving so enthusiastically it'd be embarrassing if it didn't make Gil so happy to see him there.

Suddenly, viscerally, he imagines Mikey in his mascot suit making up the new jerseys here for the Sea Lions. Maybe the rookies helping him, writing out *Roussin* with a permanent marker instead of beautifully stitched letters.

No, he won't get Coach a jersey from this place.

He glances at Sebastian's profile, the arch of his nose, the familiar shape of his jaw, beneath his neat beard.

Maybe Coach Thompson has one already. Maybe Sebastian sent him one, bothering to keep in touch with Coach, but not Gil.

Mitcher jams the car to a stop beneath the hotel portico.

"Thanks," Gil gets out.

"Catch you tomorrow." Mitcher peels off as soon as Gil gets the trunk closed.

And—oh. Sebastian got out of the car too. "Do you need something out of the trunk? I can—" Gil starts, but Mitcher is gone in a flash of taillights.

Clearly, Sebastian meant to get out too. *Terrified of Mitcher's driving?* Gil would joke if...yeah. If. If so very many things were different.

"You're not—" Gil waves toward the hotel. "I thought you lived here, in the city."

"I just moved out of my place."

"Oh."

"Team's putting me up."

Gil nods, too quickly. "Cool. Me too."

Me too? Fucking hell, of course him too, standing here outside the damn hotel as Sebastian slips through the revolving door.

Gil has to wait for it to cycle to an empty section, a couple holding hands stepping out past him. When the door spits him into the lobby, Sebastian is halfway to the reception desk.

Gil's so tired. Homesick for San Diego, the ten-minute drive from the rink to the quiet and peace of his own home. A hot, lazy afternoon floating in the pool. Teammates to hang out with, grab dinner, get excited to start the season.

Now he has the back of Sebastian's head and his silence. A throb of loneliness lodges in Gil's throat as he follows Sebastian's lead and slides his ID over to the hotel clerk.

Ten years of this, absolutely no contact, because Sebastian had let their texts and calls dwindle to nothing. *We'll keep in touch*, Gil had promised, bags packed, arms around Sebastian in their tiny dorm room, a plane ticket on his phone and a jersey waiting for him at an NHL arena.

Sebastian had just stared at him as Gil finally drew away, but Gil had kept his word. Walked out of that room toward the brightness ahead, texting Sebastian through all of it, every moment of that first day, the first practice, his very first game, all of it useless if he couldn't share it with Seb.

"Mr. Roussin?" the receptionist asks as she checks his ID. She turns to the man holding Sebastian's license and he nods as they murmur to each other, moving from one computer monitor to the next, pointing at something on the screen.

"Your room, Mr. Roussin, Mr. Martin, king bed, city view. The elevators are just down there to the right."

But they only slide one key across the counter.

"I'm sorry?" Gil asks.

"Number seventeen eighty-seven," she says, still smiling. "Would you like a second key?"

"And my room?" Gil asks. "Which one is mine?"

"Is there a problem?" she asks.

"We're not staying together," Sebastian says.

"No, we're not. There must be some mistake," Gil says.

"I have a room reserved under a Sebastian Martin and Gilbert Roussin, made by the San Francisco Sea Lions?" She leans closer to the monitor, then looks up at them, her smile still in place. "Is that a sports team? Soccer?"

"Tennis, right?" the man asks.

"We need a second room," Sebastian says.

"Hockey," Gil says. "Ice hockey."

"I'm so sorry, but we're fully booked," the woman says. "There's a baseball game in town, you see."

"Baseball," Gil mutters, turning to peer back at the entrance. Did Mitcher really already take off? Yes, he'd been halfway back to the street when Gil last saw him. "Look, ma'am, we really need a second room."

"I can get you one in a few days," she says.

"Something with two queens, at least?" Sebastian asks.

"Don't you have a place to go?" Gil asks him and then leans over the counter. "We really need two rooms."

"Sir, I'm so sorry." The woman's smile finally falters, exhaustion creeping into her expression. "Here's a second key for you two."

Right. Great. Though he can commiserate—whose job doesn't absolutely suck today?

"No, not your fault, we'll work it out," Gil says, gathering up the keys.

"If we get a cancellation, I'll be sure to let you know."

A few steps away from the desk, Gil turns to Sebastian. "So?"

"What?" Sebastian asks.

"You don't have somewhere else to stay? Can't you crash with someone?"

"I told you, I moved out of my place."

"But a friend or a—"

A friend or a—

He tries again to fill in the second word.

Sebastian's quick. The key flits out of Gil's hand, that same sharp, honed reflex that let Sebastian fish pucks off of other players' sticks before they knew what had happened.

Gil swats at the empty air as Sebastian pulls out one key, then tosses the other back to him.

Gil misses it. Bends to pick it up off the floor, his cheeks burning. It was a good throw. His own fault he whiffed on the catch.

A guy, Gil meant to say. Doesn't he have some guy to stay with who he's been...dating, is the word. Seeing. Hooking up with, at least.

Silent, Gil follows Sebastian to the elevators. No, he doesn't want to know.

EIGHT

FRANK DOESN'T ANSWER Gil's phone call.

Gil paces the hotel hallway—Steph, no, he doesn't have her number. Quickly, he swipes to Instagram, face flushing at the video posted of him in the airport with the mascot, and sends a message to Emery through the team's account.

Nothing. No returned call, no message popping up in his DMs, just his silent phone and the rows of doors stretching on either side of him, room 1787 staring back at him.

He can find somewhere else to stay, just pay for it himself and bring the receipt to the team tomorrow, though when he searches, hotel after hotel is listed as booked.

Well, good for the baseball team and all of its damn fans.

But Gil must know someone here in the city he can stay with. He's met so many guys on different teams over the years. One of them has to live in San Francisco.

Though it's not exactly a hockey town, so no, none of them have ended up here.

And he does know someone here. Sebastian.

Gil stares at the door for a long moment. He has to walk back in there and...

And what? Hang out? Sit in silence?

Find his bearings, somehow.

He swallows down the urge to knock before he unlocks the door with his key, pushing inside the room like he's meant to be there.

He is. Just...Sebastian is too.

"Tried to call Frank," Gil says as evenly as he knows how, setting his duffle bag on the desk. Casual, easy, like Dad always acts with that air of calm over his words and how he moves.

Sebastian is sitting on the side of the bed he always preferred. He's set out his phone cord, his book, his water bottle. *Shut up*, Gil used to groan when Sebastian would wake up in the middle of the night and suck it down like a camel in the desert. Once, Sebastian had squirted him with it, soaking Gil's face and pillow, and then climbed on top of him when Gil had protested, a grappling roughhouse that was stymied only by their roommates.

He could use another couple guys in here, just to break the quiet. The same sort of distraction the rink held, others moving about so the space between him and Sebastian doesn't feel so...*much.*

Well, Gil can just cling to his own side of the giant bed tonight, careful of a stray foot or elbow, and steeled against the draw of a warm body, especially in the muddled coziness of sleep, his face pressed to Sebastian's chest. *Drooling on me*, Sebastian used to say, wiping his palm over his pec and then on Gil's face, laughing, teasing.

Gil clears his throat, the noise too loud in the quiet room. Yeah, maybe not cuddled up together, bare skin and wandering hands, but the rest of it? Goofing around with each other? *I missed you* sits at the back of his throat. *Let's hang out, let's have fun again, we must still remember how.*

Stay away from him, he tries to tell himself, but it's Sebastian and no, he's never been good at that.

"It looks like there aren't any rooms available anywhere else," he offers.

"I'll talk to the front desk tomorrow, get it all sorted out," Sebastian says.

"Great. Just bad luck tonight, I guess."

"Seems like."

So they'll just...share this room. Cool. Great. How perfectly normal and not fucking weird at all.

Sebastian's texting someone. Gil can see the message app on his screen, even if he can't make out what he's writing, or to who. *You seeing someone?* Gil could ask oh so casually. His throat tightens and he clears it again.

No, something lighter. Simpler to ease into. *What's with the beard? What brought you to San Francisco? What have you been doing for ten years and did you ever, even once, think about me?*

"I caught up with Steph and Frank after practice," Gil ventures. Professional, isn't that what Sebastian wanted? Gil can do professional, keep hockey between them as an easy, simple way to be around each other, because if Sebastian can play at being normal, so completely, utterly casual about finding themselves back together again and stuck in a hotel room on top of it, then Gil can as well. "They really want to turn the team around and I guess they think they can."

"Yeah, they mentioned. Pretty impressive goals."

"Impressive," Gil echoes. Impossible, more like. Hopeless. Laughable, even.

He sorts through his duffle bag, setting out his clothes

for tomorrow, finding his toothbrush and shaving kit, aligning his shoes neatly against the wall.

Sebastian has left his sneakers in the middle of the floor, one of them tipped on its side. His messenger bag gapes open, a shirt hanging half out of it. *Still a total mess?* Gil could tease, but to broach their past feels like too huge a hurdle. Winning states, they had remembered together in the car, and then Sebastian had shut down, like a switch flicking off suddenly, a breaker blowing and the power winking out.

"Mitcher said last year was a real shitshow," Gil ventures. "And that this season isn't looking much better."

"Steph and Frank'll do alright with the team," Sebastian says.

Will you? Gil wants to ask, because half the guys talked over Sebastian when he spoke and the other half barely pretended to pay attention.

"How was coaching college?" Gil asks instead. *Hi, good to see you after a decade, you kinda suck at your job* isn't the way to break down this awful, forced casualness between them.

And yes, that's good, a gentle probe at Sebastian's life. *Tell me everything*, Gil wants to demand. Start with the day Gil left and retrace every moment since then so Gil finally has an answer of *why*.

He could ask now. Just go for it.

"Yeah, it was alright," Sebastian says.

What happened that stopped you calling me back? Gil coaches himself, but instead asks, "What made you take the leap to the NHL?"

"I live here," Sebastian says. "And this job came up, so I applied."

"Sure, but this team? Really?"

"I live here," Sebastian says again, a touch louder. "I have some commitments in the city."

Gil glances over, but Sebastian's eyes are on his phone still, his thumb moving as he scrolls. *Like what?* Gil is desperate to ask. "Right," he gets out, and when his phone rings, he reaches for it like a lifeline. "Hello?"

"Gil?"

"Hey," he says, relaxing onto the foot of the bed. "Dave, how's it going?"

"Just scrolling through Instagram," Dave says in that voice Gil's always liked so much. *I'll come over*, Dave used to tell him, calling him back when Gil would text that the team plane had landed, that he was done at the rink, that he'd finished his workout and was free to meet up. "You got traded?"

"Yeah, I did. It's been a hell of a day."

"So you're what, in San Francisco?"

"I am, can you believe that?" Gil lets out a soft laugh. "Wild, right?"

But Dave doesn't chuckle. Instead, there's a beat of silence before he asks, "Were you going to tell me?"

"What? Yeah, no, of course I was."

"I was going to pick you up tomorrow." There's an edge to the deep timbre of Dave's words. "At the airport, remember? You texted me your flight info."

"Absolutely," Gil says. "No, I was going to let you know, definitely."

"Right." Dave sighs.

Gil wants to remember the warm puff of Dave's breath against his skin, but there's an exasperation to the sound that wasn't ever there when Dave had him pressed into the mattress.

Sebastian glances over.

Gil hunches his shoulders. "You alright?" he asks Dave.

"Going to tell me," Dave repeats slowly. "You were going to tell me that I shouldn't drive to the airport tomorrow, or you were going to tell me you won't be back at all?"

"Oh, no, it's not like a permanent trade," Gil says. "I'm still figuring it all out, actually."

"What's a non-permanent trade? Explain it like I'm a nurse, not a hockey player."

"Just, it's—you know. I'm not sticking around here. My agent's working on it."

"So you are coming back? To San Diego?"

"No, I—well, maybe," Gil says.

"Maybe no?"

"Probably not."

"Probably? What does that even mean?"

"I can let you know," Gil says.

"Like you let me know that you won't be flying in tomorrow?"

"Well yeah, I was gonna, I—"

"I fucking found out on Instagram, Gil."

"Well, I was on a plane. I couldn't text you, and then I had practice and—Dave? You there?"

He pulls his phone from his ear. *Call ended*, the screen reads.

"Shitty service," Gil says, his cheeks warm.

"I get five bars here," Sebastian says.

"Yeah, it's, um. Old phone." He holds it so Sebastian can't see that it's the latest model, camera lenses studding the back of it. He stares down at the screen, like Dave might call him back. Is he mad? *Sorry*, Gil texts him and waits for a long moment, but Dave doesn't write anything. *It's a hockey thing, I couldn't come back*, Gil adds. Dave's a nurse, and the closest he ever came to the world of hockey was telling Gil not to get a concussion and show up in his ICU, so he doesn't really get it.

"Friend of yours?" Sebastian asks, his eyes on his phone.

"Yeah, down in San Diego." Gil almost says *hot as hell, hooked up with him on the regular, one of plenty of guys over the years*—but doesn't. What're they going to do, sit here and try to one-up each other? They both had the entirety of their twenties and Sebastian must have his own tales to tell, men he met, slept with, some imaginary guy Gil can nearly picture.

He frowns. He kind of hates that hypothetical guy.

And how absolutely shitty to think about.

But no, it doesn't matter. It's fine—it's not, but it is because it has to be. Their lives were entwined until they faded away from each other and if Gil learned anything over the years of silence, it's that Sebastian doesn't want a damn thing to do with him anymore. So what if Sebastian fucked a slew of guys, if he's texting one now who's putting that smile on his face as he grins at his phone. A decade was enough time for Gil to realize Sebastian was off living his own life and to get the hell over it.

He grabs the TV remote and stabs the power button, clicking through the channels and turning the volume up to fill the quiet of the room. The news, a sitcom, a crappy action movie with a blaring helicopter that threatens to make Gil's head hurt. He settles on a baseball game, the cadence of the announcer familiar even if it's the wrong sport, no hockey games to catch up on with the season not yet started.

And still, it's too quiet in here.

"So how you been?" Gil asks, his eyes on the TV. "Been a minute since we caught up."

There, casual, like he doesn't ache to know everything that's happened since he walked out of their dorm room, Sebastian staring after him as he left.

"Yeah, life and all," Sebastian says. "You started liking baseball?"

Yes, this is what Gil wanted. Easy, simple conversation. "Oh, yeah, course."

"What do you think of that pitcher?"

Gil glances at the TV. He's never seen the guy before in his life. "Total dud." On the screen, the pitcher strikes out the batter and Gil quickly changes the channel again. "You keep in touch with anyone from college?"

"A few guys."

"Like who?" Gil prompts.

"Coach," Sebastian says, still scrolling his phone.

"Coach Thompson? Yeah, me too."

Nothing. Just Sebastian crossing and then recrossing his ankles. He's taken his socks off and the hems of his jeans are worn, a few threads hanging loose.

He's ticklish right there, behind the knob of bone, the soft skin where his leg hair ends in the hollow of his ankle.

Or was, at least.

"Anyone else?" Gil finally prompts.

"Hallsy, Quizzer, that group."

That group. All brothers, like Gil doesn't know them, didn't play with them, hang out with them all the time. "So Mouser, too?"

"Christopher? Yeah."

Christopher. Who even calls him that?

Though he's of course grown up now too. How odd to think about. Chris—Mouser, they'd always called him—not the string bean he was in college, hanging around his older brothers on the team, earning a nickname by virtue of always being there. A nice enough guy, though Gil could never understand why he hadn't ever played hockey, with two brothers who were so good.

"What're Hallsy and Quizzer up to?" Gil asks.

"Selling real estate." Whatever's on his phone must be pretty damn engrossing, because Sebastian doesn't look up from it.

"Mouser, too? What, are they still letting him tag along?"

"Christopher's here in San Francisco, actually. He's got a big tech start-up situation going on."

"Oh, really? I should catch up with him. You got his number?"

Sebastian finally looks at him. He laughs softly, just a quiet exhale through his nose. "Yeah, I have his number. You gonna reach out before you leave? Non-permanent trade? I like that."

"I just meant—"

"Everyone down to our Zamboni driver knows what you mean." Sebastian's already back on his phone, tapping at the screen. "You've got one foot out the door, scrambling for a trade."

Gil checks his phone, but Sebastian didn't just send Mouser's number. Instead, a message from Melissa appears: *Working on it, sit tight*, she's written. *Thanks*, he writes back, and checks Dave's message thread, but there's nothing new. *Don't touch any of my shit when you get to my place*, he drafts to Joey, then deletes it.

"Anyone would want to get out of here," Gil says. "Seriously, you can't really want to coach the Sea Lions of all teams."

Sebastian sits up and swings his feet over the bed, bending to sort through his messenger bag. "You don't know that. It's been a minute, Gil. You said it yourself."

"Yeah, but—" *I know you*, Gil wants to say.

"And don't shit on the team your first day," Sebastian says like Gil didn't even speak. "It could be good for you here, finally get you off the third line."

Gil's face heats. Dad and now Sebastian, too? "I'd have been the second center in San Diego this year. And I would have last year, but that kid we got from Austin came in and took my spot."

"I know," Sebastian says. "I coached him."

"You did?"

"He played well, didn't he?"

"You watched my games?"

"I watched his games," Sebastian says. "But you need some work on your shot."

"My shot?"

"Just saying."

Gil laughs. "What?"

"Kind of hard to not notice."

"Notice what? My shot's fine."

"Okay," Sebastian says. "We can go over it on the ice."

"Go over—the hell?"

"Your wrists," Sebastian says.

"My wrists are—there's nothing wrong with my shot."

"Steph thinks you could use some tweaks too."

"Steph—no, I know how to shoot. And you can't—you don't know—"*Don't know anything about hockey that I don't*, he nearly says. Because Gil taught him everything from day one, tying his skates for him, showing him how to wrap tape around his shin guards, switching his elbow pads to the correct arms before any of the guys on the team could make fun of Sebastian for it. "I'm good," Gil says. "But thanks."

"Oh, okay. I'll tell Steph not to worry about it then."

"Great, yeah, because there's plenty of other stuff the team needs to work on."

Sebastian lets out a laugh. "Gil, are you for real? Steph makes the practice plan, I help her, and you follow it. You can't just opt out of working on skills you think you've mastered if Steph says otherwise."

Gil's face flushes hot. "No, I know, but..."

"But?" Sebastian prompts.

"I just—" It's jarring, the idea of Sebastian coaching him. Sebastian being here in his life again. Silence for ten years and now..."Are we okay?" Gil asks.

"What?"

"You and me. Are we good?"

Sebastian rubs a finger into his eye.

Gil's stomach flips over at the hesitation. He had lots of ideas about why Seb let them drift apart, and *royally pissed off at me* was definitely among them. *Was seeing someone else the entire time* was up there too. *Never cared about me* also topped the list, along with *didn't know how to break up with me and was just waiting until I left.*

"I guess I just, um, wondered? A lot? 'Cause I still don't really get what happened, so..." Gil scratches the back of his head. "If you want to talk about it now, I mean."

Sebastian looks down at his phone.

"Or not," Gil says. *Professional.* Yeah.

"You wondered?" Sebastian asks.

Gil straightens. "Of course I did. I thought we were going to keep in touch and you didn't—I just eventually stopped hearing from you. Figured you didn't want me to call, I guess. Did something happen? I've been over that day I left so many times. I was in class, I checked my phone, there was a voice mail, I called them back and booked it back to our room and—"

"Okay," Sebastian interrupts. He nods once and then twice. "Yeah, okay."

"What is it? Did I say something? Or do something? Or not do something? Or we had done that drill in practice the day before and I was playing against you and you took that hit and I—"

"What drill?"

"Down in the corner? Battling for the puck?" Gil leans toward him. "Quizzer laid that hit on you and I grabbed the puck and scored so your team had to do push-ups?"

"You remember a drill from that long ago?"

"You don't?"

"Why would I?"

"What was it, then? You stopped talking to me." His voice sounds too small.

"Shit, Gil. You thought it was a hockey drill?"

"I just never knew why. We promised to keep in touch, and I texted you all the time, I called you, I even fucking emailed you, and you didn't—" Gil's throat is too thick. "I thought you wanted to keep talking, too."

"Let's not do this."

"Okay." Gil pulls in a deep breath. Okay. They're not going to talk about it. That's fine. That's just more of what he's used to. But...

"No," he blurts. "We're back together again. Are we just going to ignore everything? Because we were—and then we never—it fucking sucked, Seb. I was halfway across the country. I didn't know anyone, and I was terrified, and I just stopped hearing from you. You could have up and died for all I knew if I wasn't still trying to watch your games when I could, just to see you out there."

Sebastian looks up from his phone. "You watched our games?"

"Of course I did. I watched every single one I could. And I fucking—I'd text you! During them, and it took longer and longer for you to get back to me and then—" Gil's voice is too loud. He tries to soften it and his words come out just a whisper. "Did you block my number?"

"Gil..."

"Did you? Or change yours, or—or—"

"You don't even..." Sebastian rubs his hand over his face, digging into his eyes. "Okay. Yeah. Wow."

"Seb?" *Please*, Gil wants to beg. But what's he going to do, drag information out of Sebastian that he's had ten years to give Gil?

"It was ages ago," Sebastian says. "Can't we just move on?"

Is that what you've done? Gil wants to ask. Was it a relief when Gil had thrown clothes into his backpack and let the door shut behind him, off to the airport for his flight to San Diego? "Yeah," Gil says quietly. "Yeah, it's been a while. Move on. I—yeah. Got it."

"We just both have new lives now, and you're focused on getting a trade and I'm new to the team and—" Sebastian closes his eyes, rubbing at the bridge of his nose. He still looks tired, achingly so. "This is hard for me."

"Coaching? Yeah, with this group? I can imagine."

"Coaching," Sebastian repeats. "Yeah."

"I won't make it worse, okay? Professional, I got it. I talked to Steph and Frank, and I didn't, you know, mention anything about..." Gil waves between them, but it leaves his hand feeling empty, hanging in the air.

"Thanks," Sebastian says.

"And I won't. I get it, you want the job to work out."

"I appreciate it."

"Good. Then we're...we're good?"

"We're good," Sebastian says and yeah, Gil will take it. It's a start, at least.

He holds out his fist in an old half-forgotten habit, grinning when Sebastian raises his hand like he always did, ready to smack against Gil's in the start of their special handshake.

But Sebastian just runs his hand over his face again.

Gil looks down, his fist still outstretched. Cheeks burning, he quickly shoves it into his pocket like he meant to do that the entire time.

"Shooting practice," he says even though his face still feels warm. "That'd be good, 'cause I gotta get that trade, so I need to get some points on the board." They can share hockey again, at least, that small piece of their history for the short time he's here, which is better than the nothing he's had for so long now. There can't be anything about shooting a hockey puck that Sebastian possibly knows that Gil doesn't, but... yeah. It's something, at least.

He grabs the remote. And baseball, they can watch baseball together. Hang out and—

"Hello?" Sebastian says, holding his phone to his ear. "Hi, sweetie."

Sweetie? The fuck?

Sebastian stands, shoving his feet into his shoes with no socks on, the heel flattened down. "Of course, day after tomorrow," he says, his voice warm. "Yeah, no, tell me. I want to hear all about it."

Who is that? Gil wants to ask, but Sebastian grabs his room key and he's gone, the heavy door swinging shut behind him.

Gil stares blankly at the TV. Then he turns to Sebastian's side of the room. His socks are in a heap next to his bag, his book upside down on the bedside table. Tape is wrapped around his phone charger, like it wore through and Sebastian hastily repaired it rather than bothering to get a new one.

Their dynamic isn't going back to normal. A bubble of hope Gil hadn't known he was clinging to pops. Had he always assumed they would?

Yes, he had. Assumed all it would take was just running

into Sebastian again and their old friendship would take over, smoothing over the awkward, jagged edges of silence between them, soothing the pain of the years that came and passed.

Slowly, Gil unpacks his bag: his foam roller, his set of resistance bands, an old, scuffed lacrosse ball he drops on the floor and then stands on, wincing as he presses his foot into the hard curve of it, easing the tension of a session on the ice, that too-long flight and...this. This room. Sebastian in it. Back in his life again.

He mutes the TV, straining for the sound of voices in the hall, but he can't hear anything and when Gil peers through the peephole, Sebastian's not standing by the door, nor is he in the hallway when Gil pokes his head out.

He presses the door shut again, leans his back to it and stares at the bed, rumpled on the far side where Sebastian had been sitting.

Gil sucks in a breath. His chest hurts. He turns the sound of the baseball game back on just to break the silence. It's being played just down the street, he realizes. This is the game that filled up this hotel, that brought fans to pack the stadium, the city.

There aren't half as many seats in the Sea Lions arena. And they certainly won't be full.

After the fifth inning, he lays on the bed, East Coast time dragging at him. He turns the lamp off after the sixth, letting the glow of the TV compete with the last of the sunlight seeping through the curtains.

He should be in his bed in San Diego. Or really, still back at Dad's, one last dinner with his brothers to finish out the summer before he heads to training camp. He can picture it as if none of today happened. He'd be helping Joey arrange movers from Texas. They'd be figuring out how to get his car to California, trying to convince Tommy he'd really love to take a solo road trip and drive it, wouldn't he?

And Dad would take them to the airport tomorrow, with none of the dread of today's ride but a stir of excitement in the car, a few last words from Dad on the curb, and then Gil and Joey off to play together, the season stretched out before them.

Gil lets himself be carried on the idea of that dream, trying to pretend he's back in his twin bed beneath the green comforter Mom bought him, the bed too short, his room caught in time from before he left for college. Not this bland hotel room, the TV glowing against his closed eyes, old memories on the other half of the bed that threaten to make him dwell on the time with Sebastian he's spent ten years trying to push away.

He must eventually drift off, because when he blinks, the TV's off, the room is dark, and Sebastian's across the bed, the covers pulled up to his waist, his back to Gil, his shoulders rising and falling on his breath.

But Gil must have woken at some point, because he's under the blankets, his feet sticking out just as he always sleeps.

You're ruining the bed, Sebastian used to complain as Gil yanked the sheets free on his side. *Just 'cause you have the coldest feet in the world*, Gil would say, jumping when Sebastian pressed them to his shins.

He stares up into the darkness, trying not to listen to the soft sounds of Sebastian sleeping.

It's a long time until he drifts off again.

NINE

GIL SWATS at the alarm that blares through his cocoon of pillows, but his hand just meets laminated wood and he sends a lamp teetering.

He grabs it before it can fall, squinting around, daylight haloing the edges of heavy blackout curtains, the gray outline of a dresser, a desk, a TV hung on the wall and—

He sits up. Any hotel room is familiar from years of road trips, bland walls, white bedspread, a lightly patterned rug.

But Sebastian's here, sleeping with his mouth open, his face relaxed, one arm under his pillow and his hair mussed. He didn't evaporate overnight like Gil half expected him to.

"Sebastian," Gil says. "Your alarm."

"Hmm." A deep, throaty mutter and Sebastian rolls over, fumbles his phone, and falls back into the pillow, the beeping silenced.

He did that without opening his eyes. Gil can't see his face, but he knows. Knows Sebastian, still, and he nearly smiles.

No. He turns away. He's not doing this, grinning at Sebastian beside him. He's moving on. Has moved on, hasn't he? Ten years to do it and he's *fine*.

Gil swings his feet to the floor, his back to Sebastian laying there with the sheet wrapped over his waist, his T-shirt pulled tight against his shoulders. He doesn't work out as much as he used to. Less definition in his lats, smaller deltoids, not nearly the same slope of his traps.

He's gorgeous. Different than he was, softer, older, but maybe even more attractive. The line of his neck, the hand flopped on the bed, the shape of his legs sprawled beneath the blankets, the perfect curve of his—

No.

When Gil gets in the shower, he turns the water to cold. *Waking up*, he tells himself, gooseflesh on his skin, the breath leaving him as he dips his head beneath the spray. *Focus*. He tips his head back to let the water catch him in the face, thinking of a clean sheet of ice, the glide of his skates, the weight of the puck on his stick.

Quickly, efficiently, Gil scrubs himself clean and then forces his mind on hockey plays as he brushes his teeth, pictures taking a pass and winging the puck past the goalie to score top shelf, high in the upper corner of the net, as he quickly dresses.

"Hey," he says at the foot of the bed. Louder, he repeats: "Hey, Sebastian."

Sebastian doesn't stir.

"We have practice," Gil says, loud enough it should wake him.

A snore from the pile of pillows.

Gil jumps when the alarm blares again. Of course Sebastian hit snooze. Of course he did.

An arm emerges from the nest of blankets, slaps at the phone, and retreats once more.

Gil could smile. Wants to smile.

Sleep with your feet out and you might actually bother to

wake up, he used to say to Sebastian, laughing as Seb cocooned his feet in the sheets.

Sometimes, Gil would wallop him with a pillow to get him up. Other mornings, he'd tease the sheets back, sleep-warmed skin and—

"Sebastian," he says, roughly shaking his leg. "C'mon, it's morning. We're on the ice soon."

Brown eyes peer up at him, blinking slowly. Sebastian's cheek is red above his beard, creases in his skin from the pillowcase, his hair matted on one side, sticking straight up on the other.

Slowly, Sebastian smiles. The corner of his mouth curves, his eyes soft and his voice deep and husky when he asks, "Gil?"

And then Sebastian sits up, a pinch between his eyebrows. "Right. Hey." The warmth is gone from his voice. "Yeah, I'm up."

"Me too," Gil says, which is...his cheeks flush and he shuffles back a quick step. Yeah, obviously, he's awake, Sebastian can see that. *Smile again*, he wants to prompt. What was that tiny, brief break in Sebastian's careful distance from him? Just exhaustion, he knows. Seb's brain isn't ever quite online until he's drunk his weight in coffee. "I'm gonna go down for breakfast."

"I'm coming."

Sebastian's going to stand up in wrinkled clothes, his thin white cotton T-shirt clinging to his chest. He'll shower too, probably. Soap sliding over his skin, water funneling down his neck—

Gil skips a step backward. "Yeah, no, I'll be down there when you're ready." He jams his phone into his pocket. "Hey, don't—"

No. *Stop*, he tells himself.

Sebastian scratches his hair and yawns. "Don't what?" His voice is too husky, an entirely too deep sleepy rumble.

"Don't fall back asleep." Gil quickly escapes into the hallway before he has to see Sebastian's reaction. Or lack of it. No eye roll, no half exasperated sigh of a laugh.

Downstairs, he fishes his phone out, checking for a text from Melissa. There isn't one. Dad'll already be up, so Gil can call him and check in. Joey too, since he's heading to the airport soon.

Gil hesitates, his thumb poised over Joey's name. No, he doesn't want to talk to Joey right now. And Dad...*How was day one?* he'll ask when he answers.

No, no reason to bother Dad. He'll call when he has news.

At the breakfast buffet, he piles eggs onto a plate, fills a bowl with scoops of berries, and sorts through the basket of bread until he finds whole wheat slices. He pours three glasses of water, arranging all of it on a tray he dumps on the nearest table, swinging into the seat and staring down at the food.

In San Diego, he'd snap a picture of it and send it to the team nutritionist, who'd log his meal along with everything else he ate, and each week would start with a new list of foods to incorporate, what he should cut back on, and the best way to get the right fuel for playing.

Though hell, in San Diego he'd go to the rink for breakfast, downing a smoothie chalky with protein powder in the car on the ride there and then eating with the guys from the spread the chef made fresh for them.

For all he knows, the Sea Lions players' lounge will have cold coffee and stale bagels, given how things here have been going.

Get the omelet with the mushrooms and red peppers, he should text Joey. Those small tips about being in San Diego that Gil can share for when Joey gets there, how the chef makes eggs pretty close to how Mom cooks them.

Though when he pulls out his phone again, he calls Tommy instead. "Please tell me this entire trip to San Francisco is some elaborate prank. You got me, you two won. I'll admit my little brothers get this round," Gil says when Tommy answers.

"If only," Tommy says. "Remember that time I froze Joey's skates in a trash can full of water? That solid block of ice, two little ice skates there in the middle, just looking back at him? Now that was a good prank."

"Not if we hadn't gotten them back out by the time Dad got home."

"C'mon, where's the fun, Gil?"

"I don't know fun anymore. I play for the Sea Lions."

"Nah, you didn't know fun even before this latest adventure you're on. How's it going? Good, by the sounds of it. You're really thriving there, aren't you?"

"I'm not sure I can do this."

"Aw, the team's not that bad, is it? And it could be worse. You could not be playing at all, right?"

"Don't even say that."

"Please, you'll be out of there soon enough, since you're a walking, talking force of will. I'm waiting for the news special where you simply ascend out of San Francisco Bay on the back of a sea lion and ride it to—where's the holy grail of hockey? Somewhere in Canada?"

"You don't even know what you're talking about."

"Only because I have an actual life outside of a sports game. Listen, speaking of, I hope you don't have anything you don't want Joey to find in any bedside drawers, because he's made big plans for your house."

"I hate that he's heading there and I'm here."

"Well Dad hates it too. Guess what we got to talk about

all night at dinner? We read through your coach's resume and your GM's and no offense to them, I'm sure they're lovely people, but what an absolute snooze fest."

"They think they can turn this team around. And..." Gil pokes at his eggs. They're rubbery, bouncing back against his fork. "Um, Sebastian?"

"Sebster. The Sebinator. The Seb—"

"He's coaching."

"Sebatron. What?"

"The Sea Lions. He's the assistant coach."

"Oh." Tommy pauses. Then he laughs. "Oh shit. Okay, this is worth you heading out there early. You're forgiven. Well, mostly. You still have to watch the video from last night."

"What was last night?"

"My glorious speech, you asshat. Sebastian's coaching the Sea Lions?"

"He told me in the airport, said he wanted me to know and that he—" The words feel wrong. "He wants to keep things professional."

Tommy snorts a laugh. "Yeah, good luck with that."

"That's the word he used. He didn't want me to say anything about, well. Us."

"You two being 'professional'? I'm sorry, all I can picture is that time you both tried to get into the same hockey bag, thinking you'd fit."

"We did fit."

"Tell me you didn't just make out in there."

"I—that's what he said, professional. And to not tell the head coach or GM or anyone about, you know. Everything."

"Wow, Sebstamus Prime, all grown up. Okay, so don't go blabbing about how cute you think his butt is in coach's warm-ups. That makes sense, doesn't it?"

"I wasn't going to," Gil says.

"You sure? Because I've always wondered if it's not a whole thing you players like a little too much. Someone out there with a whistle telling you to skate here, skate there, do it better, that wasn't good enough. Mind you, I only want enough details to be able to make fun of you and whatever boner you have for coaches after an entire life of being ordered around by them, but not so much that I actually have any information."

"That's not—" Gil stabs a blueberry. "Shut up."

"And gazing at his butt aside, this must be so fun for you two, back together again."

"No," Gil says. "It's not, it's—he's—he's different now." Gil swallows the lump that rises on the back of those words. That's the crux of the problem, no matter how layered their dynamic is with the years of silence. This Sebastian isn't the Sebastian Gil left in their dorm room, the one he grew up with, because growing up didn't stop that autumn day. No, they both went onward with their lives and Gil sucks in a breath, sharp against the wish that they hadn't. "We're not friends, not like we were. I don't know what's going on, I haven't for years, and this is—being back together—"

It sucks.

It's awesome. And awful.

He stabs at a piece of egg, but it slips from his fork, rubbery and too soft.

"You and Seb? Not friends?" Tommy asks. "Sorry, those words don't compute."

"I'm serious. You know we hadn't talked in ages and now it's just more of the same."

"Falling out of touch, sure, we all get busy, but what happened? Did you talk to him?"

"I fucking tried."

"I don't know if you know this about yourself, Gil, but

101

it's kind of hard to get a word in with you that's not about hockey. Did you two actually really talk?"

"I want to! But he keeps reminding me he's my coach, and he doesn't want to hang out."

"Oh, look at him wearing his big-boy pants, Sebstopher with his fancy career. Give him a chance to warm up. I'm sure it's weird for him too, being shoved back together so suddenly. But it's going to be fine, you two were, you know. Ruining my life because all of a sudden Mom made a rule I couldn't have my door shut with anyone of any gender who came over."

"She did?" He thinks back to high school, Tommy living with Mom and Lex, her then-girlfriend, for most of those years. Tommy had begged Dad to let him move in with her and when he finally quit hockey in middle school, Dad had given in. So no, Gil didn't see much of him by the time high school came around. Didn't see him at all, really.

"Yes, she did, so thank you for that. I hadn't even kissed anyone yet."

Gil tries for a smile. "Have you by now?"

"Fuck you. I knew I shouldn't have answered."

"Is that a no?"

"Look, not all of us got a next-door neighbor to mack on to our heart's content."

"Yeah." Gil shifts his phone to his other hand. A first kiss with Jessica Bertson after the eighth-grade dance, Gil's palms sweaty with nerves and so confused afterward about what the big deal was supposed to be. And then years later, in Sebastian's basement, soda bottles and video game controllers, the taste of pizza and—

Yeah, he'd gotten the idea about what a big fuss kissing was at that point. Thoroughly.

"Mom made us keep three feet on the floor and the

lights on bright enough to read," Tommy says. "Did Dad even know? Or did he just not care?"

Did he? Yes, he must have known, though he'd certainly never said anything. "Look, it doesn't matter. Sebastian hates me now."

"Doesn't matter? Fucking hell, tell that to high school me, you lucky little shit. Hooking up with your bestie—how'd you manage to mess that up so badly?"

"I didn't. He's got a hair up his ass, I don't know what's going on with him. He's just been like this forever."

"Since college?"

"Yeah."

"Since you left for the NHL, you mean?"

"We said we were going to stay in touch and then he just didn't. And I asked, but he said it was a long time ago, doesn't want to talk about it. He wants to—he said we should move on. That we have new lives now."

"Yeah, he might," Tommy says and laughs. "You have hockey, so your life hasn't changed one bit. Look, I don't know what happened, besides the fact that Mom bothering to be a good parent was absolutely awful in some ways, but it's you and Sebastian. You two will find your way back to each other."

Gil frowns. "What does that mean?"

"He's probably just feeling awkward after all this time. I hate to break this to you, but you're not the Don Juan you think you are."

"No, about Mom."

"Well, you know Dad," Tommy says like that explains anything. "But c'mon, Gil, all those years between you and Sebastian? You were friends, no matter what other fun you had. Maybe you gotta apologize, I don't know. Did you fuck up?"

"No! I got called up by San Diego, I had to leave, and

then it was like Sebastian was too busy to bother talking to me. We were going to stay friends when I left, we said so, and he knew I was probably going sometime soon, and he knew that when they called I had to go. It was the NHL. What was I going to do?"

"Yeah, he did know. We all know what we're getting into with you, Gilbert. Look, go figure out your shit, okay? Remind him that you two used to be glued together at the hip. And other anatomy parts. Which reminds me, after I go rinse out my brain with bleach, I'm going to tell Mom— again—that her responsible parenting meant I didn't have nearly the fun in high school you did."

"You wanted to move in with her and Lex. And don't call me that." *Why?* Gil had asked as Tommy packed up before he'd even had Dad's permission, before the custody battle had dragged through court again. *We all agreed you three would live here. It's the best thing for you,* Dad used to say, placidly calm as every night Tommy shouted at him in the kitchen, *If you cared that I lived here, you'd bother to actually be around.*

Though Dad was around, Gil had always thought. It was Tommy who never came to the rink, who skipped practice, who refused to come out to the driveway when Dad drilled them on their shooting, their passing, putting them through stick-handling exercises for afternoons at a time.

You have to know, Tommy had said and Gil hadn't felt much like the oldest brother then, curled on Tommy's bed with arms around his knees, watching him fill up a suitcase in the hopes he might be freed from the house.

"Take my persistence as a lesson," Tommy says. "You want to get out of where you are, you gotta whine and beg and fight for it. Though I'm sure you know that, trying to escape San Francisco. Now listen, Gilly, go make nice with your old buddy, okay?"

"Don't call me that either."

"Love you, Gilly. Bye."

"Bye," Gil mumbles. He sets his phone down and stares at his plate. Slowly, he starts eating again, one bite after the next until he's done. Get the hell off this team...yeah, Tommy's right. Gil will fight for it, of course he will. *Your mother agreed you'd live here,* Dad had said over and over, and it had never, not once, deterred Tommy from trying, and eventually succeeding, in moving to her apartment.

And Sebastian...*Leave him alone,* part of himself wages against the soft ache in his chest, where the knot of hurt has sat for so long. Sebastian avoided him for ten years, and he clearly doesn't want to strike up their old friendship like they never skipped a beat.

But...finding their way back toward each other. Gil likes the sound of that. A new sort of dynamic between them than the one he'd left behind at Rideau.

Because Sebastian didn't say a hard, firm *no,* just that he didn't want to rehash what happened. Okay, yeah, Gil doesn't have to bring up college, high school, the years they spent living in each other's pockets. He can move on, start fresh like a clean sheet of ice.

He grabs a paper coffee cup and fills it, leaving an inch of space before the rim. Does Sebastian drink his coffee black now? Grown up, moved on, living his new life he's shucked Gil from?

Gil grabs a single-serve creamer and a packet of sugar. He has no idea. And won't, either, until he can find out.

The lights are on in their room and Sebastian's hair is wet as he ties his sneakers, wearing his old Rideau sweatshirt and his coaching warm-up pants.

Yeah, he looks good in them. Gil shifts his eyes away and sets the coffee next to Sebastian's phone. "I'm heading to the rink," Gil says. "You want to share a cab?"

Sebastian's hands are still on his laces, his eyes on the coffee cup. "You brought me this?"

"Figured you still need your IV drip of caffeine to get moving in the morning, but look at you, up and at 'em," Gil says. Easy, casual, calm, like his heart isn't stuttering a bit. Sebastian'll just pour the coffee out. Leave it there to cool, refuse to drink it. Tell Gil he shouldn't have, and please don't do this again.

Gil clears his throat. The room's too quiet. "There's cream and sugar, too," he ventures. "If you still use it." *Because I don't know you anymore*, Gil wants to say. *Just like you wanted.*

But no, he does know him. Sebastian is just...more. *Move on*, Sebastian had said and of course he had, this adult version isn't the static, imagined version Gil's held for all these years of Sebastian caught still in time, poised in the last moments of adolescence.

It's Sebastian, Tommy had said. Just a new version of him, a fuller, deeper version of the Sebastian Gil once knew.

And this is Gil's chance. His only one, if he's going to get his trade.

Sebastian opens the packet of sugar with his teeth and dumps the cream into his coffee, like he always did. And he still drinks it too fast, taking a too-big sip.

"What you said last night," Gil starts. "Moving on. Yeah, that's the best thing."

Sebastian sets the lid back on his coffee slowly. "I am sorry," he says, his voice low. "Falling out of touch with you. I—you kept in touch. I didn't."

It's fine, Gil could say, brush it off, but he can't quite get his mouth around the words. "Yeah, it sucked. A lot. And it still does."

"I know I hurt you," Sebastian says. "But Gil, that drill from practice?"

Gil takes a step forward. "That was the reason?"

"No, it wasn't, of course it wasn't. But that's what you remember. I've totally forgotten about it, but you...there were other things going on than hockey when you left."

"Well, sure," Gil says.

Sebastian just looks at him. Waiting, Gil realizes a beat too late.

"Yeah," Sebastian says when Gil can't find what he's supposed to say. Sebastian adjusts his watch and sighs as he stands. "Look, thanks for the coffee. I know you don't want to be late to the rink, so let's go."

"You're pissed at me, aren't you?" Gil asks.

"I think we're both pissed off at each other."

No, Gil wants to say. He doesn't like that it's true. It sits itchy against his skin, uncomfortable when they should be laughing together, goofing around, talking and talking, all of last night, this morning, the entirety of the car ride ahead of them, at the rink—

No. Gil has work he needs to do. His own play to focus on so he can get the hell out of here.

In the lobby, Sebastian stops to refill his cup, already half empty from sucking it down in the elevator. *Don't burn your tongue, I happen to like it*, Gil used to say.

He tucks his hands in his pockets and waits as Sebastian fiddles with his cup, his phone in one hand, a second packet of sugar in the other.

They're...yeah. Gil hunches his shoulders, staring at his shoes as he waits. Sebastian's right. Gil is real fucking hurt and has been for so long, and Sebastian isn't thrilled either, clearly.

But...Gil's driven himself to the rink day after day for years now. Hux lived across town and Gil wasn't really close with anyone else enough to want to regularly ride with them, so summers with Joey were the only times he had a buddy in the car as he headed off to skate.

Seb's something less than a friend now. Or more, maybe. Complicated and confusing but...he's here and they're going to the rink together, for the first time in so, so long.

And that feels really, really good.

TEN

"Heads up, coming through," Millsy says, a bundle of plastic in his arms as he walks toward the ice.

Wrapped hockey sticks, Gil thinks as he steps out of the way, but no, it's layers and layers of cling wrap encircling a camera tripod.

Millsy grins as he takes his armful over to the side of the rink, spreading the legs of the tripod and producing a similarly wrapped camera that he attaches to it.

Sebastian has already disappeared up the stairs to the coaches' office. Gil should have made it quicker to the locker room, too, apparently, to avoid...this. Whatever this is.

"Is that all of Emery's camera equipment?" Gil asks.

"Sure is."

Gil rubs at his eyes. He's going to get a headache, he can already feel it threatening at his temples. "Did you—"

"Get it set up for her just like she asked? Sure did." Millsy presses his palm to the center of his chest. "I like to make sure I'm giving everyone a hand around here, really putting in the work to make this team the type of organization we all know we can be."

Gil's mouth opens. "Why?" is all he can get out, but no, he doesn't really want to know the answer.

"Because she knows I love caramel apples and left one oh so innocently on the counter the other day. You know what it actually was?"

"No?"

"A fucking onion." Millsy carefully aims the camera at the ice, setting it up as if it was really able to film their skate this morning, not layers of cling wrap obscuring the lens. "She's my big sister, so fair's fair. I got the plastic wrap to mess with Bloomer's stuff, but he's not actually any fun so this is much better."

"Seriously?" Gil asks.

"Yeah, he's seriously a bummer," Millsy says.

Yes, Gil needs to get out of here. San Francisco, this dreary arena, this set of teammates. He needs to absolutely, as soon as he can, get the hell out of here.

Though when he escapes toward the locker room, Millsy follows him, laughing. "See?" Millsy asks as Gil pushes into the room. "We can have fun here, just you watch."

"We've got practice," Gil says. "And our first game coming up."

"And," Millsy says. "A delighted social media manager, you're welcome."

"Alek!" comes a shout from the hallway as they push inside.

"I was never here." Millsy darts into the bathroom.

"He's an ass," Pezer says as he straps on his shin guards.

"But he's our ass," Lomsy says from the stall next to him.

The door bangs open. Emery's jaw is set. "Where the fuck is he?"

"We'll get him," Pezer and Lomsy say together.

"No!" Millsy shouts through the bathroom door.

This is a zoo. A circus. A joke, when everyone should be warming up and only Bloomer's stretching, calm among the chaos around him.

He's also the only one who stands up and crosses to Emery. "I'll help," he says as a scuffle sounds from the bathroom, laughing and play wrestling.

This is a professional team. This type of fun before a practice—sure, maybe in college. Definitely in high school. But they're all here to work, not to goof around.

"Guys," Gil says but his voice barely cuts through the din.

"Hey," he calls, louder.

But the most he gets is Mitcher motioning to him to quiet down. "Not worth it," he says. "And you'll piss off Hal."

Hal's sitting sideways in his stall, his feet up against one wall and his back against the other. The position makes Gil's back ache just looking at it, but goalies are always flexible. And strange.

And typically, worried about their spot on the team, with younger guys nipping at their heels for a chance between the pipes.

"Hal," Gil says.

"Don't," Mitcher says.

"Get dressed," Gil says.

Hal looks around, making a show of trying to find who Gil is talking to, even craning to see under his bench as if there's anything there but his skates waiting for him.

"The rest of you too," Gil says. "Guys, we have practice. Hal, get your gear on."

"Really don't," Mitcher says. "Not with him."

"It takes goalies forever to get dressed, so Hal, let's go, okay?"

Hal stares him dead in the eye, locks his phone, sets it

aside, and then slumps down farther in his stall. He yawns, crosses his arms, and settles his chin on his chest, closing his eyes and getting comfortable for a nap.

"Are you serious?" Gil asks.

"Hey, pro tip around here," Mitcher says. "Worry about yourself. You try with these guys and you'll be even worse off."

"But—" *We're a team*, he nearly says, but he can already imagine Mitcher's bark of laughter if he let that come out of his mouth.

Gil jams on his equipment and slips out onto the ice before anyone else has bothered to finish dressing. The glide of his skates is familiar, soothing, even if nothing else around here is.

How the hell is Gil going to score enough goals to catch the eye of another team if he's playing with teammates like this? They'll be trapped in their defensive zone, constantly back on their heels. Gil will be stuck down there with them, trying to run damage control instead of striding up the ice, the puck on his stick, shooting it into the back of the net and throwing his arms up in success.

Though Emery won't even be able to snap a picture of it, the way things are going, she and Bloomer cutting cling wrap from her camera because this place…it's not just a joke. It's hockey's version of hell. Gil hadn't even known that could exist in a sport as perfect as this one.

Gil skates over to Steph the moment she steps on the ice. "The guys aren't going to be on time," he says.

She dumps out a bucket of pucks. The equipment staff should be doing that for her—though Gil hasn't seen a single equipment staff member in this building.

"Yeah, they'll probably be late," Steph says.

"But we have practice."

"Yes we do."

"Aren't you going to do anything about it?" Gil asks. "We have a game coming up."

"That's right. A season's worth of them."

"So are we going to miss puck drop because these guys can't tie their skates on time?"

"I sure hope not," Steph says.

Gil lets out a soft laugh. "Coach."

"You have something you'd like to say about it, Mr. Roussin?"

Yes, of course he does. And maybe this isn't his place, only his second day with this team, but she asked, so..."I know you're new to the NHL, but this is the pros. If you don't get the respect of these guys, and get it soon, this team's going to end up even worse than last year and honestly, that's saying something."

"Respect." Steph turns to Sebastian, stepping onto the ice. "Coach Martin, we're getting a lesson from Mr. Roussin here. Care to join?"

That's sarcasm. Fuck, Gil's going to dig himself into a hole here. But he can't not say something. "These guys need some discipline," Gil says. "Consequences if they're going to mess around. Like my Dad does, he—"

"Which one is your dad?" Steph asks.

Gil sucks in a breath. She knows. Everyone knows of Bert Roussin.

Oh. She's fucking with him and...enjoying herself.

His face flushes.

"Since you know the league so well, can you answer this for me?" she asks.

Crap. This is...yeah, this is bad, whatever he started, but it's too late and she's still talking.

"What do you think would happen if I lined the guys

up, gave them a piece of my mind, and blew the whistle for sprints?"

Gil flounders, but there's only one answer to give. "They'd skate. We'd skate, all of us, until you told us we could stop." Until they grew nauseous, until some guys threw up their breakfast, until their faces were so red they tipped to purple, and their legs were weak, and taking another stride, just one more, felt like skating through concrete. And they'd do it together, all of them, over and over again until they got the message. Then tomorrow, they'd all be on time. Early even, and for every practice for the rest of the season.

"You'd skate." Steph taps her stick against his chest.

He looks down at the divot it leaves in his jersey. "I—of course I would."

"I think some of the rookies would probably go with you, actually. They think you're pretty swell with that last name of yours. Bloomer would too, because he's good like that. Mitcher, maybe, depending on his mood."

"Everyone would. We're in this together."

"You think Millsy would do sprints?"

"He'd have to. You'd cut him from the team if he didn't."

"He already told me he's looking forward to being cut. Prefers the farm team in Sacramento to this one."

"He—what?"

"And Pezer and Lomsy, they might do one sprint, maybe, before they started fucking around. I can see it now, probably taking turns pushing each other."

"Okay, them too. Cut them from the roster if they pull something like that."

"We don't have better options to call up from Sacramento to take their places," Steph says. "The same owners run both teams, which is really great, just all-around super-thrilled at the state of this organization. So right there we're down three players: Pezer, Lomsy, and Millsy, and that's half of our defense."

"Ok, but—"

"Tell me, do you think Hal would lift a single finger around this place for anyone but himself?"

"Well goalies are always kinda off."

"Exactly," Steph says. "So what did I do with Hal before this season?"

"Told him you'd trade him? Dump him in the minors too?"

"Nah. I made a bet with him based on his save percentage."

"What?" Gil asks. "Why?"

"Cause he wants money and I want a goalie to save some pucks, and I don't really care how I get that to happen."

"That's not—" not right. Not how it's done.

"That's not a bad idea. Thank you, Mr. Roussin, I knew that's what you were going to say. Listen, I take your advice and I get a bunch of guys ignoring me. Laughing too, proba-bly, and we lose what little we get from them already. This is a group of players who gave up a long, long time ago. They're completely checked out, here for their paycheck and that's it. Why would they bother to respect me? I wouldn't, if I were one of them. So Frank, me, and Mr. Martin, we're doing things this way. Okay?"

No, Gil wants to say.

But she's his coach.

"Okay," he says and nods as if he possibly means it.

"I'm so glad I have your approval, thank you," she says and yes, wow, that's a deep layer of sarcasm under her words as she skates off.

Fuck. He...did not handle that well.

"And Gil?" she asks, spinning around. "Your advice?"

"Yeah?"

"We're looking for a leader among our players, so I appreciate your thoughts. But this is the last time you'll question me, let alone explain to me how to run my team."

"I—"

"If you want to collaborate, I'm all ears. But I'm doing my job, so why don't you focus on doing yours. Or..." She pauses, then laughs.

He feels sick. "Or?"

"Or maybe I will make you do sprints, given that with you, that would actually work."

Gil pulls in a breath as she skates off, snagging a puck to bring with her and shooting it into the net, a beautiful release that finds the top left corner.

"Um," Gil says.

"You could sprint now," Sebastian says. "Just get it over with."

"Fuck."

He should. Skate away from Sebastian to some other part of the rink, though the ice feels glaringly open without the rest of the team out here, just Steph hammering another puck into the net and Sebastian suddenly too close to Gil.

"Keep at it and you might get your trade."

"She'd cut me instead of letting me go." It's laughable. He's the best skater out here, but Steph...shit. Yeah. She'd cut him from the roster and send him down to the minors, just to prove a point.

And she's right. It would work to motivate him. Just the threat of it, even.

His face burns and it's not the flush of exercise.

When she glides back toward them, Gil takes a stride toward her.

"Coach," he says. "I'm sorry. I apologize."

"Good." She keeps skating past him, finding another

puck and taking a slap shot so hard the boards shake when it hits them.

"Am I fucked?" Gil asks softly.

"I'd mind your manners for a while with her," Sebastian says. "Play nice, you know."

"I will."

"Maybe bring her a coffee too." Sebastian stick-handles a puck, bouncing it off his skate and then kicking it back up to his blade. "Thanks for that, by the way. This morning."

Don't, Gil tells himself but asks anyway, "Did you get something to eat?"

"Yeah, there was some food in the lounge."

"Anything good?"

"No."

"Figures."

He needs to skate away. Practice. Drills. Get his feet under him on this team so he can be gone as soon as he can.

Put air between him and Sebastian, really.

Warming up is soothing, long, looping strides along the boards, and then pushing himself from blue line to blue line with a harder, quick pace. It's hockey. He can do this and do it better than any of the rest of them who finally wander onto the ice.

And they are late. Pezer and Lomsy and Millsy spill through the door, still laughing. Bloomer at least looks like he's hurrying, caught behind on getting ready from helping Emery.

But Steph doesn't skate over to gather them up, just stands there, watching the team slowly emerge. Only when Hal gets on the ice, long after the rest, does she move toward him. "Good morning, thanks for joining us," she tells him.

He ignores her, skating to the net at the far end of the ice. He takes off his gloves and lays them and his stick on top of it, reaching up to adjust his long hair beneath his helmet.

She snags a puck and shoots it, sending it flying past him into the net.

"Give me a minute," Hal says, not hurrying to put his gloves back on.

"That's two." Steph sinks another puck.

"Fucking stop."

"Fucking block a shot." Steph scores again, neatly sending the puck between his legs. "Martin, get the kids started, will you? Hal and I have some work to do."

"Circle up," Sebastian calls and blows his whistle.

But Millsy just leans against the boards with a lazy smile at Emery. "Take my picture?"

"Fuck off."

"You love me."

"Bring it in," Sebastian says, but everyone's watching Millsy instead of him.

"Some trouble with your camera this morning?" Millsy asks.

"Yeah, I took a picture of your face and it broke," Emery says.

"We're getting started," Sebastian says and taps his stick on the ice. "Gentlemen, listen up."

"Hey." Gil lightly smacks Millsy's leg with his stick. It's practice time. It's been practice time for a good while now, minutes ticking by on the clock hung above the rink.

But Millsy just grabs a puck and starts bouncing it on the blade of his stick, still standing directly in front of Emery and her camera.

"Just start," Gil says to Sebastian.

"Nine," Millsy says. "Ten. Em, film me, c'mon."

"Don't bother, he can't get very much higher," Pezer says.

"Not 'cause he drops it, that's just as many numbers as he knows," Lomsy says.

Millsy bounces the puck up once more and then uses the flat of his blade to swipe it out of the air, hitting Lomsy in the chest.

"Fucker," Lomsy says, catching the puck before it can fall and throwing it back.

Millsy swats at it again, though the angle's wrong and he whiffs.

"We're going to work on some breakouts," Sebastian says, but his voice is too quiet and everyone's watching Millsy.

"Hey!" Gil says, loud enough to cut through the ripple of laughter, but Lomsy ignores him, parroting Millsy's swing and miss, exaggerated and comical.

"Eleven, twelve, thirteen, just like that, Millsy. Use your toes when you run out of fingers to count on."

"Guys," Gil says.

"We're changing up the breakout a bit from last year, so listen up as I describe our new system," Sebastian says.

"Pay attention," Bloomer says to Millsy.

"Pay attention," Millsy echoes, already bouncing another puck on his stick. "Seventeen, eighteen—shit, Pezer, help a guy out here. Ninety-teen."

Gil has to be ready to play in the coming game, and he's not going to get there with a practice like this. And Steph... well, maybe he can inch his way back into her good graces.

And if nobody else is going to help Sebastian...

Find their way back to each other, like Tommy said. *No*, he tells himself. Those phone calls he made, those texts he sent, unanswered. So no, Gil shouldn't try. Move on. Gil helped him once, yesterday, running through the drills so Millsy couldn't laugh at Seb.

Though this is for his own career. Yes. *Can't score goals*

if we're constantly on defense, he tells himself. Selfish. Self-centered, at least.

"Hey, listen to Coach Martin," he says.

Listen to me, he should probably start with. When was the last time anyone here gave a shit? *Worry about himself*, Mitcher had said, but what's the fucking point of that if he can't field an entire team on his own?

He glides forward, fists a hand in Millsy's jersey, and drags him to the side. "What'll it take to get you to listen?" he asks, his voice low.

"An authentic Bert Roussin jersey."

"Deal," Gil says.

"Wait, really? Signed, I mean. From the Stanley Cup Finals. Oh, and a stick too. I'm gonna sell that shit."

Gil shoves him a few inches forward. "Millsy's ready to go through the drill." That's at least one of the class clowns neutralized. "And I am too."

Who else can he get on board?

Bloomer, yes, hanging back next to him. He cared once, according to Mitcher. Burned out hard in this place, but maybe he has some spark left. "Blooms too." Gil gestures Bloomer forward.

"Wait, no, he doesn't like me," Millsy says when Bloomer glides too close to him. "And I want more than a jersey. Like a pair of socks. Or his favorite coffee mug. Or—"

"You." Gil grabs Lomsy. "Stand over there, away from Pezer."

"Um, we actually can't be separated," Pezer says. "It's in our contracts."

"Do not move. Don't talk to him. Don't even look at him," Gil says to Lomsy, setting him on the other side of Bloomer. He catches the eye of a rookie and tips his head for him to join them.

The kid does, and then a second one.

"We're ready," Gil says to Sebastian. "What've you got for us?"

"Breakouts." Sebastian's voice is louder this time. He points with his stick around the rink as he talks. "For now we'll start with our centers cutting toward the boards for the outlet pass from the wing. Offside wing is going to skate over hard, looking for the next pass."

Sebastian looks good up there, explaining what he wants from them. *Shut up*, Gil tells the imaginary Tommy grinning in his head.

The rookie's hand shoots up in the air.

"Yeah?" Sebastian asks.

"What do you want from the wing who made the pass?"

"Getting there," Sebastian says. "He's going to head for the far boards."

"Sorry, I should have waited."

"Hey, it's okay." Sebastian gives him a smile. Of course he does. Doesn't snap at him, doesn't send him to the back of the crowd for distracting everyone with needless questions, just encourages that type of young, eager curiosity.

This isn't the peewee league, Gil could complain. There's no time to hold rookies' hands, make sure they're feeling okay. Keep up or get out.

But. Of course this is the man Sebastian was always going to grow up to be, so very gentle with the younger guys on the team. He'll probably pull the rookie aside later, let him know it's okay to ask questions, see if he has any concerns, if he's fitting in alright on a new team, his first time up here in the pros.

Sebastian could have played in the NHL. He has the skill, the talent, the same coaching Gil got as a kid, since Dad piled Sebastian into the car too for every skills practice and hockey camp. Sebastian just…hadn't. Entry into the draft had come and gone and Sebastian never submitted his name, and then when he was eligible for development camps or paid tryouts he let the opportunities slip by him.

He will, Gil had thought for years after he left Rideau, waiting for Sebastian's name to come up on a roster, scanning lists of players now and again, sure he'd find that familiar Martin at the top of the M's.

Yes, of course this is who Sebastian was probably always going to become, not pursuing a playing career but instead out there leading others toward theirs.

Shit, Gil thinks. He likes that. Liked those traits in Sebastian all those years ago. Likes them now, too. Finds it really...

Gil frowns at the thought as soon as it bubbles up: *Hot*.

And no, the way his ass looks in his coach's warm-ups isn't helping.

Move on. Gil can do that as much as he can just stop breathing.

It was easy to stay mad at him when they were apart for so long. To pretend he'd forgotten Sebastian and that was the reason for the silence between them.

Now...now, he's fucked.

Professional, Gil thinks. Fucking hell does he need to get off this team and out of this city and the mortification of being on the Sea Lions is only part of that, because being back with Sebastian all over again?

It's the fire of competition warming his chest. The need to beat Mitcher at this drill, the need to stand out from this crowd, to get traded and be gone. To get in good with the head coach.

Not warmth buzzing through him, stoked by the soft brown of Sebastian's eyes that find Gil's. *Thank you*, Seb mouths when at least most of the guys have listened to his explanation.

Gil nods, sharp, curt. Professional.

Sebastian blows his whistle and Gil hurries off to the pile of pucks, the start of the drill.

Yeah, Sebastian looks good. Coaches well, too, at least once the guys listen to him. Gil clenches his stick, focused on hockey, and somewhere, Tommy laughs.

ELEVEN

IN THE BACK of the Sea Lions arena, amid puddles and flickering lights, Gil stick-handles a weighted ball around his feet until his forearms burn and only then does he shoot, flinging it as hard as he can at the wall.

It catches him in the thigh when it bounces back, rebounding off sore muscle. He grimaces, gets it on the blade of his stick, and shoots it once more.

Their first game is going to be the embarrassment of his career, plain and simple. No matter how well he plays, there's only so much he can do if the rest of the team is a mess.

And he needs to fucking *focus*. Get on the ice, get his work done, and not let his mind wander.

He rockets the ball hard against the wall once more and reaches to catch it on his stick, but he misses and it sails straight past him.

It rolls back again before he can even turn to chase it.

"Oh," Gil says when he sees Sebastian there, his hands in his pockets. "Hey." *Came down here to get away from you,* Gil wants to say. Of course he did, rather than trapping himself in a hotel room with Seb all afternoon and evening, breathing the same air, having to exist in the same small space. "Did Steph send you down here to rip into me after I was a dick to her on the ice?"

"Nah, I heard something slamming around back here and figured it's either an actual sea lion or you taking out your frustration like you always do. Figured I should check before the building falls down either way. But she did recount it all for Frank. She does a pretty good imitation of you."

Gil snaps the ball at the wall again and this time he catches it on his blade, stick-handling it back and forth.

"Hey," Sebastian says and when Gil glances at him, he's a step closer. "She appreciated you getting the guys to listen for once. And I was thinking I should say thanks, too. This is a hell of a team to walk into and what you did helped."

You're welcome, do you like me now, are we friends again finally? Gil works the ball faster on his stick, his hands growing tired. "Someone had to do something."

"Steph was pretty impressed, too."

"She was not. She thinks I'm telling her how to do her job."

"To be fair, you were. But she also knows you're the best player out there on the ice and it's nice that you give a crap."

Gil slams the ball at the wall again. "Great. I can be the star player on a shitty, awful team."

"You could. Steph's been talking about you being captain."

"The hell?" Gil stills the ball, straightening to hold the stick in just one hand. His chest flushes. Captain?

No, he shakes his head, dousing that excitement before it warms through him. Ridiculous to even think of it. "C'mon, of the Sea Lions? This team? And she can't want to work with me."

"The team hasn't ever had one. They've just been

making do running three alternate captains each game. She likes you—well, she likes you if you keep your attitude in check, and the guys listen to you."

"I can't be the captain." Of course he can't. He's leaving. Captains don't look for trades all season, or talk with their agents each week, an eye on any possible escape.

"You'd be great," Sebastian says. "Gil, you're born for it. You'd be the face of a franchise. Frank would build the team around you, kids everywhere in the city would know your name, be wearing your jersey."

Gil laughs. "Can you imagine what my dad would say? That'd be so fucking embarrassing. Captain of the Sea Lions, of all teams."

"Have you ever considered that maybe your dad isn't right about everything?"

"Well he sure as shit is about this."

"Yeah." Sebastian shrugs and his smile fades. "Yeah, I told Steph you'd say that."

"I'm not running my career into the ground on this team." What has he always said? "The top ceiling of my career is in how hard I work." Yeah, that's right, the image he had for his NHL days, the dream he'd held so close back in college and high school. And then the draft had come and it had been like lighting a match on a pile of kindling he'd been building since his first day on skates.

"Gil," Sebastian says.

Gil frowns. His voice sounds too gentle. "What?"

"Do you ever think that maybe this team is your best chance for the type of career you've always wanted?"

"I thought you came down here to tell me I did a good job in practice, not to shit all over my prospects. Seb, this place is a joke, you can see that as well as I can. The kind of career I've always wanted isn't here. I'm going to go do that somewhere else."

"Do you think you can?"

"What? Get traded? Of course. Melissa's on it, and if she can't make something work, Dad can."

"Yeah, your dad." Sebastian turns like he's going to walk away, though he hesitates. "Have the career you want, I mean. Is that really happening for you?"

"Not in this place, that's for sure." *Come with me*, he suddenly wants to say. They'll find themselves in a different city, a new one. They can start over, move on, like Sebastian said. Let all of the pain of the past fade away, wiped clean.

But no, Sebastian's not leaving this city. He loves this damn place, apparently, with its fog and hills and crappy team. *Commitments*, he said. Gil frowns. "This is really where you want to be?" he asks. "The Sea Lions?"

"Can't say it's where I thought I'd end up, but yeah. I like Steph, I like Frank, and I think they can really make something happen here. I get that you won't ever see the good around here, but...it's nice. Different from the rest of the NHL, which I know really drives you up the wall, but there's something to be said for that."

"Is there? 'Cause you can find another team, get the hell out of here. How long is your contract? Though you can probably get out of it, push comes to shove."

"I already asked Steph and Frank for an extension. They said they'd think about it, see how it goes for now."

"Why don't you have a long-term contract already?"

"Why do you still shoot like shit?"

"I don't."

"Well I don't either."

"Shoot badly?" No, he doesn't. Seb's shot is as gorgeous as the way he skates.

"Have a long-term contract. Keep up, Gil."

But Gil feels too off balance, rocked back by trying to match Sebastian after so long out of practice. "I shoot like

Dad taught me," Gil says. "My shot is fine. Did you not ask or negotiate or—"

"You shoot like you've got somewhere else to be." Quick, before Gil can stop him, he snags the stick out of Gil's hands. He takes the ball and moves it smoothly back and forth, then winds up a shot and unleashes the ball toward the wall.

"That's what I was doing."

"It wasn't."

"It was." Gil reaches for his stick.

Sebastian ignores him, gathering the ball back to himself. "Put some oomph into it. You're barely flexing the stick." He shoots again.

Gil steps forward, trapping the ball beneath his foot before Sebastian can do it a third time. "I'm doing the exact same thing you are."

"You're not putting the effort in, so you're not getting enough power, and your release is too quick."

"Hockey's a fast game. Of course I'm getting shots off quickly."

"Doesn't matter if you give the goalie plenty of time to track the puck, 'cause you're also broadcasting where you're aiming."

"I am not," Gil says. "Give me that."

"No." Sebastian doesn't hand the stick back.

"What, Steph teach you her little coaching trick of stealing our equipment? Yeah, looks like you will like coaching here."

"What can I say, she's a breath of fresh air." Sebastian pokes the ball with the blade, but Gil keeps his foot in place and Sebastian gives up after a moment. "No, the other reason I came over here was to tell you...listen, this morning, getting me coffee."

Don't do that again, Gil is sure he's going to say. Move on. They're not friends. That's not what Sebastian wants.

But instead Sebastian dips his head and then looks up with a small, tentative smile. "You don't have any reason to be nice to me. But you are and I—I really do appreciate it."

"Seb..." Gil chances a step closer. "What happened?"

Sebastian flips the stick over, examining how Gil taped the blade. *You use too much*, Seb had always said, trying to wrestle the roll of tape out of Gil's hands. *Leave some for the rest of us.*

"I guess I thought you knew," Sebastian said, still studying the stick.

"Knew what?"

"I hoped, at least. Which I shouldn't do." Sebastian tucks the stick under his arm. "So. Anyway. You need to take a look at the time. You've spent all afternoon working out and now practicing your stick-handling and shooting. Exhausting yourself isn't going to help you any."

"You can't just tell me I should know and then—"

"It doesn't matter, Gil. Nothing's changed. Why don't you get some dinner? Spend some time doing something other than hockey. It'd be good for you."

"I'm fine. This is what I do, and you're not—" *my coach.*

No, Sebastian is his coach.

How absolutely fucking weird.

"C'mon." Sebastian walks back to the locker room and sets Gil's stick inside.

"Hey!" Gil calls, but Sebastian doesn't stop, just pushes out the door to the alley, and hell, Gil can't keep arguing with him if he's not going to bother to stop and listen, so he jogs after him.

Is he asking Gil to grab a bite to eat with him? Is that what this is? An overture, a chance to reconnect?

Gil needs to practice. To focus on hockey.

Instead, he follows Sebastian out the door, catching him in the alley outside. "What're you up to tonight?" Gil asks as casually as he knows how.

"Got some game tape to watch from last year," Sebastian says and turns to walk towards the street. "Notes to take on some of the guys, and I want to talk to some of them too."

Gil hurries to follow. "That rookie? Who kept asking questions on the ice?"

"Jay? Yeah, he's a good kid. Nervous."

"That he'll never set foot outside of this team?"

"Playing in front of you, mostly," Sebastian says.

Gil snorts a laugh. "Okay."

"I'm serious. These kids grow up hearing 'Roussin' and he thinks he doesn't belong on the ice with you."

"Maybe you should tell him you don't think I can shoot."

"I did."

"Great, thank you." Gil stops in front of a restaurant, an A-frame sign on the sidewalk, lights glowing inside the broad windows. Tentatively, he tips his head toward it. "Want to, um, you hungry? Before you get started on your work?"

"You taking my advice?"

"Sure, Coach."

Sebastian wrinkles his face. "C'mon, that's just weird."

"Coach Martin," Gil says.

"Don't," Seb says.

"What? You said I was too focused on hockey, so yeah, let's get some food."

The door opens before he can reach for it and—oh.

"Rooster! Roussin, get it? That you out there?" Mitcher laughs, a beer in his hand.

"Yeah, I get it," Gil says. Everyone calls him that, as far back as high school. "Hey, didn't know you were in there."

"Oh, Coach too! Awesome, come grab some beers." Mitcher pushes the door open for them.

Sebastian doesn't move, so Gil doesn't either. It's the hockey season, so Gil doesn't really drink. But...he glances sideways at Sebastian. Getting a beer is technically something other than hockey.

"Wanna get a drink?" he asks. *Yes*, he's nearly sure Sebastian would have said a moment ago, but Mitcher's grinning at them and behind him, Gil can spot some of the other guys on the team. A loud, crowded room full of guys Sebastian doesn't know—Gil catches his eye. *I'll help*, he tries to telegraph. Introduce Sebastian, make sure he doesn't end up standing awkwardly by himself, a drink in his hand but nobody to talk to, unsure of how to step into an ongoing conversation.

"C'mon," Gil coaxes.

"I probably shouldn't," Sebastian says.

Please, Gil wants to beg. He clears his throat. "It'd be fun."

"Yeah, no, I'll catch you later." Sebastian backs up a step. "But you should hang out with the team, have fun. You guys don't need a coach in there with you."

"Yeah, but you're—" *you*, Gil nearly says.

Though Seb's right. It's a different type of night if there's a coach with them, a lack of the ease of players spending time together.

"Yeah, players only," Mitcher says and laughs, grabbing for Gil.

"But—" Gil hesitates against the grip on his arm. But Sebastian, that was the reason he left the rink, he doesn't want to—

Sebastian's already gone, hands shoved into his pockets, head dipped as he starts up the street.

Okay. Yeah. Moving on. Professional. Not sharing drinks at a crowded, noisy bar. Fine. Great.

It's too hot inside, the floor sticky and the music cranked up way too high. Mitcher pours him a full glass of beer and Gil takes a small sip and then sets it aside, looking around for a way to get a water. Millsy, Pezer, and Lomsy are here too and they apparently don't care about the looming game or practice in the morning or what alcohol will do to their performance, because their glasses are half empty and there's already a finished pitcher on the table.

"Wanna see if you can beat us?" Lomsy says, gesturing with his pool cue at the table.

"I don't really play anymore," Gil says.

"You can't," Pezer says. "Beat us, I mean, so it's no difference if you try or not."

"I'll just stay focused on hockey, thanks."

Mitcher grabs his shoulders. *Stop touching me*, Gil suddenly wants to say. "Because we're the only two with any hope of getting the hell out of here, aren't we?" Mitcher says. "Gotta stay sharp."

Gil out-skated him in practice today. Worked harder, did the drills more crisply, and put more effort in. Long enough here and anyone would be burnt out and, it's obviously already coming for Mitcher. Which is good, 'cause it'd be worse if Gil thought he was a legitimate threat to outshining him.

Gil shrugs him off. "That's the hope."

Mitch just claps him on the arm. "Yep, I'm with you. Steph and Frank running things? It's hard to watch, honestly."

"It's nice not being screamed at," Pezer says.

"Yeah, but what the hell are they doing instead?" Mitcher asks. "They don't have a clue."

Gil takes another tentative sip of his beer. He could join

in, throw Steph under the bus, help Mitcher list the things wrong with practice. And...he glances at the guys. Have it get back to her, he'd worry. He doesn't know this group, and they don't know him. The new guy, showing up here—none of them have his back. They don't give a shit about him. About anything, he's pretty sure, beyond the drinks they're downing and goofing around with each other, trying to eke some fun out of their day.

"What do Frank and Steph even think this team is?" Mitcher says and laughs. "Women's hockey? What a joke."

Gil frowns. Their absurd practice is one thing. But women's hockey? Maybe he clocked Mitcher wrong when they first met, not the easy, fun buddy he's going to make on this team.

"Women's hockey is great," Gil says.

Mitcher snorts a laugh. "C'mon, seriously? It's barely even hockey. Don't tell me you actually watch it."

"Of course I do," Gil says. "You see that Boston team the last few years? They're incredible."

"It's boring as all hell. And Frank and Steph? They're sending this team down the shitter, and that Martin, talk about a guy who's in over his head."

Gil pauses with his beer glass half raised. *Don't talk shit about Seb* had been his rule for years. Sebastian who was smaller than most of the other guys, who was never quite able to keep up with the ribbing and laughing of the rest of the team, who once burst into tears in the middle of math class not long after his dad died. *Not Seb*, Gil had said more than once, calling out a guy who went too far with the chirping that bonded teams together, that layer of trash-talking that floated atop their easy affection for each other.

Move on, Sebastian had told him. So no, it's not Gil's place anymore. And it hasn't been in so, so long now.

But still. "He fits in great with Steph," Gil says and

turns away from Mitcher, catching the bartender's eye. A glass of water, and an excuse to not have to listen if Mitcher wants to push the topic.

"You want some dinner?" the bartender asks, sliding a menu toward him.

Gil tries not to grimace as he reads through the list of burgers and fries, searching for something decent. "Avocado chicken salad," he finally says.

"And an order of wings," Mitcher says.

"No, no, just the salad," Gil says. "With extra avocado, please."

"Wings and tots too." Mitcher elbows him. "Gotta get your protein and carbs, don't you? You get celery and carrots with the wings, it's basically a second salad, right?"

"I don't—"

"We've got you covered, Rooster." Mitcher swings his arm around Gil's shoulders. "Look, I'm glad you're here, 'cause this team is full of duds, but these three, this is the only fun to be had."

"Fun," Gil says, glancing at Pezer, Lomsy, and Millsy.

Pezer grins and takes an extravagant bow, but Lomsy just looks down at his phone and then up at Gil. "Shut up," he says and tips his screen so Pezer can see.

"Shut up, shut up," Pezer echoes.

"Too cute," Millsy says, sticking his head between theirs to get a look. "Gilbert Roussin, is this you?"

It's an old picture, *Rideau* on Gil's jersey, and next to him, arms around each other...

They look so painfully young. Were he and Sebastian really that boyish in college? That incredibly youthful looking?

"Emery just posted this," Lomsy says. "Wow, I love it, can we print out a couple dozen and put them everywhere in the rink?"

"Wallpaper the coaches' office," Pezer says.

"I'm thinking above the urinals," Lomsy says.

"Let's get them printed on pucks," Pezer says.

"Oh, or jerseys. Team Rooster versus Team New Coach, full ice scrimmage, losers buy the beer," Lomsy says.

"Tell Coach nice haircut," Millsy says. "Can we get him here? Because I've got a few fashion tips."

His throat hurts a little. He and Sebastian were smiling in that picture, leaning into each other, caught mid-laugh. Of course they were, they were on top of the world. Living in the same dorm room, sharing most of their classes, playing together, their lives so perfectly, wonderfully entwined.

"Earth to Rooster," Mitch says, waving his hand in front of Gil's face. "Where's New Coach?"

Gil jerks his eyes away from the phone.

"He went back to the hotel," Gil says. Of course Sebastian's not here. He wouldn't want to hang out with these guys, not when he can be off by himself in the hotel room and—

And Gil's leaving. As soon as he can get the hell off this team.

So what the hell is he doing here? Sebastian's back in their room, watching game tape. By the time Gil eats and escapes this bar, he's going to be sound asleep.

When Gil gets traded, that'll be that. All that there is of Sebastian back in his life suddenly gone again, cleaved apart before Gil actually gets to enjoy it. Both of them still hurt, pissy with each other, feathers ruffled and so peeved they can't just relax and hang out. *Thanks*, Sebastian had said for the coffee. He came and found Gil just now, just like...just like he used to, making sure Gil occasionally took a break.

Stay away from him, Gil tries to tell himself but no, he

doesn't like that thought, not at all. Right now, Seb's *there* in the hotel and Gil's here and—and that's not right.

Gil shoves a handful of bills across the bar. "Can I get that for takeout?"

"You're leaving?" Mitcher asks. "Seriously?"

Years and years and Gil had no way to contact Sebastian and now he's *here*, in Gil's life and what the fuck is he doing not soaking up every single second of that? So what if it's an awful idea. He has to go, and he has to go right the fuck now.

"I don't really drink during the season," Gil says. "Or go out, actually. So enjoy your night, but I have somewhere else I need to be."

TWELVE

THE LIGHTS ARE STILL on in the hotel room, the TV glowing, the noise of a football game a low clamor.

"Seb?" Gil calls as he presses the door shut.

A dark mop of hair rises from a nest of pillows. "Gil? You came back?"

"Yeah, that was..." every night Gil's ever spent at a bar feeling alone in a group of guys.

And Sebastian's back here. So.

"Yeah, I came back. Who's playing?" Gil asks casually as if he hadn't hurried like he might skid into the room and find Sebastian gone.

But he's here, curled up on his side of the bed in the cocoon of blankets and pillows he always likes to make. His bag is gaping open, laundry thrown at it, not in it, and his shoes are in the middle of the floor, socks stuffed into them.

Gil nudges them aside with his foot, then just grabs them and puts them next to his, neatly against the wall. Yes, that's better. He likes how that looks.

"San Francisco at Seattle."

Gil glances at the TV, where rain is streaming down on

the players, and grimaces. "Another tick in the box for hockey: the weather's always the same."

Sebastian sits up and moves his laptop out of his bundle of blankets. There's a hockey rink on the screen, paused mid-play as tiny Sea Lions players stand on the ice.

"How's the game tape going?"

"I'm done." Sebastian folds the laptop closed. "Steph wants to work on shoring up our defense, changing some things up from last year."

"Yeah, probably need to." Gil feels too tall, looming next to the TV, unsure of what to do. He could sit at the desk. It's at the right angle to sit in the chair, put his feet up on the bed and still see the TV. And it's a careful, safe distance from Sebastian. Less intimate than sitting on the bed, no matter how huge the mattress is, plenty of space chastely between them.

Maybe it was a bad idea to come back here, too much time between now and going to sleep, and too much quiet to fill even with the clamor of the TV.

But...this is it. This is what he gets of Sebastian, maybe forever, this small slice of time together in this city. Fortuitous to be shoved together in this room. Awkward too, as Gil sets his bag of food down and carefully settles on the very edge of his side of the bed.

Sweatpants. He meant to take off his jeans, but it feels weird now to stand up again, especially to unbutton his pants. *Calm down*, he tells himself. *It's just Sebastian.* Even so, it's better to stay where he is, looking at the TV as if he's watching it.

Though Sebastian's far more interesting, the way he crosses his ankles beneath the blankets, and how he clicks rapidly through the channels when the game cuts to commercials.

"Here, your favorite," Seb says, settling on a baseball game.

"Great, thank you so much."

"Should have stayed at the bar."

"With my luck they'd just be watching this too."

"How was it?"

"The bar?" Gil shrugs. "Fine."

"Making friends?"

"The guys are...I don't know. No."

"Sucks being the new guy?"

Is that what it is? Because Gil had his buddies down in San Diego, the group he grabbed meals with, worked out with, sat with on the team plane and in the locker room. He'll have to find that again on whatever team he ends up on, go through the process of situating himself and figuring out where he lands in the dynamic of the locker room.

But no, it's not just being new in a group of guys who know each other. It's that all of them pale in comparison to Sebastian.

"You got a bunch of friends out here?" Gil laces his fingers behind his head as if he truly, absolutely doesn't care if the answer is a resounding *Yes, so many of them, and they're so much cooler than you.*

"I just moved recently. I mean, I know plenty of people, yeah, but that's all kind of—it got complicated."

Gil shifts to look at him. "How big is the city? It can't be that complicated."

"No, it's just—" Sebastian waves a hand, changes the channel, and then quickly changes it back to the baseball game. "Yeah."

"What about Mouser? You know, Chris? From Rideau?"

"Christopher?"

"Seb, honestly nobody calls him that."

"I see him around," Sebastian says.

"Why'd you move?"

"Hmm?"

"You said you were between places right now."

"Just a whole roommate situation. They moved out, couldn't find someone else, just a big mess." Sebastian clicks back to the football game, but it's still commercials so he flicks to baseball once more.

"Frank doesn't pay you enough to get your own place?"

"I'm hoping if I can sign something long term, and if Frank manages to turn the team finances around, then yeah. This city is pretty wild with housing."

"So you're really only on a one-year contract?"

"Yeah."

"Yeah?" He knows that tone in Sebastian's voice, knows he's not saying the whole story.

And Seb knows he knows, casting a look at Gil and then sighing. "Not a year, even, actually. I'm just an interim assistant coach at this point."

Gil sits up. "Interim? So you're not even here for the whole season? Is that what that means?"

"Yeah. It's like a non-permanent position."

Gil snorts. "Fuck off."

Sebastian turns the volume up. "Who was that guy?"

"What guy?"

"Last night? Who called?"

"Oh, just a guy."

"Boyfriend?"

Yes, Gil nearly says, except Seb'll know he's lying. "No, not a—no." Gil crosses his ankles and stares down at his feet. "You?"

"Me what?"

"Are you, you know." Is this what Gil wanted? Yes, hanging out with Seb, but his stomach twists, terrified of

140

actually knowing anything about Sebastian's life that might only deepen the yawning ache. "Seeing anyone?"

"No, I'm not doing that."

"Doing what?"

"Seeing anyone."

Gil frowns. "At all?"

"That's what I said."

"Why?"

"Because I'm not, oh go, go, go, run, get there—ah, damn."

On the screen, the batter climbs to his feet, the front of his uniform streaked with dirt from sliding toward second base.

Not doing that. What does that even mean? "You're a fan of—" Gil has to check the score bug to make sure he has the team right. "Portland?"

"When they play Philly I am."

Sebastian's not dating. Not just not dating anyone, but not dating at all. Gil chews on the inside of his cheek, his eyes on the TV. That's...interesting.

Though he has absolutely no idea what to do with that information.

Were you? he thinks of asking, but he'll just get brushed off again, he's sure. *Are you going to again?* except that sounds too much like Gil's angling to get himself in the front-runner spot of guys who Sebastian wants and, well...

"Are they in Portland?" Gil asks to stall while he thinks.

Sebastian gestures toward the TV. "Are they in Portland? Oregon? Gil."

So is he hooking up with guys? Or is he not, and that's why he's here in this hotel room, rather than the ease of finding another bed to spend the night in?

"We've been there, to that ballpark." Sebastian points

the remote at the TV. "That's Philadelphia. You get hit in the head during practice today?"

Oh, yeah, it is Philly. Gil nods, probably too quickly. "No, yeah, I just…" If Sebastian's not having anything with any guy, even casually, is that a good sign…*for me?* Gil dares to think.

Is that what he's hoping for? A reconciliation with Sebastian? Sliding back toward being buddies, being friends, and being—

No, of course not. That's absurd to even think about.

But maybe…

"We went to that game, you genius," Sebastian says. "Against Baltimore, remember? Our moms took us on the train, and they went shopping downtown and we got to—"

"Yeah." Gil grins. "Yeah, we got to go to the game just the two of us."

"Which you hated 'cause, you know, baseball."

"I did not, that was so much fun. Do you go to games here? In San Francisco?" *Because I'd go with you,* Gil tries to push out, figure out a way to say it that doesn't sound desperate and too much.

"Yeah, I just started taking—yeah, I do. Taking my mom, I mean." Sebastian's talking a little too fast. "She was out here the beginning of the summer for a while."

"Okay." Gil waits for more of an explanation, but Sebastian just picks at the power button on the remote, not pressing it, just messing with the little piece of rubber.

"How're your brothers?" Sebastian asks quickly.

"Them? Oh. Tommy's doing his art, music, whatever thing in Annapolis, and Joey, well." Gil wants to pick at something with his hands, too, like Sebastian is doing. "Probably just got in to San Diego."

"That really sucks," Sebastian says. "That he was traded there right when you left."

"Yeah, well." Gil clears his throat, focusing on the TV. "Good for him, I guess. He always wanted to play on a better team that has a chance in the playoffs."

"Do you know..." Sebastian fiddles with the remote again. "Any idea from your agent where you might land with a trade?"

"No, she just said she's working on it."

"How quickly?"

"Soon," Gil says, like he has any real idea.

"Do you care where you end up?"

San Diego, Gil wants to say, though it's a laughable idea that the team would take him back again, after having just shipped him off. Still, it's a nice thought, being able to step back into his old life as if this week never happened. "Anywhere."

"Anywhere but here?"

"Well, yeah. I mean, I know you like it here, but...well, hopefully you can pull out a sweet contract, long term, if that's really what you want. With the Sea Lions, I mean."

"It'd be nice," Sebastian says. "Probably won't turn out, though."

"No?"

"Not much I want ever does," Sebastian says.

"Geez, not with that attitude." Gil licks his lips. *Soon,* he thinks. Yeah, maybe soon. Maybe not, but this time with Sebastian is going to end far quicker than Gil's sure he's ready for. "I, uh. It's good to, you know. Run into you the other day, back home. And here, too."

Sebastian messes with the remote again, though he doesn't change the channel.

"I think so, at least," Gil says. Sebastian doesn't have to say it back. It's fine. Gil wanted to keep in touch, Sebastian didn't, and Gil's had plenty of time to deal with that.

He should have stayed at the bar. Fuck it, he can maybe go back there, he still has his pants on, he'll just—

"Mom's selling the house."

Gil sits up straighter. "What?"

"That's why I flew back. I wanted to go through some things."

Your dad's, Gil knows, but he doesn't need to say it.

Sebastian clears his throat. "I didn't know you were there. I was only out for a couple days, helping her pack."

Gil stares at him. The Martins gone from their house? Some stranger across the back fence from Dad's, moving around their kitchen, swinging on the rope swing? No, Gil doesn't like that idea, not at all. "Where's she moving to?"

"Out here, actually."

"Here?" Gil asks. "San Francisco? Why?"

"She wants to be closer."

"Okay," Gil says as if he understands. *Tell her not to*, he wants to blurt. Because if she sells that house, how will he ever find Sebastian again? It was always one last link to him. Gil could safely simmer in resentment and angry hurt because he had the ability to simply walk over there and knock on the door, especially around the holidays when he figured Sebastian might be around. He didn't, but he could have.

Though with her gone, that tie cut...Gil is going to fly out of this city at some point to join a different team and Sebastian will stay behind.

He'll see him when their teams play each other, Sebastian in a suit and tie behind the Sea Lions bench, except that'll be twice a year only, and Gil will have to search for him, find him in the other locker room. And Sebastian will be working, busy with his job, no time to catch up or hang out.

If he'd even want to.

"Seb," Gil says softly.

"Hmm?"

"Can we be friends again? We don't have to talk about what happened, but we were best friends, we spent every minute together, can't we—I get if you don't want to, you know. Hook up."

"Hook up," Sebastian repeats. "Seriously, Gil."

Heat floods Gil's chest. "Uh, do you?"

"Do I—you're a player on my team. Let's not complicate this, okay?"

"No, yeah, I just meant..." Gil tries to will the blush from his cheeks. "Can't we be friends again? I know you're my coach, but the rest of the time?"

"Gil..."

"Seb," Gil says. "That's who we are together. Friends. The rest of it—yeah, okay, hard no on that, I got you. But c'mon. We're great together, are we just going to ignore that?"

"I don't think it's a good idea to rehash everything," Sebastian says.

"We don't have to." Gil licks his lips. "And that's not a no. Can we—look, we're already hanging out. See, we can watch baseball."

"You hate baseball."

"I do not. Look at them swinging their little bats and running in a big circle, they're doing so good."

"It's not a good idea."

"To play that dumb sport? No shit."

"To—to hang out again, Gil."

"We already are," Gil says. "Right now. And last night, and at the rink today when you came to get me, and—and I don't think we're going to stop."

"Gil..."

"Are we? Because I'm going to have to drag you awake

tomorrow morning again, and we'll go to the rink together, have practice, and then what? Just ignore each other?"

"There'll be other rooms available. I—shit, I should have checked for tonight."

Oh. Yeah. Gil should have too.

Except...he doesn't really want to. "Maybe you don't think we should hang out again, but you're doing a really shitty job avoiding me," Gil says.

"You're the one who came back here."

"You came and found me after practice."

"Well you were trying to break down the rink brick by brick."

"Would have too, with my awesome shot."

That pulls a smile out of Sebastian.

Warmth blooms in Gil's chest. "Wouldn't be hard either, with that crappy building. Look, just buddies," Gil says, even though there's no *just*, not when it comes to Sebastian. "While I'm here, yeah?"

"While you're here?"

And forever, for always, for every minute of every day. Gil shrugs easily, like he's possibly able to be casual about this man. "Sure."

"I'm your coach."

"Nah, you're the goofy kid who lives across the back fence." Who's grown into the most lovely, wonderful man Gil could have imagined.

"That was a really long time ago."

"And now look at us. We're here, and we get this chance."

"Are you going to take no for an answer?"

"Do I ever?"

"Not even once." Sebastian lets out a long, slow breath. "Gil, I recently, I've been—this year has been a lot."

146

Gil feels himself lean forward, drawn in, hungry for any information about Seb's life. "Do you want to talk about it?"

"No, I want—I can't get hurt again. I can't take it."

"I won't. Buddies. Friends."

"You're leaving."

"We'll stay in touch."

"You have hockey, some new team when you leave, a whole life to settle into."

"I promise."

"You promised before," Sebastian says softly.

"I did keep in touch," Gil says. "I called you, over and over and I—"

Sebastian pulls in a breath that shakes. *Oh*, Gil thinks. He's blinking too quickly. Is he going to—

"Fine," Sebastian says.

"Seb—"

"Yeah, okay, friends, that's great."

"Are you alright?"

Sebastian lets out a choked laugh. "No."

"Sebastian, I—"

"You did call." Sebastian stares at the TV. He blinks once, twice, clears his throat. "Yeah, cool, we can hang out while you're here. You're right, we're probably going to anyway."

"I wanted—"

"Gil."

"I missed you," Gil ventures.

Sebastian forces out a quick laugh, like it can cover how he quickly swipes at his cheek. "Yeah, well, I missed you too, Gilbert."

"Funny."

"Gilly."

You're crying, Gil wants to say, but no, he's going to get pushed back again, held at arm's length. "Fuck you, I'll take it," Gil says instead, though he lets himself reach across the bed. Once, he'd have laced their fingers together, but now? A high five? Shake Sebastian's hand? Bump their fists together?

Neither of them know, apparently, because it's a mess between them, and Sebastian ends up just slapping at Gil's palm.

"No, c'mon," Gil says, "that was just awful."

"Yeah it was."

"We can do better."

"Fine, here." Sebastian holds his fist out. And Gil grins, something tight loosening in his chest as he puts his fist beneath Sebastian's.

"This is so embarrassing," Sebastian mutters.

"Do it."

"Did you not hear the part where we're adults now?"

"Do it, Seb, you gotta."

Sebastian sighs. Though there's a softening around the corner of his mouth, maybe even a hint of a smile. "Fine." And he cups his fingers into a cone, raising his hand as Gil flips his over, making a whooshing sound with his mouth, wiggling his fingers.

"Rocket power," Gil says, their hands making a rough, haphazard imitation of a rocket and its engine soaring up. "Say it."

"Gil."

"Say it."

"Rocket power, okay, what is that you got to eat? Smells good."

"Salad."

"Let me guess—egg whites, chia seeds, acai something or other, is that right?"

"I wouldn't put chia seeds on eggs. That'd be gross, and

definitely not on a salad," Gil says. "Also, I eat the yolks. Healthy fats, you know."

"Oh, I didn't know you were allowed to do that these days." Sebastian gives the bag another glance. "Honestly, that smells like—Gil."

"Seb."

"Did you get tots?"

"No, I got—" Though it does kind of smell like fried food, now that Gil thinks about it. And Mitcher had told the bartender...he peers into the bag and sure enough, there's a plastic container of salad and two other boxes, both with grease stains leaking through the cardboard.

Gil can't eat wings and tots. Not with a game coming up. "Here, you have them." Gil takes out his salad and pushes the bag across the bed.

"I'm not going to steal your food."

"I'm not going to eat it."

"Because it's spicy?"

"No, 'cause the kitchen made a mistake and it's not good fuel for—fuck you, don't."

Sebastian grins. "Don't what?"

"Don't bring that up."

"Bring up what?"

"Seb."

"Ow, ow, my mouth, my tongue, even my teeth," Sebastian says, pitching his voice in an imitation of Gil. "You took such a giant drink of that, it was—"

"You put hot sauce in the fucking water bottle!"

"You could see the hot sauce in there. You were supposed to notice. Everyone else on the team saw what was in there and didn't drink from it, but then you come along and—you know what, you can't even be mad. You put hot sauce in my toothpaste after that, Gil. My toothpaste."

"And then you just used mine!"

Sebastian rips open a packet of ketchup with his teeth and squirts it over the tots. "I don't regret it for a second. Oh, is this—gross, you want this?"

"It's not even touching the wings," Gil says as Sebastian carefully pries up a sliced avocado half.

"Did you put this in there on purpose? Ew, take it, take it."

"No, I told you, the kitchen goofed up. Oh my God, you're fine, it's not poison. Are you still going to be able to eat that with trace amounts of avocado on it?"

No, Gil waits for him to say, but Sebastian gamely picks up a wing.

Gil gasps and touches his chest. "Sebastian Martin. Look at you, all grown up."

"Yeah, tough shit. You can't just smear avocado across your food you don't want me to touch."

"My best defense. Remember when that nutritionist came to Rideau to tell us to stop eating like crap and made that so-called 'healthy chocolate pudding' for us?"

"No, don't."

"And it turned out it was coconut milk avocado chocolate pudding and you'd already had like five of them?"

"Shut up."

"And then I told you—" Gil can't hold the laugh in. "Remember? I found those pudding cups, the little plastic ones from the dining hall?"

"Please don't remind me."

"And refilled them with the avocado stuff and sealed them again?"

"Yeah, yeah, and I ate them and didn't notice, how funny. Do I have to double-check everything I eat while you're on the team?"

"Maybe you should."

"Great, and you're sure you don't have an idea of how long that will be?"

Not long enough, Gil suddenly thinks.

He frowns. Too long. Any day spent playing for the Sea Lions is far too long. He pokes through his salad, roughly enough to spill out lettuce he has to pick off the bedspread. He can't stay here.

When he looks up again, Sebastian's watching him.

"Um, my mom moving out here and—and these last few years, you asked what I was up to, I—"

"Yeah?" Gil asks, the word coming quickly.

"I—" Sebastian shifts again and his eyes find the TV. "This is weird as shit to be back together, but I'm—I guess I'm glad you're here. Until you're gone, I mean."

"Yeah, I—me too." That's not what Sebastian was going to say. Though…well, it's still pretty nice to hear. "Until I'm gone."

"And then I can eat in peace again," Sebastian says.

"Think I can manage a trade?"

"I think you've always done everything you've set your mind to."

Except keep you, Gil doesn't say.

"Anyway." Sebastian picks up the remote. "You ready for our first preseason game coming up?"

"Yeah, I'm gathering inspiration from watching the boring drudgery of baseball. Can we go back to football at least?" Gil leans over to reach for the remote.

Sebastian raises his knee, so Gil has to lunge for it, holding his salad steady with one hand and leaning over, to grab—"Don't," he says when Sebastian moves a wing too close to him. Gil can smell the spice on it. "I'll put avocado on your pillow."

"You wouldn't."

"Give me the damn remote."

"Admit baseball is the best sport."

"Never." Gil snags the remote and retreats to his side of the bed.

Fun, to play at nearly wrestling with each other.

Dangerous, too. So very much.

Gil changes back to the football game and sets the remote on his bedside table so Sebastian can't easily grab it. Even if he does, he'll end up falling asleep soon enough and Gil can change it back. Of course he will, laying in his den of blankets, once he's done eating.

Gil should go to a store and buy some hot sauce. Soon, too, if he's going to manage to get it in Sebastian's toothpaste before...

Well, before Gil leaves. Or before they manage to get their own rooms.

He glances over beside him like he can commit Sebastian to memory, his clothes in a heap by his bag, how he's eating wings in bed and is probably going to make a mess, his tousled hair, his eyes on the football game.

"Run it!" Sebastian yells at the TV, like his dad always did, on the couch in Sebastian's living room when Gil would sneak over on autumn afternoons after practice, stepping momentarily into the Martins' life so very, very far away from ice hockey.

THIRTEEN

GIL'S PHONE buzzes before the grayness of dawn has even begun to creep into the room.

He fumbles for it, knocks it off the bedside table, and pats around on the floor as it chimes and vibrates.

Beside him, Sebastian murmurs something and rolls over, taking half the blankets with him.

Dad, the screen says when Gil manages to grab his phone. He clears his throat and sits up before he answers. "Hey."

"Gil, you awake?"

"Yes, absolutely." Gil gets to his feet as if that will help prove it. "Good morning." Shoes. Socks. Pants to yank on over his boxers. He slips into the bathroom with his clothes and his phone, pulling the door shut and squinting against the too bright light. "You got news on a trade?" It's good that Dad called, he should be getting up anyway. He can work on his stick-handling for a while with the extra time, do some shooting practice, get good and stretched out before they're on the ice.

He yawns silently and rubs his eyes, trying to blink awake. He stayed up too late, watching sports and chatting.

He should know better with the season starting, such important hockey for him to play.

"Working on it," Dad says. "I wanted to hear how it's going out there."

"Yeah, good."

"Good?"

"Bad," Gil quickly corrects. "No, the place is a disaster."

"Sebastian's really coaching your team? Sebastian Martin?"

Gil shifts his phone to his other hand. "He is."

"Coaching," Dad says softly. "You know, Gil, preseason is valuable time to get ready for the season. I don't want you to lose too much of your summer training during this little jaunt to San Francisco."

Gil glances at the door. It's not soundproof. He'll wake Sebastian if he keeps talking. And this conversation...no, he doesn't want Seb to overhear.

He turns down the volume as he hunts for his room key, then slips into the hallway.

"It's been okay. Practice yesterday was—well, I got my work in at least," Gil says as he heads for the elevators.

"That's my boy. This Stephanie Morris, tell me about her."

"She's, well. Yeah."

"That bad?"

"No, no, I just—I think I might have, um." *Be honest*, Dad has always told him. *Can't help you if you're not honest with me, kid.* Gil clears his throat. "I didn't handle things great with her? Yesterday? On the ice? The guys were running late and I, well. Told her what I thought she should do."

Dad's silent. Bad reception in the elevator, Gil wants to

believe, though he can hear background noise through the phone still.

Gil can fix this. Will fix this. "I'm glad you called, actually, because I think I have to figure out how to get back on her good side."

"Don't bother."

Gil stutter-steps out of the elevator. "What?"

"You've got plenty to worry about as it is," Dad says. "And she won't be your coach for long, so that's not where you should put your energy."

"Well okay, but I—she was really not very happy with me." Gil needs to explain better, be clearer so Dad knows... his cheeks flush. Yeah, Dad has to know what he did, get the full story so there aren't any surprises when he's working with other teams to get Gil his trade. "I kind of went off about the way the NHL works and her being new to the league."

"Good."

"Good?"

"I don't want her thinking you're cut from the same cloth as the rest of those so-called players she's got. Though that Doug Mitchell, he's alright, isn't he?"

"Mitcher? Yeah, he's not bad."

"Keep your focus where it needs to be, not soothing some half-assed coach's ruffled feathers. And if anything, you helped her out."

"Well, I was kind of..." Gil grimaces. "She said she has her own plan for how to handle the guys here."

"Which is her first problem, the idea that there's anything at all salvageable on that team. You can't work with issues like the ones the Sea Lions have. There's nothing to build on."

"No, no, no, I know, I just—"

"You have a game coming up. I talked to Melissa. We're trying to get some scouts there."

"Oh. Wow. That's great, that's amazing. And that's so soon, our first preseason game, really?"

"Told you I'd get you out of there."

"No, thank you, you did. Just, I'm—with Steph, Coach Morris—" *What if she doesn't play me?* Benching him would make her point. And she knows that, too, knows exactly how to work Gil over.

Which…fuck.

"I think I need to talk to her, at least. So I don't know if you have any advice, or…" A player pissing off Dad and then going to him to talk? No, the guy would already be packing his bags.

"Don't drop this game, Gil," Dad says. "That's my advice, and that's why I called. I don't want you playing more than this one game in a Sea Lions uniform. Not if I have anything to do with it."

Oh. Just one game. He could get out of here that quickly? Really?

Though if Dad says so, then yeah, it'll happen. "I'll be ready for the game," Gil says.

"I know you will," Dad says and then he's gone, Gil's phone falling silent.

Gil eats slowly, forcing down a breakfast he's not particularly hungry for. *Fuel for the ice*, he tells himself when oatmeal sticks in his throat. Steph will play him, right? He's the only logical choice for the first line center. *Benched, Mr. Roussin*, he can suddenly imagine her saying.

A cup of coffee appears across the table and Sebastian drops into the chair, yawning as he scrubs his hands over his face.

"Sorry, did I wake you up?" Gil asks. *Is it even possible to wake you up?* he could joke. He manages another bite of oatmeal and has to chase it with a long drink of water to help it down.

"S'fine," Sebastian says. "You got up early."

"My dad called."

"At the ass crack of dawn?" Sebastian works a finger into his eye. "Did you get enough sleep? You could have just called him back."

"No, I'm fine. I want to get to the rink early anyway."

"You okay?" Seb asks.

"Early bird gets the puck."

"What happened?"

"You guys decide on lines for the game?"

Sebastian shrugs and yawns again. "Steph said we'd talk about it soon. Why, you worried?"

"No," Gil says quickly.

Sebastian snorts a soft laugh. "You'll be fine."

Promise? Gil wants to ask. But no, of course Sebastian's right, who else is Steph going to put on the ice if not Gil?

And Dad's right too. He has to focus on playing well enough to get his trade, no time for his mind slipping elsewhere. One goal and one goal only, like his entire career has been, hitting an achievement and then moving immediately on to the next.

Maybe your dad's not always right, Sebastian had said.

Dad's focused, that's for sure, on getting Gil traded. So...yeah. Dad's just not thinking this through all the way, but Gil can. He knows how to act as a member of a team, as a player to a coach. Dad taught him that long, long ago.

Get that trade, he thinks. So what if going to Steph also soothes the worry in his stomach that he acted like an ass and needs to make up for it?

Gil stands and shoves his food aside. "Let's go."

"Now?" Sebastian asks but Gil's already hurrying to push in his chair.

The lights are at least on when they make it to the rink. The door's unlocked, and sure enough, Frank's door is half open as he talks to someone on the phone. *Another GM*, Gil wants to hope, but he keeps going down the hall, not letting himself linger to see if his name is mentioned.

"Steph?" he asks as he knocks lightly on her door and then pushes it open.

"Ah," she says, "Mr. Roussin. What a delight first thing this morning."

"I came to apologize." Yes, this feels right, and when he tells Dad about this later, he'll agree. "For yesterday, on the ice."

"Apologize," Steph repeats slowly, sitting back from her laptop. She looks at Gil, then past him at Sebastian. "Huh."

"I was a total shit to you. I shouldn't have spoken to you like that, and it won't happen again."

"Is he serious?" she asks Sebastian as if Gil's not in the room.

"Gil? He's always serious when it comes to hockey."

"This isn't the latest joke from the team?"

"I'm not joking," Gil says. "You shouldn't have to deal with that kind of attitude, and I'm sorry it came from me."

"From you," Steph echoes. "This is...what's the right word? Unexpected? Unprecedented?"

"I know the team's not...well." *Normal*, Gil could say, as a start. "Respectful of your coaching. I don't mean to make things worse, is what I'm trying to say."

"According to you we can't get much worse, now can we?"

"Well, I just—" Is he supposed to agree? Keep from starting up a second argument? Because she has to know...

She grins, leaning back in her chair. "It's a joke, Mr. Roussin. Thank you, I guess. I'm not entirely sure what to do with such adorable earnestness, though it's at least a change of pace around here."

"I—okay." Gil nods once, and then again. A joke. He's joked around with coaches before, but not at his own expense. *Get out*, he's still braced for her to say, a finger pointed toward the door and his gear missing from the locker room by the time he gets down there.

"Look, you want to make it up to me?" She grabs a piece of paper from her desk. "Here, take this. See if you can wrangle the guys into being on time for practice today. Or at least make it to the building early enough that they might be on time, should they bother getting dressed."

Gil looks down at the sheet of names and phone numbers. "Call them?"

"Call them, text them, bribe them, threaten, beg. Whatever you have to do."

Make it up to her. *Get the fuck out of my sight and off my team,* she should have said.

Gil nods quickly. "I'm on it."

"Thank you. And Gil?"

"Yes, Coach?"

"Sure you don't want to stick around with us?"

"I—"

"I'm just messing with you. Of course you don't. Get out of here, scare up your teammates. And hey, thanks."

"Of course," he says.

In the players' lounge, Gil sets the list on the table and pulls out his phone. Bloomer, first. *Hey, this is Gil, just checking you're good for practice this morning*, Gil texts and gets a *Yes* in response. Okay, one down. Some of the rookies, too, to ease into things.

And then, well. *Who died and put you in charge?* Mitcher sends him. *Wrong number*, he gets from Hal.

He scrubs over his face. *See you on the ice right at 11*, he writes to Millsy. And to Lomsy, *Big game coming up, first of the preseason, you feeling ready for it? We have practice at 11, and we're getting started straight away.*

His phone chimes, a text from an unfamiliar number. *Don't need to text me too, Loms and I are a two for one deal.* Pezer, that must be.

When he's done, he sits back in his chair, stretching, working his head side to side. He'll get dressed early. Bug some rookies about jumping on the ice before practice too, see if they can get some work in. Set the precedent today that being five minutes early is considered on time.

Nothing to salvage, Dad had said. Gil sighs. No, there probably isn't, but he can at least try. Get his own practice in with the extra time.

And skate with Sebastian. He lets himself smile, just a little.

"Hey," he says when Sebastian pokes his head in the room.

"Hey yourself," Sebastian says.

"Does your doctor worry about your stomach lining?" Gil asks as Sebastian heads straight to the coffee machine.

"No, but I'm glad to know you still do."

"You know what would probably soothe the amount of shitty coffee you drink?"

"You keeping your mouth shut?"

"Avocado."

Sebastian snorts a laugh and Gil's phone chimes again.

I know we're on at 11, but I can get there early, should I? I'll come right now, Jay texts.

Great, one of them will be early. Overeager and too energetic, too. *Breathe*, Gil could just write, but no, some of the vets were helpful when he was the same way before his first game. And what had they said to him?

"Hey," Seb says.

"Yeah?" Gil asks, a response half typed to the kid.

"That's nice of you to want to even things up with Steph."

It's selfish, Gil should explain. Make sure he gets his ice time. Ensure he gets the hell out of here. But... "Well, I felt like a jerk."

"Fair enough."

He needs to go, start getting ready for practice.

Seb kicks out a chair and drops into it. *Focus*, Dad had just said. Though Gil got up early today. He's got an extra couple minutes, doesn't he? He can sit here for just a moment more, tease Sebastian about his coffee. Sit with him in this room overlooking the rink, the ice shining white beneath the lights, clear and smooth first thing in the morning.

Steph knocks on the door jamb, sticking her head into the lounge. "Hey, sorry to bother this little party in here, but I just got word from the league. Bad storm up north, delaying all sorts of travel plans, so we're not playing Vancouver tomorrow anymore. They can't make it here. Instead, we've got the Mountain Lions day after tomorrow. They're flying up tonight to beat the worst of the weather."

"The Mountain Lions?" Gil asks. "San Diego?"

Steph grins. "What do ya say, Gil, you ready to play against your old team and your little brother?"

FOURTEEN

With the hotel room air conditioner blowing on him, Gil does another push-up.

He needs a real gym, not what passes for one in this hotel but a room full of weight racks, exercise bikes, medicine balls, and resistance bands. There, he could go sweat after practice, work until his heart rate monitor beeps happily at him, push until the burn in his body blanks out every thought in his mind.

He wipes his face on his shoulder, lowers himself toward the rug, pauses, and pushes back up.

You ready for this? Joey had texted during Gil's practice.

He's ignored the message since then. Tried to type something back that has a zing to it, to parry Joey's affectionate taunt with one of his own, but he deleted everything he wrote, shoving his phone into his pocket and hurrying from the rink.

His old team, coming here. With his little brother among them. Hux and Little and Giffy and Joey across the ice day after tomorrow in their jerseys, Gil's old coach on the bench, the team's equipment staff, trainers, and assistants with them. All of them flying into the city this evening on the team plane with the mountain lion painted on the tail wing, snarling, claws extended.

He lowers down again, arms shaking, sweat dripping from his nose. Behind him, the door opens and only then does he rock back onto his knees. "You get the key to the other room?"

"Yeah," Sebastian says. "But it's a suite so I'm sure it's meant to be for you. And I got this too."

Gil rubs a knuckle into his eye as he turns. He needs to gather up his things in that case. Shuffle everything back into his duffle bag, drag himself to another floor and unpack again. Shower too. Or just get back to his workout, exhaust his body so he can sleep tonight, not stare into the darkness and dread the coming game.

Or he can tell Sebastian to just take the nicer room. What the hell does Gil care?

A pair of heels steps next to his gaping-open duffle bag. Wide-legged slacks, a sharply tailored blouse and a scarf and—

"Mom?" He's already halfway across the room, perfume wrapped around him, her hand stroking the back of his head as he hugs her.

"Oh sweetheart," she says, holding him tight.

He draws back, embarrassed, as soon as he can get a grip on himself.

But she pulls him in for another hug. "I wanted to surprise you. Thought I'd see a game."

Gil's breath hitches. "Because of Joey playing here?"

"Joey's not getting in until late tonight. I came to see you." Mom steps back to look at him, her hand on his face, her fingers smoothing back his hair. "And I know you're having a tough time, so how about an early dinner, you two? How does that sound?"

Gil's barely eaten all day. Not before practice like he

should have, and only a couple bites afterward of a bland, dry sandwich he'd forced down and chased with water like it would help the sick knot in his stomach. So no, he's not hungry, not at all.

And he's not having a tough time. He's fine, he just has to work hard enough to—

His stomach growls loud enough that Mom glances down, arching an eyebrow. "Yeah," Gil says. "I could—if you want to grab a bite."

Get out of this room for a while, at least. He should have gone for a jog, he realizes now. Fresh air, the pavement pounding under his shoes, let it burn off this hot, terrible itch in his chest. Thrown on his sneakers, pushed out of the hotel and just lost himself in the city.

Never come back, he thinks. Run over the Golden Gate Bridge and disappear into the countryside where the Mountain Lions can't find him.

"Gil?" Mom asks.

"Yeah?"

"I asked what you're in the mood for."

"Oh, I—whatever you want, Mom." He rubs the bridge of his nose. "Let me shower, okay?"

Scalding water doesn't help clear his head, so he turns it ice cold instead, stands there until he's shivering. He pulls clean clothes on without bothering to towel dry enough, his jeans sticking to his legs and he has to wrestle his shirt over his head.

Calm the fuck down, he tells himself like he has all day. This was always going to happen. He was always going to have to play against San Diego, as soon as he was traded away from there.

But to play them while wearing a Sea Lions jersey, Hux seeing him in the sorry state of this arena that they had laughed about just last year, and Joey across the ice with Gil's old team. And Dad watching on TV—

Gil's cheeks burn and he shoves his hair into something neater than the mess it is.

"Ready," he says, stepping out of the bathroom.

Mom and Sebastian fall quiet, seated close together on the foot of the bed. They both turn to look at him.

"What?" Gil asks.

"Nothing." Mom stands and gathers her purse. "Sebastian has a wonderful recommendation for an Italian restaurant. Gil, do you need a coat? It's chilly out there."

"Were you talking about me?"

"I was telling her about Buddy," Sebastian says.

"We were talking about Tommy's speech at the high school."

"Right," Gil says, looking between them. "Sure."

"I'm absolutely starving," Mom says. "And the restaurant is close enough to walk, so shall we?"

But Sebastian doesn't stand up too.

"Seb?" Gil asks.

"No, you two go on," Sebastian says. "I've got a thing, actually."

"A thing?"

"A dinner thing."

With who? he wants to ask, but Sebastian just gives them a little wave and Gil follows his mom out of the room.

Frank and Steph, maybe? Grabbing dinner with them, going over a bunch of work issues? Or he just doesn't want to sit with Gil and Mom at a dinner table, linger through drawn-out conversation?

"So," Mom says, looping her arm through Gil's as they walk down the hall.

"Mom, no, I don't want to talk about it," Gil says.

"About what?"

"About anything. How's Lex?"

"She's good. She sends her love."

"How's work?"

"Clients are finally choosing colors other than gray, to the delight of us interior decorators everywhere."

"Well that's good, I guess."

"Are you okay, sweetie?"

"You sure you want to walk? It looks like it might rain. Let me get us a car."

"Oh, Gil." She gently squeezes his arm as he busies himself on his phone.

The restaurant is small and cozy. Quiet, private tables, waiters in starched shirts with black aprons, music drifting through the room. *Sebastian went on a date here at some point*, Gil can't help but think. *That's how he knows this place. Sat at one of these tables with some terribly handsome guy, laughed at his jokes, kissed him at the end of the evening.*

Went home with him.

Gil swallows a mouthful of ice water cold enough to give him a headache.

"It's so nice to see Sebastian again," Mom says. "And he still knows his way to my heart with this menu, even after all these years. Gil, you'll have to come here all the time once you get settled in."

"Mom..."

"I just about died when my phone rang with his number. He called me Mrs. Roussin and then apologized twice because he forgot I don't use that name anymore. Isn't he just so sweet?"

"He called you?"

"Of course he did, he didn't tell you? Picked me up at the airport too, it was just so nice of him."

"He called you to come out here?"

"And he said this is his mom's favorite restaurant."

"It is?"

"I'm going to have to give her a call. It's been so long since we've had a chat, and just seeing Sebastian again is so wonderful. Plus, the two of you, back together. I know this isn't where you want to play, Gil, but it must be nice to have him so close again."

Gil takes another drink, smaller this time. "It's...yeah. Can we talk about something else?"

"We can talk about your game against Joey if you'd rather."

"I think we're ready to order," Gil says, catching the eye of the waiter and folding his menu closed. "Mom?"

"I'll start with the pinot grigio. Or no, this chardonnay sounds lovely, doesn't it? Or, Gil, should I get red? This Bordeaux seems so interesting."

"A glass of the chardonnay and a glass of the Bordeaux," Gil says. "Mom, you can pick which one you like best."

"Sweetheart, I know it's the season. You don't have to have a drink on my account."

"I don't mind having a glass." *Because it doesn't matter*, he could add. He knows how this week will go. A glass of wine isn't going to change what's waiting for him during the game against San Diego.

"My son," Mom says to the waiter, Gil's face flushing as she reaches across the table to pat his cheek. "He's perfect, isn't he?"

"I'm not." Gil takes her hand before she can pat him again. "But thank you."

"This team is lucky to have you," she says as the waiter writes down their order and leaves. "Are you making friends already?"

"Sure."

"Gil."

"I don't know. No. It's not worth it. I'm not trying to stay."

"Then it's so nice to have Sebastian, you two finding yourselves in the same place again after all this time."

Gil rips a piece of bread in half. "I guess."

"He said he really likes living here and the city is beautiful. This isn't the worst place to live. Let me look for a spot for you while you're at practice tomorrow. You can't be happy at the hotel."

"No, I can't buy something. I'm not going to stay. Melissa's working on getting me traded."

"So you can sit up north in Canada and freeze all winter? Or live in some awful city with none of the character this one has? There's more to life than hockey."

"No, there isn't."

Mom sighs and leans back in her chair as the waiter sets down two glasses of wine. Gil waits while she sips both of them, pursing her lips, head tilting to the side before she gives a nod.

"I'll have this," she says, keeping the red wine. "Now listen, Gil, Sebastian loves it out here, doesn't he? He said he's been here since he graduated from Rideau."

"Is this going to be another talk about how I should have finished my degree?"

"Well, you can always go back to school if you decide to."

"No, I'm done. I tried that. It's not for me."

Mom smiles, sipping her wine. "Yes, a real horror to have to do something poorly, isn't it?"

Gil gives her a look. "And here I thought you came to cheer me up."

"Oh sweetheart, we all know what you're like when things don't work out."

"Look, San Francisco might be good for someone else,

and maybe it is for Sebastian, but this isn't where I wanted to end up." He sips the wine and sighs. "Mom, I'm scared. What if I can't get out?"

"Then you'll honor your contract and do the best by the team that you're able to."

"That's an awful thought."

"It's what you'll do," Mom says with the same sternness that's always shown Gil how she went toe to toe with Dad. "You may not like it, but it's what you agreed to when you signed up for this life."

"I didn't think I'd end up here of all places."

"You'll find the good in it."

Gil rubs his forehead. "Have you by any chance heard from Tommy recently with critiques to your parenting?"

"Yes, he shared some feedback. And he said you and Sebastian, well. You two out here on the same team again, I thought maybe you two were getting back together."

"Mom."

"But Tommy said that isn't the case?"

"We're not on the same team. He's my coach, it's not like—" *how it used to be*, he tries to finish, but the words get stuck. Gil tears half of the bread into smaller pieces. "He doesn't want to, you know. Have anything. With me. Now."

"He said that? Gil, you two were dating, weren't you?"

He coughs around a bite of bread. "Um."

"Gilbert, I was also nineteen once. We'll call it dating and no I don't want to know any more details of what you boys got up to. But I always thought you two would stay in touch."

"I thought so too! And I did, he just started taking forever to call me back, or when he'd text it'd be like one word, and eventually—I tried, Mom. It was him who didn't want that."

"You went off on this grand adventure, Gil."

"He knew I was going. We talked about it all the time."

"Of course he knew, but he was left at Rideau without you. Can't you imagine how it would have been for him with you gone?"

"Is that what it is? He was jealous?"

"Oh Gil," Mom says. "Did you ask him?"

"Of course I did. He doesn't want to talk about it."

"Well, if you're not going to date him, are you going to find someone else to settle down with?"

"Mom!"

"What? I'm just asking. You never introduced me to anyone in San Diego, and here you are with a fresh city, a new start."

"Let's go back to talking about how I never finished college," Gil mutters into his wine glass. "I have to focus on my playing. Now, especially, I don't have time to go off meeting someone. And you know what Dad says. It's just a distraction."

"Yes, I'm entirely clear on your father's opinion on relationships," Mom says. "And tell me, Gil, is he still married?"

"Well, that's not—" Gil stops. "What?"

"It's hard to share you boys with hockey."

"What does that even mean?"

"There's never enough of you to go around. I certainly felt that with your father. Being with someone, you're right that it takes a different kind of focus and, well, I suppose there's something nice in not having to watch you and Joey get your hearts broken if things don't work out. But Gil, it's not any better to see you both so alone."

"We're not alone. I'm not, I have my team and plenty of friends. Or I will, at least. And Joey's fine."

"Neither of you are fine." Mom covers Gil's hand with hers. "Knowing you're back in the same spot as Sebastian, I so hoped, but...well. At least you'll get some time together, and that must be nice, right?"

Nice. It's amazing. So deeply incredibly special it's nearly too hard to think about, like a light so bright he can't face it straight on. "I don't—" he frowns. "I don't want to say goodbye to him again."

"Then don't," Mom says. "Gil, you can stay here in San Francisco."

Gil laughs. "No, I really can't."

"Okay." Mom squeezes his hand.

"I'll be alright when I get on another team," Gil says. "That's all I need."

"And then when you get a certain number of goals. And then when you're on the power play, and if you make the all-star team, and if your team makes it far enough in the playoffs."

"Of course," Gil says.

"And then, and then, and then," Mom says.

"It's my career. I have to have goals, you know that."

"We all know that." Mom squeezes his hand again. "Just like we know you, Gil."

"What's so wrong with that?"

"Nothing, if that's all you want. It's worked out well enough for your father."

"It absolutely has, and I can—" Gil swallows. "I can do it too, have his type of career."

"I love you." Mom lets go of his hand to lean back and catch the eye of the waiter. "And I think I'm going to need a second glass of wine."

FIFTEEN

In the hotel lobby, Gil presses the key to his new room into his mom's hand. "I'll get another room for myself. You go ahead to bed, I know you're tired from the flight," Gil says.

"Goodnight, sweetie," she says. "And I know you're not excited to play against your old team, but I am excited. Because remember..."

"It's just playing a game," Gil obediently echoes.

Tic-tac-toe, she'd made him repeat in the car when she was the one to pick him up after games, when Dad would have to dash off to Joey's team and Gil stared out the window, trying to ignore her chatter. *Tug-of-war, tag, Mouse Trap, soccer, baseball, and even hockey. They're all just games we play for fun.*

He eases open the door to his room, ready to find Sebastian asleep no matter how early it still is, and sure enough, the lights are off.

Though the bed's empty, no lump of Sebastian on it.

Okay, he's still out. That's cool. Fine.

Gil sits on the edge of the bed. Stands, paces, and sits down again.

Sebastian's out doing something. A thing. With that *sweetie* on the phone.

A friend, Gil guesses, someone he's close to, but no, he'd be staying with them if he had a choice, not crammed into a room with Gil of all people. And did he say things were complicated with his social circle these days? Maybe a niece or a nephew, then, though he's an only child, so it's not that either. A cousin, not that Sebastian has any. A long-lost cousin, Gil thinks wildly.

A dog, he tells himself. Desperate, he knows. Clutching at straws, because what is Sebastian doing, chatting on the phone with Buddy right now?

No, he's out with some guy. Blowing his back out while Gil paces around this empty room. Oh, just the thought of it, how horrible.

He grabs his phone. Does he even still have Sebastian's number? It was so many phones ago that he'd last texted him...but yes, there it is, Sebastian's name hemmed in by emojis on either side like Gil used to save contacts when he was in high school. *Shut up, it's cool*, he had told Tommy once, wrestling the phone back from him.

There's no saved message thread between them, whatever they'd last texted to each other left on some previous phone. Though maybe it's better that they're gone, the screen fresh and blank as he types.

They didn't even have avocado on the menu, he writes. *You'd have been safe.*

It probably goes to someone else's phone. Somewhere, someone with a Baltimore area code is glancing down at their phone and swiping the message away, or typing in *Sorry, think you got the wrong number*.

Can't take the chance, Sebastian writes back.

Gil grins. *You done or you still out doing your mystery 'thing'?* he writes, deletes it, then types it again.

He's just asking. Just curious. And he can turn this into a good-natured ribbing, like he doesn't care about the answer at all.

The door opens and he jumps.

"Hey," Sebastian says, his phone in his hand. It chimes and he looks down at it.

Shit. Gil hit send.

"I am not still out doing my mystery thing," Sebastian says.

"I didn't mean to send that."

"Oh, like a non-permanent text?"

"Shut up." Gil tries to pretend he's not looking over Sebastian for clues as to where he was. He's in the same jeans and sweatshirt as before, he's not carrying anything, and nothing around the room looks disturbed so...yeah, absolutely nothing to go on.

"You eat?" Gil asks casually.

"I did. How was dinner?"

Where, with who, what'd you have and did you hold hands with this gorgeous guy I really, truly absolutely hate? "Really good," Gil says easily. "Mom still loves you and all the more for sending her toward an Italian restaurant. What'd you get up to?"

Sebastian just brushes past him. "It was good to see her again."

Gil locks his phone, sets it on the bed next to him, and picks it up again. "You really called her to come out here?"

"I figured she'd like that restaurant. Should we put money on whether she's going to make Joey take her there again tomorrow?"

"Thanks," Gil says. "Really. Thank you."

"Course," Sebastian says, flicking through his phone. "You got the other room key?"

Gil looks around himself. Right. Packing. He's

supposed to be sleeping somewhere else tonight.

But he dawdles, lingering where he is instead of standing and moving toward his duffle bag. "Gave that one to my mom, but I'll go talk to the reception desk."

"Cool."

"Yeah, cool," Gil echoes.

Sebastian glances at him. *Get your shit cleaned up and go*, Gil waits for him to say, but instead, Sebastian bends over his phone again. "You feeling okay about the game?"

"No." Gil lets out a soft breath. "How can I?"

Sebastian's scrolling through his messages again. He's texting whoever it was who called him the other night, who he went out to see, sending them a bunch of emojis he quickly selects from the screen—

Gil's phone chimes. A little vomiting face with an avocado next to it.

Gil fishes around for the TV remote and chucks it at Seb, catching him in the shoulder.

"Ow," Sebastian says. "Though your arm's better than your shot. Sure you shouldn't have picked up baseball?"

"Okay, there's no need to be mean."

"Next at bat, Gilbert Roussin," Sebastian says, catching up the remote and talking into it like a sports announcer's mic. "Here he is, chewing seventeen pieces of bubblegum at once because go big or go home, and what's this? That's not an ash bat he's got, it looks to be some sort of composite material, and it's entirely too long and too thin, and at one end it's got—is that a blade on it? A hockey blade? My word, Gilbert Roussin is up here at home plate, he's wearing skates, he's brought his hockey stick, he—"

Gil laughs. The sound surprises him, bubbling up out of the worry of the day, the crush that still sits in his chest at the thought of the Mountain Lions.

But Sebastian's still going, swinging the remote as if it's

a baseball bat and then immediately switching to pantomime an outfielder shielding his eyes, backing up in the narrow space between the bed and the wall, hand up, tracking an imaginary ball.

"Home run, empty net goal, hat trick, only Gilbert Roussin can do it all, folks, you heard it here first."

Gil covers his eyes, his stomach hurting from laughing. Sebastian's ridiculous.

Perfect. So very perfect. "Stop," he gasps.

"Premier athlete, he's mastered hockey, he's mastered baseball, and up next he's tackling badminton, table tennis, and skijoring."

"What the hell is skijoring?"

"With a dog, cross country skis, it's a whole thing."

"Have you spent the last decade skijoring?"

"Nah, got busy," Sebastian says.

Busy with what? Gil doesn't let himself ask. "Dip your toe into the world of professional sports commentating instead?"

"Maybe I should have," Sebastian says.

Yes, this is what Gil wants, like he's thirsty for information of Sebastian's life, anything he can pull out of him. *What're you doing right now?* Gil used to try to guess sometimes, trying to picture Sebastian going through the banality of his days, at a grocery store, getting gas.

But it was that younger version of Sebastian that Gil kept in his mind, the mop of his dark hair, the traces of youth still on his face like that picture Lomsy had shown him. College-aged, caught in time, so entirely different from this man in front of him now.

"Why'd you leave your old job?" Gil asks.

Sebastian shrugs. "Didn't like the way the program was trending. Then the previous head coach left and it got worse under the new guy, so I started looking for something else. I know what you think about the Sea Lions, but this program, under Steph and Frank? It's got some things going for it."

"Does it? Mom was trying to sell me on San Francisco," Gil says.

"Yeah? It's a great place."

"That's what she said, that I'd be happy here if I can't get, well. Out." *I'm scared*, he had just said to Mom. What if there is no trade? What if Frank changes his mind, settles on the roster the way it is, and refuses to trade any players, Gil included?

Or what if...he swallows. What if he's just not good enough to get out of here?

When he looks up, Sebastian is a step closer to where Gil sits, slumped on the edge of the bed.

"Gil?"

"What's wrong with my shot?" he asks and he didn't mean for his voice to be that quiet.

I'd have made second line center, he'd already protested to Sebastian once. But what had Dad said? *Stuck in a rut.* "Am I not a good player?" Gil asks and it's awful to say that out loud, but it's Sebastian.

"You're the best player I've ever seen," Sebastian says, his voice simple, clear.

Gil looks up at him. "That's not what you've said about my game recently."

"Well, you don't play like you used to," Sebastian says.

"But I've worked so hard. Though I did start trying a new stick the end of last season, I think I don't like the curve of the blade, because—"

"It's not your stick."

"What is it, then? Because I'm not releasing the puck too fast, that's not it, and you said I wasn't getting enough strength on my shot."

"You have all the power in the world to flex your stick and load up on it, and you—" Sebastian waves toward him. "Have filled out. Your um, body. Since college. So it's not a strength issue, is all I mean."

Sebastian's looking at him. At his chest, his shoulders.

Gil flushes. He wants to kiss him.

No. Absolutely not. He won't lose what he's gained with Seb. Won't chance it, won't even come close. "Let's go to the rink. You can show me."

Sebastian laughs. "Now? It's late."

"It's not late at all. And what the hell happened, did you get old? C'mon, we're going."

"Gil, we're not going, you're meticulously packing up everything you have just to painstakingly unpack it five minutes later, and I'm going to sleep."

"No, I'm telling you to put your money where your mouth is, and if I'm right, you have to eat an entire avocado." Yes, this is better, a quick jab to smooth over the worry in his stomach.

"You know I won't do that."

"I know you want to go to the rink, because you're you and you always want to go to the rink and I know you."

"I—"

"You gonna deny it? C'mon, like old times."

"I can't do like old times," Sebastian says softly.

Gil's mouth hangs open on his next argument. Slowly, he closes it.

Yeah, 'cause old times...the shitty, awful showers at their local rink, throwing the deadbolt on the bathroom door so they had all the privacy in the world. Skating after hours in college, when the maintenance staff had long left and they were alone in the building, the fun of the net to brace against, bent over on the bench they sat on during games, making eye contact during the next one and Sebastian flushing slightly.

"Yeah, I know, okay," Gil says.

"I just can't."

"No, it's, I mean, that's not what I'm, you know, asking."

"Good, 'cause I need you to be clear about that."

"I am. Absolutely. And it's not even what I—" *want*, is the end of that sentence, but Gil can't get it out.

Which Sebastian knows. That look on his face, the way he reads Gil so easily.

"You're my coach," Gil says, brushing it off. Yes, hide behind that. "And it's the pros. It's not like it's college anymore, so it's not, you know, even really an option. We work together now. And besides, the guys would probably care."

"That I'm your coach? Yeah."

"No, that we're, you know."

"Gay?" Sebastian laughs. "Gil, half the team is queer."

"What?"

Sebastian shrugs. "They don't give a shit. It's one of the first things I asked Steph. After Rideau, well."

Gil stands up. "After Rideau what?"

"Nothing."

"Did something happen?"

"Nothing happened."

"But was it because we were—were the guys on the team—did they give you shit? After I left?"

"No, they were fine."

"Are you sure?"

"I am very sure."

"How sure?"

"They didn't care."

"About us? Or about you?"

"Us? You mean fucking each other senseless and the

entire team knowing?"

Gil's face flushes hot. "Seb."

"Do we have to do this sincerity thing?" Sebastian asks. "Go back to pretending you know how to shoot a puck."

"I do know how to shoot a puck. And I am serious. But, um. Yeah, did the entire team really know?"

"Of course they knew. You were just so damn good at hockey that nobody was going to give you any shit for you and me or the team'd fall apart." Sebastian lifts a shoulder. "And you left your mark there, Gil. Whatever attitude the team had before you came, they remained a very chill group of guys when you left. That's what I meant about Rideau, is all. The college I worked at wasn't like that, and when I talked to Frank and Steph, I wanted to know their stance, 'cause you're right, not all teams are okay with it. Any teams, really, it feels like a lot of the time."

"But were you okay?"

"I started dating a guy," Sebastian says. "And nobody said anything, and the next year we got some recruits who came to the program specifically because they knew Coach would be cool, and the guys too."

Gil rocks back on his heels. "Who?"

"A freshman goalie and a center. They were both pretty good. Playing in Europe now, I think."

"That's not—"

"I'm not saying, Gil."

"You dated someone? Do I know him?"

"We're not doing this."

"So I do know him. Was he on the team?"

"No," Sebastian says. "He wasn't on the team, and you can quit asking more questions because I'm not talking about him."

"Okay, but, did he even go to Rideau or—"

"Gilbert."

Gil frowns. "Don't call me that."

"Are you going to drop it?"

"I am," Gil says. "Oh shit, was it Freddy Mc—"

"Let's go to the rink," Sebastian says. "We're going to the rink. Let's skate."

"It was him, I knew it. My God, Seb, really?"

"No, it wasn't Freddy fucking McDonald. Put your shoes on."

"Was it that dude, the one at the coffee place? He always liked you, what the hell was his name? With the, you remember, the hair?"

"He liked me?" Sebastian smiles as he pulls a coat out of his bag. "I didn't know that."

"He did. It was awful. Was it, okay, no, I know, it was that guy in our English class. Hitoshi, right?"

"You're the one who wanted to fuck him. You're getting confused, you're clearly the one who got old."

"Me? Get your ass in gear. I'll be the one teaching you how to shoot, Coach Martin."

"If you can find the broad side of a barn."

Gil ties his shoe, glancing over at Sebastian as he zips up his coat.

Then he crosses the room.

"You gonna argue with that too?" Sebastian asks, adjusting the hood.

Gil grabs the hood and pulls it up over his head, and then down over his face, wrestling with him as Sebastian tries to twist away, batting at Gil.

Once, Gil would have kissed him to shut him up. Slapped his ass, grabbed it, and the wrestling would have ended up on the bed.

This is...different. Good, though. Great. Really, really great after so many years alone. Gil grins, shoving Sebastian toward the door. Yeah, he'll take it.

SIXTEEN

In the lobby of the rink, a sign in front of the doors reads *Pickup game $10, goalies skate free*.

Gil frowns. "What the hell? This place shouldn't be open for public skate."

"It's not."

Gil points. "Then why—"

"They do public skate in the afternoon. Tonight is a pickup game. If you come back over the weekend they have rock night sometimes, music, disco ball. It's very fun."

"This is a professional arena."

"And you're the pro, and this is your idea to be here, so I'm assuming this is your treat, right?"

"This is ridiculous," Gil mutters but pulls out twenty bucks.

Instead of heading toward the team's locker room, Sebastian leads him the other way, around back where the cinderblock walls are in even more need of a coat of paint and the mats for walking with skates are worn thin and torn in spots.

"Hey," Sebastian says, pushing open a door with a large *4*

on it. Locker rooms, Gil recognizes, like any rink has. Every rink—except for professional arenas, because teams don't have to share their game rinks with the public. He crosses his arms as Sebastian asks, "We were hoping to use the ice for a minute, but if you guys are playing, you got room for two more?"

A group of men stare back, bellies hanging over their hockey pants, helmets old enough they can't be safe any longer sitting on the bench near them. A handful of women too, one on her knees as she straps goalie pads to her legs. And kids. More than a couple of them, looking like they're up past their bedtime, putting on hockey gear so tiny it seems more like toys than equipment.

Gil played when he was that young. Younger, even. But not at night with a washed-up pickup team in a shitty, dingy locker room.

"Seb," he says softly, "let's go."

"You want a beer?" a guy calls and tosses two cans to Sebastian. "Yeah, you can play, but you need full gear. You got anything with you?"

Slowly, Gil takes the beer Sebastian holds out to him. "My stuff is in a, uh, different room."

The guy frowns. "You know how to play?"

"He's okay," Sebastian says. "Gets the gist of it, at least. We'll see you out there, alright? I gotta help him with his skates."

"Shut up," Gil mutters as Sebastian leads him back around the rink, cracking open his beer. "You're not really drinking that before we get on the ice, are you?"

"I gotta do something to equalize our shots or you're going to be so embarrassed it'll just be awkward for everyone."

"I don't—Sebastian!"

"C'mon, you never go mess around and play pickup?"

Sebastian asks. "Bring some cold ones to the rink with buddies?"

"I have training," Gil says. "And summer's only so long with playoffs that I have to use what ice time I can get to practice."

"You and Joey don't just go out and play?" Sebastian sips his beer.

"We get ice time together when we're at Dad's, but we're not doing—" Gil waves to the beer, himself, the ice where a little girl is already out there with her mom, whaling on pucks with all her strength, though they only slide a couple feet along the ice with the force she can muster. "This."

"Well try not to make any of the goalies cry by schooling them. Oh wait, that's why we're here, isn't it?"

Gil huffs a breath, but Sebastian ignores him, pushing into the team's locker room and hunting through the stalls for equipment that will fit him.

Gil would normally warm up before playing. Hit the exercise bike, jog the hallways, stretch out, and then take a few minutes to draw up a plan for what he'll work on while he's out on the ice.

Though tonight, apparently, he has a coach for that, who's grabbing his stick, gloves, and skates from where he and Steph stash them and sniffing at Lomsy's shin pads before shrugging and picking up his chest protector and elbow pads too.

Gil doesn't watch Sebastian as he undresses, focusing on the familiar rhythm of sorting through his own gear, shin guards, socks, pants, one skate and then the next.

"Jerseys?" Sebastian asks.

Don't, Gil tells himself. Eyes on his shoulder pads, the two straps around his ribs, and then one each around his biceps.

"Gil?"

"We're a little light on equipment staff, if you haven't noticed."

He can't quite make it across the room without catching sight of Sebastian, smooth skin sliding over muscles as he pulls on Lomsy's chest protector. The hair on his stomach is thicker than it was, his shoulders broader, his body filled out in a way he never was before.

Nice, Gil thinks and jerks jerseys out of the laundry bin. Yeah, great, Sebastian looks fucking amazing. Focus. *Professional.*

The shirts are clean, at least, even if they're not folded and waiting in their stalls for morning skate tomorrow. Quickly, he shoves two at Sebastian and goes back to his stall.

"These are huge," Sebastian says, holding up what must be one of Hal's goalie shirts.

"Get it yourself if you're so picky," Gil says.

Sebastian throws one at him, catching him in the face.

A respite, however brief, from staring at the ladder of Sebastian's ribs, the flex of his abs as he moves.

"Maybe you need the bigger size, help you shoot the puck," Sebastian says. "Is that the problem? Your arms are stuck?"

Gil could throw it back. Just like old times, hundreds of days just like this, getting dressed for a skate together, hitting the ice one after the next. He tosses the shirt in the bin instead, rooting through until he finds his own jersey.

It's not old times, Sebastian was clear on that, and Gil needs to stop fucking looking at him. "If that's my problem, I'm not solving it by taking Hal's shirts. That guy's scary as shit." Gil jams his arms into the sleeves and grabs for his helmet, pushing it on his head as he walks out toward the ice.

The kid and her mom are the only ones out on the ice still and he gathers up a handful of pucks, pivoting to glide backward as Sebastian steps on the ice a moment later.

The similarity to how he's always skated is more obvious when he's wearing equipment rather than his coach's warm-ups. Same stride, same way he holds his stick, same angle of his upper body. *Too bent over*, Dad used to tell him, pressing the butt of his stick into Sebastian's chest to coax him to stand more upright. Though skating like that always worked for Seb, his stick blade on the ice as he hurried a few strides ahead of Gil up the boards, catching his pass as they broke into the zone. *Pass it back*, Gil never had to say to him. Sebastian always did, so Gil could deke around the goalie and tuck the puck into the net, already cheering and reaching for Sebastian to hug.

Yeah, he knows how to shoot. He passes one of the pucks to Sebastian, who sends it sailing back to him and Gil sets it up on his stick, shifts his weight, snaps his arms, and launches the puck into the top corner of the net. "What a fucking beauty." He spins quickly, but the kid's on the far end of the ice, toppled over and using her stick to try to clamber back to her feet, not close enough to have heard him.

"So yeah, that," Sebastian says.

"What?"

"That's what I'm talking about."

"Yeah, I got it in the net, how fast do you think that was? Over ninety miles per hour, don't you think? Might have broken a ninety-five."

"C'mon, look at yourself. Look at where your stick ended up."

"The puck ended up in the net, thank you."

Sebastian waves an arm at the ice. "Even right now, the entire rink open in front of you, no goalie, no defense pressuring you, nowhere to go, you're still shortchanging the back end of your shot."

"I am not. Did you see that puck? No, you didn't, it was going so fast. Get a radar gun out here, why don't you?"

"Look at where your balance is at the end of your shot," Sebastian says. "I can't believe your old coach in San Diego didn't make you go over this and fix it."

"He didn't have a problem with what I was doing."

Sebastian just shrugs.

Yeah. Okay. He did, obviously, because when the GM wanted to trade Gil, it's not like the coaching staff fought for him to stay.

"Fine," Gil says. "Show me."

"Like, well..." Sebastian glides closer.

With your own stick, Gil suddenly wants to blurt because Sebastian's behind him now. No, this isn't what he meant, but there's a hand on his forearm, the press of warmth behind him—

"You got this," Sebastian says softly. "Just imagine the puck going in the net."

Gil stands stiffly. "That's what I'm doing."

"No, you're terrified you won't score." Sebastian taps Gil's hip. "Shift your weight."

"I—what?"

"The way you play these days, you're not playing to get goals. You're playing to make sure you don't make mistakes. You never used to do that."

"How is that different? What are you—" Sebastian's too close to him. Gil can't think. "I'm trying to score, of course I am." *Score with you*, he would have teased, once. Ground back against Sebastian behind him, thrown a look at him, snuck a kiss.

He keeps himself carefully, perfectly still.

"And you need to relax your grip on the stick too," Sebastian says.

"It's relaxed. I'm relaxed."

Sebastian takes Gil's shoulders, jostling him lightly. "No, loosen up."

"I'm loose, I'm good, see? I'll just shoot." He reaches for a puck, though a second puck slides over and bounces against it, both gliding off in opposite directions.

"I can shoot," the girl says around the bulk of her mouthguard. *Mei*, reads a piece of masking tape stuck to the top of her helmet. "Watch this."

Gil lets out a breath. He needs to go cool down. Lay on the ice, maybe. Press his face to it.

"I'm so sorry," her mom says, skating after her. "Sweetheart, these are Sea Lions players. They're here to work, let's leave them be, okay?"

"I saw a sea lion at the wharf." Mei swings her stick like a golf club, missing the puck and nearly toppling over.

"Easy there," Sebastian says. "Move that bottom hand down a bit. Yeah, like that."

"Yes, we did see sea lions," the woman says. "Come along, Mei. Let's see what position you'll play tonight, okay?"

"I'm playing center," she says. "And Mama says that the sea lions in the harbor are better hockey players than the team is."

"I don't—" Flustered, the woman takes Mei by the shoulders. "I'm so sorry. We'll just be over here, so sorry to bother you."

But Sebastian's laughing. Teeth showing, cheeks dimpled, his eyes crinkled at the corners. He looks...*good*. And that sound, laughter bubbling out of him, the little sniffing snort he does when he tries to staunch it, only to start again.

"Shut up," Gil says.

"Ah, she got you in one," Sebastian says. "C'mon Mei, when we play you can test your mettle against our new superstar here, maybe teach him a thing or two tonight."

"I can do crossovers," she says and demonstrates, teetering as she balances on the edges of her blades.

"I'm really so sorry," her mom says.

"We'll take it as motivation to practice." Sebastian laughs again, abandoning Gil to skate after Mei, pointing to her skate and saying something to her that Gil can't hear.

A teenager in sweatpants eventually blows the whistle to stop the players from milling around and chatting as they come on the ice and gather loosely into teams. Sure enough, Mei skates to center ice, and the guy who handed out beers assigns Sebastian to her wing and takes the other side of the center circle himself.

Gil's not really going to have to pretend to take a face-off against this tiny kid, is he? Because he's going to be here soon on this sheet of ice facing off against his former team, not playing games with old guys and children.

But she's standing there, both hands clamped around her stick, eyes staring at the puck in the teen ref's hands like she's been apparently trained to.

Gil was trained like that too, even younger than she is. Dig in, throw your weight into your stick, draw the puck to where it needs to go to get the game moving along.

He's not going to lose the draw against San Diego when he takes it two nights from now. Right here, on this same patch of ice.

Get it now, he thinks and frowns at the thought, appalled at the idea of dropping his shoulder, flexing his stick and winning the puck against this little girl. So he just stands still when the puck drops and lets Mei whale on his stick with hers, slashing and smacking at the ice, his gloves, his skates, and only finally making contact with the puck, pushing it inadvertently back behind herself.

Sebastian grabs it up with his stick, laughing, his eyes dancing behind the visor of his helmet, passing the puck gently back to her and then retrieving it again when it doesn't do anything but bounce off her stick. "C'mon, this way." Sebastian takes a handful of strides up the ice and Gil matches with a slow glide backward.

A woman with a long braid hanging down her back challenges Sebastian as he holds the puck, waiting for Mei to catch up, but he just swoops it under her stick and pulls it back behind himself gracefully, stick-handling it once, twice, then pops it through the woman's legs when she lunges. She skates away, laughing.

"See? We're doing it, just like that." Sebastian passes to Mei once more and then collects the puck again when she flails wildly at it.

"Get him," the woman calls to Gil, her stick on the ice, ready for a pass if Gil can snag the puck back for their team.

Sebastian hasn't played competitively in years, not like Gil. Gil could skate circles around him, easy.

He takes one stride, two—Sebastian curls away from him as quick as he ever was, protecting the puck with his body and then taking a series of short, hard strides back the other way as Gil crowds him toward the boards, a hand on one side of him, his stick reaching around the other.

He could slam Sebastian into the glass like this. Set his edges, drop his shoulder, and lay Sebastian out in the type of hit that would make it onto highlight reels and leave Sebastian on the ice, trying to catch his breath and hoping nothing's broken.

And Sebastian is trusting him not to, with how he's skating. He knows Gil has the angle to drive him into the boards hard and—and he knows Gil won't.

Plenty of guys would do it. Sebastian grins over his shoulder, teasing him, sure Gil isn't going to hurt him.

No, Gil won't. But he does grab the back of Sebastian's pants, a clear goading penalty their teenaged ref ignores, and Sebastian's still quick, still so fast, his hands smooth, his stride elegant, but it's Gil who works out for a living, who spent all summer building muscle. He hauls Seb backward and bats the puck away, gently dumping Sebastian on his ass on the ice.

"Holding!" Sebastian shouts, laughing. "Tripping, interference. Mei, go get him, avenge me, please."

Gil scoops up the puck, leaving Sebastian climbing to his feet, his pants covered in snow. Red line, blue line, into the zone—Gil went too quickly, because none of his teammates are with him to pass to. The goalie's ready though, coming out of her crease to challenge him, her eyes tracking the puck.

It's almost too easy as Gil handles the puck once, twice, tricking her into sinking into a butterfly just before he shoots, sending the puck up over her shoulder—

Her glove flashes out and she catches it.

Well, damn.

"You play for the Sea Lions!" she shouts, tossing her stick in the air like she just won a championship game. "I saved it! Look, I saved it, and you're an NHL player."

"Went easy on you," Gil says, making his voice light and raising his stick to give her pads a friendly whack.

That was going in the net. It should have gone in, certainly. Sebastian's just in his head now, messing with him.

"Play it," the ref calls, clearly no intention in the slow way he's skating toward them to blow the whistle and organize a face-off, so Sebastian grabs the puck from the goalie and circles behind the net, smirking at Gil as he sets up the next play.

Fine, if he's going to be an ass about it, two can play this game. Gil skates toward him, battling for the puck down low in the corner like it's a regular game, like his stats count for whether he wins this, like scouts and GMs alike are watching. Behind him, both teams cheer them each on, and he gets Sebastian pinned to the boards, a knee between his legs, purposefully pushing Seb off balance as he digs for the puck with his stick.

Seb feels good, trapped between Gil's body and the boards. Smells good too, sweaty from working hard, fighting back against Gil.

A helmet only as high as his waist joins the fray and Gil freezes.

"Mei, please let them play!" her mother calls to her, but it's too late because Mei has her gloves off and is bending to pick up the puck with her bare hands. Gil holds still, bracing Sebastian too, so they don't tumble onto her, so no skate blades come close to those tiny fingers.

"I'm so sorry," her mom says as Mei takes the puck with her, skating toward the other end of the rink which seems all the farther away for her tiny, choppy strides.

"You planned that," Gil says, still pinning Sebastian in place.

"Nah, she's just already angling for a spot at the Olympic development camp," Sebastian says. He's breathing hard, his face flushed, body between Gil's and the boards—

Gil glides backward and Sebastian slips past him, sprinting up the ice to be ready to help Mei take her shot on Gil's team's goalie.

He should go too. Head down there, get in Sebastian's way, play defense for his team, but he'd beat any of the other skaters back except Sebastian no matter how they hustle, end up stealing the show, so he only slowly drifts along the ice. It's a better view anyway than being in the thick of things, the goalie making a show of skating out to meet Mei, and then being obviously too slow to even begin to save the puck.

Though Mei's shot goes wide, missing the net even if the goalie had tried to make a save. Still, Mei throws her arms up, cheering for herself before she drops to a knee and pumps her fist in a tiny celebration of a beauty of a goal.

Sebastian rights her when she nearly falls over, sets her back on her feet, cheering, "Celly!" as she tries again, nearly tumbling once more.

Gil remembers that, his stick feeling too big, the rink so large around him, his helmet slipping into his eyes, spending half of his time falling over and the other half trying to remember what he was supposed to be doing.

Though he would have had to aim the puck at the net again and for that single miss, hit it five times in a row to make up for sending it wide once. Not be scooped into the air like Mei is in her mom's arms, both of them laughing with Mei's delight.

"You could play for the Sea Lions with a shot like that," Sebastian says, holding out his glove for her to bump his fist.

"I'm going to play for a better team than that," she says.

"Don't blame you," Gil says as her mom sets her down again. "But listen, don't ever turn pro, okay? It stops being this much fun."

Mei heads off toward the puck again, where the rest of the players on the ice are carrying it down to the other end. Gil should join them. He's playing center after all, and he has the entire ice to cover both on offense and defense. *Responsibility*, Dad always says of the position. *But also the chance to shine.*

Sebastian glides over and joins him as Gil stares after the swirl of players, still and silent in the eddy they leave with their turns and passes.

"You alright?"

Gil looks at him. *Stops being fun.* He hears the words over and over again.

"Go ask Mei for some shooting tips. I don't think I have any pointers better than hers," Sebastian says and nudges him with the end of his stick. "Gil? You in there?"

"No, yeah, just..."

"C'mon!" the woman with the braid shouts, passing the puck to Gil.

Not fun. No, hockey isn't fun. Was it ever?

He gathers up the puck and quickly stick-handles it, bumps it off Sebastian's skate blade, flips it between his feet, and grabs it back again. He grins at the surprise in Sebastian's face.

Fun. Yeah, it must have been once, for him to make it this far. For him to play all those hours as a kid. Right?

SEVENTEEN

"THAT LAST GOAL SHOULD HAVE COUNTED," Gil says as they push into the locker room.

"So here's the thing about hockey. Goals only count when they go in the net," Sebastian says. "There has to be a clear, distinct view of white ice between the puck and the red paint of the goal line, meaning the puck has fully crossed it before it can be called a—hey!"

Gil strips another piece of tape from his shins, wads it up, and throws that one at Sebastian too.

Sebastian bats it out of the air. "Is that you trying to hit the trash can?"

"It counted. It was in the net. Sorry we don't have the instant replay cameras set up, but we definitely beat you."

"We tied and you should be happy about that 'cause I counted not one, not two, but at least three penalties you full-on committed against me."

"Not my problem the ref was on his phone most of the time." Gil pulls his jersey over his head.

"And here I was thinking you paid him off so you'd have a fair chance against us."

When Sebastian emerges from his jersey, his hair is wet

with sweat, his cheeks flushed. His neck and chest are red too as he pulls off Lomsy's elbow pads and chest protector, tossing them into the stall.

Gil tugs halfheartedly at his own equipment, when what he really wants to do is stare. Sebastian looks *good*. The brightness of a hard skate on his face, the sheen of sweat on his skin as he sits and leans over to unknot his skate laces, forearms flexing, his shoulders working.

"Maybe I should have," Gil says. Yes, the easy banter of any locker room, as familiar as the glide of ice beneath his skates, the ritual of dressing and undressing again. That's better than wanting to stare at the motion of Sebastian's triceps bulging beneath his skin, the round curves of his arms, the line of his collarbone.

Safer, too. Necessary. Vitally important, even though Gil chances another look.

The tape flies toward him, arcing through the air, and he barely gets his hand up to block his face.

Sebastian snorts a laugh. "Good thing you never took up goalie."

Gil makes himself laugh too. Sebastian's joking around. Gil is the one who can't keep his eyes to himself, can't contain the *want* in him to cross the locker room, tuck his face into the sweat in Sebastian's neck and shove his hands into his pants, chasing after hot, slick, bare skin, greedy and eager.

Gil picks up his stick, tosses the wad of tape in the air, and swings at it like he's holding a baseball bat.

He misses, but it's worth Sebastian's laugh.

"Pro athlete over here, folks," Sebastian says, sweeping his hand toward Gil like there's an imaginary audience watching. "And there's that skill in baseball we're all talking about, the great Gilbert Roussin with a swing and a miss."

Gil whacks him with his stick right in the shins, way too

hard if he wasn't wearing his equipment still, but not nearly with the force of a puck that his shin guards are designed to protect against.

"Ow," Sebastian says anyway. "Oh, wait, no, that was your ego that's getting bruised."

Sebastian grabs for Gil's stick before Gil can hit him again, holding onto the blade, still laughing. He tugs, but Gil doesn't let go, 'cause Sebastian will just smack him with it if he does.

But Sebastian pulls again despite Gil's grip, dragging him a step forward. Another step.

Fine, two can play this game and Gil hauls back. But Sebastian just drags him farther, slides his hand up the stick toward Gil's and then Gil's being reeled in, a warm hand cupping the side of his neck, Sebastian's face filling his vision of the room.

Oh.

Oh.

Soft lips pressing, tugging at his, the scratch of Sebastian's beard, and the scent of his skin as Gil remembers to kiss back. Moves his mouth with Sebastian's, answering the gentle squeeze of fingers on his neck by opening his lips, tipping his head to the side.

This is...Gil flounders a hand through the air, finds Sebastian's forearm, his elbow. Grips him there, the soft, sweaty skin of his upper arm, the hard line of muscle beneath it, and holds him tight, a sound escaping the back of his throat. This is happening. Sebastian's kissing him, thumb tracing Gil's jaw, the taste of his mouth on Gil's tongue.

He tastes the same. Kisses the same too, and Gil moves with him as Sebastian presses closer, the stick clattering to the floor between them, and for a moment they break away and breathe in an old, familiar rhythm that brings their mouths back together the very next moment.

Blood pounds in Gil's ears and a shiver runs down to his stomach. Nobody else is like this. Can do to him what Sebastian does. Kisses him this same way, firm and thorough and so *right* that Gil's lost in it like the years have collapsed in on themselves, accordioning closed until they haven't passed at all.

"Can we come in?" someone calls, a sharp tap at the door.

Sebastian skips backward a step, wiping at his mouth.

Wait, Gil wants to gasp, but Sebastian's already moving toward the door to open it.

"Hey there, absolutely, c'mon in. Good game, right?" Sebastian pulls a T-shirt on as he ushers Mei and her mom inside, tucking the shirt into the open waistband of his hockey pants.

Yes. A shirt. Gil should—he stares blankly at his locker. There's one just there, hung neatly on the hook. Chest protector off, the T-shirt on.

It takes him two tries to get his arms through the sleeves.

"She asked if she could have a look around. I hope we're not interrupting."

"Of course you can, Mei," Sebastian says. "This place is neat, right? This is where the team gets dressed for practices and games. You can see everyone's stalls right here with their names on them. The goalies are over there. They get some extra space. Want to see the coaches' dressing room? That's where I hang out. It's just through here."

Gil slowly sits. He hasn't felt like this...ever. Dizzy, confused, delighted.

No, he has. A memory from so long ago that only the swoop in his chest and the pulse of blood beneath his skin brings it back. Sebastian's basement. Pizza boxes, video game controllers, an evening spent lounging against each other like it was an accident they always ended up sharing the middle of a huge couch they could have both sprawled across with plenty of space between them.

But Gil couldn't stay away from Sebastian any more than he could ease the terror that leaning his shoulder into Seb's arm filled him with. *Casual*, he would think some days and others want to curl into a tight ball, sure he was so obvious, so incredibly, terribly overt that Sebastian could see his crush plain as anything, as crystal clear as ice on a frozen pond.

Though Gil kept doing it, day after day, letting their arms slump together, their knees touch, a delirious rush of hope when Sebastian didn't pull away, when one time, finally—*finally*—he'd looked up from his controller and Sebastian had looked down at the same time, their faces suddenly too close together, the air hot and close, and they'd—

His skates. He's trying to pull off his skate but he hasn't untied it yet. In the coaches' room, Mei's chattering on about something and Sebastian's answering her, his words indistinct, only his deep voice carrying back to the locker room.

"Sign this," Mei says, pushing a puck and a marker into Gil's hands when she comes back.

There's a joke he can make, he's sure. Something about the Sea Lions not being very good, does she want him to call a friend on another team to get a decent player to sign something for her?

Numbly, he scribbles his autograph and adds the scrawl of his number next to it.

"That's my email," Sebastian tells Mei's mom. "Give me a shout and I'll get you guys some tickets."

"We'd love that, wouldn't we, sweetie?"

"You said you didn't want to watch Sea Lions games because they always lose."

"Did I say that?" Her mom's face turns bright red as Sebastian laughs. "I'm sure I was joking. Thank you for the tour and for playing with us tonight. You're welcome back to our pickup games anytime."

"Love to," Sebastian says and waves as they head through the door.

Sebastian takes off the rest of his equipment. Kicks off his loose skates, strips off his pants, and bends over to open the elastic straps holding his shin guards in place once he's yanked down his socks.

What the hell was that? Gil wants to ask.

Do it again, he's on the edge of pleading.

"I'll get us a car?" Sebastian asks, tapping at his phone, his back still toward Gil.

Sebastian's boxers are sweaty, clinging to him, stuck to the length of his thighs, the fabric curved around his ass. His back is flushed too, a mark on his skin from the strap of his shoulder pads, and a scar on his left shoulder.

Is that new? Did he always have that scar? Is it even possible Gil forgot?

"Gil?" Sebastian asks, turning to glance over his shoulder.

"Yeah, a car. Great," Gil gets out and hurries out of his equipment like he should have been doing.

Though he needs to clean up, get the sweat off of him, shower after skating like he always does in the open stalls of the team's showers. No, back in the hotel room, the steamy bathroom, Sebastian pressed under the spray of hot water, hands gliding over the slick of soap.

"Um," he says.

"Practice tomorrow, right? I'm sure you want to get back, get your rest."

Yeah, to climb into bed. Spread his legs, tug Sebastian down over him, move with him as perfectly as their mouths remember, find that rhythm together until they're panting, straining against each other, as sweaty again as if they'd just gotten off the ice.

"Are we..." Hope surges through him, hot and nearly too bright. "Going back to the hotel, do you mean..."

Sebastian yanks on his jeans, hitching them up to his waist. "Get some sleep, yeah?"

"I—oh. Yeah."

Sleep. Sebastian breathing inches away from him, the taste of him still on Gil's lips, the thought that if he inhales deeply enough he'll catch that scent of his skin, remember the scratch of his beard and how his mouth pressed so sweetly to Gil's, laughter and his smile fading into the focused heat of his kiss.

"I missed you." It falls out of Gil's mouth with no intention, absolutely no thought behind the words but oh, does he mean them.

Sebastian's shoulders stiffen, his hands on his belt stilling.

Then he shoves his feet into his shoes and picks up his phone. "There's a car two minutes away. We should hurry out front."

"I—Seb—are we—" Gil steps forward. "I missed you so fucking much, and if you want to—I just absolutely would, I —" He trips over his stick. It's still where they'd dropped it. His foot catches on it and he has to grab the bench for balance.

"Sorry." Sebastian clears his throat. "Yeah, I shouldn't have—sorry."

Slowly, Gil picks up the stick. *Sorry.* The word lands like a hit into the boards, a full-body strike that shoves the air out of him.

"Okay," he says. He puts the stick on the rack with his others, all of them neatly, perfectly lined up, waiting for tomorrow. "Yeah, okay."

A one-off. A—a mistake. A slip borne on the late night, the skate they'd shared. A misstep back in time that Sebastian's right to rectify.

Gil's beer sits in his locker where he left it. He cracks it open and takes a long swallow.

The car. They should go. And—yeah, Gil meant to get his own room. That's right, he doesn't have to spend tonight laying stiff next to Sebastian, his cheeks warm as he tries to not play their kiss over and over again, curled up on his side so his inevitable erection isn't so obvious.

"Sorry," Sebastian says as Gil yanks on his shoes. "I'm sorry."

"It's fine."

"I didn't mean—"

"No, I get it, you said you didn't want to..." Gil waves weakly between them.

Fucking confusing is what it is. Makes his head swim even as his blood's still beating too fast.

"My life is so fucked up," Sebastian says, his back to Gil as he hangs up Lomsy's equipment so it'll air out, fussing with it like he's trying to get it perfect.

It's fine, Gil should repeat. Sebastian doesn't have to explain himself. He was clear—confusing as all hell now—but clear earlier at least, and Gil can respect that.

"What happened?" he asks instead.

Sebastian braces on Lomsy's locker, his back shifting beneath the thin cotton of his shirt. Then he sighs, his head sagging down, and turns to sit, elbows on his thighs, rubbing his face.

"I got married," Sebastian says.

Gil nearly laughs. "What?"

"And divorced," he says quietly. "And I'm here in San Francisco because this is where our son is."

"Married?" Gil wants to shake his head like it'll help this settle into a shape he can understand. "You have a —what?"

"He's two."

"Who the hell did you marry?"

"And leaving my old job—housing here in the city is no joke, so I was lucky this position came with a hotel room so I can be close to him. So yeah, things are kind of a lot for me right now."

"When?"

"When—I told you I just moved out, Gil."

"When was your—" It's hard to get his mouth around the word. "Your wedding?"

"Oh." Sebastian wipes his palm over his face. He's not going to answer, Gil's suddenly sure, though Seb's shoulders drop in a sigh and he says, "Five years ago? Four and a half. We split up when Matty was a baby, so it's been over for a while now."

"Matty," Gil whispers. "You're—you have a kid?" He's a father? And a husband—was a husband? Stood with someone and promised to be theirs forever? *His mom was there*, Gil thinks, grasping at what pieces he can. Julie Martin was at Sebastian's wedding, she's a grandma to his son, and Gil...

He pulls in a breath. Five years ago he was negotiating his deal with San Diego. Working his way up from a two-way contract that had him down in the minors part of the time and with the big club when his numbers were good enough. Scraping together every assist, every goal, every second of ice time to get his stats to the point where the coach would rely on him.

Did you wear a tux or a suit? The urge to know surges

through him, like it's absolutely the most important part of this. It's Sebastian; he probably wore a button-down shirt. Yeah, that's right, that fits, because anything nicer isn't him and a wedding—

Fuck, he thinks. A fucking wedding.

"So yeah," Sebastian says. "Everything's kind of complicated so I shouldn't—it's not a good idea, is all I mean. Getting involved in anything else—I'm not really in a place for it."

"No, no, I—I get it." Gil wants to laugh. Scream, maybe. He takes another long drink of his beer, casting about for words that won't come. "That's...a lot to have happened."

"It was ten years," Sebastian says quietly.

"Yeah," Gil gets out. Ten seasons, ten pushes toward playoffs, ten all-star breaks over the winter, ten summers spent preparing for the next game to start.

Ten years for Sebastian, during which he lived his life, and ten hockey seasons for Gil, and it feels like those two can't be measured in at all the same way.

In the car, Gil folds into the backseat next to Sebastian, staring straight ahead at the fog closing in on the city.

"Wait," he says.

Sebastian looks back the way they came. "You forget something at the rink?"

"Was it that guy from Rideau?"

"Gil."

Married with a kid, too. *Adopted?* he wants to ask. Or a little boy with Sebastian's same soft brown eyes, a mop of dark hair?

Two years old. Gil doesn't even know what a two-year-old is like. Not a baby, is all he can think of. Something less than a child. Can he even skate yet?

Sebastian stares out the window, picking at his thumbnail, the city lights shining on his face. "We're not talking about that."

"Why?" Gil asks but Sebastian just sits there, messing with his nail.

He used to do that when he was waiting for the lineup to be announced before a game, sure he'd be benched even though he always ended up on Gil's wing. When they'd broken the window in his mom's garage and had to wait for her to get home and find out how mad she'd be. The morning of that last championship game they'd played in, that scratch of his nail over roughened skin that drove Gil half nuts.

He reaches across the cab. To stop him, he means to, but suddenly it's too much to grab his hand, too close, too huge a gesture, so he pokes awkwardly at the side of Sebastian's knee. "Stop that."

"I'm not doing anything."

"Quit it."

Sebastian sighs. "Fine," he says and drops his hands to his lap.

The car takes a turn at a stop sign and climbs slowly up a hill.

"You really have a kid?" Gil asks.

"I really do."

"Can I see a picture?"

"What, you need proof?"

"Well I don't know, is he—what, cute?" What is he supposed to ask about someone's kid? He has no fucking clue.

"He's the most perfect child on the planet. What do you think I'm going to say?"

"And your—your ex?" *Ex-husband*, he can't quite get out. "He's—"

"He's not up for discussion."

"Okay, but—"

"No."

Is he hot? Gil is burning to know. Does Sebastian hate him? Gil hates him. Wow, a lot, it seems from the burn in his chest. "Who asked who to get—"

"Don't."

Gil scratches his hair, drying now from the sweat. "Matty?"

"Yes, Matty."

"So who's with him right now?"

"Well, there's two of us. We all had dinner tonight, and I'll have him tomorrow."

"You had dinner with your..." *ex-husband*, Gil tries again, but flounders. "And your son?"

"We still get along. And it's nice, you know, for Matty to have us both around sometimes."

"You're a dad?"

Sebastian turns to the window. "Yeah."

Gil leans forward against his seatbelt, staring.

He's smiling. That's Sebastian's cheek curved in a soft smile, his eyes on the city lights. "I am."

"Really?"

"Is it that hard to imagine?"

"No, I—" Gil reaches for him again. Sebastian. A father. A little kid he's responsible for, who he loves, and who loves him. Gentle, Gil touches his knee again. "I bet you're a good dad."

"Shit." Sebastian leans into the window and covers his face with his hand.

"Like your dad was," Gil says.

"Thanks," he mumbles from behind his palm.

"Thanks for telling me." Gil taps Sebastian's knee again and then draws his hand back. "I've—I've wondered so much about you. Matty. Like Matthew?"

"Yeah, after my father."

"Good. That's—" Gil nods, to himself, because Sebastian's not looking. "That's good."

Gil retreats to his side as they crest the hill in front of them, the hotel there waiting for them.

He should get his own room, but the reception desk is empty when they walk in, the door to the back propped open, though nobody appears. An easy excuse, he knows, as he follows Sebastian into the elevator.

"You can go shower," Sebastian says when they're in their room.

You can get out, Gil waits to hear next. *Of my room, my life, all of it, 'cause I filled it up without you there.*

Gil slips into the shower, letting the hot water flow over him as if he can rinse tonight from his mind. That kiss still beats within him, warring for his attention with everything Sebastian told him.

He dresses chastely in the bathroom, staring at his reflection as condensation drips from the mirror. A decade on and Sebastian has a family of his own and Gil...

Tell me absolutely everything, he wants to coax Seb as he steps back into the room.

But Sebastian's fast asleep. Of course he is. *Convenient,* Gil might accuse him, dodging away from a conversation if this wasn't such classic Sebastian: mouth hanging open, on top of the covers, his foot dangling off the bed.

"Seb," Gil says. Then louder, "Hey, you need to shower too."

Sebastian rolls over and mumbles something.

Go, Gil tells himself.

But he left once and Sebastian lived an entire life without him.

It's not the same, he knows, as sleeping in a different

room of this hotel like he should be doing. Still, it feels as if anything else could happen in the space of tonight.

Slowly, Gil drags the covers out from under Sebastian, though of course he doesn't wake, he never does. *Someone else knows this too*, Gil realizes as he tucks Sebastian's feet in. Another man out there who shared a bed with Sebastian, a life, and a child.

Gil sits on the side of the bed for too long, but in the end he doesn't stop himself from lifting the covers and climbing under them, listening to the soft sounds of Sebastian's breath, once so familiar and so, so very missed.

EIGHTEEN

When Gil blinks awake, it's to the glow of sun seeping into the room, haloing the curtains and spilling across the bed.

He slept too late, if the sun's up already. He needs to get up, he has to...

Last night washes over him as he stays huddled in the cocoon of blankets. Across the mound of pillows between them, Sebastian's just a dark head nearly buried in bedsheets, his hair a mess.

They kissed. Sebastian's a dad to a little boy.

Gil lets out a long breath and only slowly does he slip out from beneath the covers, careful to not jostle the bed.

Though of course Sebastian doesn't wake up, not when Gil stands, and not when he's done dressing, the soft sounds of Gil moving around the room hardly enough to stir him.

"Hey," Gil says, standing at the foot of the bed.

Sebastian mumbles something, curling around his pillow, his eyes still shut.

"Wake up. We have practice."

"I'm up."

"Open your eyes."

"They're open," Sebastian mumbles. He yawns and burrows deeper into the pillows.

He must get up with his kid, right? Stumbling through the dark, shushing a tiny bundle of blankets held in the crook of his arms. Gil blinks. The image is too clear, impossibly too easy to imagine, this man with his hair sticking straight up, eyes half open, fumbling a bottle and murmuring over a tiny baby.

"We have to get to the rink," Gil says, louder. Sebastian in their cramped dorm room, laundry littered around his bed as Gil tried to rouse him for early morning skates. Or his old bedroom at his mom's house, when Gil would slip through the back gate, jog up the stairs, and drag the blankets off of him to coax him into the car so they'd get to morning practice on time.

A kid. A little boy. Matty.

And that ex-husband of his.

Air. Gil needs some air.

"I'll bring you some coffee," Gil says. "Okay? And when I'm back, you'll be awake?"

"I'm getting up," Sebastian says and immediately sags back into sleep, his face lax.

Downstairs, Gil fills two cups with coffee, then reaches for a third when Mom joins him. "Here," he says, passing her one of the cups. "Morning. You sleep alright? The room okay?"

"Yes, it's lovely. You look tired, sweetie."

"I'm okay." Gil touches his tongue to the corner of his mouth. Does she know? No, or she'd have told him. But if she'd heard, maybe, some detail Julie Martin let slip...did Julie like this guy Sebastian married? Is she relieved it's over now? Yes, he has to believe. Isn't that what Gil's mom always told them? *Better to split up than stay in an unhappy relationship, boys. Life's only so long.*

"Wait, before you say anything, I've got a surprise for you," Mom says. "Well, two of them. First, I looked up some places for you and a realtor called me back already."

"Mom," Gil says. "I'm not staying here. I don't need a place."

"Second," she says and steps to the side with a smile.

Hands grab his shoulders, jostling him, nearly spilling scalding coffee. "Gilly!" Joey shouts in his ear, wrapping him in a crushing hug. "Rise and shine, ready to get absolutely annihilated tomorrow?"

"Get off," Gil says, driving an elbow back into him.

But Joey dances aside. "Grabbing two coffees? Good idea, you'll need all the help you can get."

"I need them to be able to deal with you."

"Good morning, good morning, is the rink really as bad as everyone says it is?"

Everything is. Worse, even. It takes Gil too long to find the easy, joking words he needs. "Yeah, don't trip and fall in the holes in the ice. Wouldn't want to mess up your face only Mom could love."

"Boys," Mom says, but she's smiling.

"Mr. Stanley's taken a liking to your couch," Joey says.

"If you let that thing scratch my furniture—"

"He's not a thing. He's a cat and it's his couch now."

"I'm calling animal control." Gil pats for his phone in his pocket. No, it's upstairs. A reason to escape, at least, to duck away as Mom starts through the buffet, and he slips toward the elevators.

When the elevator doors close, Gil lets out a breath. Joey's really here, so all of the team is too. Gil should ask Hux if he wants to grab lunch. Catch up after a summer apart, hear how things are down in San Diego, how Joey's doing with the new team.

His jaw is clenched too tight. He forces himself to relax

it. Maybe he'll just conveniently let his phone run out of battery. Put it on do not disturb and simply forget to check it all day so he has an excuse not to reach out to Hux, to anyone.

"Wake up," Gil says when he gets back in the room.

Sebastian cracks an eye open, immediately focusing on the cup Gil puts on the nightstand.

"Joey's here. He's downstairs."

"What time is it?" Sebastian asks, his voice thick.

"Five in the afternoon."

He sits up, his eyes wild. "Is it?"

"Is it? Shit, Seb, of course it isn't. Have you ever actually slept that late?"

Sebastian frowns into his coffee. "No."

"Really?"

"I'm getting up," Seb says, though he takes another sip of coffee first, only half sitting, propped on an elbow in a way that pulls his shirt against his side.

He looks so damn good.

Gil turns, walks back across the room, refusing to stare. Last night was...he blows out a breath. *Sorry*, Sebastian had said, an apology for overstepping. Gil resolutely studies his own reflection in the window so he won't find some excuse to step nearer to Sebastian, brush against him, chase after warm skin and the hope of another kiss.

"The game tomorrow," Gil says, casting about for a safe topic. "What the hell are we going to do?"

"Oh, we're back on hockey already?" Sebastian scrubs his hands over his face. "I don't know what we're going to do."

"You're the coach."

"Yeah and I'm trying to sleep, if you hadn't noticed."

Gil sags back on the window. "I can't play against Joey.

My old team, that's my line that'll be out there, my buddies. They're going to end up laughing at us."

"We're not that bad."

Gil levels him with a look.

"Okay, we're pretty bad," Sebastian says. "Shit, I need a shower."

"You really do."

"Gross." Sebastian stands.

He's in his boxers. Did Gil know that? Not sweatpants, not shorts, but boxer briefs, and there are reddened creases across his thighs and calves from the rumpled blankets. Does he always sleep in boxers now? What did he wear before?

No, they'd end up in bed naked most of the time, skin pressed together, bodies tangled.

"We really need a video coach." Gil quickly sips his coffee. He doesn't even like coffee. He takes another drink. "It's ridiculous we don't have one. Can't we get some kid to at least put some tape together for us?"

Them, he means. He's not on this team. There is no *us*. He's not staying.

He looks back at the window instead of at the curve of Sebastian's ass as he leans over to sort through his bag.

"The best chance for tomorrow's game is if I just draw out all of San Diego's plays," Gil says, talking too loud. "Though our team's still gonna run around like a bunch of headless chickens and I've got to be putting up points, not herding cats."

"Yeah." Sebastian rubs his face. "Yeah, I know, you've said. Let me drink this, okay? And give me five minutes to wake up."

But even showered and finished with his first cup of coffee by the time they go downstairs, Sebastian still yawns in the elevator, wide enough his jaw hangs open and his eyes nearly close.

"I think a zone defense would work better than man to man," Gil says.

"I think I need more caffeine to deal with you."

"San Diego's great at moving the puck and we'll end up flat-footed, just watching them pass around us."

"Intercept it, then," Sebastian says.

"That's what I'm saying. We should practice that."

Sebastian yawns again.

"And do it so we know where each other will be, right? If I go after the puck, I want to know my D and wings are expecting it and will cover for me." So he can snag the puck for himself. Hux to Little—Gil swooping in, scooping up the puck, and carrying it outside of the zone. Blue line, red line, blue line, San Diego's goalie waiting for him—

Hammer will be in net tonight, so Gil will shoot low blocker side, but hell if he ever manages to get a puck past the guy.

Your shot, Sebastian had said.

Gil turns to him as the doors slide open. "Seb—"

"Sebastian! Mr. Coach Man, you're here!" Joey rushes over to pull Sebastian into a back-clapping hug.

Sebastian returns it with a gentle pat and another yawn. "You Roussins are a cheery bunch in the morning, aren't you?"

"Hey, Gil, I dragged this over here for you, some stuff from your old house." Joey shoves a suitcase into Gil's arms as Sebastian shuffles off to find more coffee.

Old house. *That's where I live*, he wants to protest. That's his house, his things, his car and his pool and his couch Joey's cat is shedding all over.

"Thanks," he says, poking through the suitcase. Some of his suits that Joey did a shitty job of packing, couldn't even bother to find his garment bag. His other running shoes, a handful of clothes. Beneath them, framed pictures of some of his old teams, a medal he won as a kid in a tournament and has always kept with him, proud of the memory of Dad lifting it over his head and settling it around his neck.

It's thoughtful that Joey packed all this up. Nice of him, knowing Gil won't get a chance to go back and get these things himself.

"Don't go through my stuff," he musters as a thanks, punching Joey's arm.

"Didn't even look in your nightstand," Joey says and winks.

"Boys," Mom says. "Please."

"I didn't! Could have, 'cause I was awake all night. Your mattress sucks. I'm going to have to get a new one."

"I'll sell the house out from under you if you change anything," Gil says.

"Too bad. I already got a better TV."

"Then where's my old one?"

"Gave it to a rookie. Now c'mon, tell me all about this place. Is the team as bad as everyone says it is?"

"Can we not?" Gil pulls out Mom's chair for her. "It's first thing in the morning."

"And is it true your head coach and GM have basically no professional experience and are sending the team even farther down the shitter?"

"They've got nothing to work with," Gil says. "What can they possibly do with this mess?"

"I heard the entire team doesn't get along, fights like cats with each other, and basically nobody can play."

"Mitcher is alright. He's on my wing."

"That's all you've got?"

No. Yes. Gil opens his mouth, ready to defend—what? The team? Or just throw something against Joey's onslaught, because the other option is to sit here and agree with him. "The guys have a good time, I guess. Some of them, at least, they're buddies."

"A good time? Oh boy, the stuff champions are made of. Hate to tell you this, Gilbert, but you've got twenty mountain lions to face tomorrow night," Joey says and shapes his hand into a claw.

Gil bats it down. "Don't call me that. Bloomer's good too. And Hal, our goalie, could be worse." Better too, if he bothered to try at all. Showed up on time. Took his job even a little bit seriously.

And what is Gil doing, trying to make these guys sound better than they are? It's pathetic, even to him, hearing his words. He rubs his hand through his hair and glances toward the buffet. He needs to eat, get ready for today.

Sebastian's there, a plate balanced in one hand and another mug of coffee in the other, jeans hugging his thighs, his T-shirt collar stretched out.

Gil examines the table again as Sebastian sits next to Joey. There was safety in Sebastian's clarity that he didn't want anything physical between them. *He's still clear now*, Gil tells himself. He apologized, and he's past it. So Gil needs to move on. Yes, that's the best idea. Move the hell on and stop fucking thinking so much.

"It'll be a great game to watch," Mom says. "How often do I get to see you two play on the ice together?"

Joey socks Gil's arm. "Maybe you should have stuck around so we'd be on the same team."

"Yeah," Gil gets out.

"I'm serious," Joey says. "Sucks you're not still on the team. Would have been cool."

"S'fine," Gil mumbles. Showing Joey around the team's rink, introducing him to his friends, moving him into his guest room. Someone to drive to practice with, and back home from late night games. This trip up to San Francisco would be just another game on the season's schedule, their first time on the team plane together.

Though it'd have been a hell of a shock to glance over at the home bench and spot Sebastian. See him again after all these years through the distance of the opposing team's coaching staff, someone Gil wouldn't ever have reason to talk to, let alone get any opportunity to catch up with.

And last night wouldn't have happened. *That kiss*, he thinks, and wants to press his fingers to his lips. But the rest of it, too. Chasing Sebastian up and down the ice, laughing in the locker room, stepping back, however briefly, into the days they'd played together, that had shone so brightly for so long until they'd ended.

"Gil?" Mom asks.

"Yeah?"

"I was just saying that I found some places you might like. Two condos, an apartment for lease, and a house too. It's so lovely. It has the sweetest little garden out front, and it's in a beautiful neighborhood."

Gil wrinkles his nose. "I don't want to buy anything."

"You can't keep staying in a hotel," Mom says. "What about the apartment? It's a bit far from the rink, but it's really got some character to it. I was going to go look at them today for you, since real estate moves so fast here."

"I have practice," Gil says.

"I know. And this isn't my first time picking out spots to live while the Roussin men are busy on the ice. Found that spot where your father still lives, didn't I?"

"You found that?" Gil asks. "His house?" They were already divorced when Dad moved in there, Mom living in Annapolis and the three boys shuttling back and forth.

"Well, I wasn't going to let your father live just

anywhere with my boys," Mom says. "Do you remember your dad's old place?"

"Kind of," Gil says.

"Nope," Joey says.

"You were just a baby, Joey. It was so tiny, though it was close to the rink, at least. Of course I had to find a new place. I asked him what his plan was for three boys and all the hockey equipment you'd all need and he agreed that if I found something that worked, he'd move. All that gear drying out in his small apartment, it wouldn't have worked."

"I never knew you found that house for him," Gil says.

"Well, I wanted you three to have a yard and some space to run around."

"Why didn't you just buy a house?"

Mom smiles. "Because your dad wanted you three full time. But Julie Martin was out in her yard the day the Realtor showed me the spot. We had such a nice chat about the neighborhood, even over her little boy who kept jumping on the trampoline and insisting that she watched."

Sebastian laughs. "I loved that trampoline."

Gil wasn't ever allowed on it. *What about your ankle?* Dad had said. *What if you hurt your knee?*

Years later, when his interest in tumbling and jumping had waned and an entirely new curiosity had replaced it, he and Sebastian had lain on that same trampoline, staring at the maple tree above them and through the leaves at what few stars shone in the sky against the city's lights. They'd held hands, Gil's palm sweaty, nervous the entire time that Sebastian was going to burst out laughing at him, tell him it was all a joke, a prank Gil had fallen for, this massive, all-consuming crush on his best friend and the reciprocation that seemed too good to possibly be truly happening.

"You were the cutest little thing, Sebastian," Mom says.

"Those rosy cheeks of yours, and I knew Julie would keep an eye on you all."

"I mean, Dad was there, what did she need to do?" Joey asks.

Mom touches the top of his head, smoothing down his hair. "And it was so nice to know there'd be someone your age, Gil," she says.

"Why didn't we live with you?" Gil asks. *You have to know*, Tommy had said. *Know what?* Gil wants to text him now, curiosity suddenly piquing. Would he have never met Sebastian if they had?

"I only had a little apartment," Mom says.

"So why didn't you get a house too?"

"Because your father, well." Mom puts on a smile. "Let's not rehash those years in the courts. Tell me, Sebastian, what are the best neighborhoods for Gil?"

"Mom?" Gil asks.

"Let me see the addresses of the spots you found," Sebastian says.

"Wait, I'm not getting a place," he reminds them. He's getting a trade and getting the hell out of here. *Anything?* he texts to Melissa as Sebastian and Mom lean over her phone, scrolling through a map of the city.

Working some things, hold tight, Melissa writes back. *Word is your GM is still in the market to make a move.*

That's a flicker of hope, at least. By the game tomorrow? Oh wouldn't that be so sweet, to avoid this nightmare of San Diego playing here altogether.

Gil fishes a piece of toast off of Sebastian's plate. There's too much jam on it for his diet plan, all that sugar first thing in the morning, but he's hungry and practice is coming up. Offensive systems, going over their defense— maybe they'll have a chance to practice a neutral zone regroup, which is so desperately needed, and get an idea of the best way to structure entries into the offensive zone for tomorrow.

If they even get that far up the ice. If they don't spend sixty minutes in their own defensive zone, shots hammered at Hal, Hux and Joey and Little cheering as goal after goal tallies up on the scoreboard.

"He'd love that," Sebastian says, frowning when Gil takes another bite of his food, then just pushing the plate toward him. "Yeah, that house is in a great spot. I know it pretty well."

"I'm extra excited to see it then." Mom picks up her phone. "Gil, I'll let you know how it goes with the Realtor, and Joey, I had my dinner with Gil last night, so you're my date tonight."

"I think we have a team dinner," Joey says.

"I think you're eating with your mother who flew across the country to see you." She pats his hair again. "You're a smart boy. I'm sure you can figure out how to make both work."

"Love you." Gil stands to kiss her cheek. *Don't find me a place*, he really should plead.

"I'm out too," Joey says. "Not that we need it to beat you guys, but we're having a team meeting before practice today to go over some video. Later, gators."

Gil slumps, his cheek resting on his fist as Joey and Mom leave. "Think we can beg a pro bono charity case from San Diego's video coach?"

Sebastian finishes the last of his coffee. "I might just sit you all down and tell you to look up some clips on the internet, if I wasn't worried about what videos half of you would end up using the time to watch."

"That'd be a joke if I didn't think Millsy, Pezer, and Lomsy would be the ringleaders of it."

"Let me see if there's a way to salvage this team in the coffeepot," Sebastian says. "Want any?"

Gil shakes his head. "I'm good."

Water, that's what he needs. A decent meal. He leans his forehead on his hand. A real team.

And last night to—well, to not have happened. No, that's not regret sitting in a knot in his throat. More like a stoked flicker of aching longing that he's fought so hard against for so long that he'd assumed it had burned out, the embers cooled to nothing more than memories that were easy enough to push away.

Now, he can nearly breathe in the cool night air, picture the lightning bugs dancing through Sebastian's backyard, feel the dew settling on their clothes, and the rock of the trampoline as he'd risked a look toward Sebastian to find him staring back.

A plate hits the table, Sebastian letting go of it to pull back his own plate Gil had been eating from. Scrambled eggs, a few pieces of smoked salmon, a little dish of berries, and plain whole wheat toast.

"Thanks."

"In order to get Buddy to give something tasty back, I always have to give him something else to eat," Sebastian says. "Hockey players versus stubborn dogs, frankly I'm not sure there's too much of a difference some days."

"Maybe we can go to the local pound and see if they have some rescue dogs who'll come tomorrow and play for us."

"Nah, they'd just chew up the puck."

"Be a better sight than it sitting in the back of our net."

"You'll get your trade, Gil."

He pulls his head up. "You think so?"

"I think you get everything you put your mind to, one way or another." Sebastian shrugs. "When you want something, you go after it, and when hasn't that turned out alright?"

With you. Gil swallows back the words, digging his fork into the eggs.

"Steph has some ideas for practice today," Sebastian continues, sipping at his newest cup of coffee. "I looked over them. I think it'll be good."

"Guess the caffeine's working, if your brain has come online, Coach Martin."

Sebastian pulls a face. "Don't call me that. It's weird."

"Gonna make me do sprints?"

"Fucking might," Sebastian says.

"Nah, you'd make everyone on the team hug instead of punishing us. Share secrets with each other, talk about our feelings."

"You know, that's not a bad idea."

"Let's go back to the sprinting concept." Gil takes another bite of eggs, trying to imagine it. Sebastian standing there with his whistle in his mouth, blowing it over and over again until the team is on their knees, panting for breath, and someone's inevitably hanging over the boards, throwing up.

It probably wouldn't even take that much with this team, though Gil can't picture Sebastian being that strict, that much of a hard-ass like some of the coaches Gil has had. Of course Steph likes him.

Though he's well into his coaching career now. Isn't that what he learned? That Sebastian lived an entire life out here while Gil cycled through season after season a few hundred miles south.

"So where did you live?"

"Huh?"

"Those neighborhoods you were talking about with Mom, where in the city have you been living?"

Sebastian sips his coffee.

"Like close by or—"

"Let's not do this, okay?"

"I was just—"

"No, it's..." Sebastian picks up his toast. Gil ate half of it, but Sebastian still fits the rest into his mouth, chewing as he stares somewhere past Gil. "Um. I don't know, it's just a lot? And we've got practice and this game, so."

"Oh, yeah, sure."

"And last night, I am sorry about—"

Gil waves him off. "It's fine."

It has to be, because he can't bear to sit here and hear Sebastian call it a mistake.

Hockey. Yes, that's what Gil needs to focus on. There's no other choice and there never has been. Now isn't the time to let his mind wander, but he still stares down at the texts Mom sends him of a sidewalk outside a brightly painted house and tries to picture Sebastian walking down a similar street, hand in hand with a tiny dark-haired boy.

NINETEEN

Gɪʟ ᴍᴀᴋᴇꜱ himself step out of the locker room without giving in to the urge to linger. It's a gross, disgusting room that needs a deep cleaning, someone to bother to replace the burned-out lightbulbs, and a serious look at what's causing the perpetual wet spot on the floor.

Sebastian kissed him right there.

Gil grabs a different stick than he used the night before, refusing to dwell on the memory of Sebastian pulling him in. He has practice. A game coming up.

Something in his chest flutters when he steps onto the ice and Sebastian immediately wings a puck toward him. Gil catches it on his stick and sends it back, the puck sailing across the clean sheet of ice.

"He shoots, he scores," Sebastian says, lifting the puck top shelf into the goal. "One for the record books, folks, Gil Roussin could never."

"Shut up, I can shoot," Gil says. *Come over here and show me how again*, he wants to say.

No, practice. Tomorrow's game. Focus. Joey's going to be right here, sitting on that bench with Gil's old team, and the scoreboard's going to count up the goals they dump past Hal, one and then the next and then the next.

That little girl, Gil thinks, loosening up as he skates around the edge of the rink. She chased the puck down right here, whaling on it with her stick, laughing.

"You get that kid tickets?" Gil asks, falling into stride next to Sebastian.

"Who?"

"Mei?"

"Oh, yeah, they emailed. They'll come in a couple weeks." Sebastian snags a puck and shoots it toward Gil, catching his skate blade. "Why, you wanting to pick up some of her killer moves?"

"I had a good time." Quickly, he adds, "Skating, I mean. Playing pickup. You're right, I hadn't done that in too long."

"Potted some goals too, Rooster," Sebastian says.

"Well I couldn't let that goalie think I was going easy on her."

"Gonna do it tomorrow too?"

Yeah, Gil's supposed to say. Of course he is. It's his chance to shine, scouts coming, a trade there for him to reach out and take if he plays well enough.

His stomach twists. Mei had laughed so hard her cheeks had turned bright red.

"Gil?"

"Sorry, just—" Gil shakes his head. "I gotta keep warming up."

"Gil—"

He skates away, long strides in an arc behind the net, short quick bursts of speed up the length of the ice. Slowly, the team files through the door and when Gil glances at the clock, they're more or less on time. *Good*, he should think. Progress, something around here changing, Steph and

Frank and Sebastian making a difference, no matter how small.

Not enough, he knows and his stomach jumps, his throat tight.

"Gentlemen," Steph says and blows her whistle. She taps her stick on the ice and slowly, the team gathers around her. "Big game tomorrow, first of the year."

"It's only preseason," Lomsy says.

"Yeah, like before the season," Pezer says.

"Right, the season hasn't started yet," Lomsy says.

"Hence the pre," Pezer says.

Gil closes his eyes. *One two three*, he taps his finger on his stick. Calm. Deep breaths.

Sebastian's dad taught him that. *Count it out*, Mr. Martin had told him. *Used to do it on the football field before a snap. Gotta keep your head in the right spot and it helps.*

Gil blinks. He'd forgotten that. Not the rhythmic tapping he's done for years, but Mr. Martin telling him about it in the first place.

"So this game's not really that big," Millsy says. "Kind of the opposite."

"Exactly, a game prior to regular season games," Pezer says.

"Again, pre," Lomsy repeats.

"Thank you," Steph says. "Anything else you'd like to add?"

"Plenty," Millsy says.

Steph moves quick, grabbing his stick and tucking it behind her before he can even react.

"Hey!"

"We're working on some offensive zone entries today," Steph says. "And Millsy here is working, yet again, to get to hold his stick."

A chuckle from the group.

Mei laughing, Gil thinks. Pezer, grinning, slides forward a few inches, trying to sneak up behind Steph and filch the stick back.

She grabs his too. "Defense, as a whole, will be rather incapacitated for this drill," she says and grabs Lomsy's as well. He doesn't let go, tugging back against her, grinning. "Bloomer can keep his, because he's an actual adult, but other than that, forwards, I expect you to generate plenty of scoring opportunities. Gil, Mitcher, and Jay, lead us off, please, the three of you up top here. Pezer and Lomsy, jump in and play defense. Start by that cone."

"It's mine." Lomsy tries to grab his stick back again.

It'd be mortifying if anyone in the league saw this playing out. If the guys from San Diego walked by right now, getting ready for their ice time, if a journalist was in the building, if the broadcast cameras were turned on, even if Emery was here filming.

Mei would giggle at this. Join in and help Steph tug the stick away from Lomsy.

Gil grabs the back of his pants and pulls him, and Lomsy, surprised, stumbles backward on his skates, letting go, Gil's momentum sliding him away from Steph.

"We have work to do." Gil gives him a push toward the cone.

"I need my stick!"

"Thank you, Mr. Roussin," Steph says, holding four sticks now, including hers. "Mr. Martin, I suppose you'll have to do the passing. Set them up for a zone entry if you would."

It's ridiculous, Pezer and Lomsy standing there with no sticks, Gil, Mitch, and Jay ready to bear down on them. *Kinda funny*, Gil can't help but think.

No, he's got to focus, not just give in to the urge to enjoy this scene. They have work to do. *Yell at them*, he should insist of Steph and Seb.

But Steph blows the whistle and Sebastian has the puck and quickly, crisply, he passes it to Gil.

It meets his blade with a sharp crack and he's off, his feet moving. It's easy to step aside Lomsy when he doesn't have a stick to poke-check Gil, and Jay's right there, cutting toward the net, and Gil finds him with his pass.

"Back, back!" Gil calls as Hal slides to block Jay from taking an easy shot.

Jay sends it back again and—*you don't follow through*, Sebastian told him—Gil shoots, points his stick, lingers for a moment.

He should be moving already. Dashing to get open, just in case the puck doesn't make it in—

It sails past Hal's shoulder, hitting the back of the net so hard the webbing bows backward.

"Nice," Sebastian says. He's grinning when Gil circles back to where the team's waiting.

"Get that pass off to me, yeah?" Mitch asks.

"I had the shot," Gil says.

"I was wide open."

"Well done," Steph says.

"Geez, sucking up to the coaches, I get it." Mitcher elbows him, grinning. "Nice, Rooster, gotta know where your bread's buttered, right?"

Gil frowns. "What the hell does that mean?"

But Mitcher spins away, casting one last grin over his shoulder.

Steph points at the line of defensemen. "Defense, watch your positioning. You let them walk right in on you."

"We don't have sticks," Lomsy says.

"This sucks," Pezer says.

"Yeah, Coach and Mr. New Coach, I get that you're all

pumped up, but last year was more fun," Millsy says. "Granted, I got cut before the first preseason game and made my way back to the farm team in Sacramento, but still."

"Last year we didn't do jack shit," Bloomer says.

"Well it's not like you're in a better mood nowadays," Millsy says. "Smile, or doesn't your face move that way?"

"Oh my God, Blooms, do you not know how to smile?" Lomsy asks.

"It's like this," Pezer says with a truly awful grimace.

"Yeah, see his teeth?" Lomsy asks. "He's even got most of them, all these years playing hockey, 'cause even the puck thinks he's too ugly."

Like you look any better, Gil waits for Bloomer to say. Some other chirp lobbed at Lomsy, the age-old parry and block of hockey guys one-upping each other.

A face only a mother could love, should come next. *That's why the mirror's broken in the bathroom. Gotta be the best defense our team can manage, the other guys screaming when they see you.*

Bloomer slides his gaze away to stare off down the ice, his face blank.

Good, Gil thinks, the needless chitchat finally dying away so they can get some work done.

But it feels like the air's been let out of the room, Bloomer refusing to play the game, apathy and the dullness of inertia keeping him standing still.

And not just Bloomer. The entire team, too. Sparks of humor from Pezer, Lomsy, and Millsy, but the rest of them in a stupor of burnout. Even the knot of rookies who keep to themselves just look around, silent, and one of the older guys, a fourth line winger, glances at the clock and sighs.

Fun. This game used to be fun.

"Alright," Gil says. They have a game tomorrow. They

all need to rest tonight, but fuck it. "Listen up. Defense doesn't have their sticks and I'm not entirely sure Hal's awake, so theoretically the offense should get plenty of goals in, right?"

Jay nods enthusiastically, but he's the only one.

"But guys, look at this team's stats." *Our stats*, he should say. He swallows. *We, us.* For this one game...yeah, fine. "We've got a hell of a long way to go in terms of getting pucks in the net. So I'm buying drinks for the winners. Tonight, that bar down the street. Defense, if you can manage to stop us, or offense, however many we get in. Losers pay for their own."

Lomsy throws his hands up. "We don't have sticks!"

"So try out a new concept called skating hard," Gil says. "Or do you like paying for your own beer?"

"I'm not worried," Pezer says. "Have you seen yourselves shoot?"

Your shot, Sebastian had said. He's watching Gil now, him and Steph both.

"Yes, I've gotten some feedback on my shot," Gil says. "So you shouldn't be worried."

"This is dumb as shit," Mitcher says.

"This is our last practice before our first game," Gil says.

"Preseason game," Millsy says.

"So let's enjoy it, shall we?" Gil grabs a puck. "Jay, look alive."

"We're not ready!" Pezer says as Gil starts skating.

"Is this a beer-only situation, or you buying us liquor?" Lomsy calls, chasing after Gil.

Gil skates down low, behind the net, since he has plenty of extra time with Pezer and Lomsy still getting their feet under them. "Jay!" he calls and sends the puck toward him.

Pezer dives across the ice to block his shot, taking the puck off his shoulder pad even as he yells, "Top shelf!"

"Yeah." Gil gathers up the rebound. *You got time,* he tells himself. One stride, another, puck on his forehand, pull it across to his backhand, and deftly, neatly, he lifts it over Hal's leg pad, sending the puck into the upper corner of the net.

"Nice shot," Steph calls.

"Liquor," Pezer says from his sprawl on the ice. "Top-shelf liquor, fuck you, Rooster."

"You gotta play better than that if you want the nice stuff." Gil circles back in line. He holds his glove out to bump Jay's fist. "Nice pass."

"Thanks," Jay says, flushed, breathless. "Thank you."

"Next group," Steph says and blows her whistle.

"Was that better?" Gil asks as he glides over to where Sebastian stands.

Sebastian's grinning. "Damn, Gil. Hal had no chance."

"You coming tonight?" Out at the bar with the guys, all of them raucous, too loud. *You don't need a coach there with you,* Sebastian had just said the other night. "Steph," Gil says. "You're coming, right? All the coaches, yeah? And staff? Why not?"

"If you're paying." Steph blows her whistle again. "Next group. Let's go, gentlemen."

Bloomer still has his stick, but he doesn't go for the puck Mitcher has. Instead, he lays him out, checking him in a beautiful open-ice hit that sends Mitch sprawling. Quickly, Bloomer strides after the puck, grabs it, and clears it out of the zone.

"Damn," Gil says. That's...wow, that's something there, some fire in Bloomer, just buried so deep it's barely there at all.

"Yeah, Bloomer's good," Sebastian says. "I was watching

his game tape from a couple years ago. The guy's got some skills."

"Gonna have to go against him," Gil says. He can change up the timing as he skates into the zone, try to get Bloomer to commit to the check, and then step out of the way. Or just take it, knowing he can still get the pass off, shake the hit off and jump back to his feet. Yeah, either way, it'll be a challenge. He grins, watching Millsy square up against Jay.

"There it is," Sebastian says.

"Hmm? What?"

"Hey, you two," Emery says. She's got micro spikes on her sneakers so she can walk across the ice, her camera in her hand. "Can I snap a quick picture?"

"Of us?" Gil asks.

"Get on Coach Martin's other side," Emery says. "Yep, there, like that. Smile, on three."

That picture, Gil remembers only after Emery's lowered her camera, checking the display and then nodding at what she sees. Him and Sebastian on the ice long ago, wearing navy blue, their faces boyish, their smiles huge.

"Thanks," Gil says softly as she walks away. He needs to get back in line, go through the drill again, not stand here talking to Sebastian during practice. Focus. "The pickup game, that was—I needed that."

"Nice to see you smiling again on the ice," Sebastian says.

"Well, Emery told us to."

"While you're playing, I mean."

It's just a game, Mom has always said.

"Come with me." Gil tips his head toward where skaters are flying through the drill. "You can show me your flawless shot."

"I'm not—"

"Let's see it, Martin," Steph says, nudging him forward with the butt of her stick.

She likes him. She'll offer him the long-term job here, Gil knows. Good. For Sebastian—and for his kid, the thought so weird it still makes Gil's head spin. For the team, too.

"Show 'em how it's done," Gil says, pulling Sebastian forward. "C'mon, Bloomer, do your best."

But even Bloomer can't keep up with them. One pass from Gil straight to the blade of Sebastian's stick, and then back again, the puck flying to where Gil's already skating to, leaving Bloomer flat-footed and chasing after them.

"Here," Gil calls, faking a shot on Hal to pull him to the side of the net and then immediately passing the puck to Sebastian.

"Fuck off," Hal grunts, having to slide back across the crease to be square to the threat of Sebastian's shot.

But Sebastian just sends it back again, finding Gil's stick without looking, leaving Hal out of position.

They could keep doing this all day. Did do it all day, once, laughing as their goalie finally just chucked his stick at them, Coach Thompson blowing his whistle, Rideau's rink full of the sound of them laughing.

Sebastian's not going to take the shot, Gil knows. He's here to coach, not to play. *Lucky*, Gil thinks of the team, getting a guy like Sebastian on their staff.

"Take it," Sebastian says and Gil tees up the puck, fakes once, and then sends it between Hal's legs, the puck beautifully, perfectly, finding the back of the net as Gil grins.

TWENTY

GIL SPINS HIS GLASS AGAIN, avoiding the bartender's eye so she won't lean over and ask him if his friends are really coming—again—when Jay finally walks in.

"Hey," Gil says, straightening from his seat at the bar where he's been fiddling with his phone. *Where are you?* he had texted Sebastian. *My offer to pay is going to expire if I have to sit on my ass waiting,* he wrote to Millsy, Lomsy, and Pezer. For the rest of them, he copied and pasted a quick message: *At Murry's, see you soon!*

"I..." Jay looks around at the mostly empty bar section Gil's commandeered, then at his watch.

"Yeah, not expecting everyone to be on time." Gil catches the bartender's eye. "Though I was hoping they'd at least be more punctual for drinks than for practice. Beer?"

"What're—" Jay takes a tentative step inside. "Whatever you're having."

"A pitcher of beer," Gil says to the bartender. *Nervous,* Sebastian had said of Jay and he's certainly right about that. A good skater, and he'll develop into a decent enough player, but he looks like a fish out of water here in the bar with only Gil.

Where the fuck are all of you? he thinks, casting a look at the door.

But maybe they're not coming. The lingering thought has only grown stronger the longer Gil has sat here. This will be a waste of his time, when he could be with his mom, or taking the time to focus for the game tomorrow.

Gil pours them glasses of beer as Jay settles onto a barstool, his hands fidgeting in his lap. *Fucking relax*, Gil wants to tell him. No, he can come up with something better than that. Sebastian would. "So, your rookie season, how's it going?"

"Okay. No, good, yeah, so good."

Gil takes a drink of his water, ignoring his beer glass. "Yeah?"

"I'll have a water too," Jay says to the bartender. "If you're not busy."

She points a glass around the length of the bar, empty barstools, pool tables with nobody at them, and the open tables. "Swamped."

"Sorry," Jay says.

Gil checks his watch again. Someone has to come soon.

"Food?" she asks, pushing a menu toward them.

"Oh, yeah, thanks." Jay casts a glance at Gil. "Are you eating? I can pay for this, and the beer, I can—" He reaches for his wallet.

Gil sighs. "It's all good, it's on me."

"But I didn't actually get that goal in. Hal kicked it in, on that last drill? And I think the defense actually—"

"I got it," Gil says again. *Breathe*, he wants to add.

Team bonding. That was his idea. Not sitting here with a kid stumbling over his words.

His phone buzzes. *Stop fucking texting me*, Hal has sent him. Gil shoves it back in his pocket. "So, uh—oh, geez, there you are," Gil says, jumping to his feet. "I was about to order the guac."

"Shut up," Sebastian says, holding the door for Steph. "I have Matty tonight, so I can't stay long."

"No, that's fine. Hi." *Hi?* Gil frowns at himself. Who says that?

But Sebastian looks good, jeans hugging his thighs, a plaid shirt with the sleeves rolled up and he must have just showered because his hair is wet, combed to the side.

Yeah, he looks real good.

Stop, Gil tells himself and then gives Sebastian one more glance.

"I'll have guac," Steph says. "And a cocktail and dinner and dessert. Hey there, Jay."

"Hi," Jay says, his hands tucked into his lap and his eyes darting between Gil and the coaches.

Sebastian grins at him, taking his nerves in stride. "Let's play," Sebastian says, tipping his head toward the pool table.

"I'm not very good," Jay says.

"I'll teach you." Sebastian holds a pool cue out to him.

"What, I don't get invited to play?" Gil asks.

"Oh, sorry, I didn't know if your pool skills were as shit as your shooting," Sebastian says.

Steph snorts a laugh. "Coach Martin, I didn't know you had it in you to dish out the chirps."

"Only for Gil," Sebastian says.

Gil's chest flushes warm. "I—"

"Rooster!" Millsy shouts from the door. "Get that wallet out, we've arrived."

"Finally," Gil says, willing down the bubbling happiness. The team, that's why he's here. The game tomorrow, the ridiculousness that luring the guys here to the bar was the only way to get a decent practice in.

Sebastian's just here, too. Which Gil can deal with. *Professional*, he thinks and tries again to ignore the flip in his stomach when Seb shoots him a grin.

"Oh, and look, some more actual adults," Steph says, waving at Bloomer and Emery who walk in together.

"You weren't really going to bench us all if we didn't come, were you?" Millsy asks, sipping from a beer glass he's filled too full, foam spilling over his fingers.

"Wanna test it out for whoever doesn't show up tonight?" Steph asks.

"They're all coming," Bloomer says.

"They are?" Gil asks.

Bloomer lifts a shoulder in a shrug. "I told them to show the hell up."

Millsy leans around Bloomer's bulk. "Blooms here is real good when he finally gets motivated about something."

"Well thanks," Gil says. "That's—thank you."

"That 'something' being telling everyone on the team what they're doing wrong," Millsy stage whispers as if Bloomer can't hear him.

Shut up, Gil's sure Bloomer will say, but he just leans forward, pointing at Gil's water and signaling the bartender for a glass of his own.

"Listen, Rooster," Millsy says. "You promised us food. That's the only reason I'm here, so put up or shut up."

"Yeah." Gil catches the bartender's eye. "Dinner for these guys, and the rest are coming, on my tab."

"And a drink," Millsy says. "Let's get some of that good stuff flowing. Rooster's got a pretty sweet contract, I hear."

"They'll all have light beer. We can get a few more pitchers." Gil points at the row of taps. "That one for everyone, or they're on their own."

"Except for me," Steph says.

"Yes, except for her," Gil says.

"And Em," Steph says. "Fucking hell, Rooster, you did it."

"Did what?" He turns to follow where she's looking at the door.

Hal walks in, his hands shoved into his pockets, a deep scowl on his face, and behind him, the rest of the guys.

"I'm gonna have to owe you one." Steph slaps his shoulder. "Never thought I'd see this."

"I am sorry," he says quietly. "About the other day on the ice."

"Well you sure as shit should be. Em! Over here. Mr. Roussin is buying us margaritas."

When Millsy starts a game of darts, it just becomes more of a press of bodies, everyone dodging out of the way of him and Lomsy flinging darts at the board. Gil shuffles back too, nearly bumping against the edge of the pool table.

"Think you could hit that at least?" Sebastian nods at the dartboard, pool cue in his hand.

Pezer aims carefully, rocking back a step, and it presses Sebastian closer.

Too close. Gil can smell soap.

"Funny," he says and twists away. "Jay, you want to play?"

"No, no, I..." Quickly, Jay pushes his cue into Gil's hands. "I'm just learning."

"You're doing fine," Sebastian says.

"I can't." Jay slips into the crowd.

Mitcher tosses his arms across Gil's shoulders. "Steph, come play with us. If I beat Gil, can I take his spot at center?"

"I know this will shock you two, but that's not actually how I decide the lines," Steph says.

"Put us all into a hat and pick out our names?" Mitcher asks.

"Nah, I make a list of who's pissed me off least recently."

"Then you'll want me on your team," Mitcher says. "Let's bring Mr. Social Organizer here down a peg or two."

"Not going to do coaches versus players?" she asks, nodding toward Sebastian.

Gil glances at him and Sebastian glances back. Tips his head, lifts an eyebrow.

"I don't mind being stuck with Sebastian," Gil says.

"You even know how to play?" Mitcher asks him.

"I've done it a time or two," Sebastian says.

Or for hours, day after day in the summer as they hid from the heat in Sebastian's basement. Long hours of hockey camp at the rink and then down there with sodas and chips after dinner, setting up trick shots, sinking balls into the pockets one after the next, the two of them a united front when Joey and Tommy had tried to play against them, beating them so bad Joey had gone complaining to Dad.

Wanna go head to head before tomorrow? Gil texts Joey with a picture of the pool table.

I'm feeding Mom Italian food like a good son, Joey texts back.

No phones at the table, Gil writes. *And I'll take that to mean you're still too scared.*

He gets a middle finger emoji back and laughs, shoving his phone into his pocket.

"You can break," Sebastian says to Mitcher. "Scottish doubles?"

"I'm getting a bad feeling about this," Steph says slowly. "You guys seem too happy about what's about to happen."

"Well you two went to college together, right?" Mitch asks as he racks the balls. "Play much pool there?"

"Sometimes," Gil says.

"All the time," Sebastian says.

"Okay, this might be bad," Steph says. "Mitcher, we might have wanted to think this through."

"We're good." Mitcher leans over the table, lining up his shot. He knows what he's doing at least, though he doesn't get any balls in on the break.

"Four ball, corner pocket." Gil leans over the table. He sinks it, no problem, and grins at Sebastian. "Still got it."

"Fourteen into the six into the corner," Sebastian says.

Mitch laughs. "C'mon, you can't make that."

Sebastian sets up the shot and Gil doesn't watch how his shirt pulls against his arms. Chalk. He needs chalk for his cue. A sip of his water.

"And there it is," Sebastian says as the ball neatly falls into the pocket. "Gil?"

Gil taps the side pocket in front of him. "Three into the fourteen into the one, right here."

"Shit," Steph says.

Sebastian grins, his hip cocked as he leans against his pool cue, and Gil grins back and takes the shot, turning away for a high five even as the ball finds the pocket.

"Seriously?" Mitch asks.

"That's how we do it," Sebastian says. "Fourteen into the three into the twelve into the five, far corner."

"I need another drink," Steph says.

Gil strolls around the table, leaning over to watch the five sink cleanly into the corner pocket.

"Two, maybe," Steph says.

"Yes, good idea, Coach," Gil says. "Two, this corner."

"So you guys played a lot, okay, I got it," Mitch says as Gil leans over the table. "Hockey, pool, college, you two had all the fun."

"We did," Gil says, easing the cue back and forth as he closes one eye.

"Dating, too, right?" Mitch asks as Gil takes the shot.

Gil whiffs it, the cue ball spinning off to the side. "Shit," he says.

"What?" Steph asks.

"Twelve in the corner," Mitcher says and sinks it.

That should have been Steph's shot, Gil wants to say, but he can't get his mouth around the words. Can't look at her, either.

"I'm sorry, what is this?" Steph asks.

Mitcher digs his elbow into Gil's ribs and then lines up for another shot. "No wonder you got to practice on the top power play unit today."

"It's not like that." Gil's voice is too loud, cutting over the music and the chatter of the team. Far too loud, because Millsy turns, and then Pezer does, and Bloomer too, all of them looking over.

"Oh shit, I thought it was a joke," Mitcher says. "You two really were dating? Are you still?"

"No," Gil says. "I mean yes, but not now, and it wasn't, we were—"

"Hey, it's cool, man." Mitcher claps Gil's arm. "Nobody cares. Sleep with whoever you want, God knows everyone on this team does. But damn, a coach?"

"You guys are dating?" Lomsy points a dart between Gil and Sebastian. "Oh shit, did you ask to get traded here, Gil? I was wondering how the hell you ended up here. No wonder you're so dead set on making something out of us."

Gil holds up his hands, palms out. "We're not, we're not, okay? And that's not why the trade—I didn't ask for this. Same as you all, I got stuck here, I—"

Stuck here. Wrong words, even if it's true and everyone knows it.

Steph sets her pool cue on the table. "Did you?"

"No, I didn't ask for the trade," Gil says.

"Did you two date?"

Gil can't quite look at her. Can't get any words out either and he hedges a glance toward Sebastian, whose face is red.

Steph blows out a breath. "Okay. Wow. Damnit, both of you."

"Who broke up with who?" Pezer calls.

"Yeah, Gil, what'd you do?" Millsy asks and the team laughs.

"I didn't—I got called up to San Diego, we were—"

"It wasn't serious," Sebastian says softly. Gil's stomach drops. "Gil's been looking for another trade, and I—"

"Rooster's getting the hell out of here," Lomsy says. "We all do know that, but um, details please. We need them."

"Let's have a chat, the three of us, shall we?" Steph says.

"This," Millsy says, lifting his glass toward them in a toast, "was definitely worth coming out tonight for."

Outside, Steph paces up the sidewalk, back toward them, and away again.

"Steph," Gil says. "Coach."

She holds up a hand. "I need a minute."

When she finally walks back, Gil nearly flinches at the look on her face.

"You two," she starts. "Should have told me about this. And you certainly should have told Frank, the very minute you both landed in the city. What the fuck were you thinking?"

It was so long ago. Sebastian told me not to. I'm leaving anyway. Gil swallows. Excuses only feel good to the person giving them, Dad has always said.

And besides. It's Sebastian. Gil isn't going to put it on him, slide the blame away and wipe his own hands clean.

"I—" Sebastian starts.

"I'm sorry," Gil says quickly, stepping forward.

"Gil—" Sebastian says.

"It's my fault," Gil says, louder, talking over Sebastian when he tries to cut in.

"It's both of your damn faults," Steph snaps. "And this job is hard enough. I don't need to be finding out about the two of you from a player with a chip on his shoulder the size of—of—what if this had gotten to the media first? Did you even think about that? Did you think about anything at all? The entire damn league knowing that I have a player and a coach sleeping together?"

"We're not, we're—we've just known each other for ages, since we were kids, we're—we're friends now, is all. Nothing's going on," Gil says.

"Nothing?" she asks, her voice low. "Nothing at all?"

Gil hesitates. *Don't look at him*, he snaps at himself but casts a look at Sebastian anyway.

"Fucking hell," Steph says. "Seriously?"

"Okay, but it wasn't, you know, we only—"

"I don't want fucking details, Gil!" She rounds on Sebastian. "You're on my coaching staff. He's one of our damn players. What were you possibly thinking?"

"It wasn't anything," Sebastian says softly.

The single best kiss Gil's had since...he swallows, his throat tight. "It wasn't."

Steph massages her temples.

"I'll resign," Sebastian says.

"Seb—"

"No, I should have known. You're right, Steph, and it was my idea, not Gil's, to—"

"Seb!"

"We're not dating," Sebastian says. "And we're not going to start."

Gil sucks in a breath. No, they won't be.

"But we are friends," Sebastian says and Gil spins to look at him. "And if that's a problem now that the team knows that as kids in college, we—well, whatever, I get it. I know I'm here temporarily anyway, so I understand if—"

"No." Steph's voice is cold steel. "Fuck you, both of you. You waltz in here and start to make something out of this clusterfuck of a team. Practice today? Watching the guys actually work, Gil? And Sebastian, what you said to Jay? He told me the other day he wanted to quit, to go home, and one conversation with you and suddenly he feels like a million bucks."

Gil risks a glance toward Sebastian. *Get gone*, he waits for Steph to say. It'd be better if it just came, and quickly, too, but this sounds...like a compliment?

"There is something happening here with this team for the very first time," Steph says, her voice rising with each word. "That the two of you are a part of, and hell if you blow that because players are gossiping about you. So you know what you're going to do?"

Get the hell off my team, should be her next statement, punctuated by pointing at them.

"Gil, you're going to go back in there and tell the guys exactly what is going on, so they're not left making up the story for themselves." She rounds on Sebastian. "And you."

"I—" Sebastian rocks a step back.

"You are going to make sure that this does nothing to your work with the rookies, 'cause I sure as shit need someone helping me herd the joke show of our defense and goalie situation into something resembling a hockey team. The team finding out you two used to—I don't want to know. But you're going to make it into a step forward for this group, you hear? Because if this causes damage, then I'm going to actually get mad."

"Got it," Gil says obediently.

"Absolutely," Sebastian says.

"Good." She walks toward a nearby car.

It's silent for a moment as she climbs in, then she slams the door shut and pulls away from the curb so quickly her tires squeal.

"Well," Gil says softly.

"Shit," Sebastian says.

"What's she like when she's really mad?" Gil asks.

"I don't know."

"That was bad."

"Really bad."

"I didn't tell Mitcher that. He heard it from someone, but it wasn't me. I wasn't going to—"

"No, I know. It was a long time ago, anyway."

"Yeah." Gil rubs his hands over his face. He's tired. He'd been tired and he wants that lick of anger in his chest to spark, give him some energy to deal with this mess.

But he knows with a dull ache that Steph is right. He's got to clean this up with the team.

It'd have been easier to get kicked off the roster for this than to walk back in there and...Gil grimaces. They're going to make so much fun of him. Oh, they're absolutely going to love this.

When he opens his eyes, Sebastian's a step closer. "I'm really sorry," Sebastian says. "I shouldn't have asked you to keep this quiet."

"No, I mean—seemed like a good idea at the time."

"Just seeing you again and knowing you'd be coming out here with me, and then at the airport, I just—"

"Hey," Gil says. "It's okay."

Sebastian tucks his hands in his pockets. "Alright."

Noise spills out of the bar into the night air and a car drives past, its engine and tires a low rumble over the pavement. Somewhere in the city a siren wails. Sebastian's shoulders hunch inward and Gil knows if he could see his face, see Sebastian staring down at his shoes, his cheeks would be flushed.

"I'll deal with the guys," Gil says. Yes, this is how they've always done things. Gil will go in and take the brunt of whatever's waiting for him. Teasing, laughing, the team's delight in this latest gossip. Gil will be mortified, but he can deal with it. "You get out of here."

"I can't just leave you—"

"I got it," Gil says. "See you back at the hotel?"

"I have Matty, I won't be back at the room tonight."

"Right." Gil tries to ignore the drop in his stomach. "No, yeah, I'll see you later then."

"Text me or call if…" he pauses, glancing in through the windows. Then he laughs.

"What?" Gil asks, craning to see.

"Oh definitely call, 'cause I'm going to have to hear all about this," Sebastian says. "Yeah, I'm not going in there."

"What're they—"

Oh.

Shit.

The real problem in hockey is when the team stops messing with you. It's an odd, sometimes embarrassing form of camaraderie, but it'll be all the worse if Gil walks in and everyone politely ignores him.

If only, he thinks. Through the window, Millsy gives him a cheerful wave and beckons him inside. They've moved the tables, lining them up in a long arc, the entire team sitting in chairs they've dragged behind them, Millsy in the middle, Pezer and Lomsy on either side of him.

It looks like a courtroom. Like they've set up a hearing, because sure enough, there's a single chair placed in the center of the circle of tables they've created.

"Fuck," Gil says.

Sebastian grins and slaps Gil's arm. "Good luck."

"Seb."

"I think they like you," Sebastian says.

Jay pushes the door open, turns back as Millsy shouts something to him, and then steps through it toward Gil. "Um," Jay says. "They want you in there."

"Bye," Sebastian says, already walking away.

"Seb!"

"If that's okay," Jay quickly adds.

"I'm coming." Gil takes a breath. Part of him wants to laugh at this tribunal he's facing, some giddy part that loves the depravity of hockey guys and the mischief they get up to. *But you're not my team*, he wants to protest. Somewhere else in the city are Hux, Giffy, and Little. Joey, too.

Fuck, they'll hear about this, he's sure. Someone knows someone who knows a guy with one of their numbers and they'll get pictures of this, even a recording.

Tell the guys exactly what's going on, Steph said. Because tonight, this is very much his team.

Tentatively, Gil steps through the door. "C'mon guys," he says.

"Tell us everything," Millsy says.

"These tables need to be moved back," the bartender calls.

"Yeah, move them, and stop messing around," Gil says.

"Before you all leave, I mean," she says and grins at them. "Another round, boys?"

Team bonding, Gil had thought when he suggested tonight. Pezer cheers and gathers up the pitchers to get refills as Lomsy pushes Gil to sit in the chair.

"Everything," Millsy repeats even as Gil starts protesting.

The first of many refusals, he's sure, shaking his head at

the start of their questions. Team fucking bonding, but at his expense.

Though maybe, if he's lucky, it might just make a difference for tomorrow.

TWENTY-ONE

THE CAB IS TOO crowded with all of them in it, Millsy up front chatting the ear off the driver and Gil wedged against the door in the back, Pezer next to him.

"Okay, so things cooled off when you got called up to San Diego," Lomsy says, leaning across Pezer.

Gil would cover his face with his hand if he could free it from against Pezer's ribcage. "We've been over this."

"But you would have kept the love going with new Coach."

"This is so truly none of your business."

"No, but it is," Lomsy says.

"It definitely is," Pezer says.

Millsy points at the driver. "He agrees too."

"Let me out." Gil feels for the door handle when the car slows.

But the cab pulls to a stop in front of a house, not the hotel. A nice house, modern, with huge windows, a stone path leading through a manicured little garden, and lights framing a small porch.

"You live here?" Gil asks.

"Us? Hell no. Millsy lives with his beloved sister, and Loms and I live across town. This is you," Pezer says.

"I'm at the hotel," Gil says. "By the rink."

"Oh, yeah, that's right. Okay, bye."

Gil points out the window. "This isn't—"

"Get out, see you tomorrow, have fun," Lomsy says and leans over Pezer and Gil to open the door.

Gil, squashed against it, nearly tumbles out. "This isn't me," he says.

"Tell Coach we said hi," Lomsy says, giving him a final shove and then slamming the door shut as Gil scrambles for balance.

"Hey, wait, I—"

But they're gone, Millsy shouting, "Go, go, go!" to the driver.

"Guys!" Gil calls after them, but all he gets is the sight of red tail lights and Pezer and Lomsy waving to him through the back windshield.

Coach. Gil licks his lips as he looks up at the house. *Steph*, he so wants to hope, but no, that's not her car parked out front.

He can call a cab. Slip away from here, hope nobody is glancing out the window.

But...there's only one place those assholes would drop him off. Figures.

It doesn't seem like the type of place Sebastian should be inside, let alone opening the front door to when Gil knocks.

But it's him with bare feet, in the jeans he was wearing, and a T-shirt covered with...

"What happened?" Gil asks. *Hi*, he meant to say. *I'm sorry*, he should have started with.

"Bubble bath situation." Sebastian smooths his wet shirt

over his stomach. "I was about to change. What're you doing here?"

"Lomsy shoved me out of a cab."

"What?"

"Yeah, I don't know. You live here?"

"Here?" Sebastian asks, looking at the door he's holding, the warmly lit room he's standing in like he's never seen it before. "No."

"Oh."

"But, hey, come on in. Can I get you anything?"

Gil stares around. Blonde wood accents, white walls, a gray couch and beyond it, a kitchen with wide counters and a huge, modern light fixture hanging above the island. "You don't live here?"

"I don't live anywhere right now. We agreed to get this place so Matty wouldn't have to truck all over the city." Sebastian shuts the door behind Gil.

It takes a long moment for that to register. "You bought your kid a house?"

"Me? No. I paid for half of the refrigerator and Matty's lucky his other parent handled the rest. And keep your voice down, I just got him in bed."

"It's nice," Gil gets out. Like really nice. Really, really nice. "He doesn't have to go to both your places every week?"

"You mean whatever shoebox I end up renting? No. He stays put, we do the moving around."

"That's...wow." Gil turns in a small circle. There's an odd sort of painting on the wall, splashes of soothing neutral colors that match the rug beneath the couch and coffee table.

Sebastian was really married. And still has that guy in his life. Shares a kid with him, who plays with the stack of blocks set in front of the giant TV, reads the colorful books lining the bottom row of the bookshelf, splashes bubbles all over Sebastian when Seb leaves a bar early, needing to get back for the ritual of bath and bed.

Really? Gil wants to ask, checking in on this version of Sebastian even as it stares him in the face.

"Um, so yeah, come on in," Sebastian repeats. "Anyway, what are you—why are you here exactly?"

"I have no idea," Gil says. "I would have loved this, not having to schlep back and forth every couple days." Though less than that, really, since with his hockey schedule it was often easier to just stay at Dad's.

"Yeah." Sebastian smooths his shirt again. "I remember you saying that about having basically two places to live growing up."

"This is incredible," Gil says. "But you can't just stay here?"

"No, we agreed this house is Matty's. It's not either of ours. And it's working, better than I thought it would, actually. And we're both pretty invested in, you know, not rocking the boat and making sure we keep getting along."

"So you're what, friends?"

"I guess."

"You all had dinner together."

"Gil," Sebastian says. "Don't pry."

"I'm not," Gil says and then asks anyway, "So are you two—you still like each other?"

"Not like—" Sebastian frowns. "No, we're not talking about this."

"Not like what?"

"Not like we did," Sebastian says. "C'mon. Drop it."

"Yeah," Gil says like he can possibly let the topic go. Not like they did. So once, this guy lit up Sebastian's world. Gave him that smile that dimples his cheeks beneath his beard, crinkles the corners of his eyes.

Gil glares at the dumb abstract painting and frowns.

"How'd it go after I left?" Sebastian asks.

"How do you think?"

"What did you tell them?"

"Basically nothing." Gil sticks his hands in his pockets, turning in a slow circle. "Just that we were neighbors, played in college, all that."

"So now they have every opportunity to make up the details themselves?"

Gil pulls his attention away from a pair of tiny Velcro shoes by the door. "Shit. I didn't think of that."

"Well, it'll probably be fine. It's not like they looked up the staff directory for my address and then dropped you off here."

"Great," Gil mutters. "Steph didn't end up coming back. How pissed do you think she is?"

"Very. Though I think the team's getting to the point where nothing can really shock her and Frank."

"She should bench me. Any other coach would."

"And fire me," Sebastian says. "She's right. I should have told her."

"No, it's not your fault. I could have—"

A key scrapes in the lock.

"Fuck," Sebastian whispers.

Gil turns. "Who's that?"

"What're you doing back here?" Sebastian asks as the door opens.

"Chris?" Gil asks, a laugh escaping him. "Mouser? Is that you?"

"Gil?" Chris looks the same as he did at Rideau, skinny jeans on his whip-thin frame, a T-shirt with faded lettering on it, thick glasses he peers through.

Though he's filled out a bit, less the tiny computer science kid who tagged along with his brothers on the hockey team. A nicer haircut, one that suits him, a couple days of stubble on his face that looks intentional, shoes he clearly picked to go with his outfit, didn't just jam his feet into after he'd pulled an all-nighter.

"You look good," Gil says. "Seb said you were in the city."

"Yeah, I've lived here for a while now. How've you been?"

"Good, good, and you?"

"Don't," Sebastian says softly.

"Doing pretty good, just forgot my other keys." Chris sorts through a basket on a table. "I heard you're on the Sea Lions now. That's pretty cool."

"Yeah, kind of a shitshow, honestly, but the city's alright."

"Yep, we love it here. Came right out after graduating Rideau and never looked back, did we?" He grins at Sebastian.

Gil follows his gaze. *We.*

Chris's other keys.

Slowly, Gil looks back at him. Chris, who hung around the hockey team when he didn't have his nose shoved close to a computer screen. Tagged after his older brothers, came to all the games, ran analytics for them, helping the coaches out with statistics for the players even though the team had given him a hard time about doing math for fun.

Chris, who Sebastian had always been kind to. Let him sit at their table at lunch, defended him when the teasing got to be too much.

"You two…" Just the tip of his finger moves between them. He already knows. Oh shit, yes, he very much, very horribly *knows*.

"Nice city." Chris fishes into the bottom of the basket and pulls out a keychain. "Ah, there are my apartment keys.

I'll get out of your hair, but hey, Seb, forgot to mention, Matty needs more diapers when you drop him off at school tomorrow, okay?"

"School," Gil echoes.

"Yeah, it's this great Montessori program, and they have this wonderful garden for the kids to be in. He's learning so much, it's incredible." Chris laughs. "Not potty trained yet, but future Rideau student we've got right here, and what a shoo-in with the double legacy, right?"

Diapers, Gil thinks.

"It's really just a day care," Sebastian says. "Okay, good to see you, bye."

"Yeah, yeah, I'm going. But hey, Gil, let's catch up at some point, yeah? Grab a cup of coffee?"

"No." Sebastian starts crowding Chris toward the door. "That's way too weird."

"But I gotta give him my big speech about not hurting you again," Chris says, letting himself be pushed.

"Get out, bye, I'll remember the diapers."

"And remind you the housekeeper's coming tomorrow."

"And yes, okay, have a good night, go, bye, see you later," Sebastian says and shuts the door firmly. Slowly, he turns back to Gil. "For the record, the housekeeper was not my idea."

"That's—" Gil points at the door. "That's Chris."

"Nor was the whole Montessori thing."

"You and Chris—you guys..." Gil points at Sebastian. "Holy fucking shit."

"Yeah, okay? We—yeah."

"You got married?"

Sebastian pulls in a slow breath through his nose and nods. "We did."

"You dated?"

"That's generally what happens before marriage."

"You have a fucking kid together?"

"Keep your voice down because that kid is very hope-fully asleep," Sebastian says. "Look, he's a good guy. You never really knew him that well at Rideau, but he was great. Still is."

"Yeah, you apparently think so."

"And, we got to know each other, and that was that." Sebastian turns toward the rack next to the door to grab a small canvas bag.

"Fucking Chris? That guy? Of everyone?"

"He prefers Christopher, and he's my kid's dad, and so you won't say anything shitty about him. Okay?"

Gil rocks back on his heels, still staring, but that's a hard edge in Sebastian's voice so he pushes out, "Okay."

Sebastian grabs a bag of diapers from one of the baskets and stuffs them into the canvas tote. "He was there, Gil. And you weren't."

"Okay," he says again, softer.

"I'm sure you've had your share of relationships," Sebas-tian says, his head down as he fusses with the bag. "So let's not be surprised that we both grew up."

"Yeah, no, of course." What else is he going to say—no, he didn't, not even one? Nothing exclusive and certainly nothing long term.

He was too busy. Of course he was. He had his career to focus on, he couldn't let his mind wander from the ice to picking out curtains with some guy, deciding on center-pieces and what time of year to have their wedding.

Summer, he thinks without wanting to. Because all hockey players get married in the summer, the team juggling through the weekends between the end of playoffs and the start of the next season like a revolving door of guys getting hitched, one after the next, trying not to accidentally schedule one wedding on top of another for the same day.

Slowly, he looks over at Sebastian. He married someone else. Someone who wasn't Gil, shredding a picture Gil didn't even know he had so fully formed in his mind. Chris standing where Gil should be, Julie Martin smiling through happy tears, Gil's brothers standing up there with him, his mom fussing over them both, adjusting bow ties and boutonnieres and—

"Cool," Gil pushes out. "Yeah, that you two—that's, um." He scratches at his cheek. "So San Diego plays man-to-man defense, and they run this one play where—"

"Gil," Sebastian sighs.

"This is just really fucking weird, okay?"

Sebastian hangs the bag up on a hook. *Matty* is embroidered on it in crisp navy blue letters. "Well, it's kinda weird to have you here, to be honest. And I didn't think Christopher would show up on top of it."

"Were you going to tell me?"

"I did tell you. I have a kid and got married and—"

"You married Chris!"

Sebastian gives him a sharp look and points at the stairs.

"Sorry," Gil loudly whispers. "But you did, you thought you were going to stay with him? Forever? That he was the one for you, that Chris of all people—"

"I told you not to shit on him, Gil. He's a great guy and he's family now, even if we're divorced."

"But—"

"And like I said, he was there." Sebastian's voice is soft and that's somehow worse than if he'd raised it. "When you left."

"But I—I called you, and I—"

"You called and left message after message about hockey," Sebastian says. "All about your team, and your practices, and your uniform, and your games."

"I wanted to tell you. It was so exciting, I had to tell you, of course I did, I—"

"Yeah, and it was cool at first."

"What does that mean? At first?"

"We all watched your first game." Sebastian squats to pick through wicker baskets. Diapers in one, more tiny shoes in the next. "The entire team. Coach Thompson had us over to his house, and there it was, you in the NHL, and I thought—" Sebastian laughs. It's not a happy sound.

"Thought what?" Gil asks.

"You finally got what you wanted."

"I never wanted to stop talking to you."

"You didn't." Sebastian stands to fuss with a bright green raincoat, orange dinosaur spikes on the hood and down the back. "Talk to me."

"I did, I called, and you stopped calling me back, and I'd text and hear from you after a day, and then two days, and I fucking emailed you, Seb, I—"

"You talked at me," Sebastian says.

"What does that even mean?"

"Christopher was there and you weren't."

"I would have been. I had to go, you know that."

"And the anniversary of the day my dad died?"

Gil steps closer. "I called you that day. I did. And I've thought about you every single year on that day, Seb, you didn't want to hear from me, I—"

"Yeah, you called. And Christopher got the entire team together to play football and he stood on the field even though he doesn't have an athletic bone in his body and when we were done I had three texts from you with pictures of hockey sticks and not a single fucking word about everything you left behind."

Gil sucks in a breath. "Seb—"

"Don't say anything awful about Christopher, okay? Not anything. Ever."

"I didn't know there was some secret thing I was supposed to be doing or saying. You're telling me this now? How was I supposed to know, I didn't—"

"You could have thought about it for two fucking seconds," Sebastian says, his voice rising. "Considered anything at all other than—" He stops. Looks at the stairs. "Fucking hell. Great."

"What?"

Two feet appear and above them, chubby, short legs. A trailing edge of a blanket, and a tiny hand holding a pacifier.

"Matty," Sebastian says and there's a warning in his voice, mixed with a deep, gentle warmth.

Dimpled knees, the round belly of a toddler, wearing a diaper and a T-shirt with a unicorn on it. And a grin on the kid's face as he comes down, setting both feet on each step before attempting the next one, the hand not clutching his pacifier and blanket holding the banister for balance.

"Bedtime," Sebastian says.

The little boy smiles. "No."

"It's your bedtime."

Still grinning, he takes another careful step down.

"Matty, I'm going to carry you back upstairs," Sebastian says.

But the kid ignores him, hanging onto the banister as he climbs down the last step, and then he runs faster than Gil would have thought he could on those tiny legs into the back of the house.

"I'll just—" Sebastian sighs. "I'll be back."

But Matty beats him through the rooms that apparently loop around behind the stairs, running as Sebastian hurries after him, coming back with his blanket clutched in one hand and a smile on his face.

He freezes when he sees Gil. Stares at him, all big, brown eyes, a furrow forming between them and his cheeks slowly flushing.

"Uh, hi," Gil says.

Matty screams, tears tumbling down his cheeks as his face crumples.

"My friend Gil is here," Sebastian says, scooping him up.

Matty clutches at him, sobbing into his shoulder.

"Sorry," Gil says.

But Matty only wails louder, his back arching, feet kicking at Sebastian's stomach.

"He's tired," Sebastian says over Matty's head, then ducks to kiss his wet cheeks, murmuring to him. "Yeah, buddy, you're tired, and you weren't expecting anyone else to be here, were you? This is Gil. Can you say hi?"

A wet, sobbing hiccup as Matty plasters himself against Sebastian.

Gil gives an awkward, small wave. "Hello."

Matty thrashes, shouting something through his tears.

"Yes, I know, it's been a long day and you have to go to bed, little mister. C'mon, I'll take you back up. How about another story, huh? What if we get you all tucked in again and cozy and read you another book?" Sebastian asks, unfazed, shifting Matty to his other arm as he takes him up the stairs, the shrieking fading down a hallway and then a door shuts.

Is Gil supposed to leave? Call a car and be gone when Sebastian comes back down?

No. He left once. Resolutely, he stands where he is, staring up at the stairs, the soothing neutrals of the house doing little to calm him.

What the fuck? he wants to ask of the weird-ass painting, the clean, sparse kitchen. Sebastian, with a kid? With *Chris?*

A kid's drawing is hung on the fridge, smears of crayon across a wrinkled sheet of paper. A holiday card from a couple with two kids Gil doesn't know, and a note in Julie Martin's handwriting signed *Grandma*. On the counter sits a printed version of an online calendar, days and weeks color coded with *Sebastian* written on half and *Christopher* on the other. There's no rhyme or reason to it, not like Mom's Wednesday night dinners when she'd drive up from Annapolis or the weekends they'd spend with her, at least when they didn't have games that got in the way.

The hockey season, Gil slowly realizes. The calendar's laid out to align with road trips, home stands, the occasional weekend game that will be held midday. If he pulls out his phone, he's sure it'll fit neatly to the Sea Lions schedule.

Sebastian wants this job with them. Chris—*Christopher* —is willing to work to make it happen for him.

I called you, Gil wants to protest again. Charge upstairs, explain to Sebastian exactly how hard it was to make time to squeeze in those phone calls, how thoroughly Gil had tried to share every single bit of his new life and make sure Sebastian was included.

Gil's still staring at the calendar when Sebastian walks down the stairs.

"You and Chris—Christopher—you're planning on getting this job with the team? Long term?" Gil asks before Sebastian can point him toward the door.

"Well that's the hope," Sebastian says lightly.

I can't date 'cause my schedule's too hard, Gil had told his mom once, when she'd asked why he never found someone. The distraction, the pain of trying to fit someone else into the maze of his life.

He tried, for Sebastian. Did it, even, as best he could.

Chris is going to deal with the travel an NHL coach faces, the late nights, the constant grind of the season, and do it so he and Sebastian can share their kid. And do it as his ex. Not because they're dating now, or married now, but do it through the resentment and long history together of a failed marriage.

He's a good guy, Sebastian had said.

"Um," Gil says.

"Listen, I'm sorry I got upset. It's all fine. It was so long ago, and we agreed that was behind us, so—"

"He's good. For you, I mean. Or was but he still is, too. Chris. Fucking—Mouser, I mean. I'm glad—I tried to be there but I guess I didn't do it right and I'm glad that someone—that he was."

"Oh."

It washes over Gil all over again. Married. To Chris, of everyone. Having a damn kid.

Wild, how Sebastian's life held so much in what feels like such a short time.

"What happened?" Gil asks. "That you and Chris —how?"

Sebastian straightens the calendar, neatly aligning the paper with the edge of the counter. "I just didn't really have anyone to hang out with since you and I, you know, spent every second of the day together, and Chris was there. He was a nice break from hockey."

"No, I mean—" Gil wants to wince at the image that forms in his mind of Sebastian and Chris together on Rideau's campus. What would they have even done together? Stared at a computer monitor?

No, Gil knows what they did. The narrow twin bed in their—Sebastian's after Gil left—dorm room, the way they had to shove a textbook against the headboard to keep it from creaking...

He leans against the counter. It takes a long moment to find his voice again. "What happened that you two broke up?" he finally gets out.

"Oh, it wasn't that exciting." Sebastian shrugs. "Grew apart. It happens."

"Did he do something?"

"Christopher? God no. He doesn't have it in him."

"How are you two..." The word hurts. "Friends? How does that even work?"

Sebastian shrugs. "We agreed, for Matty."

"But you broke up," Gil says.

"And we try to be adults about it. Look, it's not seamless. I have to do a very good job not making a mess in here but the housekeeper helps with that, no matter how weird that is. And Christopher sucks at sticking to a schedule—obviously, since he just came back tonight. But we try, at least. You know, let the little stuff go and talk about the big things."

"But if you work together so well why didn't you stay married?"

"Gil," Sebastian says. "Sharing a house isn't the same thing as a good marriage."

"But—"

"Maybe we should have realized before Matty, but he's the best thing to have happened to me, so I'm not exactly upset about how things turned out. Sucks for him, though. He won't remember us ever being together."

"Why didn't you just stick it out?"

"I wasn't going to stay married to someone I didn't—you know what, this isn't actually your business."

"So you were the one who wanted out?"

"C'mon, Gil. Let's not do this."

"Because who would—no, I'm serious, Seb, who would ever dump you?"

Sebastian laughs. Closes his eyes and when he opens them again, he stares at Gil. "Really?"

"Yes, really, you're—"

"Gil, please."

"So great and funny and—"

"I didn't love him, okay?" Sebastian pulls in a breath. "He's absolutely wonderful, and he's going to make someone stupidly happy someday, but I couldn't stay married to him."

"Didn't ever or didn't in the end or—"

"Gil. Enough."

"Sorry."

"You're never going to hear me say anything bad about him, alright? I know your mom and dad...well. Not ideal, the way things ended up between them, right? But Christopher is amazing. He's brilliant, he started this company, sold it, started another one, sold that too, set his parents up for life, bought this place for Matty, does all this great shit around the city, he's just..."

"What?" Gil finally asks.

"Not right for me. Which doesn't make him less incredible. I'm sure he does genuinely want to have coffee with you. That's such a Christopher thing to do. Seriously this is all so weird, Gil."

"I'm sorry you went through all of that," Gil says softly. "I—divorce. You're right, I know what it did to my parents. My mom, at least."

"I have Matty. It was worth it."

"Okay, but, are you alright? I mean you said you moved and in terms of friends, do you have people to hang out with?" *To help you*, Gil means. Take him out for a drink, listen to him through the worst days of the divorce, help him now with single parenting and juggling a career.

"I'm fine, Gil."

264

"Is that a no?"

"No, it's that sometimes fine is the best there is. I go and play pickup hockey. Not that group last night, but with some other guys. And out on the ice—you know how it is."

Yeah, Gil does. His brain finally shutting off for the glide of his skates and the weight of the puck.

"You can call me."

"With questions?" Sebastian smiles, a small, quick one. "Thanks, but I'm not gonna ask you for shooting tips."

"When I leave. If you're—if you need someone to talk to."

Sebastian plucks at his shirt, as if surprised to find it still damp. "You'll be busy with your new team."

Can't share you with hockey, Mom had said. "I know I'll be busy, but I'd make the time. I tried to, back then."

"Would you?"

Gil ventures a step closer. "I think I'd need to know how to do it better, but yeah, of course. I—I missed you. Every day."

Tentatively, Gil reaches out, lays his palm on the soft cotton of his shirt. Sebastian's shoulders are tight beneath the warm fabric.

"I wasn't only thinking about hockey," Gil says. "I was thinking about you too."

"Gil..."

Gil takes another step. Did Sebastian not know that? Or did Gil really do that shitty a job?

He sucks in a breath. It's awful, either way. Both ways. All of it, that they fell out of touch in the first place. But they're back here, finally. After far, far too long.

Gil steps into Sebastian, draws him close. Hugs him, his face in Sebastian's shoulder, his arms tight around him.

Slowly, Sebastian hugs him back. Gently at first, and then harder, gripping.

Yes, back together again.

Back for now, Gil thinks. "I'm gonna miss you all over again when I leave," Gil says thickly. Matty, this house, the coaching job he's going after—no, Sebastian's not moving away from this city. Gil will go, and he'll go alone.

"Don't."

"I am," Gil says.

"Stay here," Sebastian says, his breath puffing warm on Gil's skin.

"Seb?"

Sebastian draws back enough to look at him, soft brown eyes searching Gil's. "You're leaving soon. Again. And I want—I want you to stay. Here. Tonight."

I shouldn't, Gil should say.

But there's only one answer he has to give.

"Of course," he says and in his arms, Sebastian smiles.

TWENTY-TWO

Gɪʟ ʜᴀs ᴀ ɢᴀᴍᴇ ᴛᴏᴍᴏʀʀᴏᴡ. He needs his rest. A solid night's sleep and then to wake up in the morning ready to focus on morning skate. If he's going to stay up tonight, it should only be to run through plays in his mind.

The trick of visualization, Dad had always explained: imagine yourself on the breakaway, gracefully stepping around the defense, skating confidently into the zone, picking your spot on the goalie, and letting the puck fly.

In the upstairs hallway, Sebastian pushes a door open a crack, sticking his head in and then nodding to himself as he backs out and eases it mostly closed again.

The next door, he walks through, turning on a light inside and yes, this is Sebastian's room. Gil smiles. Very much so, with the pile of unfolded laundry in a basket, the comforter tossed haphazardly over the bed, the pillows left askew, a half empty water glass on the bedside table next to a book sitting open, spine cracked.

Boxes everywhere, too. Stacked against the wall, spilling out of the closet, pushed behind the door so it doesn't open all the way.

Just this once, Gil thinks and pushes the thought of the

rink aside. "Love what you've done with the place," he says as he steps into the room.

"Yeah, yeah, I know," Sebastian says. "But I had to pack up my old place when my last lease ran out, and I shipped things out from my mom's house, so all of this is just here until I find a new spot."

"Have you heard of a concept called a storage unit? Or is it more homey to be shoved in among your things like a sardine in a very messy can?"

"Sorry it's making your eye twitch that everything isn't perfectly organized. Are you just dying to straighten it all up?"

"No." Gil nudges a pile of boxes so they're sitting in a neater stack.

"Gil."

"What all is this?" Gil pokes through the box on top. He's giddy. He's in Sebastian's bedroom because Sebastian invited him up here. *Calm down*, he tries to tell himself, but he's got too much energy, flipping open the box to try to hide it.

Clothes, it looks like. Old, faded T-shirts, some button-down shirts—but no, they're wrapped around something, because apparently Sebastian wasn't going to spring for bubble wrap when he could use his wardrobe for packing.

"Are you going to go through all my stuff?"

"You kept this?" Gil pulls out an old plastic trophy Sebastian had carefully wrapped.

"Okay, yes, apparently you are."

"This is from—what were we, in eighth grade?" Gil tips the trophy so he can read its etching. *Champions*, it says, the letters faded and the adhesive holding the plaque peeling up in the corner.

"C'mon, that was a hell of a game. I had to keep it."

"We were like twelve years old."

"Thirteen, and I scored the winning goal, thank you. That might have been the height of my hockey career right there."

Gil sets it aside and keeps digging. "Is this your old helmet? Oh man, you loved this book. Is this the same copy? What else is in here?" Gil asks but Sebastian catches Gil's hand when he reaches deeper into the box.

Gil lets him, his stomach skipping at the warmth of his skin. This is why Sebastian brought him up here, isn't it? Yes, of course it is, or they'd be downstairs with a polite distance between them, not huddled over a box, Sebastian's hand on his forearm, his touch warm, their eyes locked.

Oh, Gil's so incredibly, so very, very nervous.

"Got photos of back then?" Gil asks. He's talking too fast. "Remember your braces? What a good look. Can I—" Yes, there, a box of photo albums, and Sebastian hands him one. Quickly, Gil flips through it. High school, not eighth grade, but it's good enough, Sebastian smiling with the bar of a retainer across his front teeth.

"Let me see at least." Sebastian grabs it back, sitting on the edge of the bed as he flips it open.

There's a desk chair Gil could wheel over, or there's just hovering as he stands, craning to see as Sebastian pages through it.

Though there's space next to Sebastian, just there, on the rumpled comforter, and Sebastian invited him upstairs, led him here to his bedroom.

He's looking at him too, an eyebrow arched. "Gil. Sit."

"I'm sitting," Gil says but he feels ungainly, too tall, and far too aware about the handful of inches he leaves between their thighs, far enough to not presume but close enough his skin pricks at Sebastian's leg so near his, mindful of where to put his elbow as he leans over to look at the pictures.

Just kiss him, he tells himself. That's why they're up here. Not to look at photos.

His stomach jumps. *Nerves and excitement are the same physiological response*, a long-ago coach had lectured them.

"I think you're forgetting how cool it was to have orange and black braces for Halloween," Gil says.

He can smell the shampoo in Sebastian's hair. Or no, that's the bubble bath maybe, drying on his shirt, the fabric still damp where it clings to his stomach.

Gil's going to see his abs. Touch the hair on his stomach. His throat is dry and he clears it.

"I think you're overlooking the fact that anyone who just wears their hockey equipment for Halloween is already a giant nerd."

"Only 'cause you wouldn't do it too."

"Not after seeing you stuff Joey into that goalie gear."

"What? We needed the whole team, though if I'd known, you could have gone as a coach, not as a—" Gil flips a few pages forward, then skips back when he gets to Thanksgiving. His breathing feels unsteady. "Yep, there you are, a superhero, how boring. Nice cape, you dork."

"It's not boring when your name starts with S and the costume's basically personalized for you."

"Is when you wear your hair like that as a fifth grader."

"That was sixth grade. Fifth was when we all went as aliens. But oh, wait, that's right. You were an alien who played hockey."

Gil gives the album a tug, but Sebastian doesn't let go of it. An invitation to wrestle it away from him, to get close and lean farther into him? Or maybe just his usual stubbornness, because the easy smile on his face isn't giving Gil a clue either way.

But—*oh*. That's a hand on Gil's thigh. Warm, through his jeans.

This is happening. A decade and Gil's back here again with Sebastian, on the edge of a bed, teetering before the fall toward each other.

So just kiss him already, Gil tells himself again.

"Please, if aliens can make it to Earth, they can easily identify the best sport we play here," he says instead. His face feels flushed. He's embarrassing himself, he knows, rambling on and on. He can't stop looking at Sebastian's mouth.

Sebastian shifts closer, his leg pressed against Gil's. "You had green paint inside your helmet for weeks."

"Is that picture in here? Let me find it and maybe we can let Frank know we need an extra-terrestrial themed night, might actually fill up the seats."

"Wouldn't you love that." Sebastian's finger draws a slow circle on Gil's thigh.

No, Gil thinks because he'll be gone, but Sebastian's still smiling and Gil can see the freckles across his nose and the tiny scar from when he took a hit to the boards in high school.

He's here now, though.

Gently, Gil kisses him. Softly, chastely, a peck against Sebastian's lips and he pulls back, breathes, waits as if there'll be a firm hand against his chest, pushing him away.

Sebastian just slides his palm higher on Gil's thigh and kisses him again.

Oh fuck yeah.

Sebastian's lips nudge his and Gil kisses him in return, tugging at his lower lip. Sebastian always liked that and he must still, because he lets Gil do it again and then a third time and Sebastian sighs against his cheek, tipping his head and opening his mouth just a little.

I missed you, Gil wants to whisper but instead he just moves slowly, like he might scare Sebastian off at any moment, like he might balk at the sudden words, the reminder of the years it's been. Just a brush of his tongue against Sebastian's lip, not the hard and wet surge forward he feels coiled in his muscles. Only this soft nudge of demure kisses that hold but an edge of the heat that builds through him.

Sex used to be so simple. So incredibly easy between them, falling into the same twin bed, hungry and eager and casual, where now Gil rests a hand on Sebastian's thigh lightly, nerves skittering through him with the thought it might be pushed away. Once, he'd have slid it higher. No, just reached for the button on Sebastian's jeans, pulled down his zipper, slipped from the bed to kneel on the floor with no worry, just the delight they'd found themselves here once more.

And he was so sure, back then. Confidently pushing forward where now he hesitates, moving only when Sebastian does, matching the tenor of his kisses, waiting, waiting, held breath and slow, careful hands.

Memories rise up, ones Gil didn't know he'd forgotten. The way Sebastian plucks at his shirt in an entreaty that he wants it gone. How he sighs when Gil scrapes his fingers through the hair on the back of his head, tickling his neck and yes, that's right, behind his ears. Sebastian likes that, Gil remembers now, pressing close into their kiss, the nudge of Sebastian's mouth a little firmer, a bit more insistent when Gil touches his thumbs into the hollows beneath his ears, tightens his fingers on the nape of his neck.

It comes back to him then, to use that momentum to tip Sebastian down onto the bed, the way their legs braid together and—*oh*—

This, he's thought about. Trapped by a layer of denim, that long ridge of Sebastian's cock in his jeans. Without thinking, Gil presses into it, his thigh between Sebastian's, and gets a soft inhale against his cheek, a gentle roll of Sebastian's hips.

Yes, this is how it used to go, the push and pull of their bodies before they'd even gotten their clothes off, a delightful bubble of frustration building at the barrier of bunched-up cotton instead of skin, the crease of fabric between them, constraining and stifling as they strained against it, rubbing into each other, panting.

Sebastian's not slowing down and Gil isn't either. No, this isn't rational thought but them lying tangled together on the bed, hips moving with each other, a warm hand up, under Gil's shirt, then tugging it off over his head, hands dipping beneath the waistband of his pants, Sebastian's hand wedged between jeans and Gil's ass, fingers digging in.

Gil's belt loosens, a fumbling hand between them. His pants, his zipper, and he groans into Sebastian's mouth, chasing after the light touch of Sebastian's fingers dancing over his cock.

But Sebastian just jerks his pants down around his thighs, his boxers, hands skimming over Gil's hips, up his sides, curling up over his shoulders and back down again, grabbing his ass and bringing their bodies flush.

Sebastian's wearing his clothes still and Gil rolls onto his side, his back, yanking fabric up, palming the bulge in the front of Sebastian's jeans. Skin, he wants skin, the coarse hair over Sebastian's chest and stomach, the shape of his body to trace his hands over. He thought he remembered but ten years and Sebastian's filled out, his shoulders broader, the coltish slimness of youth replaced with a sturdiness around his torso, a thickness to his ribs and back that was never there.

There's a difference too, in Sebastian's touch, something

less impatient and instead a slow confidence as Sebastian sits back on his knees and unfastens his pants.

Gil scrambles, kicking at his own pants, his socks, shoving them off like they burn while Sebastian finds a backpack on the floor and sets a condom and bottle of lube on the bedside table.

Gil reaches for him. Hands on Sebastian's waist, rising to his knees to get close to him. Tips his face up for a kiss and Sebastian leans down and skin to skin, Gil's arms around his neck, Sebastian's hands on him—this is perfect.

He kisses over Sebastian's neck, the line of his shoulder, scratching his fingers lightly down his chest, reaching for his cock. Sebastian's breath hitches and yeah, that's right, he always did that, does that, when Gil stroked him the first time. His breath catches again when Gil cradles his balls, mouth pressed to Sebastian's collarbone, kissing him there, fingers tugging on his balls, fist around the head of his cock. How could he have forgotten these details? The soft noise in the back of Sebastian's throat, the way Gil's thumb remembers on its own the slow circle to draw.

Or maybe that's just how he touches men, how he first learned to be with someone else and he never changed, knowing exactly the gentle press up, behind his balls that makes Sebastian's breath stutter, that exact amount of pressure, the finger Gil reaches back, stroking over his hole, yes, this is where he learned that, Sebastian's cheeks bright red, *Um, like—oh—yeah just like that, is it weird how good that feels?*

A warm hand cups his chin, lifts Gil's face and Sebastian stares down at him as Gil touches him. Eyes tracing over his, color rising to Sebastian's cheeks, his lips parting as his breath speeds up, eyes growing unfocused in that way just before he—

Gil leans up to capture his mouth in a kiss, squeezes his cock, and lets him go.

"Gil, shit, I—"

"Please," Gil says into his mouth as Sebastian gasps for air. Blindly, Gil reaches for the condom and hooks his other arm around Sebastian's neck, tugging, drawing him down onto the bed, onto Gil.

He wants this. Has wanted it since—he squirms closer, no matter that Sebastian's pressed to him, pushing him down into the mattress. Since forever. Since that last time in college, since he saw Sebastian back in Baltimore, since they kissed in the locker room, the salt tang of sweat and heat of their skin just a tease of the weight of Sebastian's body on his.

Like we used to, he nearly says but no, this is so much better. Slower, more deliberate than their younger selves, as Sebastian sits back on his knees, the flush on his face reaching down his neck, to his chest. Carefully, Sebastian rips open the condom and Gil lays back, watching as Sebastian smooths it over his cock. He's so gorgeous. He always has been but he's grown into himself now, carries his body with far more intention, nothing shy about him as his eyes rake over Gil, the bottle of lube in his hands.

"C'mon," Gil says, spreading his legs.

He's grown used to rolling over. Tucking his face into the pillow, closing his eyes and focusing on the flare of pleasure, touching himself, his mind far away from the man kneeling behind him.

Now, he stares. Watches how Sebastian squirts lube onto his fingers and then sets the bottle aside. Lifts his hips for him and lets his mouth fall open as Sebastian touches him, a slick finger slipping in.

Gil rocks against it, letting a breath out. Yes. This. And more.

He hauls Sebastian over him, his hands on his triceps, meeting him in a kiss, reaching between them to find Sebastian's cock and tipping his hips as he guides him to press slowly into Gil.

"Yeah," Gil whispers. It's a lot. Too much, nearly, but *oh* it's so good. He scoots his feet wider, his knees bent, Sebastian finally perfectly between his thighs.

"Oh God," Sebastian chokes. His face is beet-red, his back sweaty, his body trembling. "Oh Gil, I—"

Gil moves under him and Sebastian moans and rolls his hips.

Sebastian remembers too. Shaking, Gil reaches for himself, wedging his hand between their stomachs, gripping too hard, his teeth set in his lip. Fucking hell, Sebastian remembers perfectly, the angle, the pace, the heat stoking in Gil's gut.

Sebastian says something, his lips moving.

"What?" Gil gasps but then Sebastian's kissing him again, pressing him down into the pillow, hips pounding and *oh oh oh* this is what he hasn't had in the years that have slipped by, what hasn't ever been the same with anyone else, Sebastian's cock sliding right *there* inside of him, lighting him up from within in that perfect way only he can.

Gil clutches at him. Fingers dig into his shoulders, a fist in his hair, and in his ear, rough on a wash of hot breath, Sebastian whispers, "I got you, I got you."

Over and over again, Sebastian's arm hooked under Gil's knee, the two of them together, just them, only them—

Gil arches his back and Sebastian slams into him, warmth pooling in Gil's spine and as he strokes himself, gripping hard, one, two, three—he comes with a burst of heat through his body, a tingle that curls his toes, draws a gasp out of his mouth, one Sebastian answers, their lips together, fighting for breath.

He wraps his arms around Sebastian's shoulders, keeping them pressed together, skin sticking, sweaty and gasping. Lays there as his breath settles, as Sebastian finally shifts, sliding out of him, the condom ending up somewhere on the floor.

They should clean up. But Gil doesn't let him go, holding him too tight, smoothing his hair where he clutched it. He feathers his fingers through the strands, rubs his thumb into Sebastian's scalp. Gil presses his face to Sebastian's head, hair tickling his cheeks, his nose, and breathes him in.

And Sebastian doesn't move. Doesn't shift away, just lets their legs tangle together, turns his face into Gil's neck, his breath slowing, the rapid rise and fall of his back beneath Gil's hands easing until—

He's sleeping.

Gil smiles, his eyes closed, his face in Sebastian's hair. Yeah, Sebastian's sound asleep. An absolute mess on their stomachs, the bedsheets rumpled, damp, a pillow that landed on the floor somehow, and Sebastian's sound asleep, his body going lax in Gil's arms.

It's messy. It's perfect.

Sebastian doesn't wake as Gil kicks the blankets over them, but of course he doesn't. Gil could jump on the bed and Sebastian would be passed out still. Only rarely could Gil wake him for another round, walking his fingers over Sebastian's hip, finding his cock, stroking him until Sebastian finally rolled over him again, eyes bleary but his mouth already searching for Gil's.

Now, Gil curls around him. To wake him up would be a reminder of everything outside this bedroom, beyond the bounds of this mattress, and Gil likes it here. He's been trying to get back here for a decade. He's not leaving now.

Not with Sebastian to hold in his arms, a heaviness settling into Gil's own body.

Or is that happiness? He wonders as he drifts off too. Is that just the release of awful, aching loneliness and the rising memory of how it felt to sleep tangled up with this man's body, warming him through?

TWENTY-THREE

GIL IGNORES the soft noise that breaks into the room, his mind on the solid, warm weight of a body curled against his back as he drifts on the edge of sleep, beneath the arm draped over his waist, the rhythmic, soft puff of breath on his neck.

"Oh," Sebastian whispers.

Gil tucks himself closer, nosing against warm skin.

But Sebastian whips the blankets back, the mattress shifting as he rolls away, cool air rushing in.

Gil turns onto his stomach, pushing up on his elbows, blinking against the gray of early morning as Sebastian hops on one foot, pulling his boxers up.

"What?" Gil mumbles.

"Matty." Sebastian hurries out of the room.

Matty. Gil rubs his knuckles into his eye. Yes, that's right, that's a little voice calling out down the hall. He's in Sebastian's house—or his kid's or *Christopher's*, or whoever's. He came over here last night and...he dips his face into the pillow, smiling.

Yeah. Last night.

He flexes his feet, shimmies his hips. He feels fucking

amazing, his body heavy, his muscles loose, relaxed, a delicious ache from how very long it's been.

Sebastian sticks his head through the door.

C'mere, Gil wants to coax him with a crook of a finger.

"Your phone." Sebastian tosses it to him, and then shuts the door firmly.

In the hallway, a patter of small feet rushes past. Blearily, Gil stabs a finger at the screen.

When are you coming down to breakfast? Mom's written.

"Shit," Gil whispers, swinging his feet to the floor. *Give me a minute*, he texts back.

If you have time, I want to show you this place I found before your morning skate, she writes and then sends an address. *Come have some food and we can take a car over together?*

Quickly, Gil flicks to the map on his phone. The place isn't that far from him. But to get across the city to the hotel and back again, then to the rink for morning skate...

He squeezes his eyes shut. Oh, fucking hell. *Can I meet you there?* he texts, his face flaming.

A pause. Three little dots appear as she types. Disappear again, her deleting her message to restart it.

I'm at a friend's house, he types and then quickly erases it. She's smart. And she raised three boys. *Twenty minutes?* he sends instead.

See you then, she writes. *Want me to bring you something to eat?*

Please. He tosses his phone away like it's too hot to touch.

Yeah, great, him out on the town, sleeping somewhere else, and not exactly in a spot where he's going to be enjoying a slow shared breakfast. *Not a big deal*, he thinks but it's his *mom*.

Boxers, his pants—no, he's gross. They fell asleep last night and he can't see his mom like this. He has to shower, and he wore these clothes to the bar.

The first door he tries opens to a closet where clothes are just tossed on hangers, no order to them at all. The second is a bathroom, a towel crumpled on the floor, two empty bottles of shampoo in the shower and a third that's half-full, and a worn toothbrush, the bristles splayed out when there's a new one sitting in the drawer beneath the sink.

Gil opens it and scrubs at his teeth as the water heats in the shower. When he's done showering, he hangs the towel on a hook and tosses the empty bottles in the trash.

Once, when Sebastian's mom had been visiting, Gil had cleaned their entire dorm room, folded Sebastian's clothes and put them away, placed his textbooks on his bookshelf where they actually belonged, gathered up stray pens and pencils and set them in a coffee mug with *Rideau Men's Ice Hockey* stamped on the ceramic.

He wants to do the same now, though Sebastian had whined for a week afterward that he couldn't find anything, as if having all his T-shirts in one drawer and boxers in another instead of tangled together in a laundry basket was an awful sort of problem to have.

It was kind of cute. It's still cute and Gil smiles as he pokes through the mass of clothes in the closet. Suit pants that need to be ironed, a handful of ties, a pair of sneakers, and a pile of running shirts. The laundry basket shoved beneath the rack where clothes should be hung, but where only a few hangers sit, is more promising. Jeans, socks—he pulls out a T-shirt and sniffs it. Clean and it smells like laundry detergent, so Gil pulls it on, collecting boxers, the jeans, no matter how wrinkled they are, and socks.

There's a hole in the toe of one. Gil sighs and pulls it on

anyway. Sebastian always used to just steal his, though he's apparently broken the habit and gone back to wearing his own pairs far too long until they're threadbare and too thin.

Gil frowns, standing in the borrowed clothes. There's not a chance that...no, Chris is smaller than either of them. Pants that would fit Sebastian and Gil would gape loose around Chris's waist, and neither of them could get one of his tiny T-shirts on.

So no, if there's anything in here that belonged to Chris at one point, it's not this basket of freshly washed clothes, and of the few items on hangers, the suits there are tailored to fit only Sebastian.

And—cool, Sebastian's old Rideau jersey. Gil steps farther into the closet, pushing the suits aside to see it better. Though there's two of them, which is odd. It's always been tradition for the seniors to keep their own after their last home game, but to have an extra one?

61, reads the sleeve of Sebastian's as Gil looks it over, *Martin* stitched on the back, and the same on the one hanging behind it—

No. Not 61. 16.

Gil slowly pulls the hanger off the rod and stares down at the crest on the front of the jersey, *Rideau* stitched in bright white letters across the navy background.

Roussin, the back reads over a large *16*.

Sebastian has this? Gil's old jersey from so many years ago? And it's here, in his closet in San Francisco?

"Hey, so—what're you doing?"

Gil spins around. "Seb?"

Sebastian snorts softly in the doorway. "Oh sure, I don't mind, take my stuff. Nice outfit."

"You have this?" Gil asks, holding up the jersey.

"What?" Sebastian asks like he can't see it.

"My old jersey."

Sebastian flushes. "The team held onto it, you know, big star leaving for the pros, and they had it when the rest of our class graduated."

"Nobody told me that."

"Well, if you want it, go ahead." Sebastian rubs his hand up the back of his head. "I was, you know, moving, and most of my stuff isn't unpacked, but yeah, there it is."

Gil looks slowly around the room. "You unpacked these, at least."

"They were on top."

"Were you going to let me know you have it?"

"I—yeah, sure, I mean if you'd have wanted it you could have called the school, so I didn't know..." Sebastian shrugs. "But sure, take it."

"No, I mean..." Gil stares down at the jersey. Sebastian had this, the entire time. Kept it and looked at it and—

"So listen, I've got Matty up and I gotta feed him, but honestly, it's going to be way less confusing for him if he doesn't see you here, okay? He thinks it's just the two of us like normal and I'll have to explain what's going on at least twenty times."

Gil blinks. "You want me to..."

"If you don't mind."

Leave, is the end of that sentence. "Yeah," he says softly. "No, of course. I have to meet my mom."

"Take that, though, if you want."

But Gil hangs the jersey back up. He can't be carting it around with him. And—and the two blue sleeves hanging there next to each other seems more right.

"Or I can send it to you," Sebastian says.

"I'm going to see you in like two hours at the rink for morning skate."

"No, I mean—" Sebastian waves a hand. "Wherever you end up. After you get traded."

"Oh, right. Yeah. Thanks."

"Daddy!" a little voice calls.

"You have your pants on?" Sebastian asks, pushing away from the door. Over his shoulder he calls, "Yeah, see you at the rink."

"I have my pants on!" Matty calls.

"Later," Gil says.

A door opens and closes again. Still, through it, Gil can hear Sebastian's laugh. "That's not how you put pants on, kiddo."

Gil slips outside, but on the curb he pauses. His clothes from yesterday, he left them upstairs—but Sebastian can bring them to the rink. *Send them to his new address*, Gil thinks, frowning.

His shirt and pants, at least. Maybe his boxers. He'll never see his socks again, he's sure.

It's quicker to walk to the address Mom texted than to wait for a car or find a taxi, though he arrives out of breath from hurrying up one of the city's hills.

"Sorry," he says, taking the cup of coffee she holds out to him and the paper bag of food. "I was just. Yeah. Did you know Sebastian has a kid? I didn't, um." Gil opens the bag. A banana, two protein bars, and a warm, wrapped sandwich that smells like eggs and cheese. "Wow, thanks, you didn't have to get all this."

"He has a kid?"

"Matty. He's two. Thank you, this smells amazing."

"Is that where you were?"

Gil fits a bite of sandwich into his mouth, turning to stare at the row of houses before them. Trim, neat little yards with fences that line the sidewalk, brightly painted clapboards, shutters, spandrels and trim. Briefly, he imagines the team's reaction if he lived in a house painted in pastels, then chews and swallows quickly. No, it doesn't matter. These guys aren't his team and none of these are his house.

"I really don't think I should buy anything," he says.

"You were with Sebastian? Last night?"

"I'm really looking to get out of here soon," Gil says. Sebastian. He lives so close to here. Does he walk by here with Matty sometimes? Gil looks around like there's a preschool on the corner he'll spot if he turns fast enough.

"Are you two..." Mom's smiling. "Back together?"

He fits another bite of sandwich into his mouth. "And anyway I'm definitely not buying a baby-blue house."

"The Realtor left a lockbox. It's this one here, the red one. What's going on between you two?"

"Well let's go look at it, at least, while we're here." Gil starts up the porch steps.

"Gil."

"Cute place. I mean, not for me, but it's nice."

Mom ruffles his hair, but she moves past him, keying a code into the lockbox. "The sellers are willing to leave a lot of the furniture. Wouldn't that be nice? Not to have to spend all that time picking out all those details? It's a big house," Mom says, fitting the key into the lock. "Three bedrooms upstairs, and then there's another room you could turn into a bedroom that's downstairs in the back so it's a bit more private. Have you ever thought of having a rookie come live with you?"

"What, like I'm one of the old guys on the team?"

"You'd have the space if you ever did." Mom ushers him into the narrow hallway, a staircase leading up and a living room through an arched doorway. "There's all these nice original touches too. That molding up there? And these floors? The old wood is just so gorgeous. Come see the kitchen, it's just been redone."

"Most guys just get a condo."

"Most guys don't think about where their mother will stay when she comes to visit. I've spent enough of my life in hotel rooms as I follow hockey teams around," she says. "With all this space, Tommy could come too and have a comfortable spot. What if we were here for the holidays? Joey could come up too. You know you don't get enough days off to really make it worthwhile to fly out east."

Gil smooths his hand along the countertop. "I don't mind flying back to see you."

"But wouldn't it just be so cozy to spend that time here? Look, there's this little yard back here. You could get a dog."

"I travel too much."

"Luckily, I think you can afford a dog sitter," Mom says. "Having someone here waiting for you when you get home from an away game? Wouldn't that be so nice?"

"I never missed having a dog in San Diego," he says quickly. "Kind of seems like a lot of work."

"What about a cat, then?"

Gil wrinkles his nose. "A cat? Like Joey has?"

"He loves Mr. Stanley and it's so nice that he's not all by himself when he's not at the rink. If you're not going to get a pet, get yourself a roommate, at least, someone here to talk to."

"I do fine on my own, Mom."

"You do hockey. First thing in the morning until you go to sleep at night."

"Another person here, or a dog, it'd just make it harder to get focused."

She sighs and loops her arm through his. "Come upstairs and see the primary bedroom, at least."

When they step back outside, Gil squints up at the house as he finishes his coffee.

"So?" Mom asks.

"I dunno, it's fine."

286

"Fine?"

"Okay, yeah, it's great."

"I could really see you here, Gil. It's an easy drive to the rink, it's a lovely neighborhood, Sebastian said so, and wouldn't it be nice to live so close to him?"

Gil drags his foot along the sidewalk. He could see Sebastian all the time, not just at the rink. And wherever Sebastian ends up living when he's not with Matty, it won't be too far away. He'd want to stay close.

So they could hang out. Be together all the time, like they used to be. *He could come over*, Gil thinks, squinting up at the house. That primary bedroom with its gorgeous shower, the old-fashioned, ornate mantle above the fire-place. Sebastian waking up there, he tries to tentatively imagine.

His breath catches. Would he? Is that what might wait for him if...

His phone rings.

"Dad?" he answers.

"Good news," Dad says. "I told you, I'm getting this done for you."

"What?"

"Your trade. I'm getting you out of there."

"Wait. Now?" *So soon?* he wants to ask. Because he just...

No. Now. Right now, of course right now, as soon as possible. Isn't that what he wanted?

"So I've gotta talk to this Frank."

"Frank? Our GM, Frank?"

"He's not answering his phone."

"We have morning skate soon. I can check in with him then, see what's holding him up."

"We don't have time for that. I'll be there later today."

"There?" Gil asks. He looks at the bright sunshine

falling over the slope of the hill they're on, the cheerfully painted houses. "Here?"

"I'm flying in for your game tonight."

"You—you are?"

"I promised to fix this, didn't I?"

"All the way from Baltimore?"

"We've got a break in our preseason schedule, so I'm going to get a handle on what the hell is going on out there."

"Mom's here."

"Well," Dad huffs.

Mom points at the phone. "Is he—"

"That'll be fine," Dad says. "What's important is that we get this sorted out. And it'll be nice to see you and Joey play."

Against each other. With Dad, here. Watching them. Joey in San Diego's green and yellow and Gil...

He closes his eyes. No. No, no, no. The Sea Lions in their awful rink, the embarrassment of haphazard warm-ups, Dad seeing the locker room and everyone milling around, Steph joking with them. They can't even run a single play. They don't know their own power play, they can't—Dad can't—

"See you tonight," Dad says and when Gil slowly hangs up his phone, Mom rubs his shoulder, her lips pressed tightly together.

TWENTY-FOUR

GIL PACES THE BACK ALLEY, worrying at the knot on his tie. He gives Bloomer a quick nod when he arrives, and Jay a couple minutes later.

The rest of the team should be here too, by now. Gil should care that they're not. Say something when Pezer and Lomsy finally show up, strolling toward the rink like they've got all the time in the world.

He paces to the dumpster, spins, walks back.

Dad, he thinks when a car pulls up.

But Sebastian climbs out of the back, his collar unbuttoned, his tie in his hand. "Hey," he says, looping the tie around his neck. "How was the house? You didn't say at morning skate."

"The house?"

"That you saw?" Sebastian flips his collar up. "With your mom?"

"It was—" Gil rubs his palms together, trying to see down the alley past the car. "Yeah, good. Very..."

"Very?" Sebastian finally prompts.

"Um."

"You okay?" Sebastian asks.

"Big game tonight."

"Right." Sebastian quickly buttons up his shirt, fingers flexing. Gil watches but it feels like it's with a part of his brain that's been dimmed, the knowledge that he likes seeing Sebastian's hands move duller than it should be, buried beneath the twist in his stomach.

I wanted to enjoy this, he thinks even as he tries to stifle the notion. Seeing Sebastian step on the ice that morning, share a small smile with him. Let his eyes trace over him now with a rush of warmth flowing from the night before.

Gil had resigned himself, years ago, to never being close to Sebastian again. To never sharing the same space, breathing the same air...

And will they now?

No. He has to focus. Not drift on the wonder of what might come.

What might have come.

He's leaving.

"You get some rest this afternoon?" Sebastian asks.

Gil lay in bed at the hotel. He knows every spot on the ceiling, the details of the bland watercolor hung on the wall, each building outside the window. "Yeah, of course. I have to if I'm going to play well."

"You'll do great," Sebastian says.

That's not what he needs to hear. He needs a hard edge to a coach's voice telling Gil to calm the hell down and focus.

But Sebastian just steps into him, casts a quick look up and down the alley, and then adjusts the front of Gil's suit. "What's wrong?"

"Nothing."

"You sure?"

"Course."

"Hey." Sebastian runs his fingers under Gil's collar, straightening it. It tickles. "Last night, that was fun."

Gil needs to step back, put some air between them.

"Gil?"

"Huh?"

"You're a million miles away."

"I'm just—" Gil wants to fuss with his tie, but Sebastian's too close to him. *C'mere*, Sebastian would probably say if he knew of the jump in Gil's gut. He'd hug him. Hold him. Gil frowns. No, that's not what he needs. "The game's soon."

Sebastian ducks closer, trying to catch his eye. "Really, are you okay?"

"I said I was."

"What happened?"

"Nothing."

"Gil."

"My dad's coming to watch."

"Oh."

"This'll be good." Gil rubs his palms together. He wants to keep moving, it's worse to stand still.

"Okay."

"It's what I need."

"Gil..."

A car turns down the alley, bright lights against the gloom of dark bricks and the shadows of the buildings rising up above them. It's a nicer one than Sebastian took, one of the rideshares you have to pay extra for.

Of course it is. Because *that's* Dad. Getting out of his car, looking up and down the alley, his expression calm as he scans the façade of the building with its crumbling bricks.

Gil twists away, smoothing his jacket.

"Gil—" Sebastian starts.

"He's here, I—Dad! Hey."

Sebastian squeezes Gil's elbow. "I'll see you in there," he murmurs and ducks inside.

"Gil," Dad says as he softly shuts the car door. "You're not warming up?"

Gil stutter steps. "I wanted to see you."

"Big game." Dad brushes past him toward the rink. "I've coached here. Looks even worse having you playing here, kid."

Gil straightens his tie. It feels wrong, like he wound it too tightly around his neck, or like this shirt doesn't fit, the collar stretched against his throat.

Dad's hand settles on his shoulder, firm and warm. "I want better for you, Gil."

"Locker rooms are this way," Gil mutters, side-stepping a puddle. "And the offices are upstairs. I can try to find Frank for you."

Though there's a crowd to get through first. Gil clenches his teeth at Pezer and Lomsy lounging in the hallway, both of them still in their suits, ties loosened, phones in their hands as they relax, clearly no intention of hitting the exercise bikes or starting to stretch out.

"For real?" Lomsy says, pointing between Gil and Dad with a coffee cup in his hand. "Rooster, I knew you were a Roussin, but Daddy-o is here? Nathan Lomas, so great to meet you. I grew up watching you play."

Dad puts on his cheerful smile and shakes Lomsy's hand. "Looking forward to seeing you out there tonight."

Gil tries to shrug off the arm Lomsy tosses over his shoulder. Dad isn't looking forward to anything of the sort.

But Lomsy doesn't budge. "Gil ran us ragged in practice today, must have learned a thing or two from you. Rooster, how many times did you yell at us about that zone entry drill?"

Too many, because by the time they finished, they didn't have time to finesse their power play. *Move them along*, he'd wanted to tell Sebastian. Maybe if San Diego takes any penalties tonight they can just talk to the refs and politely decline the opportunity to be a man up for two minutes, since they'll be running around like chickens that whole time. Or worse—watching San Diego get the puck and go on a breakaway to score a shorthanded goal that will make the highlight reels while Gil and his team are still figuring out where to stand.

"Success is in the preparation," Dad says.

"Yep, that's where you got it from, Rooster." Lomsy smacks his shoulder.

"You didn't have to come here," Gil mumbles when Lomsy finally lets them go.

"I told you I'd get you out of here, and I'm going to," Dad says. "I just need to talk to Frank. Already ran it by your agent, so we're good there. Just need the go-ahead from the guys here."

"You talked to Melissa?"

"Course I did, I've been on the phone with her all week. I talked to my team's GM. You remember Bob, right? You might have to play wing instead of center, but I think I can get you a spot."

"A spot? You mean on your roster, playing for you?"

"If I can't get you on another team, I can at least get you on mine. I need to offload some of our guys anyway. They're not pulling their weight. We're going on a deep playoff run this year, Gil, and we need the right people in place to do it."

"There's really a spot for me?"

"There's a spot for a forward. You gonna go after it?" Dad jostles his arm.

"Of course," Gil says quickly. "Of course I am."

"Good. Then show us what you've got tonight, yeah?"

"Yeah," Gil says. Nods. "Yeah, I—I will."

"No going easy on your old team."

Gil frowns. "Easy on Joey? Never."

"You can fly back with me tonight. How does that sound? Get your things packed and we'll head straight to the airport."

The hotel room. It fills his mind quickly, his half of it neat, Sebastian's half scattered with socks, his phone charger, a small-scale model of the hurricane that hit his bedroom at his son's house.

Wait, Gil thinks. Tonight. Achingly tired from the first game of preseason, clean, crisp sheets on that king bed, Sebastian's weight pressing him into the mattress, their bodies moving together. *You played great*, Sebastian will whisper, ignoring Gil's mistakes, focusing on what he did well, fingers laced together, foreheads touching.

But. No. Baltimore. Playing for his hometown team. Playing for Dad.

"That'd be perfect," Gil says. Yeah, packing his things tonight, putting on Baltimore's orange and blue instead of this awful red and gold. Landing in the familiar airport there, back in his bedroom to sleep, finding a house to buy in neighborhoods he's familiar with.

He can see Tommy whenever he wants. Mom, too.

And Sebastian—here in this rink with this team. Trying to shape them into something better, one at a time. Gentle with each of them, Steph joking around with the guys, wheedling and coaxing and charming them toward a better sort of hockey. Sebastian with his son, finding a spot to live, carving out more years of his life here in San Francisco. *Buddy will be here*, and Gil frowns at the thought. What does it matter if the Martins' dog is out here in California instead of in Maryland, the Martins' house sold, strangers across the back fence?

Focus, he tells himself. Hockey. The potential of a trade, there for the taking if he can just reach out and grab it. It's up to him to work hard enough, push himself as far as he needs to, and then stretch and push even more.

"Baltimore," he says like he's trying the word out.

"Excited to watch you tonight, kid." Dad squeezes his shoulder.

Gil stares down at his feet, letting himself be hugged into Dad's side. Yeah. Dad watching. This team, and Gil out there. *Fuck*, he thinks.

"The offices are up here." Gil leads Dad toward the stairs.

Sebastian's walking down them and he pauses midway. "Hey, Mr. Roussin, that you?"

Dad laughs. "Sebastian? I guess it's true that you're really coaching?"

Sebastian holds out his hand and shakes Dad's. "Yes, I'm really coaching."

"And here I didn't think I'd ever see you at an NHL rink. Or at least anywhere but in the stands of one."

"Well, look at me now."

"Now how about that. You ready to wrangle this supposed team?"

"Dad," Gil says softly.

"Need me to look over the game plan?" Dad claps Sebastian's arm.

"I think we got it," Sebastian says. "Hey, mind if I steal Gil for a minute?"

"Not at all. Point me toward your offices," Dad says. "I got a trade to finagle."

"The offices? If there's something you need, I'd be happy to get it for you."

"Just your GM," Dad says.

"You have a pass?"

"Seb," Gil murmurs.

"A pass?" Dad laughs again.

"Players and staff only up these stairs, I'm afraid," Sebastian says.

"Dad needs to talk to Frank," Gil says.

"He's up here, right?" Dad points to the stairs. "It'll only be a minute." He doesn't wait for an answer, just heads up them with a last clap on Sebastian's arm.

"Sorry," Gil says. Weakly, he calls out, "Dad?"

But Dad keeps going, disappearing up the staircase.

"I'm sorry. He's just..."

"Like that, yeah." Sebastian lets out a breath. "Well, Frank'll have to deal with him. It's not like we have security."

"Do we even have passes?"

"There's a box of blank ones in a closet, but nobody has any idea how to print anything on them."

Gil tries to picture it, a security guard up there telling Dad firmly, politely, to turn back, that he needs ID, that he requires permission, that they can't just let anyone wander around. Gil's face flushes. Of course people aren't allowed to walk around arenas on their own. Press passes, player's badge, staff with lanyards around their necks and cards to swipe to open locked doors. Any arena has all of that, exactly like they should.

"Gil?"

"Dad said he can get me traded to his team tonight."

"Oh. That's—playing for your dad? Really? That's what you'd want to—okay."

"As a wing. He doesn't have room for me at center."

"You hate playing wing."

"If I can play well enough tonight, the spot's mine." *I*

can't do this, he wants to say, but that's ridiculous, he has to do this, this is what he wanted: a way out of here, off this team.

But no, he's going to choke. Go out there and fumble the face-off. Miss every pass coming toward him, get his feet tangled like a little kid, like it's his first time on skates.

Dad's here, watching him. None of the distance of at least a TV broadcast between them, but him right here in the arena. What tickets did he get? Probably just called a guy who knows a guy and he'll be sitting behind the bench. Gil gave Mom his comped tickets for the players' box, so she'll be sitting with other families, whatever kids have come to the game, partners and spouses and dates, but Dad...

"I have to go."

"Gil—"

"I need to warm up, I have to—I'm late, already."

Sebastian tugs on Gil's suit jacket to straighten it. "You really might be out of here tonight?"

"That's the plan."

"Okay." Sebastian nods, squinting down the hall.

Gil loosens his tie. He needs to get changed. Dressed. Warmed up, like Dad said. Why hasn't Gil started that by now? He's not going to be ready.

"Hey." Sebastian steps toward him.

Gil twists away, heading for the locker room, the exercise bike where he can sweat out the extra energy dogging him, get his head on straight.

When he puts on his gear, he does it carefully, focused. *Calm*, he tells himself, his pulse jumping too hard beneath his skin. Right shin pad, then left. Right sock, left sock, right leg into his pants, then his left leg. Hitch them up to his waist, tie the laces, tighten the belt, and sit again to put his right foot into his skate. How many times has he gotten dressed for hockey in his life? Practices, games, tying his right skate, his left, tape around one shin and then the next.

Feet appear in front of him, shiny dress shoes and ironed slacks.

Sebastian, he thinks. Warm hands, fingers light through his hair. *It'll be okay,* Seb saying, drawing him into a tight, long hug and holding him until Gil's pulse calms.

But when Gil looks up, it's Mitcher.

"Is that your dad?" Mitcher asks. "Can I get an introduction?"

"What?"

"In the hallway out there, your dad? Bert Roussin? I'd love to meet him. What a hell of a player he was."

"He's out there? Um, yeah, just...yeah." Gil stands, feeling awkwardly too tall in his skates. Nobody else is even getting dressed yet. *Get ready*, he wants to snap at them, but oh, the clock—no, he's early. Really early.

Early enough that Dad's still in the hallway, done with his chat with Frank, but not yet headed up to his seats.

"Get ready to say goodbye to that," Dad says when he sees Gil, pointing at Gil's red socks.

Gil looks down at himself. "Yeah?"

"They're not pulling you to sit out this game ahead of a trade, so you'll still be out there, but I've got my GM watching you tonight and I did a number on that Frank."

"Working a trade?" Mitcher asks, squeezing Gil's shoulders.

"This is Mitcher," Gil says. Gone, really gone? He'll be on the visitors bench next time he plays here.

If Dad gives him playing time. Gil frowns, watching Dad and Mitcher shake hands. Of course Dad'll give him playing time. That's ridiculous that he wouldn't have a starting spot on the Baltimore roster.

"I'm on left wing. It's been a real pleasure playing with

Gil at center for my line," Mitcher says. "And I gotta say, Mr. Roussin, I hope I don't sound like too much of a fan, but watching Baltimore the last few years? I love the systems you're running for your team. You're miles ahead of the rest of the league with handling the puck in the offensive zone."

"Just Bert, please," Dad says. "Nice of you to say so. I got some pushback from our veteran forwards when I shook things up."

"The game changes," Mitcher says. "We gotta change with it."

"That's what I always say," Dad says. "So Mitcher, is it? Have you been stuck here on this team for long?"

Gil's sweating. Shouldn't the arena be cooler than it is? The ice'll be shitty if they don't keep it cold enough, slushy and slow, pucks jumping over the blades of their sticks, taking the wrong bounces, hard to predict where they'll end up.

Gil should check. Find someone who works in the building, make sure everything's working just right, exactly as it should.

But it's just Steph he bumps into, wearing a slim, dark dress with a blazer over it, her skates traded for a pair of heels.

"Mr. Roussin, glad to have found you. You'll be starting tonight."

"Starting?" Gil asks like he's never heard the word.

"With Mitcher on your left wing, and Jay on your right. Talk to him, would you? I'm a little worried he's going to shit himself. Calm him down, okay?"

"Okay," Gil says. Calm. Yes.

"And breathe too, Gil. I know you're excited that the great Bert Roussin is here, you ever heard of him? Apparently he's a big deal. I wouldn't know." She leans in, holding up her clipboard like she's telling him a secret. "Women's hockey, and all."

He's supposed to smile at that. A joke, her teasing him. A good thing he went back and apologized to her, of course it was. *Nice of you*, Sebastian had said. "Where's Sebastian?"

"Martin? I sent him to try to herd Hal toward the locker room to get dressed. You need him?"

"I—yes."

"I'll grab him," Steph says.

Gil sags back against the wall as she walks off. Mitcher and Dad are still talking. *Go over there*, he tells himself. Be friendly, be polite.

It's cooler closer to the ice, and there's a rack of extra sticks to slip behind so he can lean against the cold concrete wall, hidden from the arena by the curtain that hangs in front of the tunnel leading to the bench.

He should get his stick, use the extra time to get some practice in. Focus. Get back to work.

"Gil?" Sebastian asks, peeking around the rack.

"I'm fine."

Sebastian steps closer. "Hi," he says. "Look at me."

"I have to, I—"

"Nope, just right here, okay?"

Warm hands in Gil's, Sebastian's eyes on him. Slowly, Sebastian takes a breath and lets it out. What's he doing? Gil has to *go*.

"I can't wait to watch Matty play sports when he gets bigger," Sebastian says.

He's talking too quietly. Gil can barely hear him over the music pumping through the arena, over the pounding of his blood.

"Or get into music or be in a play, whatever he wants to do. He was a tiny baby and the only thing he could manage was to chew on his fists, but someday he'll be up there, having worked so hard, practiced so much. I will be an utter wreck I'll be so proud of him getting to show off what he can do."

"Seb—"

"You're okay," Sebastian says, so seriously that Gil's probably supposed to believe him. "You're nervous. It's a big game. Your dad's here watching, Joey'll be out there. It's okay to be anxious. That's all this is. Just take a breath."

"I don't want to."

"Just one." Sebastian squeezes Gil's hands.

"Play. I don't want to play."

Who said that? Not him, of course not him.

"I know," Sebastian says and something fractures in Gil's chest, watery and weak. "But you love hockey, Gil. You're going to do great."

"I'm not, you said I can't shoot, I don't play well anymore, I'm not good enough to—"

"You're going to go out there and just play." Sebastian steps closer, their hands crowded between their bodies. "It's only a game."

It's not. He can't.

Sebastian squeezes his hands again.

"Okay," Gil gets out.

"You got this."

"I don't."

"I'm going to be right there with you. Now say it back to me. You got this."

Sebastian, on the bench in his suit, leaning down to talk to players, conferring with Steph as the game develops, patting them on their helmets in encouragement.

"I—" Gil has to swallow, his mouth dry. "I got this."

"There you go." Sebastian squeezes his hands once more.

When Gil steps on the ice for warm-ups, his skin itches with the feel of cameras on him. On TV, there's a split screen of him, of Joey, and of Dad, somewhere in the arena watching them.

Sebastian steps out onto the bench. He doesn't need to be out here. Coaches don't come out for warm-ups.

Gil takes a breath and skates a long, slow lap around their half of the ice, trying to ignore the swarm of green and yellow circling the other end.

"Rooster!" someone shouts. Hux, of course, grinning at him from across the red line. "Hey, Baby Roo! Get over here!"

"Ready to get your ass handed to you?" Joey calls to him, stopping with a spray of snow that covers Gil's skates.

Gil fumbles for a water bottle, pretending he's thirsty. He can see Seb from the corner of his eye, his dark slacks, the shine of his dress shoes.

Sebastian leans his elbows against the boards, hanging over them and grinning at Joey. "They're letting you skate with the big kids?" he calls in a joking, half biting chirp.

Joey laughs, delighted by being teased, and Hux circles toward him, making exaggerated baby-talk noises at Joey.

"You got this," Seb says softly, his words just for Gil.

Gil squirts water in his mouth.

A tap, a gentle one, on his helmet. *One, two, three*, right in a row. Gil sucks in a breath.

"Thanks," he gets out.

"Go herd this bunch of cats into something like a warm-up," Sebastian says and yes, that's a good idea, easier to deal with than the looming game. Warm-ups, Gil can handle warm-ups. Line rushes, shots on Hal, loops around their half of the ice to get the feel of their skates.

"You gonna stay out here?" Gil asks. *It's fine if not, it's fine, it's fine, it's—*

"Course," Sebastian says.

"Thanks," Gil says again and makes himself glide away.

Sebastian, on the bench. Here, at the rink. What the hell would Gil do tonight if he weren't here?

And how, possibly, can Gil ever go back to playing without him?

TWENTY-FIVE

Was it just two days ago that he was playing pickup here?

The national anthem blares through the arena as Gil stands on the blue line, his helmet in his hand.

That little girl, Gil remembers. Her slow, clumsy, exuberant way up this same sheet of ice, cheering for herself as she went.

He holds his stick too tightly as he glides to center ice for the opening face-off. She'd had such a good time.

"Ready?" Joey asks, across from him at the face-off dot.

Oh. Of course. San Diego's letting Joey start the game. *Roussin*, both of their jerseys say, the camera high above them as they bend over, filming their backs. The announcers are mentioning Dad right now, cutting to a shot of him in the crowd. Of course this is all arranged for the showcase of the Roussins here in this building, because there's no way Joey's got a top line spot.

Or does he? Already?

Gil's stomach jumps.

"No," he says and it surprises Joey, his head coming up as the whistle blows and the puck drops.

It gives Gil an extra half second. *Use it*, he tells himself, digging for the puck, his shoulder against Joey's. He's faster on draws, he should get it, but Joey shifts his weight, both of them going down to their knees—

"C'mon," Gil grunts. *Not fair*, he means, though a stick flashes in his vision, and it's his team, red socks behind it—

A cheer goes up as Gil jumps back to his feet, chasing after the play as it rushes down the ice.

But that's the goal horn. And arms thrown in the air, gold and red on the sleeves of the jersey, Hux cursing and smacking the puck away from the net as Mitcher celebrates.

"That's how we fucking do it!" Mitcher shouts, hugging Jay. Gil gets grabbed too.

We scored? he wants to ask. *When?*

"One on the board, let's do it again boys, whad'ya say?"

"Not bad," Steph says when they get to the bench, a pat each on their helmets. "That's what we like to see."

"I didn't—" Gil stops. *I didn't do anything*, he was going to say. No. They scored. That's good. That's shocking, actually. Caught San Diego flat-footed, probably overly confident about this game.

But Mitcher scored. Gil fell down.

He hunches forward, staring at the players on the ice whizzing past him. *You've got this*, Sebastian had said. He feels sick.

On the ice, Hux passes to Little. Joey's not out there but no, of course he isn't, because if his line got scored on only seconds into the game, he got pulled. Gil glances down the row of offensive players between him and the end of the bench, the bustle of coaches, and sure enough that's San Diego's coach bent over, talking to Joey and fuck, Gil knows that stance he has, the body language, the quick way Joey's nodding, trying to get him to just shut up and get the lecture over with, finish having his ass handed to him.

Sorry, Gil wants to tell him. But what was he going to do, let Joey win that draw? Of course not. Dad's watching.

"Go," Steph says as the puck zips down to their defensive zone and then back again, patting Gil's shoulder. He jumps the boards, joining the play, his stick on the ice, head up—the puck zings toward him from Pezer's pass before he heads to the bench too and then Mitcher and Jay are out on the ice with Gil. Zone entries, just like they practiced. He steps to the side and the San Diego winger takes the bait like Gil knew he would, opening up a lane to pass to Jay.

Good. Yes. *Go*, he tells himself and he streaks toward the net, Mitcher crossing below him to get to the far post as Jay brings the puck in wide, faking a shot from the top of the circle, then passing smoothly, evenly to Gil—

A roar goes up. *Goal*, he wants to believe in the moment before the whistle blows, but no goal horn sounds and the puck sits idle, coming to a stop below the goal line where Gil shot it wide of the net.

What?

Oh.

Joey. On the ice, perfectly still.

"I didn't fucking see him," Mitcher is shouting, tackled to the ice.

"That was bullshit," Hux screams in Mitcher's face, his gloves off, reaching for the collar of Mitcher's jersey. "Fucking bullshit, you fucking little—"

When did Joey even get on the ice? And why isn't he moving?

"He fucking tripped into the net!" Mitcher roars back. Fists swing, and someone grabs Gil's jersey, too, drawing him into the fight. Gil stares blankly at the guy's face, someone new to San Diego, who he doesn't know, and his grip loosens, surprise in the guy's expression when Gil

306

doesn't start to fight him but instead slowly kneels on the ice.

"Joey?" he asks. "Hey, Joey, are you—Joey? Joey!"

Joey's eyes blink open. A grin. "Did I save it?"

"Are you okay?" Gil asks. The replay's on the jumbotron, Joey sailing through the air from Mitcher's hit, feet clear off the ice, striking hard into the post of the net. "Is your head okay? Joey?"

"Easy there, kid," a voice says. The trainer, the Mountain Lions' trainer, Sammy, who saw Gil through months of rehab for his ankle. "There you go, you're alright. Can you sit up?"

"I'm good," Joey says, rolling onto his knees.

Gil grabs his arm, helping him as he stands. Behind him, the sound of punching and the crowd cheering. Gil keeps himself between the fight and Joey, leaning close to him. "Did you hit your head? That looked bad."

"Just knocked the wind out of me," Joey says. "Who was that? I'm going to lay him out."

"You sure?"

"That I'm fine? He's not going to be when I'm done with him."

"Joey, your head went right into the post."

"I'm fine. What're you gonna do, call Mom down here? Fuck off, Gil. I'm good."

Gil lets him go, Joey adjusting his helmet as he glides back to the bench, Sammy jogging next to him.

Though Joey doesn't head down the tunnel from there. Just exchanges a few words with Sammy and then he sits on the bench, grabbing his water bottle.

"Hey!" Gil shouts, but Joey and Sammy don't look over.

"Where's the concussion spotter?" Gil asks as he gets on the bench. "Seb? Sebastian—" Coach Martin, he should be calling him right now. Gil grabs the sleeve of his suit, clumsy in his gloves. "That hit, is Joey okay? His head, on the replay, and he was just laying there, he should be in the quiet room, his head—"

"Gil." Sebastian's voice is quiet below the crowd that's still stirred up and the music that blares in the pause before play resumes.

"Yeah?"

Sebastian squats down, bending so he's eye to eye with Gil. "You're going to be pissed as all hell at yourself if you don't do your best this game."

"He had a concussion a couple years ago, so if he gets one again—"

Sebastian touches his shoulder, not so different than one of Steph's pats, but Sebastian's hand stays a moment longer. "The team's gonna take care of Joey, okay? Focus on your game."

I can't, he nearly says. But no. *I don't want to*, he really means. The idea of Joey hurt over there—

No, what is he doing?

Dad's watching him. Three periods to play and he needs to not fall over himself at face-offs, not let himself get distracted. Dad came all this way just for this game, and he's here, somewhere in the arena, his eyes on Gil, even while Gil's on the bench.

"Okay," he says softly.

"I'll try to get an answer for you, though," Sebastian says. "I know you're worried."

"Thanks." Gil turns back to the game. But still the urge to peer down toward Joey on the other bench lingers, pulling his mind from the ice in front of him, Sebastian still standing just behind him.

———

"FUCKING HELL!" Pezer shouts, jumping around the locker room. "We did it! We did it!"

"You did it!" Lomsy yells right in his face.

"No, you did it!" Pezer hollers back and they hug, nearly knocking over the trash can.

"Well damn," Mitch says. He's smiling. Of course he is; he got two goals.

Gil should be smiling too. He got an assist on the second one.

Joey missed a pass in the third period. Gil yanks at his pads, tossing them onto the hooks in his stall. Jersey and socks off and dumped in his locker, his skates left on the floor in front of the bench—he pulls his shirt off over his head as he heads for the shower. Joey should have had that pass, but it looked like he just misjudged it, his stick in the wrong spot for where the puck was heading. And that hit he took from Bloomer a shift earlier—his head didn't connect with the boards, but it looked hard enough to rattle his teeth.

Fucking don't, Gil had wanted to snap at Bloomer on the bench. But no, it's hockey, of course Joey's going to take a hit when he goes for the puck.

Gil towels off haphazardly and shrugs on his suit jacket as he pushes into the hallway, wet hair dripping into his eyes, his body still flushed from the game so he feels like he's sweating under his dress shirt and his slacks.

Sebastian's in the hallway. Gil nearly bumps into him.

"Your dad went that way," Sebastian says and points.

Oh. Yeah. Gil nods. He should be finding Dad right now.

Joey, he thinks, peering toward the curtain that separates the hallway between their locker room and the visitors'.

"Real good game, Gil," Steph says, reaching to shake his

hand before he's even realized she's standing there too. *I have to go*, he wants to tell her, not be caught here in the hall as she holds onto his hand and claps his arm. "I think you really did something for the team, fired them up with the way you were playing out there."

"Thank you," Gil gets out. Some of the San Diego players are in the hallway down there. He can just see them if he peers past her.

"Not a single person expected us to pull out a win," she says. "I have to admit, I might have been among them."

"You did great too," Gil says, the words formed by habit. Did she? He can't remember, just knows he stared at her as she spoke in the locker room between periods, her words rushing past him.

"I'm real proud of you all." She finally lets go of him to smack Sebastian's shoulder. "I think we might really have something here, between the two of you and these guys."

"Good," Gil says.

"Good?" She smiles up at him.

There's something in the way she's looking at him. Oh, yes, that's right. Needling him about staying. But no, Gil can't. He has to go, right now.

"I have to find my brother," Gil says.

"Oh, thought you were looking for your dad," Steph says. "If you want him, he was just talking with Frank."

Right. Okay.

Gil's stomach clenches. So this is it, then. Dad'll come back, a smile on his face and Gil will...he glances back toward the locker room where Jay's gathering the shirts and socks that fell short of the laundry bin. He'll pack up his gear. Wrap his sticks together, be on a plane tonight.

And Sebastian...

"I—" Gil starts.

"Yeah," Sebastian says softly.

"What about that win?" Mitcher's arm curls around Gil's shoulders. "Fucking beauty, wasn't it? And here I didn't think we'd pull that out."

Bye, he needs to say to Sebastian. Let him know he'll gather his things from the hotel room and that'll...that'll be it. The door snicking closed, Gil's duffle in his hand, and a car taking him to the airport.

Good, he thinks. It's what he wanted. "I gotta find Joey," Gil says and ducks away, pushing through the curtain to the crowd of equipment managers, trainers, and coaching staff in the hallway on the other side of it.

His old coach shakes his hand. Sammy, the trainer, gives him a one-two punch, light on his arm. "Hell of a game," Sammy says. "How's that ankle feeling these days?"

"Joey?" Gil asks.

"Whining that he doesn't need stitches, just superglue his face back together, that'll be fine." Sammy laughs. "Joey! Get out here, your big brother wants a word."

Gil grabs Joey's chin as soon as he steps into the hallway. His jaw is bruised, and yeah, there's a cut there, a bad one. "You okay? Bloomer do that to you?"

Joey smacks his hand away. "I can't believe you beat us, but hey, at least you didn't score. Who's that guy? Putting up two goals?"

"Mitcher," Gil says. "He hit you in the first period."

Which Joey should know. He had all game to watch the replay and he'd laid a solid hit on Mitcher only a couple shifts later. Retaliation, Gil had thought, but had Joey not known that's who he was checking?

"Hell of a player," Joey says. "Sucks he's stuck with you lot. C'mon, Gil, get off."

But Gil leans in to look at the cut. "Does it hurt?"

"Yeah when you shove your finger into it." Joey smacks at his hands again.

"Little Roo definitely took a bruise to his ego, too," Sammy says.

"Is his head okay?" Gil asks.

"Was it ever?" Sammy asks.

Joey laughs and gives Gil a shove backward.

"You seem off," Gil says.

"Fuck you, is this you telling me I didn't play well? You guys didn't win by that much. We almost had you."

"No, it's not. I'm worried about you."

"You're as bad as Mom. Oh, look, what'd you do, call her? Hi, yes, I'm fine."

"My boys," Mom says, cupping Gil's cheek and then examining the cut on Joey's face. "Honey, that'll leave a scar. Don't you want that taken care of?"

"Mom, I'm fine. And call Gil off. I'm good, okay?"

Mom frowns, but she draws her hand back from him. "What a nice game, you two. That was so fun to watch. And Gil, everyone in the team's box was just so nice. What a treat to get to meet them. You'll have to have them over once you get settled."

Gil glances down the hallway. No, he's leaving. He won't need to learn all the names of the players' families. And besides, he knows the guys in Baltimore, most of them anyway.

Of course he's not settling down here. No red house. *No Sebastian*, he thinks and suddenly, clearly pictures the polished wood floor of that primary bedroom littered with stray socks.

No. Back East will be great. Mom can come to whichever games she wants to, a short drive up from Annapolis. He'll be close enough to stop by for lunch with her on his days off, meet her for dinner without a flight across the country. *Good*, he thinks. Yes, great. All of it.

"I'll let you two go." Mom squeezes Gil's elbow. *Before*

your dad gets here, she doesn't have to say, an old, uncomfortably familiar dance like they're two ends of a magnet, a careful distance kept between them as Mom slips out of a hockey rink through one door, Dad entering another one.

Though they'd both come to his first college game. Sat together, even. Well, near each other, at least. Julie Martin had been between them but that had been good enough, that he'd been able to look across the rink from the bench and see them both there. *Embarrassing,* he had whispered to Sebastian when really, his chest had glowed warm that they'd both managed to come and be in one space for an entire evening, just for him.

Stay, he wants to say now, but no, it's a fantasy that they'd all share a moment together after the game, laugh that the Sea Lions really did pull out a win, spend a moment as the four of them before they scatter again.

"Mom," Gil says. *Bye, I'll see you at the hotel in a bit,* he needs to say next. "You think Joey's okay?"

"I think he'll be even more handsome with a scar, but really Joey, no, don't pick at it."

"It's itchy."

"His head," Gil says.

"Gil, shut up, would you? You're as bad as Mom."

Gil frowns. "You just said that."

"Well you fucking are."

"Language, Joey, please," Mom says.

"You just said I'm as bad as Mom. You said it a minute ago."

"Maybe I fu—sorry. Maybe I mean it." Joey leans past him to call down the hallway, "Hey, take him back, would you? He's such a pain, you deal with him."

Gil turns. It's Sebastian Joey's talking to, just there, ducking through the curtain, his eyes on Gil.

"I really don't think he's okay," Gil says.

"Hey," Sebastian says and to Gil's surprise, he catches his arm. "I need to talk to you."

"Coach Sebastian," Joey says and plucks at the lapels of Sebastian's suit. "Look at you, big boss man. Do you make Gil do extra sprints?"

"I'm going to leave you boys. Goodnight, safe flight tonight, Joey," Mom says.

But Sebastian catches her eye and shakes his head. "No, don't—not yet. Gil, I have to tell you something."

"It's that you have to do extra sprints," Joey says.

Gil peers past Sebastian. "See? You just said that again."

"It's a fucking joke!"

"Joey," Mom says.

"Gil," Sebastian says. "Gil, Frank just told me that Mitcher—hey, look at me, okay?"

"I don't think Joey's alright," Gil says.

"I'm going to go," Mom says. "I—oh." Her mouth presses into a thin line.

Gil can feel Dad behind him, even before he turns. "Dad. Hey."

"Boys, what a game," Dad says. "Well. Hello there. How are you?"

"Hello, Bert," Mom says.

The air feels thick. Yeah, Gil shouldn't have wished for this. It's awful, Mom's tight smile, Dad's sharp, short nod.

A touch on his arm. Sebastian's still holding Gil's elbow and through his suit jacket, his dress shirt, he can feel Sebastian's thumb moving, stroking gently back and forth.

Gil wants to lean into him. *Let's never be like this*, he wants to whisper. Shake on it, bump their fists together and make a rocket of the gesture, laughing at their dumb, childish game.

Bye, Gil needs to say to him. He's about to leave here

with Dad, pull away from the warm, soothing touch of Sebastian's hand on his arm.

"Gil," Seb whispers. "I'm so sorry."

"About what?" Gil asks, though he doesn't bother to wait, just turns to Dad. "Hey, do you think Joey's okay from that hit?"

"Gilbert!" Joey says, throwing up his hands.

"We'll get you next time, kid," Dad says, smacking Gil's shoulder.

"Get me what?" Gil asks. "Joey, don't call me that."

Sebastian draws him a step closer. Softly, his voice low, he says, "Baltimore took Mitcher. Frank just put through the trade."

"The hit in the first period against the net, Joey's head—he—what?"

"Can't say Doug Mitchell didn't play his heart out tonight," Dad says. "Gil, we'll get you on the next round, you know how it is, yeah?"

"Mitcher?" Gil asks. "He hurt Joey."

"Part of the game, kid. And there he is," Dad says as Mitcher pushes through the curtain. "Looking forward to having you. You're going to fit in great."

"In Baltimore?" Gil asks.

Mitcher grabs his shoulders, pulling him into a hug, Sebastian's hand falling away. "Fucking thank you for that introduction, Gil. You're next out of here, okay? So I'll see you out there on the ice, on a real team, yeah? I gotta go get my things, but wanted to say thanks, really."

"You're leaving?" Gil asks.

"Pack up, Mitcher," Dad says. "I'll get us flights. You've got practice in the morning."

"Dad?" Gil asks.

"Sorry, kid," Dad says. "But he put on a hell of a show."

And Gil didn't. He hears it, even if Dad doesn't say it out loud as he follows Mitcher back down the hall.

Gil stares after them. Mitcher? Heading to Baltimore?

That was my trade, he wants to call out. Chase them both down. Shove his gear into his bag and toss Mitcher's back in his locker.

"Wow," Joey says. "That's a gut punch."

"Did your father really just…" Mom murmurs something softly, then rubs his arm. "Gil, sweetheart, I'm so sorry."

"Sucks," Joey says and gives Gil a quick, hard hug. "Sorry, man. But hey, you guys won, right? That's something."

Is it? Gil wants to ask but his mouth isn't working.

"Bye," is all he gets out in a mutter when Joey waves toward them, heading to the team bus and from there, the airport.

Back to San Diego. To Gil's house, with his team.

His old team. While Mitcher flies east to what should have been his new one.

And he's…here.

"Frank traded Mitcher?" he asks again, softly.

"We got a new goalie out of it," Sebastian says. "A good one."

Gil closes his eyes. That means that if Frank had traded him, the return wouldn't have been as much. Prospects, maybe. Or draft picks. A lot less than what Mitcher could bring in with his level of play, the talent and skill he brings.

"That was an awful thing your father did to you," Mom says.

Gil works his fingers into his eyes. He could argue, but he's suddenly too tired. He can't look at that flickering light in this wet, dirty rink any longer or the ache in his temples will bloom into a sharp pain, worse even than the knot that sits hard in his gut.

A hand cups his arm again. "C'mon," Sebastian says. "Let's get out of here."

That same soothing, slow rhythm of Sebastian's thumb starts up. Gil's chest aches. And with it...Sebastian's grip is firm, his hand warm. *Relief*, Gil realizes slowly. That's a deep, coursing relief, bewildering him, delighting him. *Don't*, he should be saying to Sebastian right now. Let him go, Gil needs to sort this out, undo the trade that just happened, find a way out of this mess. But...*thank you*, he wants to say to Sebastian. *Please never stop*, he wants to whisper and when that warm hand draws Gil forward, he follows.

TWENTY-SIX

OKAY, Gil thinks as the city passes by out the window of the car. The sights of San Francisco, these streets just outside the rink, the traffic light they have to wait at, the hill the car climbs.

He's here. Another trade might come, but not soon. No, Frank wants the team to get settled into its current roster. Maybe this winter, at the trade deadline, Gil can hope to be moved, or next summer during the draft or the flurry of activity when teams are allowed to talk with unrestricted free agents.

But he'll be here until then. Longer, even, maybe.

"I guess I'll take that place."

"Hmm?" Mom turns toward him in the backseat, Sebastian up front with the driver.

"The house."

"Oh sweetie, you don't have to decide right now. You can take some time."

"I thought you said the real estate market here moves quick. I gotta make a decision."

Mom squeezes his hand. "Sleep on it, at least. Give yourself some time to be upset."

"No, I..." He's here for now. For a while. *Fuck you*, he thinks at the idea of Mitcher flying to Baltimore tonight. But...

Sebastian turns in the front seat, looking back at him.

"I should get settled in soon, get a place that isn't a hotel room." Stop living out of a suitcase, arrange movers to bring up anything he really wants from San Diego, and get used to his life here. Stock some food in the fridge, if the team isn't going to provide it for him. Maybe hire a trainer, a nutritionist, the type of staff that should be at the rink each day but he'll have to find if he wants to make the most of his time here. Put up enough points, make a big enough name for himself that at the next opportunity, it's him who's chosen.

He can do it. Be the top choice, the obvious option.

And until then...streetlights flicker over Sebastian's profile. Sebastian can let him know the good spots in Gil's new neighborhood. The best grocery store, the good restaurants.

Gil will see him plenty. All the time. *I'm pissed as fuck*, he had texted Joey, but traitorously, secretly, a little glow of delight warms his stomach.

Sebastian. After all these years, Gil gets longer with him than he ever would have guessed.

"I can email the Realtor, if you're really sure," Mom says. "But Gil—"

"I gotta move on," Gil says. "This'll be good. The house, I mean."

Sebastian turns around again, glancing into the backseat, but not at him. He and Mom exchange a look that makes Gil frown.

"I'm fine, I'm good," he says.

"Okay." Mom pats his leg. "Okay, Gil, okay."

At the hotel, he stands silently in the elevator, only

murmuring a "Good night" to Mom as she kisses his cheek when she steps out of the elevator on her floor. *I'm okay*, he wants to call after her one more time, but just shoves his hands into his pockets. When the doors open onto their floor, he follows Sebastian to their room.

He...yeah. He gets to sleep here tonight.

"Hey," he says softly, turning toward Sebastian.

"Gil..."

"I'm fine."

"You're not."

"I am."

"Come sit," Sebastian says, cross-legged on the bed, his shoes off, and gently, he pats the space next to him. "That was a shitty thing for your dad to do to you."

"It's okay."

"Gil—"

"No, it is." Gil tugs at his tie. He wouldn't tell anyone else this. Can't tell anyone, the kind of words only reserved for Sebastian, ones he can barely think but are safe to share with this man. "I would have hated playing for him."

"Gil?"

Gil sinks onto the bed next to Sebastian. It's easier to not have to look at him, but at his own hands fisted in his lap. "It would have been awful. I'd have been terrified, every single day."

"Oh, Gil," Sebastian says and reaches for him.

Gil goes, folding into his side, tucking his face into Sebastian's neck. Fingers sift through his hair gently, smoothing it off his forehead, rubbing along the curve of his ear.

"Thanks for coming out for warm-ups," Gil murmurs into the smooth, warm skin of Sebastian's throat above the collar of his shirt. Gil squirms a little, shifting, and there's the stubble on his neck.

"Of course."

"And before the game, too."

"Well, you kinda looked like you were going to puke."

"Yeah, like you when you see an avocado."

Sebastian's hands slip inside Gil's suit jacket, warm and strong. "I know you wanted to get out of here. Being stuck here is your worst nightmare."

"I think playing for Dad would have been just as bad." Gil sits up a little, just enough he can see Sebastian's face. "Besides, there are some benefits here."

Sebastian's voice drops. "Yeah?"

"A couple I can think of."

Gil kisses him. Yes, perfect. Sebastian's mouth, soft and eager, the brush of his beard. Gil presses closer and when he pulls back to breathe, he whispers, "I'm glad you're here."

Gil gets to be here. Has to be here, but gets to, too.

He straddles Sebastian, kisses the soft skin of his neck, nosing into the collar of his dress shirt. Sebastian sighs, hands drifting down Gil's back, holding his waist as Gil explores the length of his throat, up behind his ear. Slower than normal, though normal was being kids and chasing the thrill of naked skin and groping hands, and last night was borne on a decade apart.

Now, Gil takes his time. He's got enough of it, the season stretching out ahead of him. The rest of the night too, no alarm needing to be set for the morning, the day free to make of it what they will. They can find this deeper sort of patience together, Sebastian rubbing at his back but not clawing his shirt from his waistband, tipping his head for a kiss but not the shove into the mattress that might have come once.

Sebastian holds his face when they finally break apart, a wet smack of their lips, a shaky, shared breath, Gil's forehead against his.

Though Sebastian draws back enough to look at him, his thumb rubbing Gil's cheekbone, his eyes tracking over Gil's face. "You're really staying?"

Gil lets out a soft breath. "Seems like."

"You're going to be great here."

Gil loosens Sebastian's tie, silk sliding against silk as he pulls the end through. "Let's not talk about hockey," he says, not when he can part Sebastian's shirt, one button after the next, his undershirt clinging to his pecs, curving around the trunk of his torso.

"Gil Roussin?" Sebastian asks as Gil dips down to kiss the hollow of Sebastian's throat, slipping his fingers beneath the hem of Sebastian's T-shirt and tracing soft skin at his waist. Sebastian's hips flex once, lightly, his body moving up into Gil's touch. "Not wanting to talk about hockey?"

"Shut up," Gil says at the tease in Seb's voice. *Put your mouth to better use,* Gil could tell him, lowering his own zipper, cupping the back of Sebastian's head in his hand.

Instead, he works Sebastian's belt loose. Nudges the hem of his shirt up a few inches and kisses the soft skin below his navel as he eases Seb's slacks and boxers down to his thighs.

Gil really fucking loves Sebastian's cock. It smells right as he brushes his lips down the length. Feels right in his hand, the thickness, its length. Tastes right too as he laps at the underside, trailing his tongue up to the head and licking softly.

Sebastian lets out a sigh, relaxing back against the head-board, his head tipped back. He's watching, Gil knows. He doesn't need to glance up to check; he can feel it in the hand Sebastian rests on his head, how he brushes Gil's hair back. He wants to see, he always has.

It's part of the fun as Gil teases down the length of his

cock, not taking it in his mouth, just lips and tongue dragging down the shaft to his balls.

Sebastian sucks in a breath as Gil presses a single, soft kiss to the thin skin there.

"C'mon," Seb whispers when Gil does it again.

C'mon what? Gil could tease, coax out of him, words that'll turn Sebastian's cheeks bright red, but he'll say them anyway, hand fisting in Gil's hair, hips rocking as Gil works.

Though maybe asking for what he wants doesn't embarrass him as much anymore. Gil doesn't want to know that if it's true, so he just gives in to it without teasing out instructions. He knows what to do. Sucks Sebastian's ball into his mouth, then the other one. Breathes over skin wet from his spit and then does it again. Licks back up the shaft of his cock, fingers around Seb's balls now, tongue teasing at him, circling the head, before he dips down.

"Gil," Sebastian chokes out.

At least he's good at something. And oh, is he, as Sebastian's hips start to shift, the pace of his breathing picking up.

Or maybe it's just practice. *Put in the work,* he thinks and fucking hell did he, sucking this dick until it was second nature, knowing when to back off, when to press firmer, learned through the skittering shake of Sebastian's breath, the soft, desperate sounds he made.

Gil draws those same noises out of him now. A flick of his tongue over the head of Sebastian's cock over and over, spaced with slower swipes and yeah, that's the choked-off sound in the back of Sebastian's throat. Pulling off to go back to his balls and the frustrated groan that ends with a pleased little sigh.

Sebastian's into it. Gil can feel it in the tension in Sebastian's body, how he grips his own cock, aiming it back at Gil's mouth.

Gil dodges it, sets his lips on the shaft, his head sideways as he gazes up, Sebastian's face knotted, his mouth open.

It won't take much more to get him off. A steadier rhythm, some intention behind it, just the right spot that makes Sebastian's thighs shake and oh, Gil hasn't done that yet has he, hasn't turned Sebastian into a limp, whimpering mess beneath him. He will, though, Sebastian's body so familiar for Gil to work over, to focus on, a squeeze here, circling his tongue—

Hands haul at his arms and Sebastian's hips tip back, his cock slipping from Gil's mouth. For a moment Gil chases after it, lips parted, but Sebastian pulls away.

"C'mon," Gil says. "I was just getting started."

"Yeah, I know." Sebastian's voice is hoarse and his stomach is flexing on his breath, his sides moving in and out.

Gil skims fingers across his chest. "Lay down. I'm not done."

But Sebastian crowds into his space. "You lay down."

"You're no fun," Gil says, turning his face when Sebastian kisses him. It doesn't dissuade him, Sebastian's lips tracing over his jaw, down to his neck. Sebastian doesn't stop, just crawls over Gil, guiding him back on the bed, finding his way to Gil's mouth and kissing him, a heavy, warm weight. Gil fishes between them for Sebastian's cock, but Seb grabs his hand, curling it up around his neck instead so Gil's left holding him, returning kisses that are too soft, too gentle.

"C'mon," Gil says, squirming under him.

"Relax," Sebastian whispers.

"I am."

"Gil."

"I want you," he says and hooks his leg around Sebastian's.

"Shit, Gil."

Gil pushes up against him, squirming out of clothes, tugging at Sebastian's too until there's bare skin between them, and when Gil draws his knees up Sebastian's sides, there's no annoyance of boxers, just his cock nearly in the right spot, if Gil can just—

"Okay, okay, wait, hold on." Sebastian leans over Gil to his bag and fishes through it.

Yes, this is what Gil wants. He grips Sebastian tighter, yanking him back onto him, curling a leg over his and holding him tight around the shoulders, kissing him and kissing him.

"Too much?" Sebastian asks as he nudges against Gil, guiding himself in, his cock slick, wet.

Ah, yes. Gil rocks his hips up and Sebastian's breath stutters. "Like that," Gil says, grabbing Sebastian's ass and pulling him against him. Yes, that deep stretch, nearly a burn, the little spark of pleasure—he closes his eyes and rides it as Sebastian finally joins him in moving together.

Fingers brush hair out of his face, off his forehead. "Gil," Sebastian whispers.

"Yeah."

"Look at me," Sebastian says, a palm against Gil's cheek.

Gil curls his arms around Sebastian's neck. Holding him, keeping him close. "I missed you," he whispers.

"Gil, oh—"

Gil tips his chin up to kiss him, but just a soft peck, a gentle tug on his lower lip, and then brushes their noses together, moving slowly, surely, with him.

"Just like this," Gil says and keeps that same rhythm, keeps his eyes on Sebastian, too close to focus on and too close to look away.

Heat builds slowly, Gil's hands resting on Sebastian's back, feeling his muscles bunch and lengthen again, Gil's cock trapped between them. When Sebastian shifts, it's to take Gil's hand, his fingers still slippery with lube, their hands tangled, slick, his cock hitting Gil just right inside of him and hands stroking.

It's intense. More so than just straining against each other, the quick, hard fuck Gil is so used to these days. No, this is far more intentional, a slower path to sweat breaking out on his skin, gooseflesh prickling over him, a heat in his stomach that starts as a dull ember and quickens.

"Seb," Gil gasps.

"I got you." Sebastian kisses him again, once, softly. "I got you, c'mon now."

I can't, he starts to think. It's all too unhurried, the space of Sebastian's movements inside him too drawn out, the rhythm of their hands nearly sluggish, and he wants it to last, wants to linger here, safe and warm. But he's pulled along anyway, a deep heat growing, his hips tipping up with each slow thrust, chasing after the singe of pleasure.

When he comes, it's a deep well of pleasure bursting up inside of him and he gasps against Sebastian's mouth, spilling over his hand. Sebastian lets out a soft, low noise and follows him a moment later, hips stuttering, his face pressed against Gil's as they still, skin cooling.

Slowly, the rest of the world forms around them again. The hotel room, the city lights through the gauzy curtain, the hum of traffic, a wail of a siren, and the beeps of car horns.

"I'm glad I'm here," Gil whispers.

"You are?"

"I'm glad you're here too."

"Yeah." Sebastian nestles closer.

"And that we found each other again," Gil whispers.

Fingers soft in his hair. The press of lips to his forehead and a tight squeeze of those arms around him. "I am too."

They need to clean up. They will, soon. At some point,

Sebastian will get up, come back with a washcloth. *Don't*, Gil's gotten in the habit of saying, embarrassed to let anyone else help him, a sickening twist of vulnerability in his gut that always cuts the moment, cleaving it in half and sending Gil into the shower, the door shut behind him.

He'll let Sebastian, though.

But for now, Gil pulls the blankets up over them, cozy in the air conditioned chill of the room. Yes, for now, at least, he feels okay. Better than okay. Good, maybe, and he yawns, kicking at the sheets until he can get his feet free.

"Don't mess up the bed," Sebastian mumbles into his hair.

How many times did they have this argument? Gil smiles and squirms closer.

"It's the best way to sleep," Gil says.

"It's the dumbest way to sleep. Aren't your feet cold?"

"No, your feet are the ones that—ah! Don't touch me with them!"

Sebastian just laughs, tangling their legs together, shoving his freezing toes against Gil's shins.

"I'm gonna get you socks to sleep in for your birthday," Gil mutters.

"Too bad you just missed it."

Gil blinks into the dark. Yeah, Sebastian's birthday was a couple months ago. But Gil hadn't missed it. He remembered it all that day, though the picture he'd had of Sebastian in his mind had been him in college, not this man laying next to him. *I didn't*, he starts to say, but Sebastian's drifting off already and Gil listens to his breathing as it evens out, the soft drum of his heart and when Sebastian shifts, snoring once before rolling onto his side, Gil follows, tucking his arms around him and making sure the blankets are just right, so Sebastian's feet don't get any colder.

TWENTY-SEVEN

In the gray of the city's morning fog, Mom rubs Gil's back as she hugs him goodbye. "I know staying here isn't what you wanted," she says. "I'm so sorry, sweetie."

Gil closes his eyes. "I'm really okay."

"Okay isn't good enough for you. I'm glad you have Sebastian, at least. And I'm glad I got to see you."

"Thanks for finding me a house."

She touches his cheek. "I'll come back out when you're settled in, alright?"

"Have a safe flight. Text me when you get home."

He waves as her car pulls away from the front of the hotel. Only when it's out of sight does he tip his head back and blow out a long breath.

He feels...okay. He woke up next to Sebastian and—yeah. He lets himself smile.

The rest of it? He needs to head to the gym and get a workout in. Eat a decent breakfast, not just the quick oatmeal he'd had while Mom ate before her flight. Call Melissa and talk to her about what comes next for his career, what his options are, and what he needs to do to make them a reality.

Though first, he stops and fills a coffee cup for Sebastian.

"Rise and shine," he says as he opens the door to their room.

The gym, he thinks, then sets the coffee down and crawls over Sebastian, kissing warm skin over his shoulders, knocking aside the pillow Seb drags over his face to press kisses to his throat, his jaw, his cheeks.

"Get up, get up," Gil says, fishes a hand down Sebastian's body, beneath the tangle of the sheets at his waist, and finds his cock. "Okay, you're up."

"You shower?" Sebastian asks.

"I'd be happy to take another one." Gil draws his eyes down the length of Sebastian's torso. "But the Realtor called. I gotta get back to her."

"Tease," Seb says, pushing up into Gil's hand.

"We got all day." Gil gives him a squeeze and rolls off him. And more than just this one. So many of them, that Gil never thought they'd get.

Sebastian emerges from the bathroom naked, toweling off his hair and then leaning over the back of the desk chair, his chin on Gil's shoulder as Gil taps at his phone.

"Can I see it?" Sebastian asks.

Gil reaches for the button of his pants. "You saw it last night, but yeah, hold on."

Sebastian snorts out a laugh and bites the tip of Gil's ear. "Your house. Where is it?"

"Not far from your—Matty's—a couple blocks."

"Hmm, a neighborhood only tech bros and pro sports players can afford." Sebastian bites his ear again. "Oh wait, that's the entire city. I'm gonna live under my desk at the rink."

Gil tips his head back, chasing the scent of soap. Sebastian looks so fucking good. A beard, who'd have thought? "I can get a desk set up for you at my place," Gil says. "But you know what? You deserve better, like the entire dining room table. You can live under there like a troll."

"Nibble your ankles?" Sebastian asks and Gil laughs, dodging as Sebastian tries to bite his ear once more. "Hmm, that's a nice sound."

"What, you scurrying around beneath the furniture? My poor mother, she thinks you're such a nice boy. If only she knew."

Sebastian tips Gil's chin with one finger and kisses him slowly, thoroughly. Gil melts into it, leaning back against him, letting that slow, meticulous way Sebastian has sink through him, lighting a low burn in his belly.

"No, you laughing," Sebastian murmurs against his mouth. "Get in bed. I'll see about those ankles."

Gil laughs again, twisting away. "I gotta send this email to the Realtor or we'll be hunting for desks together."

"Coffee, then," Sebastian says, breath hot against the side of Gil's throat. "The good stuff, I mean. There's an amazing place on that block. I've been going there since we found that house for Matty. You can show me the place and we'll get some breakfast. Gotta keep you fed."

Gil should be eating the eggs from the buffet downstairs, not ordering off some coffee shop menu, at the mercy of whatever they have for food. Pastries, cookies, and bagels, probably.

"You're buying," Gil says. "I can't afford both this house and your coffee habit."

They walk across the city rather than take a car, the fog lifting slowly as the sun arcs up overhead, the hills rising and falling beneath them.

Gil takes Sebastian's hand and when he smiles at him, Seb grins back.

It's a pretty nice neighborhood. Gil could have ended

up way north in Canada, in the crowded metropolis of New York, down south in Florida or Texas. This isn't bad, as far as cities go. Maybe not what he would choose, but some of the streets they stroll down are even cute, all of it so different from the acres of suburbia surrounding San Diego that Gil only ever saw through a car window, nothing in his neighborhood more walkable than the trip down to his mailbox.

It reminds him a bit of Annapolis, those weekends Mom had them and they'd venture out from her small apartment to explore the city, racing Joey down the sidewalk, the wind coming off the water.

Baltimore too, maybe, though Dad never took them into the city much. Ever, actually, now that he thinks about it. Just to the rink and back home, trip after trip of driving that same route.

"This is it," Sebastian says and pulls open a door, holding it for Gil. "After you."

"What a gentleman."

"See? I am nice. Tell your mom." Sebastian's smiling. A lot. Giddy, nearly, or maybe that's Gil, his stomach flipping delightedly as they step inside and he leans in for a quick kiss.

It's nearly better than the slow linger of making out. Casual, light, the familiar ease of a soft peck as they go about their morning.

The cafe is a nice place, with bells on the door that chime as it swings shut behind them, donuts neatly lining a pastry case and a pretty decent menu that Gil reads through.

"The breakfast scramble," Gil says to the guy behind the counter. "With whole wheat toast, please. And what cheese comes on it?"

"Goat cheese."

"Ugh, no, just cheddar," Gil says. "And a water."

"Double espresso?" the guys asks, glancing at Sebastian. "Or something else this morning?"

"That and a bagel," Sebastian says. "Extra—"

"Cream cheese," the guy says.

Sebastian nudges Gil with his elbow as he hands over his credit card. "Told you this place was good. I'm gonna snag that table by the window, okay?"

"Your water," the guy says to Gil. "And silverware and the espresso for your boyfriend."

Gil freezes. Across the cafe, Sebastian grabs a packet of sugar from the stand with extra lids and napkins.

Boyfriend.

Warmth rushes through his chest.

"Thanks," he says.

"The food will be just a moment."

The little cup of espresso is hot when he picks it up and he juggles it with the glass of water, the fork and knife he has to scoop up too.

Boyfriend. He...wow, yes. He likes that. A lot.

His cheeks feel warm as he slips into the chair Sebastian kicks out from the table for him. "I don't know how you drink that," he says, watching as Seb dumps in sugar.

"I don't know how you wake up in the morning without it. Wake up and work out, too. I bet you already did today, didn't you?"

No, because he'd laid in bed too long, watching the gathering dawn glow over Sebastian's skin, tucking his face into the crook of Sebastian's neck and breathing in his sleep-warmed scent until it had been time to go meet Mom.

"Nope." Gil grins. "Later, though. We have all day."

"Is that what this is? A real day off?" Sebastian asks. "Didn't know you had it in you."

Gil nudges Sebastian's ankle beneath the table. "Drink your coffee, Martin. You're gonna need your energy."

"Yeah, we'll make sure you get in your cardio."

"Gotta win a cup somehow, right?"

Sebastian glances up as he takes another sip. "All that work for a cup of coffee?"

Gil laughs. "Stanley Cup, obviously."

"Well that's one place to set your sights, I guess."

"Course it is. If you ever got your day with the cup, you'd probably fill it with espresso and just dive in."

"And you'd put a protein shake in it and jog around holding it while doing your training."

"You know, that's not a bad idea."

"What would you really do?" Sebastian asks, leaning back in his chair. "If you won it?"

"If? When, please."

"When?"

"Of course when." Gil shrugs. "And I don't like to think about it too much, you know? Focus on the game, that's what comes first. Daydreaming doesn't help anyone."

Your head gets stuck in the clouds and you forget your feet on the ice, Dad had said. He's smart about that kind of advice, always has been.

Probably gave Mitcher plenty of tips on the flight back last night.

Did he have Mitcher over to stay with him when they landed? Rather than shuttle him to a hotel, did Dad give him one of the extra empty bedrooms in the house?

Gil's, maybe. Mitcher sleeping in his bed beneath his green comforter, stepping onto the ice this morning as the newest of Dad's players.

"Hey," Sebastian says.

Gil takes a long drink of water. His stomach hurts a

little. "Gotta keep my head on straight, right? What else is the point?"

"The point?" Sebastian slides his hand across the table, tapping Gil's knuckles. "There's a hell of a lot more out there than a shiny silver cup."

"Well sure, but that's what matters."

"Gil," Sebastian says softly. "Your desire to go for something is admirable. Your single-minded focus and inability to fail really, really isn't."

"What does that mean?"

"You and your drive. Do you ever get sick of it?"

Yes, Gil thinks but that's not the right answer. Dad took Mitcher, not him. "It doesn't matter if I do. I've only got so many years left in my career, so there's only so many chances."

"Chances left to win, you mean."

"Of course to win. Why else am I here?"

"To play hockey?"

Gil laughs. "C'mon."

Sebastian sets down his cup, staring at the black swirl of espresso. "Really?"

"Really what?"

"You're really going to keep trying to leave. Now or at the trade deadline or when your contract runs out, you're going to get out of here?"

"Yeah, of course I am," Gil says. "The Sea Lions? I can't be here, not any longer than I have to be. You know that."

"I know that," Sebastian repeats. He rubs his hand over his face. "Wow. Shit."

"What?"

"I should know that, you're right."

"Seb?"

"Have you even considered that you could stay? Work with Steph and Frank and build this team into something and you're—you have one foot out the door still, don't you?"

"I mean, yeah. Of course I've thought about being here. I'm going to buy that house and all 'cause I'll be stuck here for a bit, but my agent knows, and Frank knows. If I find a way out, of course I have to take it."

"You could stay with me," Sebastian says softly. "With the team and the city and with me."

"What are you talking about? I'm with you right now, I'm here, and we can—"

"You're here for now," Sebastian says. "And then what? You'll just leave again?"

"Why are you—what's wrong? Yeah, if I get a trade I'll move again, but you know that, you have to know that. And it won't be soon, we have time. Frank's not shifting the team around again for months at least. This winter at the soonest."

"Months," Sebastian says and laughs.

It's not a nice sound.

"Seb?"

"I can't fucking do this again, Gil. Stay here while you go."

Sebastian lets out a choked sound. Another laugh? Gil leans forward across the table, his stomach turning. This morning, last night—they're good, of course they're good. Better than they were, even. Adults now, who've gone through life and found their way back to each other.

"We'll stay in touch this time, right?" Gil asks.

"Stay in touch? When you move?"

"It won't be like last time," Gil says. "I can talk about things other than hockey, check in with you, ask how Matty is."

"Matty," Sebastian says.

"Look at me, Seb. What's going on?"

"Gil, it's exactly the same as last time."

"No, it won't be because we'll talk and we can see each other and—"

"See each other? When?"

"During the summer and when our teams play each other and—"

"During the summer? A couple months a year?"

"I—Sebastian, look at me, what's wrong?"

"I'm not your convenient fuck buddy while you're in town."

"Whoa, what?"

"If you wanted to be with me, you'd want to be with me. Then and now."

"I do want to be with you. I did then, of course I did. Do. What's going on with you?"

"You," Sebastian says slowly, "wanted to get called up to the NHL."

"Well yeah, of course, but—"

"And now you want a trade. But oh, sure, we'll see each other sometimes. Great."

"We can be together, and sure it'll be tough sometimes during the season, but—"

"You don't have to leave at all." Sebastian's voice cracks.

"I do, of course I do. You know what this team is like." Gil reaches across the table. "Come with me, if that's the big deal. There are so many teams out there, we could end up somewhere amazing."

Sebastian pulls his hands back. "I have a son."

"And there are planes and we could make it work. Or I could try to go somewhere nearby, out here on the West Coast, that'd be alright, wouldn't it? Seb, I missed you so fucking much for so long, I was so lonely. I don't want to go through that again."

"Then don't," Sebastian says.

At the table next to them, a woman glances over. Gil drops his voice and leans toward Sebastian. "Seb—"

"No, I can't—fucking hell. I can't do this with you. You are so great, you are my best—no. I've finally fucking learned, I think. I need someone who'll put me and Matty first."

"But of course I do, I would, I—"

"Gil, you want me when it's convenient for your hockey career. I knew—I fucking knew, what the hell is wrong with me? I always knew if you had to choose, which it'd be. And I was right. Am right. Dammit, Gil."

"Seb—"

"Don't," Sebastian says and stands. "I'm so sick of you arguing."

"Wait, wait, I—"

"You don't take no for an answer. You don't change, not ever. You beg and work and worm your way into getting what you want, just like your dad taught you, but you never gave a shit about what I want."

"That's not true, I—"

"You don't have to go through that again, because you could be here. You could choose to be here and choose—choose me, Gil, this time around."

Gil lays his palm on the table. The woman's watching them, now. "Where are you going? Sit down, let's talk about this, we can—"

"No. This time—I've at least fucking learned something by now. I'm not coming second to your dad's dream for you and the fact that you're a fucking adult and he says jump and you ask how high."

"What the hell does my dad have to do with this?" Gil asks.

"This was such a fucking mistake to be with you again. I

knew it and I did it anyway." Sebastian shoves his chair in. "I have to—I gotta go."

"Wait, go where? We have all day, you wanted to see the house. We can eat and go there, don't you want to hang out? Because we have time, we—"

"Yeah. I do want to hang out. But you're leaving again, Gil."

"Seb—" Gil can't get around the table fast enough. "Wait, where are you going?"

"I have to get some air."

"Are you coming back?"

"I'll just—I'll see you later, Gil."

"Today? Or like—practice? Tomorrow?"

The cheerful bells on the door chime as Sebastian pushes through it. Is he—? Gil cranes to see the hand Sebastian wipes over his face.

"Seb?" he calls, though the windows are between them and then the sidewalk's empty, Sebastian hurrying around the corner and gone.

"Here's the bagel." The guy sets down a plate. "And the breakfast scramble with cheddar."

Gil stares at him.

The guy glances at the door, then at Sebastian's empty seat. "Can I get you anything else?"

I think I fucked up, he nearly says.

Fucked up big time. *How?* he wants to ask, like the guy can replay the conversation for him, walk him through it, even as he steps back behind the counter and returns to his work.

Gil's phone buzzes and he grabs for it. *I'm sorry*, he'll lead with and figure it out from there.

But it's Dad, and when Gil answers, he's already talking: "Kid, I've got good news for you. I think I found you a way out of San Francisco."

338

TWENTY-EIGHT

"I don't understand," Gil says.

"Your agent, Melissa, she's on the phone with the GM right now," Dad says.

"With Frank?" Gil asks.

"No, Peter, your GM."

Gil's GM is Frank. Peter is the GM down in San Diego. He opens his mouth to remind Dad of that, peering through the windows again like Sebastian will reappear. *Just kidding!* he'll say, arms held open for Gil to crush himself against his chest.

I'm sorry, Gil will repeat over and over again. He's sorry, he's so sorry, just come back, please.

"You're heading back," Dad says. "The Mountain Lions have a spot for you."

"What?"

Dad chuckles. "I've been so excited to tell you this, kid. Peter owes me a favor after pulling the rug out from under you and he knows it, so he's working to get you back on the team."

"So I can play with Joey?" Gil asks. His house. Hux and his other buddies. His life down there.

Sebastian, he thinks, staring down the sidewalk in the other direction like Seb might have circled the block on his way back.

"No, that's the spot that opened up. You were right about his head last night. The doctors say Joey needs some time before he can be back on the ice."

"Wait, wait, wait, what doctors?"

"He's fine," Dad says. "What's important is that this is what you need, Gil. You can't stay where you are, and we couldn't get you out of there last night, but this'll work just as well."

"If he's fine why are there doctors? He can't play? For how long?"

"You know how the league is these days with you boys and your heads. When I played, we'd be back on the ice straight away, just shake it off."

"Concussions are a big deal, Dad."

"Joey's fine," Dad says. "They're babying him. I don't know how this generation of players will ever learn to dig deep and perform if someone's holding your hand all the time. What happened to playing through a headache?"

"How bad is he?"

"Trust me, I've spent all morning on the phone with the joke of the doctors San Diego has. When you're back down there I don't want them getting in the way of your playing time either if you get a little bruise or bump."

"Is Joey in the hospital?"

"He'll be out soon. Now, Gil—"

"He is?" Gil asks. "Is he alone? Are you going out to see him?"

A pause. A long one. "I have my team to coach. I can't be flying across the country every time you boys need something. I'm sure your mother will be there."

"Mom's on a flight back east right now," Gil says. "Does Tommy know? Is he coming out?"

"Well, she'll turn right around, of course she will, never misses an opportunity to fuss over you boys."

Gil frowns. "Don't talk about Mom like that."

"Gil, I need you to focus. You've got your life ahead of you here. Don't concern yourself with Joey right now, he'll be okay. You need to take care of yourself, so get your head in the game and get after this opportunity."

Sebastian's bagel sits there after Dad hangs up, laden with cream cheese. Gil peers out the window again like he might be back for it.

Dully, Gil picks up his fork and digs at his eggs. Some part of his brain registers that they taste good, even as they feel like sludge in his mouth.

His phone buzzes. Melissa texting him: *I'm working on this trade back to SD, I'll keep you in the loop as soon as I hear something.*

Thanks, he taps back, stares at it, and finally sends it.

It'd be good to know how hard you want me to push for it, she adds. *And what you're willing to negotiate on.*

Anything it'll take, he should write.

Instead, he picks up his phone.

"Gilly," Tommy crows when he answers. "What's good? Hey, I watched your game last night, maybe on a super-illegal stream. Don't tell anyone, okay?"

"Joey's in the hospital."

"What?"

"That hit in the first period last night? I told him he wasn't okay, and he kept playing and I don't know what's going on now, but Mom's in the air, she's flying back your way and I think his team is on the road again later today."

So if they haven't left San Diego yet, they will. All the

players, the trainers, everyone packing into the team plane and flying away, everyone Joey knows in the city.

Hux's wife could go over and see him. Gil could call her, but no, they have a toddler and isn't she pregnant again? Or did she give birth already and they have two kids now? Gil rubs at his face.

"You have to go," Tommy says.

Gil laughs. "C'mon."

"Just fly down there and fly back," Tommy says.

"I have practice tomorrow morning."

"Then get your ass in gear and go now," Tommy says. "He's there all by himself?"

"You can fly in, can't you? If you head out now—"

"Then I'll make it there late tonight after visiting hours or first thing in the morning. Gil, just jump on a plane, how long is the flight? An hour?"

"Tommy—"

"And I can miss work but you can't?" Tommy asks.

"It's not work, it's practice. You know I can't skip it."

"Fucking hell, what happened? Did you just talk to Dad?"

"I—what? Yeah, I did, he called to tell me. And he wants me to—to take Joey's spot on the roster. That's why he called. He thinks I should get my agent to push a trade through, since now San Diego's out a center and Joey won't be back for a while."

"Dad wants you to..." Tommy trails off, the line going silent.

Gil pulls his phone away from his ear but no, the call hasn't dropped. "Tommy? You there?"

"Dad wants you to do this or Dad has already gone ahead and done this and you're currently packing your bags?"

"No, it has to go through my agent and San Francisco's

GM first, and there'd be some negotiation. I have to call Melissa, actually."

"You," Tommy says, his voice slow and clear. "Have to go see Joey."

"I can't, of course I can't."

"C'mon, you got an in with your coach, right? Seb will let you go, and he'll talk to the front office for you, smooth things over."

Gil picks at his napkin.

"Gil."

"I, um. Sebastian's kinda mad at me."

"What did you do?"

"That'd be awful, right? To really push for this trade and take Joey's spot on the team?"

"Yes, of fucking course it would, are you even asking that?"

"Okay, no. I—I just, um."

"You just have a moral compass aligned to point north toward *hockey*, come hell or high water? Tell Seb to call me, we can commiserate."

"I'm not that bad," Gil mutters.

"No, because at least sometimes you come up for air from following Dad around like a little duckling and feel moderately confused at why everyone is fed up with you. Better than Dad at least, who sees that same thing and just thinks everyone's a fucking idiot for not living life like he does."

Gil frowns. "Dad doesn't do that."

"Dad didn't talk to me for a year."

"What? When?"

"When do you think? When I quit hockey."

"But we were kids, he wouldn't have—no. I mean, maybe he was busy and you felt like that, but he wouldn't do that."

"No? He wouldn't?"

"No way, you aren't remembering that right. Yeah he was disappointed, but I'm sure he just—" Gil pauses, staring blankly around the cafe. That was when Tommy had moved in with Mom, wasn't it? Yes, because Gil's team had gone to states that year and he'd left for the tournament and come back home to find Tommy's bedroom empty.

"Oh, Gil."

"Dad didn't talk to you?"

"Not until Mom finally reamed him out."

"What—she did?"

"Yeah, c'mon, Gil. You know this. Dad dragged Mom through hell when she wanted a divorce, took her to court and made sure she didn't get us, didn't get money, didn't get anything, not against Bert Roussin."

"Wait, no, that's not—"

"She finally threatened to sue him for full custody rather than their Frankenstein arrangement where Dad got to do whatever he wanted and she saw you guys when it was convenient for him. Probably would have won too, but then how could Dad be elbow-deep in your hockey careers?"

"That's not how it was."

"So he started talking to me again when he realized he wouldn't win in court a second time, not with his playing days behind him and all that shiny fame fading. So he let me live with Mom, and look at us now, we couldn't be closer."

"You are?"

"No, we aren't. My God, Gil."

"Oh."

"Go fucking see Joey or I'm going to fly to San Francisco after seeing him myself and I'll hide your skates."

"I think they lock the locker room when we're not—"

Tommy groans and the line goes silent again. Then, his phone beeps and when Gil checks the screen, the call's ended.

Actually, the locker rooms probably aren't ever locked. They'd need an equipment manager to care about details like that. Someone at the rink to oversee that type of thing. For all Gil knows, there's a pickup game happening right now and one of the teams is changing in their room, pushing aside the team's gear and setting a cooler of beer in the middle of the floor.

Gil rests his face in his hand. Tomorrow, Jay will be scurrying around to collect the laundry after practice, and the guy in the mascot suit—Mike? Mikey?—will be hanging up jerseys before the skate.

And Gil needs to be there. Of course he does, he can't just miss a practice. There's no excuse for that, unless he's the one in the hospital. Even when Hux's kid had been born, he'd hustled back to the rink, showing off pictures of a wrinkly little face above the bundle of blankets, and he'd apologized to everyone for missing a team meeting.

Absurd, Tommy would say about that. That Hux had left the hospital at all that first day his baby was born. That he felt the need to tell everyone on the team and the coaching staff that he was sorry.

Good guy, Dad would probably say about him.

Seb would probably already be on the plane if it were Matty who was hurt.

But Joey's an adult. He's fine. Besides, Mom really will fly back as soon as she hears the news, and for all of Tommy's bluster about missing work, he'll go with her. Yeah, it'll take them longer to get to San Diego, but not much. And until then, Joey probably has his phone to keep him busy, and he can even watch his team's game on a TV in the hospital room.

345

Though with a concussion, is he allowed to look at screens?

And does he even feel well enough?

You good? Gil texts him.

Get your bell rung? he adds when he's done with his food and still hasn't heard back.

Maybe Joey doesn't have his phone. Was he rushed there? No time to grab some things to keep him comfortable. Dad didn't say.

And Gil…Gil's not going to call Dad right now to find out.

Instead, he fiddles with his phone like he can make a text come through. Get Sebastian to call him, explain it was just a misunderstanding, they're good. Watch his screen light up with a picture of Joey rolling his eyes at the indignity of a hospital room with an entreaty for Gil to break him the hell out of there.

He jumps when it does ring, a San Francisco number on the screen.

Gingerly, he answers it. "Hello?"

"Gil, it's Frank. You're on speaker with Steph too."

And Sebastian, he waits for but no, it's just the two of them.

"Um, hello."

"We're calling about San Diego," Frank says.

Let me out of here, he should say, with the same fervor as Joey trying to get discharged and back on the ice. Yes, let him go, end this awful string of days, and fly away from this city to return only as a visiting team, touching down just long enough for a single game they'll win with ease.

"Gil?"

"Oh, sorry, yeah. I just—my brother?"

"What about him?"

"He got hurt last night in the game, that hit from Mitcher."

"I'm sorry to hear that," Frank says.

"Is he going to be okay?" Steph asks.

"It's his head, so I don't really know, and—" he blinks. It feels better than it should that Steph asked after Joey. That Frank, probably pissed as all hell that Gil's trying to pry himself free, still cares enough to say what he did. "His team is on the road later today and he's down there all alone in the hospital."

"So you need to go down there?" Frank asks. "We're calling about the trade, obviously, so we need to know if it's a round-trip ticket."

"If it's a—what? That'd be okay? If I had to go down?"

"Of course that'd be okay," Frank says. "It's your brother."

"It's just practice tomorrow morning," Steph says. "It'd be great if you're back for our next game, but it's just preseason. If you need to miss one practice, it's not the end of the world."

Gil laughs. "What?"

"It'd be funny, probably, if you weren't back for the game, 'cause I'd put Jay in as starting center just to see his eyes get as big as saucers," Steph says and laughs. Quickly, she clears her throat. "Or I'm going to end up doing that anyway if this trade goes through."

Gil touches his fingers to his forehead. His mind is racing. *Breathe*, he tells himself and oh, that's Sebastian's voice in his mind, the memory of Sebastian's hands wrapped around his, so very warm. *One, two, three*, Sebastian's dad had taught him when Gil was a kid, calming him, helping him.

"I can't give you an answer about the trade," Gil says. *Because Melissa is the one to do that*, he means. No, because

—because Tommy's right, it's a hell of a shitty thing to do to swoop in and take Joey's spot on the roster. And besides, he's here and Joey's by himself. Gil stands, before he quite means to. "I have to go see my brother, make sure he's alright. I can call you—I mean, my agent can, whatever, but right now, I just—" *Get your shit together*, he snaps at himself. Focus.

"Of course," Frank says. "You take care of your family. We'll be here when you can think about hockey again."

"Thank you," he says. "I'm sorry about this, but thank you."

"Don't be," Steph says. "Forget hockey for today, okay?"

Gil laughs as he hangs up. No, he won't. He can't, he's pretty sure.

But he can go to the airport right now, not even bother to grab anything from the hotel. Be in San Diego by the afternoon and see Joey in person, which helps slow his pulse.

Though it picks up again as he climbs into a cab and it pulls away from the curb, as he scans the sidewalks to see if he can spot someone walking, dark hair and a beard, hands probably in his pockets. Sebastian can't have gotten far, he has to be somewhere in the first few blocks, but Gil keeps watching all the way to the highway, peering through the window for a glimpse.

TWENTY-NINE

Gil turns his phone back on the moment the plane's wheels touch down in San Diego. Quickly, he scrolls through the incoming alerts, Tommy's flight details for him and Mom, getting them in first thing in the morning, a voicemail from Mom that says nearly the same thing as her text—*Is Joey okay?* A longer, calmer voicemail from Tommy after Mom talked to Joey's doctors, saying that he was awake and responsive, and—

Gil sucks in a breath as the plane taxis.

Heard about Joey, Sebastian wrote at some point in the hour and a half Gil spent in the air. *Hope he's okay.*

Gil's thumb hovers over the screen. *I'm sorry*, he writes and quickly deletes it. *Are you okay?* he taps out next, only to erase that too.

I miss you, burns through his mind. *I fucked up*, he could write. *Can we please talk?* he sent to Sebastian ten years ago and he wants to write that again now, like all this will have made a difference in Sebastian's answer.

What if this is it? The last text from Sebastian that will ever come to Gil's phone? Does he want to mar it with a string of his own messages?

"Hey," the guy next to him says.

"What?"

The guy motions to the aisle. It's empty. Gil jumps up, bangs his knee on the seat in front of him, and hurries out of the plane.

There's no luggage to wait for at baggage claim, no bundle of sticks and his equipment bag this time—and nobody recognizes him, no hockey bag to sling over his shoulder, heads turning at the Mountain Lions logo stamped on the side, fans pointing when they recognize the green and gold.

Not him, though. Not by his face, because he slips through the airport without anyone glancing twice at him.

Kids across the city will recognize you, Sebastian had said. Gil frowns and hurries to where a line of cabs wait.

I probably won't be at practice tomorrow, Gil types to Sebastian. Deletes that too, and instead taps out, *I'm in SD to see Joey right now*, then erases that as well. He fiddles with his phone as the cab drives through the city, whacking it into his palm over and over like it'll jar loose a useful text.

But nothing comes before the signs for the hospital do, directing ambulances one way, cars headed for the parking garage the other. Gil gets out at the main entrance, staring up at the façade for a long moment before he heads inside. Last time he was here, it was for his ankle injury.

I'm scared, he wants to write to Sebastian. Tell him. Tuck himself into his arms, whisper it into his shirt, and clutch him. *I wish you were here with me*, he would add. *I wish you'd come with me, I wish I'd never said anything about the damn cup, I wish you didn't hate me again*.

Focus, he tries to tell himself. *Sebastian,* he thinks, like he can conjure up the warmth of a hand slipping into his as he pushes inside the hospital alone.

He finds his way through the fluorescent-lit maze, his

stomach twisted. Down the hall to the sign where each floor is labeled, to the elevators, up, up, and out, through double doors and around a corner. He walks quickly and wipes his hands on his thighs, his palms sweaty.

"Roussin?" he asks at the nurse's station. "Joseph Roussin? I'm looking for my brother, is he—Dave."

A man in navy blue scrubs looks up from a clipboard. "Gil?"

Gil rocks a step back.

"Hi," Dave says.

"I—you're here?" Yes, Dave is here, he's here right now, eyebrows raised as he takes Gil in.

"I work here," Dave says.

Right. *Don't do something stupid on the ice and end up in my ward,* Dave used to tell him. Gil sucks in a breath. This is the hospital the team uses, this is where Gil first saw him after an appointment for his ankle, bumped into him in the elevator, got his number, dropped him off sometimes after he spent the night at Gil's place.

"Thought you were up in San Francisco," Dave says. "Though I'm not going to flatter myself this is a social call."

"I was, but I came down, I had to—Joey. He's here, right?"

"Ah, figured the last name, big old hockey injury, all of that wasn't a coincidence. Yeah, he's here. He's sleeping." Dave goes back to his clipboard.

Gil steps closer. "Is he okay? Can I see him?"

"I'm not his doctor, Gil."

"Yeah, but is he gonna be alright?"

"I'm a nurse. You know that."

"Okay, but will he be okay? He'll wake up, won't he?"

Dave sighs. "Yes, because he's taking a nap."

"So he'll be alright?"

"You can wait for him in his room. It's right in here."

"Wait, are you saying he's not okay?"

"I'm not saying anything because I'm not his doctor and I just got on shift."

"Which is it?"

"What it is, Gil, is that he's in the hospital for observation overnight because he—and you—have a career where you get your brains bashed around your skulls. You're not okay to begin with, thinking that's a good idea," Dave says.

"So he is alright?"

"I," Dave says slowly while gesturing Gil through a doorway, "am continually impressed with your communication skills. He needs his rest, so keep it short, alright?"

There are a few beds in the room, but Gil recognizes Joey right away, even with his face pale against the sheets and an IV dripping into the back of his hand, a hospital gown loose around his neck.

"Joey," he whispers, but Joey doesn't stir, his heart beating on the monitor, his chest slowly rising and falling.

I'm sorry, Gil wants to say, like maybe Joey can hear him, even if he isn't awake. Gil should have made a bigger deal last night, should have made the trainers check Joey in front of him, should have told Joey, the medical staff, everyone to take this seriously. It's his little brother, and he can't be here, dark smudges under his eyes, his legs looking too skinny beneath the thin blanket.

"Who fucking died?"

Gil snaps his head up at Joey's croak. "Joey?"

"You look like you're going to start crying. What're you doing here?"

Gil rushes forward, sitting next to his hip, reaching for Joey's hand before he snatches his back, scared to touch the IV line. "What happened?"

"Sorry about your car. Is that why you came?"

"My car?"

"I hit a guardrail," Joey says. "And they're keeping me here for it. They won't let me leave."

"You have a concussion," Gil says. "Is that what happened? You tried to drive? After your plane landed last night?"

"I'm fine," Joey says.

"I called you," Gil says.

"My phone's dead. It's in worse shape than I am." Joey sits up a bit, though he winces.

"Wait, wait, let me help—"

"Get off, Gil. I was just tired from the flight, got in the car, and yeah, must have drifted off. It's just the fender and the hood. You don't need to ream me out for totaling it. It'll be fine once it's fixed."

"I don't give a shit about my car."

"Can it be my car, then?"

"No," Gil says. "What the hell were you doing driving with that hit to your head? And playing the rest of the game? Joey, you need to be careful."

"I told you, I'm fine. You're the one who seems like a fucking mess. This entire thing is just being blown up. Dad said he'd talk to the team doctors, get it all sorted out."

"Dad talked to them? Did he talk to your doctors here at the hospital too?"

"Yeah. No, I don't know."

"You don't know or you don't remember?"

"I don't know, because I keep getting poked and prodded and I'm kind of over it. Are you springing me from this place?"

"No, no, you have to stay here, make sure you're okay."

"You sound like Mom."

"And you sound like Dad," Gil says, hearing his words and only then realizing how true it is. "What did Dad mean, getting things sorted out?"

"You know how the league is with head stuff these days," Joey says and yeah, those could be Dad's words. "Making sure they're not going to sit me forever just 'cause I got a bump."

"I think you're going to be out for a while," Gil says slowly. Does Joey not know? He'll be placed on long-term injured reserve for a good chunk of the season, depending on how bad his head is and what his recovery looks like. "Did Dad talk to you about that?"

"For a while?" Joey laughs. "Of course not, don't be ridiculous. What're you going to do, come back and play while I sit around with my feet up?"

"Joey," Gil says softly.

"Can you get me some clothes from the house?" Joey asks. "And my phone charger? I'm like this close to snagging a date with a real hottie. I can't fall off the face of the earth right now."

No, Gil should say. He can't swing by the house, because he needs to leave for the airport if he wants to be back in San Francisco tonight and on the ice for practice tomorrow.

Joey'll understand that. Of course he will. Tease him for rushing down here, but probably be soothed to know his hospitalization is less important than ice time.

Not the end of the world, Steph had said and Gil wants to laugh because damn but does willingly missing a practice feel like it.

"Yeah, I'll get your charger," Gil says. "I don't know if they'll let me back in this evening by the time I get to the house and back again, but I'll bring it in the morning."

"Check on Mr. Stanley, too."

"That cat of yours? Maybe I will."

"I think it's trash day," Joey says. "I didn't take the bags out. I never made it back."

Gil wants to ruffle Joey's hair, but no, he has to be careful around his head. "I know when fucking trash day is."

"And you should probably get the mail."

"Who trusted you with this house anyway?"

"Also, don't look at the nice pan Mom gave you for your birthday last year."

"What happened to my pan?"

"Your stove burners are way too hot. I don't know what to tell you, it wasn't my fault."

"You thought you could cook? You do need your head checked. Let me go tell your doctor." There, that's a lighter note to leave on, and Joey cracks a small grin. "Get some rest, yeah? Mom and Tommy'll be here in the morning."

"They're coming? The three of you. I'm fine, really."

"Of course they are. We all are." *If you don't count Dad*, Gil doesn't say. And not *of course*, not for Gil himself. It still itches at him that he's not prepping for practice tomorrow.

"Well thanks, I guess." Joey lifts his eyes toward the ceiling, blinking quickly.

Gil touches his shoulder and slips out the door.

The nurses go silent when he walks toward them. All of them, not just Dave, who glances up, raising his eyebrows at Gil. "How's he doing?" Dave asks.

Dunno, I'm not a doctor, Gil could joke, but he doesn't have the energy. "Fine, it seems," Gil says. "I'll be back tomorrow."

"Good, you can take him with you in the morning then. I didn't know being a pain in the ass was genetic."

Gil tries for a smile. "Is he that bad?"

"I figured he had to be your brother when they brought him in, is all I'm saying, and not just 'cause you two look alike."

One of the nurses taps Dave's arm with her pen. "This is the guy?"

"Stop," Dave says, brushing her away.

"I'm Gil," he says and gives a quick, awkward wave. "Hi."

"See ya," Dave says and Gil nods, stepping past him.

He stops, though. Dave might not be here tomorrow and there's something Gil should say, he's suddenly sure. Words that will leave things between them better than the last time they talked, that quick, stilted phone conversation.

Sebastian had been there, listening to it. Baseball on the TV, that hotel room back in San Francisco Gil had woken up in just this morning, warm sunlight and their bodies pressed together, the sweet smell of Sebastian's skin.

"Dave," Gil says.

"Got work to do," Dave says, stepping away from the nurses' station.

"Wait." Gil half jogs a step after him. "I didn't know I wasn't coming back."

"Oh, let's not do this."

"No, I'm sorry. You were right. I should have let you know right away."

"Did you get hit in the head too?" Dave glances at the nurses, all of them watching him, and pulls Gil a few steps farther away. "Look, it was never serious, right? We agreed on that and yeah, a heads up would have been nice, but it's fine."

"I could have told you though and I'm sorry. I wasn't thinking."

No, that's not true, is it? He was thinking, just not about Dave. His mind was on his career, the next step in the process of moving forward, frantic to get out of the trade to San Francisco. He'd been consumed with thoughts of hockey.

Like always, he can imagine Tommy grumbling. What had Mom said? It's hard to share Gil with hockey? There's not enough of him to go around?

"I was thinking about hockey," he says. No, that's not quite right either, is it? "I was focused on that, I mean, not on you."

"Are you really Gil? Because I can't just let anyone in to see patients."

"I was focused on myself, actually," Gil says slowly, because really, where does hockey end and he begin? Hasn't he been so entwined that for all that matters, he and hockey are part and parcel? Isn't that exactly what Sebastian was trying to tell him? "I was just thinking about me, not about you. I'm sorry for being an ass."

Dave rubs his hand over his mouth. "Okay."

"Is it?"

"I don't know, Gil. No. Yes. This wasn't serious between us. Do you think it is suddenly? Is that what this is? Because we had fun, but I'm not looking for a relationship."

"No, I just—" He's saying this to the wrong person. Gil sucks in a breath. *Sebastian*, he thinks. "I'm sorry. That's not what I mean. I'm just trying to not be a dick."

"You want to do something with yourself, convince your brother to give up hockey, okay?"

"Give it up?" Gil asks and laughs.

"A few more hits to the head and there won't be a happy ending to the story, so save this new personality trait you've discovered and use it on him, 'cause I'm working and you're in my way."

"Sorry." Gil steps back and Dave goes, bent over his clipboard as he ducks into another room.

The nurses are all looking at him. Quickly, he escapes

back down the hallway, stabbing at the elevator button like he can make it arrive that much quicker.

Outside, the sun's setting behind the palm trees in the parking lot, a beautiful evening forming around Gil, none of the fog of San Francisco, the strange chill despite it being the tail end of summer. No, the weather here is always perfect. *Not complaining*, Hux always said, lounging in Gil's pool, just another perk of playing for the Mountain Lions.

He's lived here for ten years. It shouldn't feel odd to stand in the warm glow of evening, but his skin pricks and his shirt chafes against him.

Sebastian, he thinks again. *I'm sorry. I miss you. I love you.*

I hurt you. He pulls in a breath. Hurt him badly. Once, years ago, and then again just now. It's a gut punch to sit with that thought. *I grew up*, Gil had been thinking over the past few days, brushing aside what he did when he wasn't much more than a kid.

But now...no, he knew better. Knows better. Should know, at least.

It's a long cab ride through evening traffic to his old house. He holds his phone in his lap, staring down at his reflection in the screen. He's been here before, counting the passing seconds as his messages to Sebastian go unanswered, feeling them stretch into minutes, nearly an hour as traffic swarms around him, cars honking and the light from the sky fading into a dull darkness lit only by the streetlights.

THIRTY

GIL's favorite protein bars sit in the kitchen cupboard where he left them, but they've been shoved to the back of the shelf, behind a different brand and a different flavor, the box in front ripped open and nearly empty.

On the counter beneath them, Mr. Stanley blinks yellow eyes, his fluffy gray coat making him look massive, though if Gil were to pick him up he knows it'd confirm the cat's made mostly of fur.

And attitude. The cat stares at him, sticks its leg in the air, and starts licking its butt right there on the counter.

"Gross," Gil says, but the thing doesn't even pause.

Well, at least Gil hasn't canceled the cleaners yet. Just one more thing on the to-do list in being uprooted suddenly to a new city.

Upstairs, his clothes are still in the dresser drawers, his suits hanging in the closet. The same sheets he'd last put on the bed, right before he flew back to visit Dad, are still on it, though the comforter's tossed back, the pillow dented from Joey sleeping here, in Gil's bed.

Ass, he thinks fondly. Couldn't take the guest room.

No, of course not. He didn't think Gil would be back here and if he ever was, it would be for a visit only.

Though now Gil could be back for good. Strip these sheets off, grab a clean set from the closet and get into his own bed. Wake up tomorrow and pull on one of the green T-shirts in his drawer, a number 16 in yellow on the chest, and step right back into this life.

And Joey? Gil chews on the inside of his cheek. Gil could pick him up from the hospital, bring him back here, and try to keep him quiet. Drive him to doctor appointments and then what, make him watch while Gil heads to the rink? See him in the trainers' room getting checked out week after week, and even when he comes back, he'll be in a non-contact jersey for a good while, unable to take a hit until he's cleared for it? Make him watch while Gil channels all the anger and embarrassment of being sent up to San Francisco into a hell of a start to a season?

Which Gil would. He can feel it itch at him, the desire to jump right back into things here and prove himself, make his GM certain he should have never been sent off, no matter how appealing the return was.

Stuck in a rut, Dad had said all that time ago, back in Baltimore. *You don't play like you used to*, Sebastian had told him.

Gil pulls the bedroom curtains aside, staring down into his backyard, the pool he loves so much, his grill set right there next to the chairs where he lounges on his days off. It's not a bad spot for Joey to recuperate. The neighborhood's quiet and it's not like the weather ever sucks for days spent by the pool, laying out and getting a tan.

His phone chimes and he pulls it out of his pocket quickly. *Dave*, the notification reads, a stethoscope emoji next to his name. He's sent a list of names of doctors, one after the next, and a message with it. *Don't know who his doc'll recommend for a specialist but these guys are good.*

Thanks, Gil types.

I appreciate what you said, Dave adds. *If you're back in town, want to meet up? You do kind of owe me one.* He sends a winking face. An eggplant, a peach.

Gil drops his phone and sits on the edge of his bed.

The room closes in tight around him. This wide-open bedroom, white walls, the gray bedspread, all of it shrinks toward him and he wants to yank at the collar of his shirt so he can breathe.

Meet up again. With Dave. Who would drive right over here. Park where he always does, jog up the stairs, and push Gil down into this mattress just as he has dozens of times.

It wasn't that long ago that Gil left to visit Dad. The eggs in the fridge downstairs are still good, if Joey hasn't eaten them. He left clothes in the dryer and for all he knows, they're still there, boxers and socks and shirts and two pairs of jeans.

He could walk back into this life and it won't have changed. He can invite Dave over tonight and Dave will slip out afterward and they won't talk again until one of them is bored and horny.

Tomorrow, the team will fly back into town, which leaves him plenty of time to make it to the rink for the Mountain Lions practice. He can jump right back into the drills he knows from memory, the familiar rhythm of arriving to the rink early enough to enjoy the full spread of breakfast, hanging out with the guys, getting geared up for the coming games on the schedule with meetings with the video coach, all of them watching tape together.

And then drive back here. Sit by that pool, sleep in this bed, get up and do it all over again, day after day, hoping this is the year they make a deep run into the playoffs, that maybe he can make the jump from the third line up to the second if he hustles hard enough, if he makes sure that when Joey's fit to play again, it's Gil the coaches choose. Give everything he has for that chance, day after day as the season grinds along, no thought for anything else in his life, and no space for it to begin with.

Though didn't he already give everything? He gave up years for this team. His entire twenties, nearly. His last three years of college and the chance to earn a degree, the health of his ankle, and living on the same coast as his family. All of that and he still got traded anyway.

And he gave up Sebastian.

He swipes Dave's message away to stare at Sebastian's words. If Gil stayed in San Diego, they'd sit there until Gil gets a new phone, their text thread getting pushed farther and farther down the list until it's so far from the top as to be nearly gone already.

It's already halfway down his screen, behind the travel alerts from his flight, Melissa's message, Tommy's text, and Dave's too. He could let it drift lower, down, out of sight.

Maybe they'd run into each other again, someday. Gil will look over at the bench when they play the Sea Lions, embarrassed he ever wore that jersey, and spot Sebastian behind the bench.

They wouldn't say hi. Not on the ice, not in the hallway between locker rooms. No grabbing a quick meal the night before the game, none of the handshakes turned hugs between guys in the league when they run into each other on road trips, chances to catch up with each other after trades and contracts have cleaved them apart.

Staying here in San Diego would mean the end of everything with Sebastian. Shutting the door on this reunion they've been granted. Saying goodbye to him again, this time without a long hug and knowing full well to not hope Sebastian will ever again light up the screen of his phone.

Or—he squeezes his eyes shut.

What an absurd thought, though it rises through him all the same.

Or Gil could go back to San Francisco. Put his relationship with Joey above anything to do with hockey. Skate for a coach who lets him miss practice and even a game to take care of his family. *Captain*, they might offer him and he wants to laugh, that same high, shrill sound that rose up in him when Melissa first called to tell him he'd been traded.

Sebastian's up there. And if Gil went back to him...

Maybe, Gil thinks. What, he doesn't know, but that's one step better than slamming the door shut between them and locking it.

Still, his hands shake when he reaches for his phone, his thumb hovering over Dad's number.

Nearly, Gil balks. There's safety in going forward with a life in San Diego, knowing Dad is proud of him playing here, slipping back into what once was and wrapping himself in that familiarity.

But Sebastian was familiar too. And now he's going to live out his life in San Francisco, tearfully applauding when Matty manages to hit a T-ball, even if he runs around the bases the wrong direction.

Sebastian doesn't care about the prestige of the team Gil plays for. If he plays, even. How he does, what his stats look like, the final shape of his career when retirement finally comes.

Someone who puts me and Matty first, Sebastian had said. That's all he asked for, as simple, as easy as that.

And in the equation of that choice, this lonely, empty house doesn't even begin to compare.

Maybe—*maybe*—he can make something work with

Sebastian. And compared with the certainty of another ten years without him, that *maybe* is absolutely enough.

"Kid," Dad answers and Gil has to squeeze his eyes closed against the familiar warmth in Dad's voice.

It's going to fade when he starts speaking. Isn't that what Tommy went through? Trading Dad for living his own life?

Gil tightens his grip on his phone. "I'm not taking Joey's spot. I can't."

"Of course you can. I got you both trained to play the same way, you can just swap in for him."

"No, it's not right. I'm not going to fight with my own brother for a spot on the roster."

"Well you don't have to. He's got a long road ahead of him and he needs you to take care of the team while he's out. You're doing him a favor, Gil, letting him get the rest he needs."

A son out of the game for however long. Forever, maybe, Gil's throat closing up at the thought of Joey never playing again. And his other son playing for a team like San Francisco. No, that's not what Dad trained them for. The early mornings at the rinks, the long weekends at tournaments, juggling two hockey schedules and Dad's career to make it to ice times, get rostered on the right teams, the money and time and effort to shape him and Joey into the players Dad wanted them to be.

"I'm sorry," Gil says. He means it, too, gratitude rising up in his chest—because despite everything, he loves hockey, *loves* it—but right next to that is horror at the idea that to make Dad happy, Gil has to tell Joey he's brushing him aside and taking his old life back. "But I can't come play in San Diego. I can't do that to Joey."

"Why not? It's an open roster spot. It's got to go to someone, so why not you?" Dad asks and yeah, there's the slip in his tone, his voice lower, his words a bit slower like he needs to make sure Gil is hearing him. "You're just putting your name on the roster before they bring up a prospect or trade for another center."

"Then let them," Gil says.

A pause. "What are you saying?"

"That I'm going to tell Melissa to put the brakes on this trade, and if it's too late to get her to stop it, then I'll call Frank and try to talk him out of it."

"You're not making any sense."

"I am." Maybe for the first time, he gets a glimpse of what Tommy sees in Dad. Sebastian too, right? His exasperation with Gil's dad, the hurt in his eyes. Gil sits up straighter. Sebastian, who said he doesn't want to come second to Dad's ideas for Gil's life. And who did, for so, so long.

Yes, that's what Gil can fix. Is fixing, his hand sweaty on the phone, his stomach jumping with nerves. "I'm staying in San Francisco," Gil says as evenly as he can, reaching for that calm, smooth tone Dad uses so well.

His voice sounds too high, his words rushed. But still, he said them.

"Gil, please," Dad says. "You can't be serious. San Francisco? At least get the hell out of there. I'll talk to my buddy in Edmonton, we'll get you up there."

"I'm not done in San Francisco," Gil says. *No kid of mine will play there*, Dad had said. "I have opportunities there. Frank and Steph are rebuilding the team—"

"That head coach is a joke and that GM is even worse."

"And I have a chance to be captain, maybe."

Dad laughs. He actually lets out a laugh.

Gil closes his eyes against the sound, breathes in slowly, lets it out. He feels sick.

"Captain of a team like that? My God, Gil."

What had Sebastian said? Gil clings to it, when the rest of him wants to apologize, skip backward on his words, hear the *Good job, kid* he's chased after his entire life.

"Any other father would be proud," Gil says and yes, that helps, a frisson of anger clawing through him, indignity he has to have this conversation. *One, two, three* he taps against his phone case. *Look at you go!* Sebastian's dad had cheered when Gil had lobbed a football all of ten feet.

"This is your career, Gil. This isn't about pats on the back. You need to get your head in the game and get focused on what you've been building for your entire life, not toss it away on some sort of whim."

"Dad, thank you, really, for everything it took for me to get this far. But I've got to do the rest, alright?"

"Gil, this isn't the time for some teenage bullshit, you thinking you can—"

"Bye, Dad. Hey, I love you. And really, thank you."

He stares down at his phone, sweaty fingerprints marring the case after he hangs up.

Dad doesn't call back. No angry text message comes either, just his screen dimming when he doesn't touch it to keep it awake, and then turning off.

What had Tommy said? It was a whole year Dad went without speaking to him? Gil sucks in a breath. Well, they're playing Baltimore later this fall. He'll see Mitcher on the other team and Dad behind the bench. And if they don't talk by then, that's a chance to try.

And maybe this silence from Dad is better, at least, than not hearing from Sebastian. Gil chose this one and no matter how his stomach twists, he's right.

"Hey," he says when Melissa answers his call. "I don't want the trade."

"I'm hearing differently from your father," she says. "Loudly. And repeatedly. Gil, what's going on?"

"I don't—" He swallows. "You, um, you work for me, right? So I don't want you to deal with him anymore. Or talk to him, even. He's—I'm your client, not him."

Silence. "Really?"

"If that's okay," he says.

She lets out a loud breath. "Thank fucking God."

"Yeah?"

"I gotta go make some calls, but I think you're good. Frank didn't want to see the back of you and to be honest, San Diego wasn't offering much to begin with. I don't think they know your value, Gil, letting you slip away twice."

"Thank you," he says.

"Don't thank me, just go play some good hockey. And hey, your brother? Joey? I heard about him. I hope he's okay. Don't rush him back on the ice. That's how careers end."

"I'm going to take care of him," Gil says. *Instead of Dad*, he means.

And maybe Melissa hears it, because she says, "Good on you."

Gil sets his phone on the foot of the bed when they've hung up, pressing his hands up into his hair and pacing. He'll go to the hospital in the morning, to drop off some things for Joey and hopefully see Mom and Tommy. And then the airport for the quick flight back up north. He'll make it in time for the next game day, even if he misses practice in the morning.

And from there, preseason will wrap up soon enough, another couple games on the schedule before opening night.

He waits for the sick flush of embarrassment to flood his chest, but it doesn't come, just a lump in his throat.

Sebastian.

Gil needs to make things right with him. See if that door's unlocked at least, and if he can inch it back open and have some sort of life together in San Francisco, whatever shape it might take.

Which means he's done here in San Diego, in this house he so proudly bought. His furniture, his things in the kitchen, his TV and his lounge chairs—he'll leave them for Joey. And if Joey can't stay on the team, Gil will figure it out from there, but he won't be living here again.

No, he'll be back up north, where Sebastian is.

That house, he thinks. So close to where Matty lives. Seb will...maybe he'll come over. Maybe he'll even bring Matty over, someday. Yeah, Gil can—what do kids need? Outlet covers? Baby gates?

A tiny hockey stick, that's for sure. A net in the backyard.

If he wants to play. *Whatever he wants to do*, Sebastian had said. Yeah, Gil can figure out how to hang out with him without playing hockey. Music. He'll call Tommy for pointers. Or go watch him in a play. Gil was a tree once, in grade school. Sebastian was a rock, and they got in trouble for talking to each other too much.

Gil can make it to a play. Probably, with his schedule.

I need a day off, he could say to Steph and Frank. *I know it's unconventional, that you should say no, but it's a family thing.*

Maybe. But first, he has to find Seb and apologize.

He grabs a suitcase from the closet and empties his drawers, jogs down to the laundry room and retrieves the clothes from the dryer, shaking the creases out of the jeans that have sat there for too long. He can leave all of his old San Diego clothing from the team, he doesn't need any of that, but he wants to take some books with him. He'll need to have some other things shipped, like his framed jersey from World Juniors and the signed team photo his coach had sent him from Rideau when he'd been first called up to the NHL.

It's on the bookshelf downstairs, too big and too fragile to fit into a suitcase. When he picks it up, he and Sebastian stare back at him, Sebastian's face cleanly shaved, both of them with haircuts a decade out of fashion, so young he can barely believe they were old enough to be in college.

He'd left a few weeks after this picture had been taken, but caught in time before he'd flown away, he and Sebastian sit shoulder to shoulder. And wow—yeah, those are Chris's brothers there too. *Christopher*. Who Sebastian fucking married and had a kid with.

Gil lets out a quiet laugh. Who else in this picture had been at that wedding other than Sebastian's new brothers-in-law? Plenty, Gil's sure. All guys Gil lost touch with, traded for the next team photo on the shelf, of his rookie year in the minors.

That picture, Gil can leave. It can sit in a box for years and maybe someday, he'll pull it out again. But this one, his old team, those last days of his life at Rideau, he takes to the dining room and sets with his framed jersey, those books, everything he'll need shipped to him, the picture of him and Sebastian resting on top.

THIRTY-ONE

Tommy groans when Gil wafts the cup of coffee near him, shifting in his stiff hospital chair in the hallway outside Joey's room and blinking open his eyes.

"You brought coffee?" Tommy asks, reaching for the cardboard tray. "Did you get hit on the head too and suddenly turn into someone with a single thoughtful brain cell?"

Gil bats his hand away. "That one's Mom's. This one is for you, and I got you some food too."

"Let me guess, egg whites mixed with protein powder and juiced kale?"

"I missed you too, you little shit."

Tommy leans forward, hugging Gil around the waist. "I can't believe you came down here."

"How is he?"

"Pissed, cranky, making Mom wait on him hand and foot while he whines. She's in there with him now." Tommy collects his coffee cup and breathes out a laugh. "If I'd known it's just classic Joey, I might not have exchanged a night's sleep for that wonderful cross-country flight."

"Good movies on the plane at least?"

"Mom was crying pretty much the entire way here."

"Shit."

"Is he going to be okay?" Tommy looks at him. "Guys come back from concussions, right?"

"Of course they do," Gil says as confidently as he knows how.

Will Joey be one of them? Hopefully. Maybe. *Please*, Gil thinks.

He hands Tommy a muffin and peeks into the room where Mom's sitting on the edge of the bed, smoothing back Joey's hair.

"Morning," he says, handing Mom her coffee and bending to kiss her cheek. "Been a long time, hasn't it? Haven't seen you in a while."

"Hi," Mom says, barely managing a smile at his joke. "You're here."

Gil holds a pastry bag in front of her. "I'm here and bearing gifts. Hungry?"

"No," she says, her voice too soft.

Gil presses her breakfast into her hands. "Well eat up anyway. You're always trying to feed us, so fair's fair."

"What'd you bring me?" Joey asks. "Hi, by the way, good morning to you too, Joey, I'm so worried about you."

"I brought you a helmet," Gil says. "And one of those giant inflatable balls for you to wear around."

"Funny."

"Doctor's orders. It's here in your chart, next to how awful you are as a patient."

"Boys," Mom says, smoothing back Joey's hair again.

"Yeah, you gotta be nice to me," Joey says.

"No way." Tommy pushes in to sit on the bed next to Mom. "You're hogging all the attention, Joey."

"Don't kick me, you oaf."

"It's your head that's wrong. Move your knee, I want cuddles." Tommy squirms closer.

"Gil, help!"

But Gil just saves Tommy's coffee for him as he wriggles onto the bed, stretching out next to Joey and getting an arm and a leg over him.

"Love you, Joe Bug," Tommy says as Joey tries to scoot away.

"Don't call me that."

"Get on the other side, Gil," Tommy says. "The only cure is snuggles for our baby brother's poor little head. Too bad that hit couldn't have made you better looking."

"I'm not sure hospital policies allow all three of you in the same room," Mom says.

"Could have fixed this entire problem," Tommy says, patting gently at Joey's face with his entire palm.

"Tommy's the problem," Joey says. "Get off."

"I think this thing is the real issue." Tommy pokes Joey's nose.

"Gil!" Joey calls, trying to twist away from Tommy's hand on his face.

"Tommy, stop," Gil says.

"Thank you."

"Cause you got Dad's nose too," Gil says.

"My IV!" Joey wails as Tommy lunges across him toward Gil.

Mom stands up, slipping out from between the three of them. She's smiling, just a little. "I'm going to go find a nurse, since the way this tends to go, one of you will end up injured."

"It's me, I'm injured, help," Joey groans and lets out a little *oof* when Tommy puts his weight on his stomach.

Fighting with Joey for that roster spot? Gil sits where

Mom was, watching Joey trying to shove Tommy off. No, no way.

Let some other guy be the one dogging Joey's days, the one Joey has to fight against, work harder than, be better in every way. Just let it not be Gil.

"Baby brother," Gil says and pets his hair in an intentionally poor imitation of Mom. "Little Joe Bug, you got us good and worried."

"I can't breathe," Joey says, though he's laughing.

Tommy peers at the monitors beside the bed. "Does one of these switch you off? Especially your mouth hole?"

"Maybe we can turn you off and back on," Gil says. "Have the doctors tried that yet?"

"Joey's a medical marvel," Tommy says. "Mostly how bad he smells. I read it on his chart."

"I can't believe you're both fucking here," Joey says. "Tommy, go home, would you?"

"What about me?" Gil messes up Joey's hair as much as he dares to with his head injury. "Oh wait, that's right, you and your damn cat are living in my home. It tried to sleep with me."

"Get used to it when you move back in."

Gil sucks in a breath. "You talked to Dad?"

Joey's still smiling, trying to drive his knee into Tommy's leg, though he's mostly just tangled with the blankets. "Yeah, he said you'd be back down here. We finally get to play together. Sorry, Tommy, I don't think you're going to make the San Diego roster. San Francisco, maybe."

"Hockey's stupid," Tommy says.

"You're stupid," Joey says.

Tommy puts his weight on Joey's knee so he can't move. "You're getting traded again, Gil? Nice, that must be a relief."

"Joey, what did Dad say when you talked?" Gil asks. "Tommy, stop."

"That you're back. How cool, right?"

"Did he tell you the details of the trade?"

Joey laughs. "Don't tell me I'm headed somewhere awful."

"Joey," Gil says. Gently, he takes Tommy's arm, guiding him off of Joey, making him sit up. "What'd the doctors say to you?"

"To not let you clowns in here."

"You're not going anywhere," Gil says. "You're not getting traded."

"Thank fuck for that. What's worse than San Francisco? Montreal? Ew, can you imagine?"

"You're going to be put on long-term injured reserve," Gil says as gently as he can.

Joey just laughs. "I'm fine. Be better if you brought me some damn breakfast, though. Tommy, give me your muffin."

Gil waits for Tommy to make a show of fitting half of it in his mouth and chewing so Joey can see it, getting crumbs all over the blankets. But Tommy's just looking at him, mouth tight.

"This sucks," Tommy says.

"Do you remember talking about this last night?" Gil asks.

"I remember you talking with that hot nurse," Joey says. "He's a good looking dude."

Nobody's explained this to him, the reality of his concussion and how long his recovery will be. Maybe the doctors don't even know yet, and it could be some time before one of them comes in here and takes Joey through the details.

But if San Diego is already looking to fill Joey's spot at

center with a trade? That's enough of an answer of what Joey's playing time will look like for the next few months. The season, if it takes that long for him to get back on his feet.

Dad should be here, explaining everything to Joey. Or someone from the team, but they're in another city, focused on their preseason. Eventually, someone will check in with Joey again, but who? Hux has his family, Coach is thinking about the season, and Joey's new to the team; he doesn't know the captain or any of the guys yet.

So no, there's nobody other than Gil to have this conversation with him. Fuck. Gil's not cut out for this. *Lie to the doctors and get back out there*, he's been trained to say since he first got on the ice.

Dad was the one who told him that, and now those words gum in Gil's throat when it's his little brother he's looking at, thinking of him ending up with an injury that'll derail his life, not just his career.

"Joey," he starts, floundering for what to say. An argument against throwing away the rest of his life for the sake of hockey? No, Gil isn't the one to do this. He knows one way of life, and one only.

And it's fucked up plenty for him. So not for Joey too, not now.

"You have an entire life to look forward to after your career ends," Gil says.

Joey laughs. "So?"

"So you need to take care of yourself now. San Diego's looking to fill your spot on the roster. They expect you to be out for a good long while, in order to get better."

"But I feel fine, I'm good. This is all ridiculous. I'll be back by the start of the season."

"That's the trade I got," Gil says carefully. "To come back and play center while you're out. Dad pushed for it."

"What's wrong with that?" Joey asks.

"Joey," Gil says softly. "I said no. I asked Melissa to pull the trade. I don't want it. I'm—I'm going back to San Francisco, actually. Later this morning, I have a flight."

Joey taps at his temple. "Okay, maybe I did get hit hard, 'cause you're making no sense."

"I'm not fighting with you for a roster spot," Gil says.

"So? We'll beat some other guy out together," Joey says. "What's gotten into you?"

Sebastian, Gil thinks.

"I want to be your brother, not fuck up things between us when our coach pits us against each other."

"A week in San Francisco and you're giving up, just like that team always does. C'mon, Gil."

Gil blinks. Isn't that what he was so pissed at Sebastian about? Giving up on Gil, on them, before they'd even tried to make things work?

Though of course Sebastian did. It hurts nearly too much to think about now, but Sebastian, back at Rideau, left alone when Gil took off...would it have worked between them? Gil had a new life to live, the shiny, bright limelight of a new prospect brought up to the big show. And Sebastian, lonely, left behind to their old team, every moment in their dorm, on the ice, a memory of what they'd had and what Gil had walked away from.

The breath leaves him. He did that to Sebastian. Did it and only talked about the NHL when he did call and never thought about the reality of it, not until now. How badly that must have hurt, to watch Gil choose hockey and not once, not ever, look back.

"I'm not giving up," Gil says. "But coming back to the Mountain Lions is what Dad wants me to do. It's not what I want to do."

"Wow," Tommy says.

"I want to go back to San Francisco," Gil says. "And I want you to focus on getting better." Yes, that's what Sebastian would say if he were here. He'd be perfect to talk Joey through this, remind him of the years waiting for him after his career as a professional hockey player ends, the fact that the team cares about him as an asset, an investment to make them money, not about him as a person.

Not tough enough, Gil had thought of Sebastian's coaching. He needs to apologize for that. For that and for so, so much more.

"I'm fine," Joey says.

"You've got to take care of yourself," Gil says. "Because nobody else is looking out for you, okay? I am, Tommy is, Mom is, but the rest of them? They want you scoring goals, not thinking about headaches and if you're a little dizzy sometimes."

"But Dad said—"

"Dad is..." Gil sighs. "Dad's Dad."

"Well damn," Tommy says.

Joey snorts a laugh. "What the hell does that mean?"

"That he—he has his ideas for how our careers should go," Gil says.

"Better than you do," Joey says.

"Different," Gil says. "I'm going back to San Francisco. Sebastian's there, he and I—he's pissed at me for this same kind of stuff and I know all of this sounds absurd given what Dad's always told us, but I think he's right."

"Wait, I thought you were pissed at him," Joey says. "Because he fucking ghosted you, right?"

"I am. I was. But he thinks I chose hockey over him, and I did."

"What, when you left for the NHL? You had a contract, and we only have so many playing years in our careers," Joey says. "What were you going to do?"

Gil looks down at his hands. "There're only so many guys like Sebastian."

"Aww," Tommy says.

"Gross," Joey says. "What the hell, Gil, are you turning into a complete sap?"

"I've lived this life Dad's made for me. We talked last night, he's really—" Gil lets out a hard laugh. "He's not thrilled with me. But I gotta do my own thing and if there's any chance with Sebastian, I have to take it."

"You're going to end up single on a shitty team," Joey says.

"Yeah," Gil says. "I might. That's a real possibility."

"Or you could be here in San Diego, heading to playoffs."

"I want Sebastian more than I want that," Gil says softly.

"The hell?" Joey asks.

Tommy touches Gil's shoulder. "Good for you."

"What if he thinks it was him I didn't want?" Gil asks. "What if he thinks it was something wrong with him, not my head being so far up my own ass?" Oh, that hurts nearly as much as the thought of Sebastian alone in their dorm room after Gil left, still surrounded by his things. The thought that Sebastian might have wondered if it was something about himself that wasn't good enough for Gil, didn't measure up to hockey.

Convenient, Sebastian had said. Someone to fuck when Gil was in town.

No, he's—he's the love of Gil's life. Isn't that what this feeling is? The deep calm that wells up in Gil when he's around Sebastian? The give and take of joking with him, the hours they can spend together doing nothing? How much more he feels like himself when Sebastian's in the room and how desperately he wants to reach for him when he's not.

"I have to go," Gil says. "I have to go see him."

Gil's always felt like this. Always loved him. And he went and walked away and hurt him. *Thank you*, he thinks now of Christopher. Someone there for Sebastian when Gil wasn't.

Now, though...he has a chance. A slim one, after yesterday, but he'll take it.

"Call that nurse in to check his head too," Joey says to Tommy. "What the hell, Gil. You're going back to San Francisco? To stay there?"

"I have to talk to him, and depending on how that goes —" Gil sucks in a deep breath. *Fucking done with you*, he's ready for Sebastian to say to him. Yeah, he might be, but Gil won't know until he tries. "I don't know. I'll figure hockey out after it."

Joey laughs.

Tommy doesn't. "Good," he says.

"Well, I'm trying," Gil says.

"C'mere." Tommy holds his arms out. "Join the cuddle."

"No." Gil twists away when Tommy reaches for him.

"Snuggle time."

"I have to go."

"Grab him so he can't tank his career," Joey says. "Gil, what the shit is wrong with you?"

"Roussin hug time," Tommy says.

"Mom!" Gil calls out. "Help!"

"Hit the call button, the nurse is hot," Joey says.

"I already fucked him," Gil says.

"Gil!"

"And he's mad at me too," he says.

"You've got your own style." Tommy messes up his hair. And then he gets his arms around Gil's chest and he's not a professional athlete, not at all. He's a string bean compared to them. *Goes running*, he claims, though he tapped out at five miles last time Gil dragged him out for a jog.

Now, he manages to drag Gil onto the bed. "Good thing we always like you," Tommy says. "Even when you're a fucking idiot."

"Playing in San Francisco, seriously. Willingly, too." Joey wriggles beneath them. "Air, please, I need some."

"And pissing off men left and right," Tommy says, squeezing him tight.

And his coaches, Gil's sure. And his dad. And now the nursing staff, when one pokes their head in, frowning. Not Dave, at least.

But Sebastian's who matters. "I have no idea what to say to Seb," he admits.

"Start with the part about being sorry you're so fucking stupid," Tommy says.

"And how the dick's apparently so good you'll give up your entire career," Joey says.

Gil shoves his knuckle into his ribs and Joey yelps, squirming and laughing.

"Boys!" Mom calls from outside the door. She'll come back in here in a moment and remind them that they're ostensibly adults. That other patients are trying to rest, nurses and doctors trying to work, and to please get off their little brother, he's in the hospital of all places.

Dad would complete the picture. But he's not here and he's not coming.

Sebastian, too, and Gil closes his eyes at the thought, leaning into his brothers.

THIRTY-TWO

THE RINK IS quiet when Gil gets there, practice long over and what looks like public skate happening on the ice, a bunch of kids holding onto the boards for dear life, a few who are more adventurous tottering out in the open.

Among them, a couple teens race by, comfortable on their skates, whizzing through the crowd, knees bent, heads low as they fly. They slow only when a toddler who is mostly helmet and snow suit tips over, too top-heavy to manage to balance.

Matty's that size. But that's not Sebastian helping the tiny kid back onto his feet, and Gil heads down the hall toward the locker room with relief that he has a few more minutes to figure his shit out.

Terror too, at how long this has taken, leaving the hospital full of a bright shine of hope that faded into anxiety on the plane and now sits like a twist in his stomach.

Focus. Now's not the time to give in to that fear, but to channel it. He takes the stairs two at a time, straightens his shirt, and taps his knuckles on the door to the coaches' offices. "Seb?" he calls.

But when the door swings open, it's because Steph has leaned forward in her chair, kicking it open with her foot. "Gil, you're back."

"Hey." He looks through the room but only Frank is there, lunch spread on the desk between them.

"How's the brother?" Steph asks.

"He's okay, got released this morning. My mom and brother are with him."

"Glad to hear it," Frank says.

"Thanks for letting me go down there. Is Sebastian around?"

"Just us," Steph says.

"I, um—" Gil scratches his nose. Sebastian and then hockey, that was the order he'd planned, but here they are, staring at him. "My agent—San Diego?"

"I heard a wild rumor you don't want this trade to go through," Frank says.

Gil sags a bit. "So you didn't finalize it." Another worry following him onto the plane and then off it, as the harried anxiety about Joey faded into a clearer picture of the mess of Gil's life.

"My phone went from ringing off the hook to a quick message from your agent and that was it," Frank says. "There was no trade to finalize."

"Okay, so I'm—I'm still here."

"Well, part of me is waiting to hear the punchline of the joke of the last eighteen hours," Frank says. "But yes, you're still here."

"I'm sorry, I didn't—I'm not going to San Diego. Obviously, I mean, because it's your decision and you don't care what I want at the end of the day, but I know my dad—I'm so sorry about him. I can't be okay with that trade. I don't want it, I didn't ask for it."

"Breathe," Frank says.

"I can't play in San Diego," Gil says, forming the words slower, more clearly this time.

Steph eyes him. "Choosing against San Diego isn't the same as choosing us, Gil. It's worth it to ask, are we just your last resort?"

Yes, Gil nearly blurts in the wake of the horror of Dad's plan to send him to San Diego.

Breathe, he tells himself, repeating Frank's calm tone.

Sebastian had spelled out that other future. This future, because this is the office Gil's standing in. The team building itself up, season after season, trading for draft picks, developing prospects, pulling in players with new signings. It's a hell of a long road to reach playoff contention, let alone make a deep run toward the cup, and that—Gil sucks a breath in. That's a dream that might have to wait. Might never actually happen before he has to retire, his body giving out before the spark to hoist the cup over his head does.

But the promise of playing time? Having a say in the leadership of the team, securing his spot on the top line, getting to have some effect on the younger players? That's not an everyday opportunity in this league, and it's not waiting for him at any team but this one.

Because I'm not good enough, he thinks like a stab to his chest. Because the best he can do is be a top player on a shitty team.

No. The top player on a team he'll help build until they're as good as any other in the league. He'll grow with them, with Sebastian's coaching. Help him. *Fun*, he thinks. Like hockey used to be.

"You're not just convenient or a temporary option because it's available," Gil says. "You two are creating something here and I want to be part of it, if there's still a spot for me. I get it if there's not, if you're going to move me anyway because I came in here with a shitty attitude and obviously have been trying to get out since day one."

"That has certainly been clear," Frank says.

"And—and if you did take a chance on me, I'd want there to be some changes. If we could talk about that type of thing."

Steph leans back in her chair, her arms crossed over her chest. "What changes?"

Gil wants to laugh. Where should he even start? "Jay does the team's laundry."

Steph frowns. "He does?"

"I don't know how that started, but it has to stop. We can't have rookies treated like that in the locker room. And attitudes like Mitcher—if another one like him comes around, that has to get nipped in the bud."

"I thought you two were getting to be friends," Steph says.

"Guys like that are toxic to a team and it's good he's gone," Gil says. "Bloomer, someone like him stepping up, having a bigger voice. That's the type of guy we need."

"What're you going to do about our goalie never showing up on time? Barely giving a shit?"

"Talk to him?" Gil shrugs. "I'm—I'm not sure, but I can try. He and Bloomer and some of the guys—they seem really burned out, real low morale around here and I know the organization isn't the best—"

"The front office is in shambles," Frank says. "We've got a budget of five dollars. I have dozens of job postings up and only a handful of applications because everyone in the hockey world knows this place is a joke."

"Then we'll figure it out without a budget and with a skeleton staff. That's what we've been doing anyway and we won, didn't we? Beat the Mountain Lions and I'm not going to lie, that felt pretty good," Gil says. "We can try to talk to the ownership, see if we can work something out. If not, picking up spirits around here doesn't have to be expensive. It'd be great to have a chef here at the rink, some decent trainers and equipment staff, but that's not what the heart of a team is."

Frank lets out a soft laugh.

Steph lifts her eyebrows. "You've got a big vision, Mr. Roussin."

"You two do too."

"And you really want to throw in with this team? Here?"

"I have some—some things I want. In a contract. If I'm going to work this hard here, I—" *Last chance*, he thinks. *Sebastian*, he tells himself. "I want a no-move clause in my next contract. And I want to sign that now, as an extension. So if you do trade me, or this doesn't work, I have a say in where I go." So he can stay close. West Coast at least. Be able to see Sebastian easily enough if...*if.* "And you have to hire Sebastian, too. Long term, not just a temporary contract."

Steph and Frank look at each other, something silent passing between them.

"Look, I know it's unconventional that he and I—well. A coach and a player, it's not a good look, I get it. But if he's not here, I'm not here."

Steph blows out a slow breath. "Then that's going to be a problem."

No. Gil needs him. Of course he does, how can he play hockey anymore without him? And how can he leave Sebastian alone ever again?

Gil steps forward. "We've played together our whole lives. We can be professional at work, we've done it before.

And we're not—he—I have to talk to him, and I'm just hoping something will work out between us, but if that's a deal breaker, us being together, or us even having used to be together, then—he's more important to me than this team. I'm sorry, but he is."

"I don't give a shit what the two of you are doing," Steph says.

"Steph," Frank says.

"Look, I don't, okay? Frank thinks we should care," Steph says. "But so many things are ass-up around here, what you do in your free time is your concern, as long as it doesn't get in the way of hockey and as long as neither of you make it a problem."

Gil sags, relief warming through him. "So you're going to offer him the job?"

"I did offer him the job," Frank says. "And we had this discussion about professionalism with him, too. And Gil—have you talked to him?"

"I was just looking for him, that's why I came here. I tried to call him and text him but—" Shit. Professional. One of his coaches so pissed at him he won't pick up his phone.

Steph and Frank look at each other again.

The bubble of hope rising through Gil's chest bursts. "What happened?"

"He turned it down," Steph says.

"What?"

"Which is why it's not a good idea for a player and a coach to be involved," Frank says.

"Frank, shut it," Steph says. "Gil, he obviously wants the job, but he turned it down when it became clear you'd be playing here. He asked about you and your agent had just called and—"

"Steph," Frank says.

"Frankie, please."

Frankie? Gil looks between them.

Steph sighs. "We're in love, if you can't tell."

"I, um."

"Really happy together." Steph laces her fingers through Frank's. The look they share this time is fond exasperation.

Frank finally sighs and shrugs. "Yeah, we don't have much of a leg to stand on telling you two you can't be together," he says.

"We're not," Gil says softly. "Together. Where is he? I can talk to him. I can fix this, if it's because of me, I've been —I need to apologize to him."

"I don't know where he is," Steph says. "But Gil?"

He looks up from their clasped hands, Frank rubbing his thumb over Steph's fingers. "Yeah?"

"Please go get him, because this team is shit, but maybe a little less so with him around."

Yes, that's absolutely true. It's who Sebastian is, making everything around him a little better.

A lot better. The team, his family—and Gil's life, too.

He nods. Steps back and starts down the hallway, breaking into a jog.

———

IT TAKES Gil two tries to swipe the key in the hotel room lock. He knocked, so Sebastian could just open it for him so he doesn't have to fumble, his hands shaking.

But when he gets it open, the room's neat. Clean too, the bed freshly made, new towels hanging in the bathroom, the top of the dresser and the TV stand and the desk all tidied.

It looks so empty.

Gil crosses the room in two strides, hunting the bare

floor next to Sebastian's side of the bed for any stray sock left there.

But Sebastian's not here and none of his things are, either.

Gil turns in a circle, searching for a note, a clue, an explanation, but it's just his own belongings looking back at him, his harried reflection in the dark TV.

When Gil calls him, it goes straight to voicemail.

"Fuck," he whispers.

He left, Steph and Frank had said and no, Sebastian wasn't anywhere in the rink, certainly not on the ice and the lounge and locker rooms there were empty. If he's not here at the hotel...

Gil doesn't bother with the elevator, just jogs down the stairs, sure that it's faster to have his feet moving, legs churning than having to stand still and watch as the floors light up in an achingly slow descent.

The nice neighborhood over there, he nearly blurts to the cab driver because fucking hell, where is Sebastian's house? He has to scroll back through their texts for the address and it takes him two tries to read it correctly.

He jerks his shirt smooth as he gets out of the cab, dumping a wad of bills and waving off whether he needs change. Okay, yes, this is it. That neat path right there, that huge, heavy, modern wood front door against the sheer white of the rest of the house.

Focus, he tells himself. Get his head on straight, get a grip. He knows how to do this, the pause before everything truly begins, the world holding still for the space of a breath.

No, this is nothing like the start of the game, the silence before a face-off.

This is so, so much more important.

His hand sweats as he knocks on the door and he can't catch his breath.

"I'm so sorry," he blurts when the door opens.

Chris looks him over. "Gil?"

"Is—hi. Hello. Is Sebastian here?"

"He's not." Christopher doesn't widen the door and invite Gil inside, he can't help but notice, just stands there blocking the way.

"I, um, need to talk to him? And he's not answering his phone."

"Yeah." Chris glances back into the house, and then steps out of the door, leaving it resting ajar against the door-jamb behind him. "I imagine he isn't."

"Okay, so yes, I fucked up, but I want to—I gotta talk to him. Where—is he really not here?"

"He left," Chris says.

"Where? What? When?"

"He'll be back, he has Matty again in a few days, but he's not around here, Gil, and I'm not telling you that so you can show back up when he is. He's miserable, so leave it alone, okay? Don't you think once was enough, and to do this to him all over again?"

"He—he really left?"

"I don't think he wants to be your backup plan, Gil."

Gil sits slowly on the front step.

Sebastian leaving the cafe, his breakfast uneaten. *Lonely*, he'd said. Left at college as Gil chased his shiny new future, and Gil was ready to leave him in San Francisco once more, a single parent, looking for a job, a spot to live, while Gil headed off to return to his old life and better team.

Sebastian must hate him. How couldn't he? Gil left him bruised once and then he went and poked that old wound again.

Of course Sebastian wasn't going to stay with the Sea Lions if Gil was on the roster, of course he turned Steph and Frank down. To work here and have to see Gil every day? Worse than being left at college, when Sebastian had to sleep in their dorm room Gil had left, had to skate on the team he'd so suddenly quit, had to live out the life Gil had slipped away from for something brighter, better.

Slowly, Gil looks up at Chris. "I'm really glad he had you."

"What now?"

"In college. And now, he said you guys are still friends, and I—I'm glad he wasn't alone."

Isn't now, either, it seems. Chris knows where he is, and isn't about to tell Gil, so wherever Sebastian lit off to, he stopped to check in. Probably told Chris all about what happened, and it'd just be more of the same that Chris has already heard about Gil, confirming the worst of him.

"I'm pretty awful," Gil says.

Chris sighs. "No, you're not."

"I did some horrible things to Sebastian."

"Yeah, well, that's true." Chris opens the door to glance inside, then half closes it again and sits beside Gil. "The two of you...he's like a moth to a flame with you, Gil."

"Did you and he—was that my fault too?"

Chris shakes his head, staring out at the street. "We loved each other. We still do I guess, but he was right to split up. I was pissed as hell at him, told him he gives up too easily, that he cuts his losses, all that, but he was right."

"I tell him that too."

"Yeah, well, guess we both know him. But I know him when you're not around and when you are, and Gil, what he and I had? It can't compare. It's not even in the same league. It's like a learn-to-skate program when you two are playing pro."

"Nice metaphor."

"Well, thanks. I've had plenty of time to sit around

feeling sorry for myself when it comes to Sebastian. What a great guy he is."

"Yeah. I'm really sorry about your—your marriage." Gil is. What an odd, strange feeling about Chris and Sebastian, when the thought of them together still turns Gil's stomach. But...but Seb cares about this guy. *Family*, he thinks, glancing back toward the house where their son is.

"I am too, but I'll find that someday," Chris says. "Seb wasn't it for me. Not that I regret the stop along the way with him. It was fun in college, and then we stuck together afterward, and kept sticking together, and getting married seemed to make sense and so did having Matty. In retrospect, we were real good friends. Still are, which is pretty awesome. Not many people can say that about an ex."

Gil picks at his jeans. He can't; that's for sure. Unanswered texts, Seb's phone off when he called. He probably just silenced the ringing as soon as he saw Gil's name on his screen, or—Gil swallows—blocked his number. Of course he did. Gil doesn't get some easier answer like he's communing with nature somewhere he doesn't have service, or he's on a plane and has his phone turned off as he—

Oh—home. Sebastian went home. To Baltimore, to be with his mom. Of course he did.

"He's flying back east," Gil says.

"I'm not getting involved," Chris says.

"Did the house sell yet? His mom's? Has she moved? Can you tell me that at least?"

"You know, Seb's right about you. You're like a dog with a bone when you get on something."

"That's not a no."

"But it is, officially, me not saying anything because he told me not to, and whatever happens between you two, Seb and I have to keep our shit together for our little guy."

Gil's stomach clenches. He couldn't have done that for

Sebastian, promised that commitment to peace at all costs. No, he'd dug a trench between them even without the importance of a kid involved. Of course he did, look at his mom and dad. Sebastian was smart to not keep in touch with him for all those years. To protect himself as best as he could from Gil ravaging his life.

But Gil won't do that this time. If there is a this time. *Please*, Gil thinks, *let there be a this time.*

"Papa," a little voice says and the door swings open.

Sebastian will be back, because of this little guy, Matty, standing in the doorway on his short legs, his pudgy hands held out to Christopher for him to wipe.

"How did you manage this?" Chris uses the hem of his shirt to dab at whatever's clinging, glistening, to Matty's fingers. "Is this—Matty, is this soap?"

"I washed my hands."

"Oh no," Chris says. "Sweet pea, what did you do? Gil, I'm sorry, I've got a bit of a situation. Matty, you were napping so nicely just a few minutes ago, weren't you?"

"I'm sticky."

"Yes, you're very sticky." Chris hoists Matty onto his hip. "Let's not touch anything, okay? We're going straight to the bath."

"I don't want a bath."

"I'll go," Gil says, backing down the pathway. It's hard to watch Chris and Matty there—the two Sebastian won't give up on, not ever. Who love him. Simply, unconditionally, and above all else.

"I'll go to Baltimore. To get him," Gil says.

"You will? Now?"

"Yeah, I've got to." Gil wipes his palms on his jeans. Sebastian might slam the door in his face, which, well, Gil wouldn't blame him. But he has to try. And more than that, Gil has to know if Sebastian knows it's Gil's fault, that it has nothing to do with Sebastian, not at all, because he's—he's perfect. Absolutely and utterly wonderful.

"Well good luck, I guess," Chris says. "I mean, he'll be back in a few days. You don't have to rush all the way out there."

"I do," Gil says. "I actually, really, really do."

THIRTY-THREE

It's odd to direct the cab past Dad's house and around the block, but Gil does no more than cast a glance at the driveway. Dad's car is gone, the garage closed, the house clearly locked up for the day. Of course, because Dad's still at the rink no matter that evening's settling over the neighborhood, and he won't be done with his work until late tonight.

And by then...Gil smooths his palms down his thighs. By then, well. Something will have happened, one way or the other.

The Martins' house looks the same as it always has, bordered by Julie's neat, cheerful garden, the red brick path, and their brightly painted green door.

Lights shine inside, a lamp on in the living room and the overhead lights bright in the kitchen. At least that means someone's still awake, that rushing here with evening edging into night won't leave Gil stranded on the curb.

"Thanks," Gil says to the driver as he pays him. *Stay*, he nearly asks him but no, he's in this now and if Sebastian doesn't want to see him, Gil can go to Dad's.

If Dad will take him. If the Martins' door isn't locked to him and Dad's too. *A year*, Tommy had said.

Well, Gil can call another car if he needs to, go down to Annapolis and stay at Mom's, even if she's in San Diego still. Her wife, Lex, will let him in, of course she will. Or he can get a hotel room at the airport, ready to take the first flight west he can get on.

Or...or this will work out here, with Sebastian.

Gil's never once knocked on this door. Thrown it open, sprinted inside, and been turned around by Mrs. Martin to take his shoes off before he can streak any more mud across the floors. Snuck out of it late at night, just for the freedom of the dark sky and streetlights, no actual destination but it didn't matter on a summer night, Sebastian next to him as they wandered. Slipped in through it, as quiet as he could be on the stairs, easing open Sebastian's bedroom door and then jumping on him, laughing, hammering him with a pillow.

Gil tries to not fidget as he hears footsteps. He's guessed wrong, Sebastian's not here, Gil jumped on a plane for no reason and Chris laughed at how Gil thought he'd figured it all out. Or he is here and before Gil can get out the beginning of his apology, Sebastian is going to shove this painted door closed and leave Gil here on the front steps, hating himself.

Well, Gil probably deserves it. Maybe he can at least manage to get out how sorry he is first, let Sebastian know that Gil knows he's the one who fucked up. Twice, now. He smooths his shirt and sets his shoulders.

"Gil?" Julie asks as she opens the door. "What're you doing here? Did I know you were coming?"

"I—no. I'm looking for—Sebastian? Is he here?"

"Come in," she says, opening the door and gesturing him through. "He's upstairs, he just got in. Were you on the same flight?"

No, because Gil had studied everyone at the gate and as

they got both on and off the plane. "We weren't. I wanted to —can I talk to him?"

"Well sure, of course you can. Is everything okay? He was so quiet when I picked him up, said he wanted to come back and help me finish cleaning out the house, but I know you boys have preseason."

No, is the answer. No, Sebastian's not okay and Gil isn't either, the picture in his mind too clear of Sebastian slumped in the passenger seat, staring out the window as Julie asks him what's wrong.

"I just need a minute," Gil says.

"This isn't about Joey, is it? Oh, Gil, I heard today. I was going to try to get in touch with your mom."

"He's alright," Gil says. Was that just this morning he was in San Diego? Waking up in his old house, visiting the hospital? He slips his shoes off like an old, dusty memory, one his body still knows how to do, where exactly to place them by the door. Sebastian's are there too, one scuffed sneaker laying on its side.

"I'm so happy to hear that," Julie says. "Do you need anything? Something to eat or a drink?"

"I'm okay, I just want to, um. Sebastian?"

"Go, go, of course. He's in his room."

Gil used to charge up these stairs. *Boys!* Julie would call when they'd race back down them. *You're making the entire house shake!*

He heads up them slowly, his hand on the banister. There, a mark in the drywall where Sebastian had knocked his hockey stick into it. A chip on the balustrade where a stray puck had landed before Julie had shooed them back outside. The landing upstairs, where they'd once built a fort out of couch cushions and blankets, refusing to let Tommy and Joey into it until they'd realized Julie was feeding Gil's younger brothers cookies and Gil and Sebastian had whined at the unfairness.

That house in San Francisco has a banister not too different from this. Someday, maybe, there will be the chance to walk up those stairs, Sebastian waiting for him at the top.

Sebastian's door is closed, a strip of light shining beneath it.

Gil takes a breath. Oh shit. This is it.

Julie let him in. So Sebastian didn't get in her car at the airport and start in on everything wrong with Gil. That's some sign of hope, maybe, and he taps on the door.

It's not latched, so it swings open at his gentle nudge.

The room's already nearly empty of everything that made this space Sebastian's. The posters on the walls, the books heaped haphazardly on the bookshelf, piles of laundry that Gil always had to step over, all of that gone, leaving behind familiar furniture turned foreign for the blandness of the room.

Now, the walls are bare, the shelves emptied, and the only clothes on the floor are the ones spilling out of Sebastian's messenger bag. Buddy curls on top of them in a tight circle, as if he doesn't want any part of himself to touch the spare, vacant floor.

In the far corner, Sebastian stands at the window with his back to the room, a drill in one hand, the other braced on the wall, his shirt stretched across his back.

"Mom, are you sure the curtain rods have to come down, because—"

"—Hi."

Sebastian goes horribly, perfectly still.

Gil should have given him some warning, he realizes as Sebastian slowly turns. Asked permission to talk to him, had Julie come up first and let Sebastian know Gil was here.

397

Given Sebastian the choice to see him, instead of just barging into the room.

He looks...Gil sucks in a breath. He looks mad. That's shock coloring his face, but his jaw is set too, his face a steely sort of calm.

"So you managed to get traded to Baltimore after all?" Sebastian asks.

"What? No, I—" Shit, how was Gil going to start? He had an entire flight to get this right. Ten fucking years to prepare and now his mouth is dry. "I'm playing for the Sea Lions. I talked to Steph and Frank, and they said you— You're here, you're not there, so I came out to find you and— I called you? Your phone was off."

Sebastian turns back to the window and reaches up to set the drill in the screw that holds the curtain rod's bracket. "I'm busy, Gil. And I already told them I'm not taking the job."

The drill whirrs, a sharp, shrill sound, and Buddy lowers his head like he can sink further into Sebastian's clothes.

"Seb," Gil says over the squeal.

The drill skips out of the head of the screw and Sebastian turns it off, though he keeps his back to Gil. "There are other coaches out there. Steph'll find someone. The team'll be fine."

"I'm not here to talk about hockey."

Sebastian lets out a breath. "Sure."

"I'm not," Gil says.

"Look, I've got a lot to finish for Mom."

"I came out here to—shit, Seb. I'm so sorry. I wanted to tell you that. And that I know that I fucked up with you."

Sebastian turns, his arms crossed, the drill still held in one white knuckled hand.

He's listening. He doesn't look happy, but he's listening, when he could be pointing Gil toward the door.

This is really it. This moment is everything, time poised still before Gil dares a step forward and it jars back into motion.

"All this shit with me and a trade and leaving San Francisco and Rideau, and being awful at keeping in touch with you—that's on me. It wasn't anything you did or didn't do. I'm just good and messed up and I see that now and I wish—"

Oh, he wishes just so damn much. His chest hurts. His throat, his stomach, his whole body, and beneath that stammers the patter of his heart, his pulse racing too fast, his hands sweaty, and a flushed, prickly feeling on his skin.

Focus, he tells himself.

"Seb, when I left for the NHL, I thought...you'd always been there, yeah? And I just assumed you would be. And I didn't even consider—" ever, really, because it hits him all over again, makes him suck in a sudden, sharp breath. "I had been there for you, too, and then I just left. And it's shitty as all hell that I was ready to go and do that again, chase after a trade and leave you in San Francisco. You were right. I was still looking for a way out and I'd have spent every second possible with you and then packed up and left again."

Sebastian crosses his arms tighter. "Well, I think I learned my lesson this time. I'm not waiting around for that to happen again."

"I know. You shouldn't. Sebastian, I was so fucking wrong, for so long. I'm done letting my dad run my career—my life, really. He's divorced, he makes no effort to get along with Mom, Tommy can't stand him—he lives alone and all he does all day, every day, year after year is hockey. That's going to be me if I keep on this way, isn't it?"

Sebastian's eyes cut to the side. *Yes*, his expression says.

"I get that now," Gil says. "Finally. It took me so long. Way, way too long."

Long enough that of course Sebastian couldn't wait for him anymore. He deserves better. Deserves so damn much.

"I'm sorry," Gil says again.

"Is this why you came all the way out here? You have a game tomorrow night."

"I had to come."

"What, to make sure there'd be more than one single coach on the bench?" Sebastian asks, letting go of himself to fiddle with the drill. "That you're not throwing your lot in with a team that's even worse than you imagined?"

"No, I had to, Sebastian. The game doesn't matter. You have to know."

"That you're sorry? Thanks. I do appreciate it."

"I love you," Gil says.

Sebastian's hand fumbles on the drill.

"I love everything about you. You're this incredible, wonderful guy, you're hilarious, and you're so ridiculously kind. You take such good care of everyone around you, and I never did that for you."

There's still a hardness around the set of Sebastian's mouth. Caution in his eyes, but...Gil takes a step forward, daring, timid. The very tip of Buddy's tail wags. Something soft shifts in Sebastian's expression too, a loosening in his body.

"I'm in love with you." Gil inches another step closer. Buddy wiggles toward him, scooting on the pile of clothes. "I have been since before I knew what that even meant. I want you to be happy. And I want to be the one to make you happy, and to be there for you, and watch you have this career you're absolutely made for, and be this awesome father to Matty and—Come home with me, back to San Francisco."

Sebastian stares at the floor between them.

"Seb," Gil says softly. "I won't make this mistake again. If you can count on us—I understand if you can't, but if you could, I'm going to do everything differently this time around."

The moment hangs still for one breath, for a second, a third. *I love you so much*, Gil wants to keep babbling. *It's you, it's been you since I first met you.* Words he could stammer out, arguments he could form to convince Sebastian and persuade him back to Gil.

But...No. It's Sebastian's choice, and all Gil can do is wait. *Answer*, he used to think, his phone clutched in his hand as he called Sebastian, listening to it ring and ring.

Now, across the years since then, Sebastian slowly looks up.

"You really mean all this?"

"I do," Gil says, his heart hammering like he's been sprinting across the ice. "Can you—is there any chance you can trust that? We're good together, you and I. We always have been."

"Are you really throwing your lot in with the Sea Lions? Giving up all of your dreams?"

"No, because we're going to win a cup."

Sebastian laughs and it's the sweetest sound Gil's ever heard. "C'mon."

"You never know, we just might. You gonna be there when we do it? Get your name on it too?"

Sebastian doesn't answer, just sets the drill down on the windowsill. "Gil, this is a lot."

"I know. And if you ask me to leave, I'll go. When we're back, I won't bug you in San Francisco." It hurts to push the words out, but Gil keeps going. "I know the hockey world is pretty small out there, but I'll steer clear of you, if that's what you want."

Sebastian sniffs, shifting to stare at the wall. A poster of a band they'd both loved had hung there, and even with it gone, there's a perfect rectangle left on the paint, a slightly different color from its time there.

"That's not what I want," Sebastian whispers.

Hope flares bright in Gil's chest. "Then when you're back in the city, can I take you out for dinner? Can we start over again, as adults, now that I'm trying to grow the hell up?"

Buddy stretches forward and noses into Gil's hand, his tail thumping. He was a puppy once, bouncing into this room and they'd shoo him away, shut the door against his whining so they could be alone together, could dump their clothes on the floor, turn up the TV loud enough nobody would hear them.

The TV's gone now. The rug, the decorations, the clutter of Sebastian that made this room his, and it's not coming back again. Moving out, moving on, and Gil's breath lodges in his chest. He never thought he'd make it back in here again. Never get this chance with Sebastian. *So don't fuck it up*, he tells himself. *Focus.*

"You're my best friend," Gil says. "And I want to do a better job being yours."

"Gil," Sebastian says and his voice cracks. "You better be serious. I can't go through this again."

"Hockey's just a game," Gil says. "And it can't ever be more important to me than you are."

Sebastian rubs his wrist across his eyes. "Fuck."

Take a chance. Make the shot. *One, two, three*, Gil taps his thumb against his fingers and then reaches his arms out.

"Can I hug you?"

"Yeah," Sebastian whispers and steps forward.

He's perfect. Fits perfectly into Gil's arms, Sebastian's face pressed into his shoulder, his arms closing tight around

Gil's ribs. Gil smooths his hand over his back once, twice, again, and then again. Sebastian's shaking, or maybe Gil is, grief and regret and a terrible, aching guilt. But beneath it, his face pressed into Sebastian's hair, Sebastian's body crushed against his, burns a bright spark in Gil's stomach.

"I'm sorry I didn't keep in touch," Sebastian whispers into Gil's shoulder. "I wanted to. I kept picking up my phone but I fucking missed you so much—if I could do that over again, I'd change it."

Gil cups the back of his head. "I would change so much."

"I love you too," Sebastian says and something in Gil's chest splinters, warmth flooding him.

"Shit," Gil says and laughs and Sebastian huffs a wet, muffled laugh of his own and Gil squeezes him. "Really?"

"Yeah, really."

"Fucking hell," he whispers and Sebastian nestles into him.

He gets this. And more importantly, Sebastian does too. Seb doesn't have to face his life alone, the yawning openness of figuring out how to stitch together one day into the next. No, Gil's going to be there with him. Gets to be there, like he was once. Tonight, and tomorrow too, and then the next day. They'll fly back across the country, the start of the season waiting for him...

Gil shakes his head to clear it, tightening his arms and dipping his head to kiss Sebastian's soft hair, wiping hockey from his mind to focus on just right here and right now, and this man he holds in his arms.

THIRTY-FOUR

GIL SHOULD BE WARMING up for the game. Instead he paces the length of the hallways, side-stepping a puddle that's formed beneath a drip and listening to the hum of fluorescent lights.

One of them is flickering and it feels like it's in time with the beat of his pulse.

No, maybe he doesn't need to jump on an exercise bike and get his blood moving before stepping on the ice. Maybe this is enough, staring at the closed door to the coaches' office, walking down past it, turning, and pacing back again.

When it finally opens, he jumps.

"Well look at that, you weren't hard to find," Frank says. "C'mon in, we were just coming to get you."

"Me?" Gil's voice sounds too high-pitched.

"Yes, you." Frank ushers him in. "Take a seat. We won't be long, we've got to get you guys on the ice."

Gil sits gingerly in one of the empty chairs, trying to catch Sebastian's eye. Gil gets a glance, a quick one, but there's no answer in it of how things have gone, the direction of the conversation, why it took so long once Gil walked him up here.

"So," Steph says. "The two of you patched things up, it seems?"

They held hands the entire plane ride, though maybe that was Gil refusing to let go, fingers laced together, leaning as close to Sebastian as he could get with an armrest between them.

"We're good," Sebastian says and Gil lets himself relax the tiniest bit.

Yes, good. Woke up spooning good, got on the same plane good, and came here, Sebastian giving him a baleful look as Gil ushered him toward this office. *Just ask for your job, go for it, what's the worst that could happen?*

"So we don't actually have any policies in this organization about relationships," Frank says. "Mostly because we don't have policies and because this is barely an organization. I don't have an HR office, I don't have an employee handbook, and honestly I have no idea how to handle this with the team. This is definitely a first for me, to have a captain and a coach doing—whatever you two are doing."

"Dating," Sebastian says softly.

Gil melts. He wants to crawl into Sebastian's lap, tuck his face into his neck, burrow there and never, ever leave. Dating. Fucking dating, fucking hell *yes*.

And then he catches up to what Frank said. "Coach?" he asks, sitting forward in his chair. "Yeah? That's happening?"

"I want to find a new offensive coach when I can, move Martin here back to defense," Steph says. "Because I think it's a good idea that Sebastian not coordinate the offense long term with you playing first line center, Gil, but it's also not like I have a pile of other people to help us right now. We'll adjust as we need to once we bring some more staff on."

"But you're—" Gil wants to reach for Sebastian. He fists his hands in his lap. "Coaching? Really?"

"I need to know this isn't going to be a problem before we go any further," Frank says. "Sebastian says he's good, so Gil? You're going to be leading a locker room with a bunch of guys who know you're in a relationship with the coach. What's that going to be like for you?"

Amazing, he nearly says. Sebastian and him—he wants to grab him, hold him so tight they don't ever have to be apart again, like he can squeeze shut the years between Rideau and now. "We're good," he says with a calmness he doesn't feel. It's hard to not break into a too-big, goofy smile. "We've done this before, in college, and we figured it out, we…"

Slowly, the rest of what Frank said catches up to him. Leading the locker room. Coach and captain. First line center…"Oh."

"You said you're staying." Steph tosses a wadded-up ball of red cloth at Gil. "This isn't my vision for how the conversation would go offering the captaincy on this team, but you're right for it. Or at least, I hope you are. Congratulations, you're the first captain of the Sea Lions franchise. I think it'll be a good look on you."

It's his jersey, red and gold and on the chest…

He hasn't worn a C since high school. Staring down at it now, he realizes he never thought he would again. No, he wasn't on that trajectory in San Diego, where the veteran group was strong, and there was no indication he was in the pipeline to move into a leadership role.

Here, though…he traces it with his fingers, surprised to find himself a little choked up.

Although it's been a hell of a day already. Days, really.

"Thanks," he gets out. "Did you tell the team?"

"We'll leave that to you," Steph says.

"How does it feel?" Frank asks.

"Terrifying," Gil says. "Awesome, I don't know. This team's got a hell of a long way to go."

"All the way to the cup," Steph says and this time, Gil doesn't laugh, just strokes his jersey, staring down at it.

Downstairs, the team's milling around the locker room, though for once, Gil's the last one in here. Even Hal's kneeling as he puts on his equipment, tightening the straps of his leg pads over his calves, and Jay has his helmet on already.

The room quiets, all of them looking at him.

He feels short, standing in his shoes while they're all wearing their skates. Smaller too, without the barrier of his equipment. Vulnerable in a way he doesn't particularly like, but it's fitting, somehow. "I'm sorry I missed practice yesterday," Gil says into the silence.

Lomsy snorts a laugh. "Gonna miss this game too if you don't get your shit on."

"I had to go see my brother," Gil says. "He was in the hospital."

"He alright?" Bloomer asks.

"Mitcher laid him out good, so when we play Baltimore, no going easy on him, okay?"

"You're sticking around that long?" Bloomer asks.

"I am. And Se—Coach Martin is here too. We both are."

Pezer makes an obnoxious kissing sound and then laughs at his own joke.

"Shut it," Gil says. "You don't have to be comfortable with the fact we're together, but let's keep it professional at least."

"You two are really dating?" Bloomer asks.

It's hard to not break into a huge smile. "Yeah, we are."

Bloomer lets out a soft laugh. "So that's just allowed now?"

"Frank and Steph said it's okay," Gil says. "Are you—do any of you have a problem with it?" He looks around the room, a jump in his stomach.

"It's a bad idea," Bloomer says.

Millsy turns to look at him. "C'mon, now you bother to care about something? Seriously, Blooms, way to pick your moment."

"It is," Bloomer says.

"Yeah, it's not conventional," Gil says. "But he and I—it's not going to be an issue for the team. For any of us, you guys—what we do here is too important for that."

"And really, how could we care when you two are so cute together?" Millsy asks.

"Thanks, Millsy." Gil's gotta work with these guys. Which means making inroads with them, not just finding them irritating, lazy, a pale imitation of what professional players should be. Steph is already working on it. Sebastian too. And Gil can, as well. Has to, really, so he catches Millsy's eye. "Are you seeing anyone? Because we're looking for more coaching staff. Oh wait, that's right—I hear you can't make it past a first date."

The team laughs at that, the sound rippling around the room as Millsy groans.

This is the right tempo to the conversation, teasing, poking at each other. He'd be more worried if Millsy weren't being obnoxious, and if he wasn't comfortable dishing it right back. Bloomer...well, Gil will talk to him. Of course it'll take some time for everyone to get used to the idea.

"Things are changing around here," Gil says. "We're taking turns with the laundry, at least until we get an equipment staff. I'll do it tonight after the game and I'll get all our socks and jerseys set for practice in the morning. Who wants tomorrow?"

Jay slides forward. "I can do it. I don't mind."

"Millsy?" Gil asks. "Lomsy?"

"You think either of them know how to run a washing machine?" Pezer asks.

"Sounds like you just volunteered," Gil says to him. "Pezer's got tomorrow. Bloomer, maybe you can take the next day because we need an actual adult to follow up on whatever shitshow he'll leave behind."

"Do we have to?" Lomsy asks.

"Yes, unless our new plan to win is smelling so awful nobody will get on the ice against us. Because guys, enough of this bottom-of-the-league shit. Everyone's on time for practices from here on out. And by on time, I mean you're getting to the rink an hour early and I'm leading off-ice warm-ups, just like we all used to do on any other team we've ever played on. After morning practices, clear your schedules because we're having lunch together, my treat until we get a chef, and with it, a team meeting."

"Every day?" Lomsy asks. "C'mon."

"Every damn day," Gil says. "We win three in a row and maybe you get some time off."

"This sounds like a pain in the ass," Pezer says.

"No way can we win three in a row," Lomsy says. "What the hell's gotten into you?"

"Coach got in there," Pezer says and the room laughs again.

Gil's face flushes. "Guys."

Millsy leans forward and snags Gil's jersey. "Makes sense," Millsy says, showing it to the room, the C bright gold against the red. "Could have just said, Rooster."

"Give that back. I was gonna."

"Not until you tell us the details." Millsy holds it away to taunt Gil into grabbing for it.

"I just talked to Steph and Frank and they gave that to me. I was about to—Mills, give me that."

"Oh, no, we don't give a shit about how they decided the captaincy, of course you were going to get it." Millsy waves the jersey in the air. "Even if we voted, 'cause honestly it would have been you chasing us all around to make us bother to vote. Wouldn't it, Rooster?"

"Warm-ups are starting." Gil points to the clock. "I need to get dressed. Yes, I'm your captain. This isn't how I was going to announce it, thank you Millsy for this lovely moment."

"You and Coach Martin," Millsy says, dancing a step away. "We need the details. You didn't tell us jack shit the other night."

Gil goes after him, but he's in his shoes and Millsy's in his skates, the blades sharp enough that Gil's careful. And it makes Millsy taller than him, too, so he can easily keep the jersey out of Gil's reach. "Millsy, seriously."

"First date," Millsy says. "Oh wait, you two were high school sweethearts, right? So I'm just going to assume the school ice rink."

Lomsy's hand shoots in the air as if he's asking a question. "Be honest. Have you two fucked in the showers here yet?"

"Lomsy!" Gil snaps.

"That's a yes," Pezer says. "Which shower? Was it Hal's?"

"Fucking better not have," Hal says.

"We didn't—Pez, stop it."

"It was, wasn't it? Pulled that curtain shut and went for it, 'atta boys." Pezer holds his hand out for the jersey and Millsy tosses it to him. "Who's little spoon? Or, wait, does

Coach draw drills for you in bed? Ten reps, Rooster, get 'em done good."

"C'mon," Gil says, knowing he's blushing.

It's not a bad group of guys. Not like some teams out there. Lack of drive, zero confidence, and morale couldn't be lower, but the lot of them? No, not bad at all. Far from it. There are locker rooms where with this type of thing going on, Gil would be terrified. Now, he's just embarrassed, putting his hands on his hips instead of lunging for the jersey again and quietly, secretly pleased that at least some things can bring the guys together, even if it's messing with him.

"Gentlemen," Gil says. "Please."

"See, Rooster, you can date our coach, but you'll catch shit for it." Lomsy snags the jersey from Pezer.

Everyone's laughing. The entire room, even Hal has a grin on his face, and Jay, though he sobers when Gil looks at him like he doesn't want to be caught joining the teasing.

"Well, that's a nice sound," Steph says.

They all turn. How long has she been in the doorway? Long enough that behind her, Sebastian's cheeks are flushed red.

"Team bonding, starting off strong, I see. Get your ass into your gear, Captain. Be a good example for them."

"Gil's little spoon," Lomsy stage-whispers.

Gil finally snatches his jersey back. "You guys are the worst."

"We literally are. Thought you were going to change that," Pezer says.

"Gonna fucking try." Gil shoves the jersey in the back of his locker and reaches for his skates.

In the hallway, waiting to hit the ice, Gil goes down the line of them, tapping each of their helmets. "You're going to do great," he says to Jay, smacking his shoulder. "Go get 'em," he says to the rest of the guys, giving fist bumps to everyone as they walk past. Hal should really lead them out onto the ice, Gil just behind him, but this is a start, at least. One step and then the next, to start it off.

He pauses before he joins them, staring down the hallway at the ice, lit up bright, the team circling their half of it as Hal heads to the crease.

"Ready?" Sebastian asks softly.

"I think so. Though I have this coach who told me I can't shoot for shit," Gil says. It's hard to talk around his smile.

"Yeah? Did you bother to listen to him?"

"Nah, he was so cute I couldn't focus. But I'm totally gonna ask him out, see if he wants to get some private training in, if you know what I mean."

Sebastian adjusts the collar of Gil's jersey. "Yeah?"

"Yeah."

"I might be up for it. Just not at the ass crack of dawn, okay? You think that 'Rooster' nickname is 'cause it goes with Roussin. Hate to disappoint you, I started calling you that at Rideau because you can't manage to sleep past dawn."

"That was you?" Gil gapes. "You came up with that?"

"C'mon. You knew that."

"No fucking way, I didn't."

"Well," Sebastian says and smooths his hands down Gil's arms. "I was also pretty into your cock."

"Sebastian!"

"Go get 'em," Seb says, turning Gil toward the ice and swatting his ass. "I'll be right behind you."

Yeah, on the bench. Watching as Gil skates out there.

"I love you," he says before he goes.

Sebastian smiles. A real one, his cheeks dimpled

beneath his beard, his eyes lit up and shining. "It's nice to hear you say that in a hockey rink."

"It's nice to be here with you."

"Well, get the hell out there. And yeah, I heard the guys. I might have some drills for you tonight."

Gil goes, catching up with the team, and as he steps onto the ice, he's still laughing.

BISCUIT IN THE BASKET

If Sebastian shoots, he'll score.

Learning to trust the idea that he might actually get to be happy is one challenge facing Sebastian. The other? Gil's single minded focus.

Read this sequel novella for free at:
www.kitoliver.com/biscuitinthebasket

ENJOYED LIGHT UP THE LAMP?

Reviews are a huge way to help this book reach more readers. Honest reviews written by readers like you help show those browsing that Light Up the Lamp is worth a try.

If you've enjoyed Light Up the Lamp, I would be so grateful if you could take a minute to leave a review on Amazon or Goodreads (or both!), as short and brief as you'd like.

Thank you so very much!

ACKNOWLEDGMENTS

This book has many hands in it, but above all the guidance, cheerleading, and enthusiasm from my editor, Sarah Calfee, has shaped this novel into what you're reading today. What a fun project to get to collaborate on, and what a grand adventure our work together has been!

Huge thanks also to Jules Hucke for wrestling the prose into a readable shape with her copy edits and proofreads. Also, of course, to Elle Maxwell for another beautiful cover. She brought the Sea Lions to life by creating their logo and drew the perfect images of Gil and Sebastian for us all to enjoy.

My husband has been the rock-solid support he always is as I worked on this book... and as I headed to the rink once, twice, three or more times a week for 'research'. And most definitely, this story wouldn't exist without all the hours my mom spent driving me to hockey practices as a kid. This sport is one of the greatest joys of my life, and I wouldn't have it without you.

Finally, I want to recognize and thank those who continue to make the world of hockey a more inclusive and welcoming space. Professional hockey is a far cry from the depiction here in this book, and on almost every level, the culture around hockey needs to change. My teammates who I play with each week are happily excused from that claim, but I am too aware that I am of the few and the lucky who get to dress in a locker room inclusive of queer folks. At the national stage, journalists, players, and organizations are fighting to realize the goal of every team, and every locker room, standing for that same embrace of diversity for racial differences, sexual orientation, and gender identity. You are all inspiring and give me hope for this sport I love so much.

ABOUT THE AUTHOR

Kit Oliver's days are spent writing, thinking about writing, having just written, or preparing to write. When not mulling over plot points and dialogue, Kit can be found reading or outdoors - or reading outdoors - often with one or more of the family dogs for company.

Kit writes contemporary queer romance novels full of bantering, bickering, pining, and kissing (and then some) that always end in Happily Ever Afters. Kit may take writing seriously, but believes that above all else, books should be fun to both create and consume. Kit's stories are based around a strong sense of humor, a deep love of complex characterization, and the joy of two people finding each other and falling in love.

ALSO BY KIT OLIVER

The Place Between

A Place to Go

Another Shot

Cattle Stop

While the Sun Shines

Roll in the Hay

Light Up the Lamp

Biscuit in the Basket

Printed in Great Britain
by Amazon

41176633R10249